Inspector Pim and the Blood of Inferium

Inspector Pim and the Blood of Inferium

Riley J. Perrie

To request permissions, contact the publisher at rileyperriewrites@gmail.com

Hardcover: 979-8-9871189-4-8
Paperback: 979-8-9871189-1-3
Ebook: 979-8-9871189-5-5

First paperback edition November 2023.

Edited by Lorelei Jensen
Proofread by Sera Amoroso
Cover Design by Mykenzi Griffin and Kyannah Durocher
Cover Formatting by Susan L. Markloff
Author Photograph by Gaelle Perrie
Interior Formatting by Riley Perrie
Chapter Art by Raphiel Diederich

Printed in the United States of America

Keys to Kingdoms Publications

authorrileyperrie.com

PRAISE FOR INSPECTOR PIM AND THE BLOOD OF INFERIUM

"Filled with gritty adventures and a star-studded cast, Inspector Pim is an explosive first book in this must-read detective series. Author, Riley Perrie, has outdone herself with all the twists and turns included in this page-turning mystery. If you're a fan of Sherlock Holmes or Hercule Poirot, this is a story you don't want to miss!"

—V. ROMAS BURTON, AUTHOR OF FORTIFIED

"Filled with grit, high stakes, a delicious steampunk-flavored world, and characters who are both complex and surprising, Inspector Pim and the Blood of Inferium is two-parts Agatha Christie and one-part pure genius! Hang on to your seats—this is one wild ride you won't be able to put down!"

—AJ SKELLY, BESTSELLING AUTHOR OF THE WOLVES OF ROCK FALLS SERIES

"Mysterious and bloody, Inspector Pim is a stunning steampunk masterpiece. Full of shocking twists, wholesome romance, and complex characters, you'll be chasing clues the whole time—make sure to hold onto your hats!"

—SERA AMOROSO, AUTHOR OF THE MAKRIA CYCLE

"Reminiscent of Sherlock Holmes, this riveting story captivated me from beginning to end. With a host of colorful characters, intersecting storylines, and prosaic depth, this mystery is sure to keep you on the edge of your seat until the last page is turned."

—ALISSA J. ZAVALIANOS, AUTHOR OF ENDLEWOOD

I would like to dedicate this book
to my Lord and Savior Jesus Christ,
Who gives me all ideas and inspiration
to write and point to His truth.

And to my sister, Gaelle,
your constant support and ideas while I
wrote this book meant the world to me.

AUTHOR'S NOTE AND DISCLAIMER

Thank you for picking up this book. Inspector Pim and the Blood of Inferium has a special place in my heart. I wrote it in fifty days, and the characters blew me away. I loved being able to bring them to life in such a short time.

I've written this little note to let you know that this book will not be for everyone. It tells the story from multiple different points of view that jump around. It is told in three parts—before the war, during the war, and after the war. These parts are in no particular order, so I warn you that to read this book, please pay attention to all the dates and POV headers. I have a list of dates and ages in the back of the book to help you along.

I also want to point out that this is a work of fiction, and while it has certain elements that are reminiscent of the early 1900s, this book is in no way historically accurate, and I never intended it to be. It is just a fun little story.

The dates start in 1864 and move around from there. I realize the American Civil War occurred during most of the same years that are mentioned in this book. I, in no way, intend to take away from that period of history, but I also decided to keep the dates as I felt led to do so.

I urge those reading to be over the age of 15 because of the themes of murder that are present in this book. Some other disclaimers you should be aware of before reading are: mentions of abuse, blood, death, disease, murder, sex, sickness, some mild cussing, rape, and war.

CHAPTER 1
After the war: 1864-S: Inspector Leo Pim

Seperium Year 1864-S Constable Bruce. STOP.
To Investigator Pim. STOP.
Murder in Seperium's High Countryside at Dwell
Hall. STOP.
The lord of the hall, Lord Caldwell, murdered
around 2100 14th of
Oktobor 1864-S. STOP.
One suspect in custody. STOP.
Requesting your immediate assistance. STOP.

I stare at the telegram for longer than I should. These cases always seem to bore me. Another marital squabble, I'm sure. As usual, I will have the proper suspect in custody and taken care of immediately. Another glorious achievement for Inspector Leo Pim. Soon, no one will be able to dispute that I'm the greatest inspector in the world. Not that anyone is disputing now, but they will.

"Marisa!" I call through my open office door.

My stout secretary appears in the doorway. "Yes, Inspector Pim?"

"Please call a cab. I have to be at Dwell Hall before sunset."

"Of course, shall I pack you a lunch?" she asks.

Lunch sounds good, but no, this case won't take long.

"No, I'll be back before dinner." I turn, looking out the window at

Seperium City.

Airships dot the sky and cast shadows that resemble beetles or dragonflies on the buildings. Men and women, dressed in their finest ruffles and silks, walk the smoky paths down below me, while others ride in fancy cabs that run off diesel fuel. The diesel engine—a marvelous invention if I do say so myself. Only someone as brilliant as me could have come up with something of that capacity. Shame. That person is dead now, but I wish I could have met him.

"Your cab is ready," Marisa's voice disrupts my thoughts.

I nod, grabbing my top hat and coat. "Thank you, Marisa. You can take the rest of the day off."

She bows her head of dark ringlets. "Thank you, Inspector."

CHAPTER 2
Before the war: 1849-S: Leya Barrett

"Leya!" Mother hisses, glaring down at me. "Take your ruffles out of your mouth! You're not a child." She turns her head, looking toward the window of our moving motorcar.

But that is precisely what I was. At that time, my mother only saw me as her seven-year-old daughter who would one day get married to a rich High Seperium Council member and create a whole family of High Seperium Council members. Only, at the age of seven, I didn't know that, but I'm getting ahead of myself here.

I dream of becoming a pianist and holding grand concerts for a cheering audience that will beg me to play every night. The only problem—my current audience are the porcelain dolls my father buys me after he's been away on long business trips.

He's home tonight, and he got me another doll. This one is pretty, with a beautiful purple dress that flares at her knees in a huge poofy skirt. She has golden ringlets and antique gold filigree watches as her belt and wrist adornments.

I hug the toy to my chest as I spit the itchy high-collar ruffles out of my mouth. I was only chewing on them to keep the uncomfortable fabric away from my neck, which I'm sure has a red welt on it the size of an airship. I don't know why Mother insists I wear this ridiculous thing anyway. Her dress doesn't have any neck ruffles, so why should mine?

Mother wears a navy-blue dress adorned with black lace pulled tight over her bodice and buttoned to the notch in her neck. Her dark hair is pinned underneath a giant hat the size of a chandelier. It's decorated with little glass birds and leaves. I wish I had a hat, but she'd told the maid to roll and pin my hair the night before so my dark hair would have perfect ringlets by morning. Of course, that meant I had to sleep like the dead in a casket, and not move all night. It was torturous. On top of all of that, I have to join my parents at their boring party.

Father sits next to Mother, his leather-gloved fingers entwined with hers. His black velvet top hat sits in his lap, and a dark blue silk tie, that matches Mother's dress, peeks out from his silver vest and black jacket. His hazel eyes smile from behind his bushy beard that tickles when he hugs me. I hope this party will at least have other kids there. Someone I can talk to who won't be an adult shushing me into silence.

The carriage halts, and the door opens to reveal a young Seperium officer. He hasn't been an officer long because no medals adorn the left shoulder of his gray uniform. I know because my father taught me.

Father steps out and reaches in to give Mother a hand out. Once she has successfully exited the carriage, he extends his hand to me, and I take it just as my mother had, like a proper lady. Mother looks pleased when I step off the last carriage step and release Father's hand.

She takes Father's arm and walks on the red, carpeted stairs up into the most beautiful building I have ever seen. It gleams brightly against the darkness of the night. Inside, lights shine down from glorious gold and silver chandeliers. Women and men on giant raised platforms scattered throughout the room dance and sing in perfect synchronicity, so no matter where you look, each performer sings and dances the same way. Guests dance and mingle in the middle of the checkered marble and metallic floor.

I look around, noticing that I've lost sight of my parents. Having been so in awe of the beauty surrounding me, I forgot to follow them. Panic sets in my heart as I push and shove other guests aside. People are everywhere, but none of them are my parents.

"Excuse me," I gasp, squeezing between two people. "I'm looking for my parents," I say as I scramble past a couple in matching velvet garments. I stumble onto the open dance floor, where couples are dancing around and around in a circle.

"Tip, tap. Tip, tap. Here is the night for splendor and entertainment!" The performers sing, blazing throughout the ballroom. It's such a gorgeous display of color and steps that I am instantly mesmerized and forget about my quest to find my parents.

"Leya!" Mother's shrill voice shocks me out of the reverie. I feel her snatch my arm, pulling me away from the dancers. "What do you think you're doing?"

"I—"

"Come with me right now!" she growls in a harsh whisper. "You were supposed to be with me and your father. How dare you leave our side!" She drags me with her to the other side of the room where she sits me at a pleated tablecloth covered in dozens of steel roses. "Stay here, and don't you dare move for the rest of the night!"

"But Mother, I—"

"Don't you talk back to me—"

"Michele?" Someone takes my mother's arm and hauls her away, leaving whatever she had left to scold me with on the tip of her tongue. I want to scream after her and tell her that it wasn't my fault. There were a lot of people, and I couldn't keep up. How is that my fault?

"Psst . . . hey," a voice beside me whispers. I turn to see a young boy about my age peeking his head out from behind a marble column. He wears a light blue vest with gold sleeve ruffles and white knickerbockers that give way to knee-high black boots. His long black hair is pulled into a ponytail at the nape of his neck. But his eyes—they are dark, almost completely black and the shape of watermelon seeds. I've never seen eyes like his.

He smiles at me, a gap-toothed smile showing a front tooth missing. He glances around the room as if waiting to see if someone will stop him before sprinting to my table.

"May I?" He gestures to a chair.

I glance around nervously. Would Mother be upset if someone sat next to me? "O—of course." I nod and he sits. "I—"

"So, the plan for tonight is to get a rat into the room, maybe one or two if we can spare it. It'll cause quite a hoot!" He laughs, his gap tooth reappearing.

I stare at him, dumbfounded. "Excuse me. I have no idea what you're talking about. Where did you get rats, and why would you even want them?"

He stares at me like I'm a foreign object. "You must not be Ceklia."

I shake my head.

"Oops, I must have the wrong table." He looks around the room. "I'm sorry to have bothered you." He gets up to leave.

"Now, wait a minute," I say, grasping one of his gold ruffles. "You don't just sit at my table, talk about rats, and then leave. You have to introduce yourself. It's proper."

"I mistook you for someone else."

"Well, un-mistake it then." I release his sleeve and shove my hand in his face. "My name is Leya Barrett . . . and you are?"

He hesitates before taking my hand and shaking it like a gentleman would—but a gentleman wouldn't walk away without properly introducing himself in the first place.

"Gabriel Hoek," he states.

"Nice to meet you, Gabriel. Now what is all this talk about rats?"

CHAPTER 3
Before the war: 1849-S: Gabriel Hoek

I stare up at Leya, who is climbing over the balcony railing. Somehow, she has even managed to get up there with the caged rat under her arm. I've just met this girl, and I'm completely certain she's crazy. I'm sure she's much more fun to hang out with than Berren's friend, Ceklia. I'm glad I allowed her to help me with my brilliant plan. I just hope no one notices what we are doing before Leya can complete her mission.

She reaches the top and opens the rat's cage above a decorative silver banner. She giggles as the rat crawls out onto the decoration and heads toward the center of the room.

If my calculations are correct, the rat will decide to drop down on some poor unsuspecting High Seperium member, creating mass hysteria that will be remembered and talked about for many parties to come. I smile, thinking very highly of myself.

"Leya!" The scream comes from somewhere behind me, and I freeze, looking up at Leya again, who has just started climbing down over the balcony's railing. She looks at the crowd, her face pinching in fear as one of her hands slips from one of the rails and she drops a little.

"Leya!" I move forward, even though I know I can't stop her from falling.

"Leya! Get down from there this instant." A woman appears through the crowd that has gathered at the base of the outcropping— Leya's mother, I assume since they look similar.

Guilt strikes my heart. What if Leya can't get down? What if she falls and hurts herself? If that happens, it'll be my fault—mine. Leya centers herself, her other hand grabbing a lower ledge as she starts her descent.

"Rat!" someone in the crowd yells and several others break out in screeches of terror. People start running around the vast room, heading for any nearby exit. A laugh rises in my throat before I can think better of it. These people and their pompous parties are the most fun to pull pranks on.

"Gabriel!" Leya's voice rises above the commotion, and I turn to find her lying on the ground with tears streaming down her cheeks.

No.

I race over to her.

"Are you hurt?" I kneel beside her.

"Yeah." She shivers, her voice breaking. "My arm."

"I'm gonna get someone to help." I stand trying to see if I can find Leya's mother. I see her, trying to push her way through the crowd that is hastily shoving her toward the door. Anger blazes in her brown eyes as she shouts at the panicked people keeping her from her daughter. I turn back around and find a man kneeling over Leya. She seems calmer now.

I start toward them but a rough hand on my shoulder holds me in place. I hear the tap of his cane hit the stone floor.

"Gabriel," Father's voice rises above the commotion.

I gulp and look up to meet his narrow eyes.

"Did you cause this?" he continues.

I start to shake my head, but then think of Leya. If I lie and say I had nothing to do with it, then Leya would be in big trouble. She doesn't deserve that.

"Yes, Father, I did."

Stillness sweeps over the ballroom with the absence of guests to fill the space. It only makes me feel worse. I look back toward where Leya was, but she is gone now. Tears well in my eyes. I didn't even get to say goodbye.

"You will be punished when we get home. You will think about the consequences of your actions and then you will write and deliver a letter of apology to the Barretts. I think their daughter's arm is broken." He starts toward the door, pulling me along with him. "She's a pianist. She won't be able to play for weeks now."

More tears fall down my cheeks. Leya won't be able to play piano because of me? What if she never plays again? She'll hate me forever, and I just met her. I don't want anyone to hate me.

Little did I know as my father dragged me back home, that this would be the beginning of a life-long friendship. Little did I know that Leya wouldn't hate me because of that night, but when she did start to hate me, it wouldn't even be my fault . . .

CHAPTER 4
Before the war: 1849-I: Vienna Sinclair

I race through the disgusting streets of Lower Inferium. Home by 1700—home by . . . The thought anchors itself in my mind. I'm supposed to be home before dark, that's what Mama said. I clutch my precious books to my chest and glance at the sky above me, but through the smog, I can't tell if the sky is truly dark or not yet. But I know that once it becomes pitch black, drifters will haunt the streets. Stealing, destroying, killing . . .

Shivers run down my arms, persuading me to move faster. As an eight-year-old girl living in Lower Inferium, I have been no stranger to the horrors humans can afflict on one another. I just have to make sure I'm never caught in the middle of it.

I round the corner and stop, immediately realizing that this place isn't familiar to me. I hurry to leave, but a faint, "Help me." Chills my blood and forces me to stay still.

Move! I tell my feet, but they don't obey me. Mama always says to never help someone so close to lights out. I glance behind me and see the shape of a body sitting on the ground with his back pressed against a sludge-covered brick wall. I blink, forcing my face away from the man.

"Please . . ." the man says, and this time I recognize his voice. Dropping my books, I spin on my heels and race toward the body. His features become clearer as I near him—Papa. Dark blood pools beneath his body. A queasy feeling settles in my stomach—I'm going to throw up. This man lying before me can't possibly be my father. This isn't real.

"Papa?" I gasp, but my voice is no stronger than his.

"Vee . . ." He can't even manage to say my name.

Tears start down my cheeks. I have to get him to Mama.

"Papa, can you stand? We have to go home," I grab his shoulder and try to lift him. He cries out in pain, twisting just enough so I can see the blood flowing from a cut on his side. It looks big, terrible. I've got to stop the blood flow—that's what Mama taught me. I pull my jacket off and ball it up, pressing it against his side. He winces, his face contorting in pain.

"Papa, I—I know it hurts, but home is just around the corner. We h—have to at least get home. C—can you do that?" I stutter, willing my tears to clear so I can stare into his eyes.

He nods. "For you, I—I will try."

He grunts, using me as support as he carefully lifts himself away from the ground. The next few seconds are torturous as we shuffle the block toward home. Thoughts fill my head. How did he get stabbed? Will the person who hurt him come back? We round the corner and my eyes light on our small, black-bricked house.

"We're almost there. J—just a little bit farther," I tell Papa.

The golden light spilling from our front window never seemed so inviting. Papa stumbles, crushing me with his weight as he falls.

"Papa, no!" I shout, scrambling out from underneath his arm and shoulder that pinned me. I don't think, instead, I race toward the house.

"Mama!" I scream, pushing the front door open. "Mama!" I race into her outstretched arms.

"Vienna, what's wrong?"

"Papa—he—we, come on!" I grab her hand, forcing her into the street where Papa lies.

"Harold!" Mama yells, bending down to help him up. "Vienna, get inside." Her voice is frantic, and when I don't move, she screams, "Now!"

CHAPTER 5
During the war: 1862-S: Doren Caldwell

The doctor's eyebrows scrunch together as he studies the report in front of him. I look at him from my spot in the hospital recovery room. The pristine ceramic walls have become an impenetrable prison for my mind and body over the last three days, blurring into boring nothingness. I hope I can leave soon.

The doctor looks up at me. "Unfortunately, your condition is permanent. There is nothing—" he continues to tell me the full details of my report, but I don't hear him. My mind is stuck in a constant loop.

Permanent.

I am permanently crippled. I will never be able to walk again, not without mechanical help anyway. What about the war? I can't possibly fight now. What kind of man will I be if I can't help my city? I'll be an outcast for the rest of my life. They will think I hurt myself on purpose—at least, my father already thinks I did. For the rest of my days, I'll be known as a coward. Fear knocks in my gut; I don't want to be known as a coward.

"Did you hear me, Mr. Caldwell?" the doctor's voice fades back into my mind.

I focus on him, trying to keep the fear out of my words as I say, "No, I'm sorry, can you repeat that?"

"You will have a specialist work with you for a few months to build your physical strength. When he thinks you are ready, we will discuss an operation to put you into a mechanical apparatus that will help you walk again."

I nod. "Of course, and . . ."

"You won't be able to fight again. I'm sorry, but you can work once we get your physical strength built back up."

"Right—um, and I can go home soon?"

The doctor nods. "Yes, after a few more days, and a couple of sessions with the specialist, you will be able to go home."

"Thank you, Doctor," I say, and he leaves.

Home. I will be going home. Not as a hero, but as a disgrace. Tears well in my eyes at the thought. The war had given me a chance to redeem myself, to right my wrongs, and come back home—a son worthy of being called a Caldwell, but now, my past will always haunt me with no chance of redemption. I will always be thought of as a coward and a disgrace.

CHAPTER 6
Before the war: 1849-I: Rosea Dierich

I was ten years old when my entire life came crashing down . . .

Skipping home through the dirty streets of Lower Inferium, I sing a song called *Through the Night* to remind me where I have to go.

Through the night—left turn.

I will hold you—right turn.

The multicolored dress my Grams helped me dye with leftover fruit and vegetable seeds has a huge black grease stain smeared down the front of it. I don't mind because it adds more color to the already psychedelic dress. Don't ask me how I got the stai—okay, I'll tell you. I got it because I punched Billy Bomn in the face. In all honesty, he deserved it.

He called me fat, and I'm not fat. I'm chubby, and Grams says it's good to have a little meat on your bones. She's smart like that. Grams is a lot like me. She's one of the smartest and spunkiest women I know . . . not that I know many people, but let's not focus on that detail.

The door to my family's apartment is open when I round the corner. Odd. I walk to the entrance, peering inside. The place is destroyed. I mean, not that it was particularly clean to begin with, but even I know our apartment shouldn't look like this. My heart starts to pound while staring at what little belongings we had broken and scattered across the floor. Shards of glass dishes and splinters of wood are all that is left of our kitchen.

My breath comes out in short, quick gasps as I study the scene. "Mom? Dad?"

I shouldn't go inside. Whoever did this could still be here. I shouldn't but I step inside, racing through our apartment to the one bedroom.

"Mom! Dad!" I search, but they're not there. It's just as destroyed as the kitchen. Panic sets into my heart. Where are they? Did someone take them? They should be home by now.

"I knew I shouldn't have stopped to stare at a mural I'd seen on the side of a building. Why didn't I come straight home? No, maybe they would have taken you too then," I say to myself.

A hand clamps me on my shoulder and pulls me out of the small apartment. I scream, trying to wiggle out of their grasp, but their hold is too strong.

The people who did this are back. I'm gonna die. They're gonna take me too. They—maybe they'll take me to where my parents are. I stop struggling, thinking that's not so bad. I blink, suddenly looking at my captor, but she's not a captor at all—she's Grams.

Grams pulls me into the street. "What are ya thinkin'! Goin' in that place?" Her eyes are as menacing as a blue flame; they give way to a road-map of crow's feet and wrinkles. Her white hair snakes across her shoulder in a long white braid.

"I—" Tears start to stream down my face, as I wrap her in a hug. "They're gone—I thought you were gone too. I thought—"

She hugs me back, rubbing small circles into my back. "I'm 'ere. I got ya. I won't let ya be alone."

"Grams, do you know what happened? Where are they? Who took them?"

She pulls back, looking into my eyes. "No, I'm sorry, Rosie. I don't know, but we'll never stop lookin' for 'em, okay? We'll never let 'em be lost forever." She hugs me again.

"Shouldn't we call the constable?"

"Oh Rosie, no one's gonna 'elp us. It's all up to us now."

Grams was right. From that day forward, we were on our own. We picked up the broken pieces of a family that had been torn apart by greed.

I didn't know it at the time, but my parents had set something in motion that no one could have been prepared for. That I wasn't prepared for— until I had to be.

CHAPTER 7
After the War: 1864-S: Inspector Leo Pim

The ride through Seperium's High Countryside is a drab bore. I hate the countryside. It's so . . . dusty. I put my handkerchief to my nose once more to block out the fine particles. I much prefer the smoky city.

What is the difference, you might think? It's simple. I love the smell and the sounds of the city. Except for the rumbling motorcab, the countryside is just itchy, dry, and soundless. I'm jolted to the side as the cab hits a pothole.

I grumble and right myself. Another thing the steel-paved city streets don't have—potholes. In the city, I never have to worry about being thrown to the side of a motorcar. Hopefully, this ride will be over soon.

I glance out the window and find rolling hills leading to large manors made of marble, steel, and glass. The mansions aren't that bad to look at, but I don't think I would ever want to be a Seperium Council Member because there is no way I will ever live out here again.

The motorcar rumbles to a stop and the driver opens the door for me. "Dwell Hall," he announces and holds his hand out. "That'll be 4000SEM."

4000!? That's ridiculous! I want to say, but the driver delivered me all the way out to the desolate countryside. Pulling my purse from my coat pocket, I place the golden bills into the man's hand.

"Thank you, sir." He tips his head at my generous 200SEM tip. I nod, placing my top hat on my head and starting up the path to Dwell Hall.

The manor is spread out into three main wings—right, left, and center. The right and left wings are at least four stories tall, while the center wing has three. Large windows in the right and left wings easily take up two stories and are surrounded by gleaming steel that gives way to sparkling quartz. Quartz and steel steps lead up to the center wing, and vases filled to the brim with purple and pink hydrangeas line the steps like a welcome mat.

A man, wearing the golden uniform of the countryside constables, stands at the landing of the stairs in front of steel double doors that are crafted with adornments of roses, vines, and birds. Steel knockers molded like a cluster of roses lie against the doors.

"Inspector Pim," he calls as I near the top, his dark mustache fluttering with each word. He greets me with an outstretched tanned hand.

"Constable Bruce." I shake his hand. "Nice to meet you. Now, what can you tell me about the case?" I nod to the doors behind him.

He starts toward them, ushering me to follow. "Last night, we got a call that the lord of the house, Lord Doren Caldwell, was brutally murdered in his study. His wife found him when she went to tell him good night. We were notified a few minutes later." He leads me into the foyer which is an open room with a high domed ceiling. Double staircases on the right and left lead up to a balcony of sorts, and more doors sit underneath the overhang. Constable Bruce hurries to the left, leaving little time for me to further inspect the entryway.

"The telegram said you have a suspect in custody. Is it the wife?"

"Well, yes, and no. Her father, you see, is a very influential man, and wouldn't let us take her to prison, but he allowed one of my deputies to watch her overnight. The other suspect is a man by the name of General Gabriel Hoek, who recently started staying at Dwell Hall as a guest. He is very close to both Lord and Lady Caldwell."

I roll my eyes. A lover's dispute then.

"And there is something else you should know . . . The Caldwells had a dinner party last night, inviting several different guests. Some of them were wartime friends of General Hoek and Lord Caldwell."

"You didn't think this was pertinent information to include in the telegram?"

"His wife said he saw the guests out for the night, so he was alive when they left."

That means absolutely nothing. Anyone could have come back.

"Have you asked any of the other guests this?"

"We're getting a list together and issuing Council Orders to bring them into custody. We have a few located and are watching them currently."

This case is starting to get a bit more complicated than I initially thought. *Stupid, brain! This is why we don't assume things!* Perhaps, I won't be back in Seperium City by dinner. I should have had Marisa pack me lunch.

Constable Bruce opens the door of the study for me, and I stand in the doorway while I inspect the scene of the crime.

It's a nice office—one story, full of books on either side with a large mahogany desk sitting in front of bright windows. My eyes narrow on the splatters of blood decorating the desk, chair, and once pristine windows. Whoever murdered the lord was exceptionally strong to have splattered blood so aggressively, since the windows stand at least two feet from the desk chair. It's highly unlikely that it was the wife . . . unless she had help.

"And the murder weapon?" I ask.

He sighs. "We have no idea where the weapon is. It was a blade. The suspect we have in custody didn't have any weapon on him, but that doesn't mean he didn't stash it somewhere. I've had officers looking for it since."

Blast it! It would be easier if I knew what the murder weapon was, but no matter—I'm sure we will find it eventually.

"I assume the lord's body is on ice?"

He nods. "Yes, when you're finished up here, I can take you to see the body."

I step into the chilling office. It carries the stench of death—a heavy and suffocating feeling, draping over the room like a weighted blanket. This case won't be as easy as I thought, and that makes me ecstatic. The thrill of the mystery fills my heart. I finally have an investigation that will put my bored mind to the test.

CHAPTER 8
Before the war: 1849-S: Leya Barrett

"Bed rest until your ribs heal," the doctor's orders ring through my head. I hate this. I hate sitting still, but it's not like I have a choice. In addition to my arm being broken, I broke two ribs. Part of me is glad I succeeded in delivering the rat as promised, while the other part of me is angry that I helped that stupid Gabriel in his ridiculous scheme.

Only, I wish I could blame the entire thing on him. Delivering the rat to the banner had been my idea. Gabriel told me I didn't have to because he was afraid people would see me, but I had to prove to him that I could do it, just because I wore a stupid neck ruffle didn't make me any less of a great schemer. Especially since his plan had been nothing short of genius. Even though I had been writhing in pain at the time, I wanted to laugh so hard at the hysterically screaming adults rushing by me, but now I am forced to sit here in my drab room and stare at the wall.

My pastel pink and blue-lined wallpaper is quickly turning into a blurry kaleidoscope of craziness or boredom. I'm not sure which is driving me more insane at the moment. Stuffed animals bury my play table and giant dollhouse. My father made it with leftover cogs and warped metal parts from his steel factory. When I'm not forced to sit here, I will finally clean the room like my mother asked me to do a million times yesterday—maybe that was a stretch. I hate cleaning my room.

The door opens to my right, ushering a maid and Mother inside. The maid sets a tray of breakfast on my bedside before opening the large curtains to the left of me. Bright sunlight floods the space, expanding like a fire, and I have to squint to focus on my mother and the maid scurrying out of the room behind her.

"Seriously, Leya, I told you to clean this room yesterday," she scolds as she sets volumes of books on my bedside table. "I brought you something to read."

"Lady Barrett." Our butler, Mr. Graneur, joins us and addresses Mother, "Lord Hoek is here to see you."

Mother arches an eyebrow. "Send him to the parlor. I will be there shortly to receive him." She glances at me before following Mr. Graneur out the door.

My heart pounds ferociously at the mention of Lord Hoek. Does that mean Gabriel is here too? If so, are they here because of yesterday? *Of course, they are.* I glare at the doorway, waiting to see if the boy from the party will appear there or not. He has plenty to say to me.

At least, he better be here to apologize. It's because of him that I am on bed rest. *It's your fault too . . .* I shake my head. Even if it is, I will never admit that to him. We don't know each other enough to admit faults to one another. After all, it was *his* plan.

A pair of interesting, dark eyes appear sideways in the doorway— Gabriel's eyes.

"May I?" he asks, standing fully in the doorway.

I turn my nose up at him. "Are you here to apologize?"

Out of the corner of my eye, I see him hang his head. "Yes."

Suddenly, I feel bad. He probably got punished because of his manic plan. Maybe even worse than I had—besides bedrest, that is.

He steps into the room, his head still bowed. "I'm sorry, Leya." He lifts his head, glancing at my cast. "Does it hurt?"

I shake my head. "Not too much, but I don't think I'll be climbing any balconies soon."

His gap-toothed smile appears but falls shortly after. "My father says you can't play piano anymore."

My heart sinks as I look at him. "He's right, but I'll be playing in no time, so don't worry about it. I forgive you." I smile at him.

"You do?" His narrow eyebrows raise.

"Yup."

And it was at that moment that I knew Gabriel and I would be best friends for the rest of my life . . . *or so I thought.*

CHAPTER 9
Before the war: 1849-S: Michele Barrett

Stepping into the parlor, my eyes narrow on the mid-northern man who leans against an intricate silver cane. His son stands beside him with a forlorn look on his face. I recognize the boy immediately—the one I had seen encouraging Leya to climb the balcony, and, I assume, the same boy who introduced rats to our gala.

"Please take a seat, Lord Hoek." I smile, gesturing for my guests to sit.

He does, pulling his son down beside him. I'd been acquainted with Lord Hoek since my husband introduced me at a dinner party once, but I had never met his son and didn't know he was such a troublemaker.

"Lady Barrett, I'm sorry to arrive unannounced, but I felt that this could not wait." He looks at his son.

The boy stands up, a slip of paper in his hands. Bowing his head, he extends the letter toward me. "I'm very sorry, Lady Barrett. Please accept my humblest apologies."

I raise a dark brow before taking the letter from him and setting it beside me. "Children like you should neither be seen nor heard, nor pulling pranks with rats and girls." I wave my hand, dismissing the boy.

He stutters, "May I—"

"May you what?" I snap, looking into his eyes.

"May I see Leya? I want to apologize in person."

"You think—" I start at the same time his father says, "Gabriel, I think Lady Barrett's daughter needs time to rest."

He turns to his father. "Father, I'm here to apologize. I will not leave until I have told Leya I'm sorry."

Lord Hoek meets my eyes, waiting for my response. I have to give the boy credit. He has gumption, and gumption is good. "You may apologize to Leya." I stop and call for a maid. "Follow Gertie, she'll take you to her."

The boy bows his head. "Thank you, Lady Barrett," he stammers before following Gertie.

I look at Lord Hoek after they're gone.

"I'm willing to pay for all of Leya's medical expenses until she is fully healed. I'm very sorry for my son's behavior."

"You should be. If your son was properly taught, he wouldn't have been pulling such terrible pranks at a Council gala. Where is the boy's mother for heaven's sake!"

Lord Hoek's eyes grow sad before he looks back. "My wife died in childbirth. I've been looking for a suitable wife since—someone to raise my son."

Guilt stabs my heart. "I'm sorry to hear. I didn't—I offer—"

The door to the parlor swings open, introducing my husband, Wellan.

"Samuel!" Wellan shouts, stepping into the room with his broad shoulders and stocky build.

"Wellan." Lord Hoek shakes hands with him.

"What brings you to Claren Hill?" Wellan asks, sitting beside me.

"My son, Gabriel, caused quite a fiasco at last night's gala."

"Ah, yes, the rats." Wellan's eyes look down, a troubled expression settling over his face.

Lord Hoek nods. "I brought him today because he wanted to apologize to you and Lady Barrett and Leya. He's speaking with Leya now, and I've offered to pay for Leya's medical expenses until she is well."

Wellan nods. "That's very generous."

"I'm extremely sorry with how my son behaved, and as I was telling your wife, he doesn't have a mother to help teach him right from wrong," Lord Hoek says.

"Indeed, and—you and Michele didn't speak of anything else?"

I quirk my head at my husband. What does he mean? What else would Lord Hoek and I have to possibly talk about? "What are you referring to?"

Wellan looks at me. "Well, my darling, Samuel and I struck a deal last night."

"Oh." I look at Lord Hoek, who nods.

"You see," Wellan continues. "Samuel owns a weapons factory in south Inferium, so we have become business partners. Barrett Industries will be providing all of Hoek Weapons' metal supply."

I smile at my husband. "Wellan, that's wonderful."

"Indeed, it is. It means I won't be traveling as much. I will be closer to home, and instead of leaving for days on end, I will take a train every day to the office and be home for dinner."

My heart soars. My husband will come home every day. Perhaps now, we can finally try for a second child, as we have always wanted to. I take Wellan's large hand into my own, and he squeezes it.

"I have another request for both of you that I would like you to consider." I focus on Lord Hoek. "Since Wellan and I will be in the city during the same time, I was wondering if perhaps Gabriel could stay with you. You said yourself that he needs a mother, a constant presence in his life to help him grow up and become a suitable gentleman."

What? He wants *me* to watch his son? *Raise* his son? "I—"

"I would like you to consider it before you say no. I know my son can be a . . . handful, but I think this would do him a world of good," Lord Hoek's face is hopeful and sincere.

"I—" I start, looking at Wellan for guidance. His hazel eyes meet mine.

"It's your choice, my darling."

"I will consider it, Lord Hoek," I hear myself say.

If only I had thought better of those words all that time ago. Maybe my precious daughter wouldn't have lost everything.

CHAPTER 10
Before the war: 1849-I: Vienna Sinclair

I peek into the bedroom to see if my father is awake before I head to the library.

"Vienna," his voice rings across the space as his eyes meet mine. He smiles. "Come here."

I race into the room, hugging him gently so as not to open his wound. Mama said that if I hadn't gotten there when I did, Papa would have died.

"I'm proud of you, Muffin," Papa says, kissing the top of my head.

"What happened? Why were you—"

"It doesn't matter now. What matters is that my daughter is a strong little girl who saved her father's life." His dark eyes shine. "You know what you could be one day?"

"What's that?"

"A nurse. Someone who helps people like you helped me. Someone who isn't scared when they see a little blood, but instead, does everything in their power to help that person."

"But I was scared."

He brushes my dark curls from my forehead. "I know, but a lot of people are too scared to even help, and you were scared of what would happen if you didn't."

"I wouldn't have helped if I hadn't recognized you."

"I'm glad you did recognize me, and I'm glad you thought about it before rushing to help me. Others wouldn't have even considered that drifters might be lurking around."

I smile. "You think I can really be a nurse?"

He nods. "I know so. You're a smart girl, and you have a good heart—qualities that are perfect for a nurse. Plus, if you do really well, you might be transferred to a hospital in Seperium."

"Seperium?" I gasp in awe, thinking about the majestic floating city that hovers above Lower Inferium.

"Yes." Papa smiles. "Maybe one day."

Suddenly, I remember why I'm here. "Oh! I'm going to the library."

"Have fun, Muffin. Home before dark." Papa's eyelids droop with exhaustion.

"Home before dark," I echo, before racing out of the room.

Grabbing the books I need to return, I head out to Inferium Library. It was less of a library and more of a home for moths and bugs at this point, but every once in a while, I find a good book with most of its pages.

I head through the streets of Lower Inferium, keeping my head as low as the thick hanging smog, and tucking my books to my chest. Even in broad daylight, the streets aren't safe, and Mama always tells me never to forget that.

As I near the once magnificent library, I hear a sound. It's faint, but I can tell that it's beautiful, flowing like a warm breeze. Curiosity takes hold of me, but I stop myself. I'm not supposed to stray from the path, but the sound . . . it's like a beacon. A call that needs to be answered, tugging my heart, and pulling me off the path. Perhaps, it won't be so bad.

I follow the sound, rounding a grimy corner and finding myself face to face with a large group of people who are standing in the middle of the street. Here, in this sectioned-off street, people of all shapes and sizes, wearing bright, colorful dresses and suits, dance and sing.

"Disgrace! How shameful! Look at them!" They sing, stomping to the music of a band that sits on a makeshift stage behind them, filling the dark world with a life long-forgotten.

"How they fool us so!" Acrobats are thrown into the air, spinning and twirling. They remind me of flags waving in the wind. I start to push and shove my way through other onlookers to get to the front of the line.

"Look at this!" Dancers come right up to my face, bowing as they sing their song. Their feet move to the rhythm in perfect synchronicity.

"Do they think they ever—"

"Think they ever . . ."

"Stood! A! Chance!" The song ends in a crash of cymbals and drums as the dancers explode in a glorious array of colors, reminding me of a rainbow. Just for a moment, grim Inferium glows with beauty.

"It's beautiful, isn't it?" a voice asks.

I jump, locking eyes with a girl who is a few years older than me. I had been so enthralled I hadn't noticed her come stand next to me. Her blonde hair is pinned back behind her round, pale face. She wears a red leotard with a frilly skirt over her ample figure.

"I—yes," I say, gaping at her because she's part of the display I had just witnessed.

She smiles at my astonishment, sticking her hand out. "Rosea Dierich." She flashes a bright smile. "And don't you forget that name. I'm gonna be famous one day!"

I shake her hand. "Vienna Sinclair. I—I'm gonna be a nurse," I introduce, twirling my dark hair in between my fingers.

"Grim inferior!" Rosea smiles even wider. An older woman off to the left of us calls Rosea over. "Coming, Grams!" Rosea yells. Walking backward toward the woman, she addresses me. "There's one more performance, stay for it, and afterward I'll introduce you to Grams. She's amazing, and you'll love her!"

"I will," I call back, my heart swelling with happiness.

Little did I know at that time that Rosea would become one of my closest friends—one of the few I could lean on in the hardest of times.

CHAPTER 11
Before the war: 1849-S: Leo Pim

I stare at the large casket. My parents would have been proud of it . . . not that they could have picked it out.

Tears smart in my eyes, but I swallow them down. I won't cry. Not when my peers stand a few meters away. I'm already the odd kid who is too smart for his own good. Now I'm the "orphan kid" and I refuse to be known as the "crying kid" too. At least, they have enough decency to be respectful today and not pick on me.

I'm sure school tomorrow will be hell. I wish my parents had enrolled me with a private tutor, but now they can't possibly do that. They didn't deserve what happened to them—death by a motorcar accident. A gruesome ordeal, I had been told—dead on impact.

The tears are back, and instead, I study the casket as the pallbearers place it into the funeral hall's incinerator. The casket is stained in the most beautiful rosewood finish with carvings of birds and flowers vining around the wood and garnishing it with elegance.

It's exquisite, and I have to credit myself for helping Aunt Madelyn pick it out. Someone moves to stand beside me, speaking of . . . Aunt Madelyn's eyes are focused on the casket as well, her dark eyes veiled by an exorbitant amount of black lace that folds and falls all the way down her dress like a cape.

She sniffs. "It was a beautiful ceremony."

I glance at her. "It was."

The fires start to envelop the casket through the glass. The incinerator is a large cast iron furnace that reminds me of a fireplace, except for the fact that it has a glass door where you can watch the flames destroy. The orange glow casts eerie light on my aunt.

"It's decided that you'll be living with me," she says.

I assumed as much, and nod. I'm fine with the decision. A twelve-year-old boy with an enormous inheritance can't possibly live on his own. It means I will be moving from Seperium High Countryside into Seperium City to live in Aunt Madelyn's flat. I'm fine with that decision too. I much prefer the hustle and bustle of the city. Plus, it means I'll be moving away from that ridiculous school my parents had me enrolled in. Maybe I can beg Aunt Madelyn to let me have a tutor for my studies.

Aunt Madelyn is my mother's sister. A widow, who owns one of the most prestigious dress shops in Higher Seperium. She knows elegance and class like no one else. We are cut from the same cloth, and that makes me happy. I will be fine, and as I watch the flames lick my parents' casket, I breathe a sigh of goodbye and don't wipe away the tear that falls onto my cheek.

CHAPTER 12
Before the war: 1849-S: Riel Mjorn

Sunlight streams through the window of RN Prosthetics, illuminating the letters Father had painted on the glass years ago. Apparatuses, modeling father's creations, fill the front of the shop, along with a measurement table, and a wall filled with pictures of current styles and available material.

From my spot in the back of the shop, I stare agape at Lady Merella, whom my father is outfitting for a porcelain prosthetic arm to replace the stub that used to be her left arm. It's covered in bandages now. It was only last week that Lady Merella had been in the shop with *all* of her limbs. Even though I am only nine years old, I know she had her arm removed just to wear one of my father's hand-crafted porcelain prosthetics.

I mean, I understand why. Father's prosthetics are particularly beautiful, but to mutilate yourself just to be able to wear one? What a disgusting notion. The society of Higher Seperium is supremely prideful. If they can buy something, anything, to make themselves look more beautiful or perfect, they will waste no expense to make it happen. Lady Merella is one of those who has no fear of using her precious money to make herself perfect.

She picks out a pastel pink prosthetic arm that is trimmed with rose gold and veined with quartz. The arm itself is quite heavy, and only made useful by the rose-gold cogs and mechanics underneath the porcelain covering. Her white hair is pinned underneath a pink and black lace hat. Her facial features have been stretched across her cheekbones in a way that makes her look ghastly but takes away any wrinkles she must have had once. I'm sure she was quite a beautiful lady before she had an operation to keep her vanity intact.

Vanity, vanity, everything is all vanity . . . I remember a sentence from a book I read once. Whoever the author had been, I'm almost certain he was referring to High Seperium citizens.

I start to fiddle with the mechanical necklace my father had made for me. It has a little compartment covered by gears and wires that can only open because of the button on the bottom. I have a little piece of porcelain from the shop inside it. I pull the piece out and palm it as my thoughts wander to what Lady Merella's life was actually like. Did she truly want to cut her arm off? Or did she only do it because others had? It seems like a horrible existence to me, doing things because everybody else does.

Father looks at me as he checks the measurements on the prosthetic she picked out. He signs: *'Erase that expression and get me a 2mml wrench. Her arm is a bit larger than the original attachment I had for this prosthetic.'*

'Father, why do you stand them? They mutilate themselves to be able to wear your beautiful designs.' I sign back.

He looks at me with an expression that seems to say, "I know." *'I can't do anything about it. I can't tell them not to do it, but I can't not sell to them either. Their vanity helps us be able to continue making pieces for the people who do need them. Unfortunately, Riel, it's a vicious cycle. Now, hand me that wrench.'*

I look away, wanting to say more, but I decide not to argue and hand him the wrench anyway. He's right. The people, who mutilate themselves, do spend enough money for us to make prosthetics for those who need them. The Council allowed my father to donate one or two prosthetics a month to help someone down in Lower Inferium. I have never been there, but from what I've heard, many of the factory workers are missing limbs due to work accidents.

Most people don't survive injuries like that, but the ones who do need artificial limbs to continue to work, or they have to work without them. I shudder at the thought. How can people keep going if they've lost something so important as a hand, or an arm, or a leg? Father says they have to, otherwise, they and their families will starve. I'm glad we can provide some relief for a few of them, but who's to say if our donated prosthetics ever make it down to Lower Inferium?

I sigh. I'm being skeptical again. Father says he personally delivers his donated work to the elevators. He says they go straight to the hospital in Lower Inferium and onto whoever needs them. I just have no proof of that, though, and that's where my skepticism lies. Maybe it's because I was taught to stay hidden. To the citizens of Higher Seperium, I'm an abnormality; being born deaf doesn't fit into their perfect society.

So, my parents decided to keep me hidden until I could be properly introduced into society, which requires me to learn and study until I can understand people's mannerisms and facial expressions to determine what they are saying. Sometimes as practice, my parents speak to me until I can read their lips. I can't speak, because I've never heard the sounds, so my voice can't physically recreate them, but I can write to communicate. Once I get introduced, some people will still call me an abnormality, but at least I won't be stupid.

Father looks at me again before disappearing into the front of the shop with Lady Merella's newly outfitted prosthetic arm. I glance out the window to watch the exchange. She seems delighted with her new attachment. She hands Father a huge bag full of SEM—400,000 to be exact—before she exits the shop with a content smile on her face.

I try not to be disgusted by her delight, but my nose wrinkles anyway, and my sour expression returns. I don't care if Father sees it again. I will never stop expressing how wrong I feel about Seperium's vanity.

CHAPTER 13
After the war: 1864-S: Inspector Leo Pim

While I stand in the Seperium Countryside Morgue waiting to see the victim's body, I review what I learned during the full inspection of the office. I noticed two things: blood splatters outlined where the body had been sitting in the chair, and the weapon was either a long dagger or a rapier. Those things alone tell me Lord Caldwell was a young, scrawny man.

Now, how can I tell those things? One: his body wasn't big enough to fill out the entire chair, and two: the imprints in the chair were not worn down by him, meaning that he recently took up sitting in the chair. Meaning, he recently became the Lord of Dwell Hall.

Also, I couldn't find any newly commissioned portraits, but did find several portraits covered with dark curtains. Upon further inspection, the man portrayed in those pictures looked like a man who could fill that specific desk chair. The only thing I couldn't figure out were the interesting cuts in the back of the chair. Equal in size, and never in the same place. At first, I thought the knife or rapier had gone through him, but if that were the case, blood would have stained the chair as well. Perhaps, a closer inspection of his body will tell me.

The mortician appears from behind grim double doors to my left. "You may inspect the victim now," he says, and I follow him into the chamber. After helping me into a warm suit, he leads me into the chilled room where a body half-covered by a cloth lies on a metal table.

A satisfied grunt escapes my throat as I study the victim, and I am quite excited to find I was right. Lord Caldwell is, indeed, not a large man, and appears to be in his mid-twenties. He has shoulder-length blond hair that is spread out over the examination table, and a metal apparatus snaking around his torso and extending in bars down the outer sides of his legs. My eyes narrow on the metal parts, the culprit for the odd cuts in the chair? I hadn't considered the fact that he may had been injured.

"He's a cripple?"

The mortician nods. "He's paralyzed from the waist down. He was hurt during the war. His medical reports show he only recently learned how to stand and walk with the apparatus's help." I nod and continue to study the body. It seems my assumption that the weapon is a narrow dagger or rapier still proves to be true.

Several thin stab wounds lacerate his thoracic region, chest, and neck—seven in total. Hmm, interesting number. Already, I know the suspect had to have been someone Lord Caldwell trusted because if he hadn't trusted the suspect, he wouldn't have been sitting in the chair while his guest was standing. He would have stood and continued to stand while his guest was and sat only if his guest decided to sit.

The mortician points to a laceration in the middle of his chest, close to the victim's heart. "This was the first stab. You can tell because of the way the blade was forced into the victim's skin. There was a jolt that caused excess scar tissue here"—he points to a nicked mark on the side of the first cut—"before the suspect was able to drive the blade into the victim's chest, or it could have been signs of a struggle, but if that were the case . . ."

"The victim would have most likely been standing, not sitting."

He nods at my words. "This first blow killed him. The next six were unnecessary to his death. This was a vendetta—seven means something, either to the victim or the suspect or both."

I study the laceration again. "At what angle do you think the blade was driven?"

"Straight across." The suspect had to have been standing beside him before making first contact then. Especially since the angle at which the blade penetrated Lord Caldwell's chest couldn't have been made if the suspect had been on the other side of the mahogany desk.

I look at the mortician. "Thank you. Please send a copy of the report to me when you send it to the prison."

He nods. "Of course, Inspector."

CHAPTER 14
Before the war: 1849-S: Wellan Barrett

"I think it's a good idea. Lord Hoek is an upstanding gentleman who has just been dealt a rough hand of cards in his lifetime. I'm sure losing his wife wasn't easy," I say to Michele over the table covered in decadent breakfast foods—pancakes, waffles, fruit in colorful assortments of apples, berries, and exotic pineapple, and bacon . . . plenty of bacon.

My wife sighs, nibbling on a piece of pineapple. "I understand. I think I'm going to say yes. Lord Hoek is right. I can offer some assistance to that insolent boy."

"Of course, you can! Who better than you to help tame that wild boy? Plus, I think it'll be good for Leya to have someone her age around."

Michele tosses her fork to the table with a loud clang. "You think I will allow that boy to be anywhere near my daughter? You saw how he influenced her at the party!"

"Yes, but if you are going to say yes, my darling, I think you have to take into account that he and Leya will more than likely be spending time together. They'll be living under the same roof for Seperium's sake!"

"Not if I can help it."

"What? Do you plan on locking the boy in a closet? Only to appear when his father is around? How will that help him?"

"I don't plan on locking the boy up, Wellan." She rolls her eyes.

"So, you plan to lock Leya up?"

"I think this discussion is over with!" She stands.

"Michele," I whisper her name, and she sits back down with a sigh.

"You have to understand that bringing Gabriel into our home means treating him like our own. If you don't want to do that, and you don't want Leya around him, then tell Lord Hoek no, and let's move on."

"But I can help that boy. *We* can help that boy."

"Then let's help him, but not at Leya's expense. Understood?"

With a slump of her shoulders, she nods. "I won't lock Leya up. You're right. If we are going to do this, then we are going to do it right. Leya and Gabe will be tutored together, but if they get into too much trouble or cause trouble, I will have to separate them."

"Of course, my darling. Now, that seems much more rational to me."

CHAPTER 15
Before the war: 1860-S: Inspector Leo Pim

"There is a radical group known as The Rosaries who are causing trouble in Lower Inferium. Their leader is a woman named Crémant Rose. She started this whole ordeal a few years ago by painting murals on factory buildings. Since then, her following has grown, and many strikes and protests have been started in her name."

I glare at the report in front of me, knowing what Chief Zorman wants me to do. I'd rather die than step foot in Lower Inferium. I mean, I knew becoming an inspector would put me into places and situations I didn't quite want to be in, but I never expected my first big case would place me in the filth of *Lower Inferium.*

I stare at the chief. "And I expect you want me to find her?" Despite the case being in the disgust of Lower Inferium, I won't let this opportunity pass me by. An elusive vigilante? It sounds right up my alley.

Chief Zorman looks me over. "Yes. Her words are stirring hope into the hearts of Lower Inferium citizens. They're starting to get . . . *ideas,* and the High Council is pressuring me to find her and make an example of her publicly. Unfortunately, the Lower Inferium Inspector on the case seems to not be interested in doing what he can to find her and putting a stop to her. The fool probably believes the nonsense she's spreading."

I salute him. "You can count on me, Chief Zorman."

"Just bring her into custody before this mess gets out of hand," he grunts and hands me the report and a letter with his wax seal. "Show this at the police station down there, and Chief Hampton will get you a nice apartment to live in until you've found her."

I take the paperwork, stuffing it in my breast pocket. After telling my secretary I won't be back for a couple of days, I slip from the department, deciding to walk to the Inferium elevator instead of taking a cab. After all, it's only a few blocks. I breathe in the air. Scents of oil mixed with gasoline and a little bit of fresh bread from the bakery nearby assault my senses. It smells expensive. It smells like Seperium.

I like investigations where I have to find someone who definitely doesn't want to be found. My mind is ready for a difficult case. Of course, I'm not thrilled that I must visit Lower Inferium, especially after all the horror stories I've heard, but it can't possibly be that bad, right? *I might eat those words,* I think, but I ignore them. I'm not wrong. Never have been, never will be.

"Crémant Rose," I try the name over my tongue. It's almost as polished as the wine it is named after. Whomever this woman is, she had to have tried or drank plenty of the expensive wine, and if so, does the suspect really live in Lower Inferium? From what I hear, they don't have high-quality wine among the citizens. Maybe I should start with finding the wine. If I find the wine, I'll find the woman, and then I can be back in Higher Seperium in no time flat and forget I ever had to step foot in Lower Inferium.

CHAPTER 16
Before the war: 1853-S: Riel Mjorn

Father glances behind him, before motioning his head in the direction we are walking as if to say, *"Keep up, Riel."* I know I'm falling behind, but it's not like a porcelain prosthetic is easy to carry long distances, especially since I'm only thirteen, and don't quite have my father's muscle strength yet. I race to catch up with him.

The station looms ahead. It's a giant machine made of steel and glass that sits in the middle of High Seperium. The glass compartment wraps around an enormous metal railing and pulley that lifts it up and down from the grand floating city of Higher Seperium to the land of Lower Inferium. A large hatch door in the middle of the glass stands wide open where passengers seat themselves in the elevator.

Higher Seperium is very beautiful, and it only stays that way because all the farms and factories are on Lower Inferium. I know that because of a book I found once. I thought it was a book about mechanics, but it just turned out to be a book on mechanical engineering feats. The citizens of Lower Inferium are either farmers or factory workers. All their hard work immediately gets shipped up to Higher Seperium, and maybe, just maybe, the Council leaves a little food and supplies for Lower Inferium.

I sigh. I shouldn't let my imagination run with things.

I have no right to assume how the Council does or doesn't do things for Lower Inferium. At least they allow us to donate expensive prosthetics. Like today, Father and I will be personally delivering his three hand-crafted donations to the hospital down there. It will be the first time I get to step foot into Lower Inferium, and I'm curious to see what it actually looks like. All I've had to imagine it with are stories from the customers who have visited, and they never have anything nice to say.

I stop for a minute. I'm hoping I'll get to see some bugs. I've heard Lower Inferium has a lot of them. I've been obsessed with them since I saw spiders making their webs in my father's shop. Technically, those aren't bugs. I just wanted to figure out how these creatures survive in a world where they have to hide away like I do.

My favorites are butterflies, but I don't know where you have to go to see them. I have seen them in pictures. Anger fills my mind as I think about one of the pictures I saw in a book once of scientists pining the butterflies' wings down to study them better. The fact that they can be so heartless appalls me. What did the butterflies ever do to them?

I feel Father's hand on my shoulder, pulling me forward. Oops, I got stuck again. I do that a lot when I start to think about things that upset me, like—never mind, I'm doing it again. I jog to match my father's pace.

Two men approach us from a building to our right.

"Fine day for a nosedive," one of the men with a bulbous nose and large mustache, whom I assume to be the elevator operator, says. I'm glad my lip reading has improved so I don't have to wait for my father to translate in secret.

Father nods in acknowledgment, looking up at the bright sky and breathing in the crisp air. The other man takes Father's bag and the two prosthetics safely packed away in the leather cases he had been carrying.

"Indeed, it is," Father says, before clapping a hand on my shoulder. I look up to study his lips. "Breve, this here is my son, Riel."

Breve moves forward, his hands signing, forming words I understand without having to study his lips. *Nice to meet you, Riel.*

Surprise widens my eyes and I know it shows on my face. The second man comes back and takes the prosthetic I hold.

'You don't have to look so surprised,' Breve continues. *'My wife is deaf. In fact, I helped your father and mother learn sign language after they found out that you couldn't hear them.'*

'You did?' I sign back.

He smiles. *'That's right. It's so nice to finally meet you. You are a very special person, Riel. Don't let anyone tell you any different. Got it?'*

I nod at his words. *'It's nice to meet you too.'*

I never met someone, other than my family, who could communicate in sign language. Of course, I haven't been a part of society for very long, but now that I am smart enough to walk the streets of Higher Seperium, I'm determined to find others like me . . . just to see if they exist, and this man is married to a deaf person.

How did she become a member of Higher Seperium society? Did she have to hide away before she could be introduced, like me? Or was she forced to hide until she miraculously met someone who would love and marry her for who she is—imperfect and all? I have so many questions, but this is not the time or the place. Maybe one day, I will get to hear Breve and his wife's story.

'Could I meet your wife one day? I've never met anyone like me before.'

'Of course, she would be honored to meet you, and share what she knows.'

'Thank you.'

Breve turns to my father. "Make sure you're back before sunset. After the sun goes down, the lift stops," he says, but signs for my benefit.

Father nods, ushering us toward the glass compartment. "We won't be down long. Thank you, Breve."

Breve tips his top hat, sending us off with a toothy grin. I settle onto a chair inside the machine, and Father sits down beside me. I notice the prosthetics strapped safely onto a rack beside us.

'Where exactly in Inferium are we going?' I ask as the hatch door closes after us, shaking the entire compartment.

'Lower Inferium Hospital. We'll be meeting with Dr. Greenwood who makes sure that all of our donated products find deserving persons. He's a good man, and I think you'll like him.'

The elevator starts to move, nearly jolting me out of my seat. It shakes with more force than a hundred motorcars. I clench the seat with both hands to keep myself still. I see Father laugh at my distress, and I glare at him.

As we descend, the sun starts to disappear, slowly eaten away by smoke and ash that blackens the sky like midnight. My heart leaps into my throat as little golden lights start to appear through the haze. Buildings and houses made from black bricks and iron appear like sleeping coffins—filled with darkness and possibly death. I try to see the factories, or even the farms where most of the Lower Inferium citizens work, but I can't see far through the smog.

The elevator lurches to a halt, and it takes all my willpower not to fall out of my seat. The hatch door opens, revealing a broad-faced gentleman with smears of grease and oil slathered against his face. Bits of smoke escape the lit cigar hanging from his lips. A dirty thread-bare hat sits upon his head, hooding his eyes as if that can help him escape the reality of the world he lives in.

Father stands, shelling out a few SEM as he passes the man before taking his packed prosthetics and stepping out into the street. Grabbing my prosthetic, I race to catch up.

The second I step out into the street, I gag and wish I had a free hand to cover my nose. The stench nearly suffocates me. How do people live like this? The smell of the streets alone is enough to kill someone. How do people breathe? I can't even inhale without feeling like I'm going to puke. Maybe I won't be able to see some bugs after all. The thought disappoints me, but at the same time, I feel relieved. I don't want to be down here longer than I have to.

Father looks back at me, and I hurry to stand close to him. I know I'm not supposed to wander. The streets of Lower Inferium are anything but safe . . . or clean for that matter. Rotting garbage and feces litter the cobbled streets we walk on, soiling our boots. Bile rises in my throat, and I have to swallow to keep the feeling in check. A rat the size of my head scurries in front of us, and I almost fall over in fright.

People walk past us with their jackets pulled tight around them, and their heads lowered to the ground. No eyes even glance our way, as if acknowledging our presence, might lead them into a situation they can't come back from. Shivers break out across my skin. I knew Lower Inferium was bad, but I didn't understand it was this bad. It makes my skin crawl to think people *actually* live here. How do they stand it? How can they?

CHAPTER 17
Before the war: 1854-S: Leya Barrett

These are the times when I want to strangle my mother. Okay, not actually kill her, but maybe just enough so she understands how I'm feeling right now . . .

"Hold still!" The seamstress swats my hand, nearly stabbing me with one of her pinning needles in the process. I glare at her. I don't care how many times I get stabbed. I just want out of this—this contraption. "I'm almost finished," she mumbles, fastening a ridiculously large blue bow to my side. I want to gag. Even at twelve years of age, I can't get excited by this pinned disaster of material.

Apparently, I am going to my first women's tea party, which to me, sounds terrible. I'll have to sit there in this horrifying dress, talk to women much older than me, and pretend that I like tea. Mother thinks it's the perfect time to start introducing me into society—perfect for her.

She never seems to ask me what I want, and what I want is to torch this ridiculous dress. I'm completely certain she won't like that very much. The thought makes me smile. Anything that can put my mother into a shocked, horrified, or overdramatic frenzy makes me happy. I shift my shoulders, wanting to rip the fabric away from my skin.

The seamstress huffs and says, "There, I'm finished. Take it off slowly, or we'll have to pin the whole thing all over again."

I groan inwardly. As much as I want to rip this stupid thing off, I know Mother will just make me hold still again. Maybe she'll even order the seamstress to sew the dress on me, that way I can't destroy the pin-job. I would like to say my mother is beneath that, but I'm not so sure.

I roll my eyes and carefully take the fabric off and hand it to the seamstress. She huffs with a satisfied grunt before scurrying out of my room. Gertie helps me back into my afternoon dress and tells me that Mother wants me to join her for tea in the parlor at 1500 sharp—to continue teaching me how to be a proper lady, no doubt. Is there any way I can feign a terrible illness, so I don't have to have tea with Mother today . . . or ever?

"Psst . . ." the voice comes from my balcony. I glance behind me where Gabe stands behind the glass, sticking his tongue out at me. I hop over, opening the door and allowing sunlight to pour its warm streams over me. Gabe takes my hand and pulls me out onto the balcony. I gladly oblige, happy to be doing something that doesn't involve my mother.

"Come on, I have something to show you." Before I know it, he's jabbering about some sort of wings he's made or something.

Of course, I was right in my prediction that Gabe and I would become best friends five years ago. When Mother and Father introduced Lord Hoek to me and told me that Gabe would be staying most, if not all, of the time with us, I was ecstatic. Since then, Gabe and I spent almost every second he was here together. Learning, eating, napping, and most importantly of all, coming up with schemes that made my mother want to rip her perfect brown hair out.

Some of them included: releasing barn cats into the house until they clawed and destroyed Mother's perfect furniture, replacing all of the spices in the kitchen with spicy crushed pepper—the entire kitchen staff had red, itchy eyes and sniffles for a week. Of course, that one didn't quite go as planned because I never meant to harm the kitchen staff, but Mother was furious, so it counts. And many others that included: leeches and frogs, mud, and whatever other gross things we could get our hands on to bring into the house.

Of course, my mother always threatened to separate us because of our hair-brained schemes, but she knew she couldn't do much to punish us because Gabe had nowhere else to go—aside from the fact that she is forcing me to go to a grown-up tea party in an ugly dress . . . Never mind, maybe Mother gives the perfect punishment by contorting me into a proper lady.

Gabe pulls me through the square, manicured green gardens of Claren Hill, crosses over the driveway, and stops on the other side of the barn where Father has left-over metal pieces piled into what looks like a rickety mountain that can crumple at the slightest sound or vibration.

Gabe and I aren't supposed to be anywhere near it, but that has never stopped us before. In front of the pile, Gabe has created a contraption that looks like a pair of wings one could strap to their back. I smile and race over to inspect his invention.

"Wow! It looks amazing!" I exclaim, gently touching the left wing.

"Be careful!" he cries, moving to stand beside me.

I take an incredulous step back, crossing my arms over my chest. "Does it actually work? Or are you pulling my leg?"

"Ew, why would I want to pull your leg?"

I roll my eyes. "It's just an expression people say when they're sure someone is trying to fool them."

"Oh." He fiddles with the metal contraption that holds the wings together. The part that—I'm assuming—is either strapped to your waist or shoulders, so you can fly.

"Well, does it?" I glare since he still hasn't answered my question.

He looks at me. "Of course, it works, and I'll prove it to you."

"You'll prove it to me? Fine, if you're so certain that it works, you should jump from the barn roof," I say, even though I already feel in my gut that this is a bad idea.

"Ley—"

"Well, come on!" I start toward the barn. "You said it works. Don't be such a coward."

CHAPTER 18
Before the war: 1854–S: Gabriel Hoek

I stand on the edge of the barn roof with my wings strapped to my back. I'm still not sure how Leya convinced me to get up here. *Because you couldn't admit that you hadn't tested the wings yet . . .* I pridefully promised Leya that my invention works. Now, I'm standing on top of a barn about to fall to my death with a crazy metal contraption as my only parachute.

I gulp and the ground spins, swirling in a dizzying frenzy that almost causes me to fall over. I'm gonna die! I always knew that Leya would be the death of me, but I never factored in my own stupidity. Why couldn't I just admit I wasn't sure and wanted to test it out first from a much shorter height? Why had I let her convince me to do it from the barn?

She called me a coward. My pride is on the line now, but is pride worth dying for? The thought deflates my new-found resolve. Maybe pride is a fickle thing to hold onto. Maybe it's all stupidity, because standing up here about to get myself killed, is stupid. I don't want to die. I want to know if these wings work, but not at the expense of my life.

Leya stares up at me from her spot where she is safe on solid ground. She looks a little worried, but it might just be my imagination.

"I'm not gonna jump," I yell.

She sighs with relief. "I think that's a good idea. Get back down here then. I'll feel much better when you're on the ground."

Me too, I think before I help myself down the same way I went up—from the tree growing on the right side of the barn.

Leya meets me at the bottom with a big hug. "Thank goodness. I know it was my idea, but I thought it was stupid. I knew you didn't test them, and I shouldn't have told you to jump from the barn. I just—I did it to make Mother angry because I was upset over the dress ordeal, but I didn't know how to take it back, and I'm sorry. I can't lose my only friend," she mumbles into my neck.

I hug her back. "I—I should have just told you that I hadn't tested them out yet. I just—I didn't want you to think I was a coward."

She pulls away, her brown eyes with the little orange flecks in them swell as if they are drowning in an ocean. "You could never be a coward to me. You're the bravest person I know. How else could you stand to be friends with me?" She laughs.

I smile. "I think that would make me more stupid than brave."

She wipes her tears. "Probably."

I take my wings off and set them on the ground, sitting under the shade of the tree and patting the ground beside me.

"What did your mother do this time?" I ask as she sits down.

She glares, ripping grass up with her fingers. "She wants me to go to this stupid tea outing, and she was having me fitted for a ridiculously ugly dress. I think she does it on purpose to make herself look better."

"I don't think—"

"Come on, Gabe, you've seen some of the contraptions she's put on me, and they're never beautiful like the dresses she wears. It's like she wants me to be ugly." Her eyes pin me, the flecks of orange burning like fire.

"I guess you're right. Have you ever asked the seamstress to make you something else? Like, have you ever said that you hate the design?"

"She works for Mother. She doesn't take orders from me."

"Yes, but you can always play the card that says you will be the one wearing it."

She looks away, contemplating my words. "I guess I could try it, but what if Mother tells her to change it without asking me first?"

"Well, then at least you tried. There is no harm in trying, except when it comes to falling to your death." I fiddle with my wings.

Leya giggles. "Right, no harm done." She shoves my shoulder, nearly pushing me over. "Thank you."

I shove her back, and she *does* fall over. "You're welcome." I stand, strapping my wings to my back again. I hold my hand out to help her up. "Now, let's go test these things from a safer jump."

CHAPTER 19
After the war: 1864-S: Inspector Leo Pim

"Inspector, I think you've had a long enough day. I don't believe it necessary for you to interrogate the suspect right now," Chief Lecten says in response to my request as we sit in his office over cups of hot tea.

"With all due respect, Chief, I'm not one to sit still when there is a case to be solved. I know you and the Barretts are ready to press charges against General Hoek, but I have to inspect all sides of the story before we charge someone with manslaughter. After all, that is what you hired me for.

"We have several more people who were at that dinner party, and in my mind, all of them are potential suspects. Even though Lord Caldwell saw them out for the night, one of them could still be the killer. I can't interrogate all of them yet, but I can ask General Hoek some questions while I wait," I finish, taking a sip of my tea.

Chief Lecten glares, a blue eye cutting me with a knife. "Fine, you may interrogate the suspect. I'll have Pierce bring him up."

I stand with a nod. "Good day, Chief!" I shout with a giddy bow in his direction.

He rolls his eyes and points toward the door. I want to linger just to see how long I can keep pestering him, but I have a suspect to interrogate, and despite my initial protests, I am getting quite tired and hungry. As if to emphasize this thought, my stomach rumbles with the force of an avalanche. I glance around the desolate halls, hoping no one heard that . . . not that I care, but still.

I open the door to the interrogation room. It's cold, musty, and dark. I wrinkle my nose at the sight. It's much different from the one in Seperium City. That room is still completely closed off without any windows, but at least it has enough adequate lighting for me to actually see the suspect.

The door opens behind me, and a man, whom I assume to be Pierce, shoves a shackled man into the room. General Gabriel Hoek is decently tall, not as tall as me at six foot three, but tall enough. He has black hair that has been cut short due to his profession. A barely perceptible white scar mars skin under the right side of his chin. His chiseled jawline is free of hair, making him look younger than twenty-two. His narrow brown eyes look over me without a hint of fear.

He's not scared in the slightest. This means one of two things: one, he is completely confident in the fact that I don't have enough evidence to convict him, or he knows he's innocent, and the deeper I dig, the more his innocence will be proven. I'm leaning toward the latter because the guilty always will be found . . . something about your sin will find you out and all that.

I sit down on a metal chair on the other side of a metal table. Metal, metal, and more metal—it's not even pretty metal either. High Seperium Countryside has no sense of class even though it is filled with the richest people in all of Seperium. Pierce locks General Hoek's chains to the table and then leaves us to get to know each other.

I sigh deeply. "I'm going to skip formalities because it's just going to waste time I don't have. I already know who you are, but you don't know that I am Inspector Leo Pim. I was assigned this case after I heard that you murdered Lord Caldwell." I'm goading him, but he doesn't say anything as his eyes flash with a mixture of pain and anger. Smart man.

I try again. "Why did you kill Lord Caldwell? From what I hear, you were war buddies until he lost feeling in his legs due to an explosion. He was shipped home, and you were left to fight. Though, I think you did shockingly well for yourself if you were able to make general. So, tell me, what did he do to make him deserve death by your hand?”

Tears form in the suspect's eyes. Have I broken him already? Disappointment settles in my chest. I really thought this case was going to be harder.

“Nothing,” he answers, his voice rugged and raw like metal sliding against metal. “Doren deserved to live a long life. He is—was one of the best men I know. Whoever decided he needed to die; I hope justice comes swiftly to them.”

His tear-stained eyes harden, a burning fire fueled by vengeance. Not my killer then, but I have no evidence of that. In fact, all evidence points to this man sitting before me. He's strong so he could have easily driven the blade into the victim's chest and ripped it out with enough force to splatter the walls and windows.

“If you believe that so strongly, then why did you kill him? Are you begging for justice to be executed against you?”

“Whatever the Council decides is best. I've lost one of my best friends, and because of these chains, I won't be able to attend his funeral. I hope you find the killer soon and make them pay for what they did to Doren.” He turns his head to hide the tears starting to stream down his cheeks.

CHAPTER 20
After the war: 1864-S: Gabriel Hoek

Boy, this guy really likes the sound of his own voice. As much as he spoke about not wasting time, he sure does like to fill the silence with meaningless chatter.

Inspector Leo Pim is a tall man with dark hair and bright blue eyes that inspect and over-analyze everything around him. His hair is short compared to the current style and parted down the right side with a thick swoop falling over his brow. He looks like a pompous snob to me.

After not allowing me to introduce myself, he purposely accused me of killing Doren just to see if it would get a rise out of me. He'd have to do better than that to break me. I didn't kill Doren, but no amount of protesting will get a man like Inspector Leo Pim to believe me. If I'm the only suspect in custody, then that must mean all evidence points to me. If that is the case, then who framed me for Doren's death and why? I'm sure I have plenty of enemies, just none of them who would be able to sneak into a Lord's house, murder him, and frame me for his death.

Inspector Pim asks the question again, and I give him the only adequate answer I can form without absolutely saying that I didn't kill Doren. That in any universe, I could never fathom killing Doren.

. . . and for Seperium's sake, I can't get these tears to go away. It's not like I can openly grieve either. I can't cry in the seclusion of my own home, or rip or tear or break anything to make the pain go away. Instead, I'm locked in a cell where anything within reaching distance has been bolted to the floor. It's suffocating. I want to scream, but I can't even do that without them thinking I'm insane and deserving of a mental institution.

I can't believe Doren is dead, and I can't believe I'm the main suspect in his murder. Never in a million years would I think that Doren deserved this. Never. He didn't deserve to become a cripple. He didn't deserve to be brutally murdered in his own house. He didn't deserve . . . I stop the intrusive thought before it roots.

If anyone deserved her, it was Doren, and he got her until she lost him. It only makes more tears stream down my cheeks. How is she holding up in all of this? Her scream when she found him last night still echoes in my mind—a constant reminder that this isn't a dream, even though I desperately wish it to be so. I wish to wake up so I can see my smiling best friend again, to wake up so I can hug him once more. So I can hear his dorky bird call of a laugh again. I just want to wake up, but this isn't a dream.

CHAPTER 21
Before the war: 1854-I: Vienna Sinclair

Papa and I stand in front of Lower Inferium Hospital. It's a grim-looking building made out of dark bricks with metal bars covering the windows that face out onto the street. Metal double doors stand as the entrance. They are covered in cogs, and Father pulls a lever set into the side of the building to start the cogs whirring and chugging. The doors swing open inwardly, revealing a pristine white room. A woman, who sits at a desk directly in front of the entrance, raises her head as we step inside. The doors clang to a close behind us as if spurred on by some sort of magic or trickery.

"We're here to see Dr. Greenwood," Father announces to the woman.

She smiles, looking up and down. "Are you here for the internship?" She directs the question at me instead of Father, her pretty blue eyes looking at me with the warmth of a summer rain.

I nod. "Yes, I'm Vienna Sinclair. I passed a test directed by Dr. Greenwood a couple of weeks ago."

She smiles. "I know. Dr. Greenwood hasn't been able to stop talking about you since. He says you are one of the brightest participants he's ever seen. I know he's very pleased that you will be shadowing him for the next few years. You're thirteen, right?"

"Yes, I am, and I'm very pleased to hear that the doctor thinks so highly of me."

She grabs a stack of paper from her desk before moving around it to stand in front of a set of double doors to our right.

"Follow me," she commands, opening the door and ushering us into a bustling hallway. Men and women wearing white coats and pinafores respectively, run and weave among the white hall as if they are master craftsmen creating a patchwork quilt with their patterns. It's chaotic, and yet, beautiful at the same time—like the performances from Rose's traveling troupe. They all have a place. They all have a job.

It sets my heart pounding in my chest because soon that will be me. Soon, I will learn the steps and be a part of their intricate dance. I smile up at my father, and his dark eyes glance down at me with a spark of pride.

"My name is Miss Dottie," the receptionist continues with a laugh. "I realize I didn't introduce myself earlier. You'll probably be seeing a lot of me."

She stops at a closed door with a golden plaque that reads *Dr. Ralph Greenwood.* Dottie knocks, and a gruff "Come in," replies from the other side. She opens the door and ushers us inside.

A man sits behind a large metal desk with books lining the wall behind him, papers sticking out from between the volumes. A small window illuminates the room from the left. Dr. Greenwood looks at us from behind round spectacles. He has a halo of white hair encircling his head that has been combed neatly and matches his square-trimmed white beard and mustache.

"Vienna!" He smiles standing to his feet. His mechanical leg whirs and creaks as he steps toward us to shake my father's hand.

"You must be Mr. Sinclair. Your daughter, Sir, is as bright as the sun—ridiculously smart and brave."

Father chuckles. "You're telling me. I know she didn't get any of her wits from me."

"I'm sure you're being modest, Sir." Dr. Greenwood turns to me, offering his calloused hand.

I take it, shaking it firmly.

"I'm so pleased to welcome you to Lower Inferium Hospital. I won't layer this job with a veneer of honey. The hours are grim, and the work is gruesome. You will be worked until you're so tired you can't stand. You will be forced to watch people die because there is nothing more you can do for them, and you won't be able to tell them the truth.

"But you will gain knowledge and experience no one else at your age will ever have the opportunity to do. You will get to be a part of people's healing process—the ones that are strong enough to fight and survive. Unfortunately, the hardest part will be trying to help people who don't want to fight because no amount of effort on your part will get them to fight for themselves. Are you ready?"

I nod once, my resolve set. "Yes, Doctor."

Doctor Greenwood's honey-colored eyes shine with delight. "Wonderful! Let's get you settled."

CHAPTER 22
Before the war: 1860-I: Rosea Dierich

"The Rouge Rosea!" My stage name rings through the *Drunken Pig,* one of the usual places I love to perform a good skit.

I can't help the smile that spreads across my face as the stage lights illuminate me wearing a bright red, sequined one-piece with ginormous puffed shoulder sleeves and cape. It's the first night I get to show off this creation of mine, and I know it's gonna dazzle the crowd, or maybe they're just looking at my fanny. I have to admit it looks good though. The place is packed, and cheers erupt from the stuffy room full of cigar butts, factory workers, and men over the age of fifty.

You shouldn't assume things, Rosie . . . Grams' voice echoes in my head. She's right. Not all of the people in the room are over fifty. Sara's barely twenty, but I wouldn't consider her a fan of my singing.

The musicians begin to play over the cheers, drowning the patrons into silence.

"Baby, you're so cold," I start to sing as the music rises and flows. I step over the stage, moving to the choreography Grams had instructed me to use for this song.

1 . . . 2 . . . slide.

"Your hands on my skin. This feels like a sin."

Sultry finger pointing, a slight lift of the left shoulder, and . . . doe eyes.

Cheers erupt from the house.

"Dancin' with the dead at night."

Flutter those eyes; deep, confident look; step . . . left, right; spin; and boom. Pose.

"Where do I begin? I'm never gonna win."

Deepen the vocals, make eye contact with someone in the crowd, point, and step down.

I lock eyes with a pair of light blue gems, belonging to a nice long pair of legs with an expensive glass of wine beside him—wine so expensive almost no one ordered it, but this gentleman . . . He sits at the bar, looking almost disinterested, which kinda pisses me off. Buddy, this is my best performance yet, and you aren't going to ruin it for me. I almost forget not to smile as I decide that he will be my victim. Hoots and hollers ring through the crowd as I step into the house.

"I'm sayin' save yourself from the devil in red."

I stride toward the man, taking lengthy strides to elongate my long legs and wide hips.

"She's all in your head."

I tug at the tie tucked into his vest. The man practically jumps onto the bar behind him, his face cringed as red creeps from his ears to his face. Oh! A shy one?

Catcalls make their way around the room.

"Tryin' to take her up to bed, so you keep her close instead."

I turn with a sly look in my eyes, stepping into the man's personal space and using my fingers to "walk" up his chest. He audibly gulps, and I almost laugh in delight. Almost. I lean against him, my lips hovering over his for a second before I step back for my big finish.

"Save yourself from the devil, the devil, the devil in re-e-e-ed, the devil in re-e-e-ed!"

And the crowd goes wild. When I turn to look back, the man is gone, but he left a full glass of expensive wine on the counter. I frown. Hmm . . . maybe I was too much for him. No, that couldn't be. I'm not even too much for myself. At least, I got a free glass of wine out of it. I hope he paid before running away.

CHAPTER 23
Before the war: 1860-S: Inspector Leo Pim

I stand in the street gasping for air, but of course, there is no breathable air. I put a handkerchief to my nose, but it does little to stifle the stench. In fact, it only makes it harder to breathe. I had to get out of there. I swear I still feel that woman's fingers tapping my chest. I shudder.

You stupid dolt! The only reason she chose me is because I made *eye contact* with her. If only I had kept my head down and drank my wine like a good man, none of this would have happened. I only looked because her outfit was so outlandishly bright and covered in sparkles, it forced anyone within a six-hundred-meter radius to look at it whether they actually wanted to or not.

I feel so violated. I found the wine, but there had been no one else there drinking the stuff. Now, I will admit it was good wine, but the glasses were hardly clean and . . . I gag. I can't believe I drank out of one. I gag again.

Clearly, everyone was lying when they said that Lower Inferium was disgusting. They made this—this abomination seem like a sugary confection of wonder. They forgot to mention how extremely abominable, revolting, repulsive, abhorrent, detestable—I can go on and on!—this place actually is.

I convulse at the thought of where that woman's hands have been, and she *touched* me. I can't get over that fact. I'm supposed to be on the lookout for the vigilante, and yet, here I am trying not to throw up the two sips of wine I did drink. I need a bath. I need a concerto. I need Higher Seperium. That's it, I'm leaving. I can't stand this place. I thought it wouldn't actually be that bad, but it's worse. I start toward the Seperium elevator. Forget the belongings I brought with me. They'll have to be burned anyway.

But the case . . . the thought stops me dead in my tracks. Yes. But the pull—the mystery of the chase.

No! I'm not going through this hell just for a case. Chief Zorman will just have to find somebody else!

But you want to find out who the vigilante is. I stop, then shake my head. No, I don't want to know who the vigilante is. I see a light flash from a building ahead of me, catching my eye. The light stops, settling on an image that taunts me.

It's a mural of the vigilante herself—*Crémant Rose*—depicting her in a red costume and captivating mask as she looks down at the city of Lower Inferium. A ruby rose is clutched between her teeth with a full moon shining in the background behind her.

My heart starts to pound. It's a sign—literally. I can't give up on this case. She's taunting me. I have to find her, if not for the High Council, then for me—to prove to myself that I will not be bested by a coward in a mask.

CHAPTER 24
Before the war: 1854-S: Leya Barrett

My knuckles turn white as I squeeze Gabe's hand. I hadn't been able to let go since this morning when I watched my mother collapse at breakfast. I know Mother and I have our differences, and she drives me insane, but I never wished any ill will on her. I'm terrified.

The hallway inside my house feels like a never-ending tunnel of despair. The gold and dark blue drapes hanging from the window directly across from us seem too cheery as they frame the sun's rays and illuminate the little bench Gabe and I sit on.

What if she's going to die? *Okay, Leya, stop thinking like that. You have to be rational, and rationality says one little fainting spell isn't going to kill your mother. She's stronger than that.* My brain is right. Mother is stronger than that. She will be fine, but still . . . I can't seem to let go of Gabe's hand. His presence is a constant comfort that I'm scared to release. Maybe I'm staying calm and haven't cried yet because he is here.

We've been sitting on this little gold and blue bench for over an hour now, waiting for the doctor to reappear and tell us what caused her to faint. Okay, maybe it hasn't been an hour, but it feels like he's been in there forever.

Father hurries down the hall with a servant trailing after him, who is begging for his coat. Father takes off his coat and hands it back to the servant, nearly dropping it on the floor in the process. I stand as he nears, dragging Gabe with me. Finally, the hall doesn't seem so unending.

"Is Mother—"

"I'm not sure yet, Sweetie," he says, kissing the top of my head. "I'll talk to the doctor, and then let you know." His hazel eyes swirl like a storm. He's worried—and that realization does little to comfort my heart.

"Okay," I whisper as he lets himself into the room. Tears well in my eyes; I'm going to cry. I can't cry, not over Mother. She'll be fine. She has to be.

"She'll be okay," Gabe's voice grounds me, drawing me back to the hallway and his dark eyes. "Don't cry, because if you cry, I'll cry. She's like a mother to me too, and if we start crying, we'll never stop."

I nod, blinking away my tears. "Okay, for you, I won't cry."

He squeezes my hand, and we sit back down. "What do you think happened?"

"I don't know. What if she's sick?"

"I don't think it's physically possible for your mother to get sick. I think she'd tell it that it's being insolent and yell at it to hide away, and I'm certain it would." He laughs, and I can't help the giggle that escapes my throat.

"You know I'm a hundred percent certain she would say something like that."

The door opens, and Father steps back out into the hall with a large smile on his face, the doctor in tow behind him. They shake hands.

"Thank you, doctor. We will see you in a couple of days," Father says, and the doctor nods.

"I'll see myself out." And then the doctor is gone.

Father looks over at Gabe and me, a grin on his face that he can't seem to wipe off. So it must not be bad news. "Your mother is pregnant. You're going to be a sister," he says to me and then throws me into one of his bear hugs.

"That's wonderful news!" I squeal, glad that my mother's not dying.

"Indeed, it is, but your mother is on bed rest for the next few days. She was doing too much and will need time to recover." He sets me down.

I nod, excitement pooling in my gut. "Does that mean I don't have to go to the women's tea party on Katurday?"

He chuckles. "Yes, you are off the hook for now."

I sigh with relief. "Thank goodness."

"You can go in and see her now, but make sure that you let her rest for the next few days. No getting into trouble. You hear me?"

"I hear you." I pretend to be mournful about my situation. No getting into trouble? Whatever would I do?

"I have to get back to the office. Promise me you won't get into trouble." Father's green and brown eyes look me up and down.

I nod. "I promise." For my father, I would obey.

He looks at Gabe. "Keep an eye on her."

Gabe nods. "I will."

"Hey! Why are you making deals with him? He's usually the one instigating the trouble." I pout, crossing my arms.

"That's not what I've witnessed. He comes up with the plans and you happily carry them out. There's a difference." Father laughs.

"No one said it was a crime," I mumble.

Father chuckles once again and kisses the top of my head. "I really must be going, I love you, Sweetie."

"I love you too, Father."

Gabe turns to look at me after Father has left, a mischievous glint lighting those dark eyes.

"Don't even think about it," I say, trying not to smile at his antics. "You heard him. We must be on our best behavior, but that doesn't mean we can't cause some trouble *after* Mother has recovered."

"I'm going to hold you to that . . . big sister." He smirks, and I playfully punch his arm. Despite his teasing, I'm really excited to become a big sister. I will make it my personal mission to navigate my little brother or sister through the world of our mother. Oh, the trouble we'll be able to get into . . . and with Gabe by our side, we'll be unstoppable.

Gabe grabs my hand. "Come on, let's go see your mother."

CHAPTER 25
After the war: 1864-S: Inspector Leo Pim

Sitting in the dining room of Higher Countryside Brasserie, I glare at the list lying in front of me. Any one of these names could be the killer in Lord Caldwell's murder.

Leya Caldwell: the wife
Gabriel Hoek: the main suspect
Riel Mjorn: Lord Caldwell and General Hoek's war-time friend
Vienna Sinclair: hmm, a very interesting name, considering her background. How did she get to this party?
Rosea Dierich: ? come back to her later.
Lord Wellan Barrett: the wife's father
Lady Michele Barrett: the wife's mother

A small list, but a detrimental one. All of these people had been at the Caldwells' house that night, and even though the wife testified to the constable that Lord Caldwell saw his guests out, it does little to tell me the truth of the matter. Any one of these names could have come back, or never left at all. I'd already questioned the five servants working that night and all of them had been home at the time of the murder with families to testify.

Food suddenly appears on the table before me. Dishes full of decadent masterpieces—roast duck in rosemary-mushroom sauce, lightly steamed broccoli and brussel sprouts in olive oil and garlic, fresh steamed rolls topped with fromage, and Galette De Rois garnished with a layer of honey and cinnamon.

I thank the servers and dig in. The duck melts in my mouth with a perfect burst of savory flavor. I hum to myself. One thing the rich do know how to do is eat. The food is one of the only things I can accredit to the High Seperium Countryside. I know it'll be a chunk of my paycheck, but I can look past that for right now—not that I care about the cost of things anyway, but still. I've had a long day, without lunch, might I add, and an interesting murder case that is only getting more intriguing by the second.

At first, I thought this was a simple lover-meets-husband and lover-murders-husband case, but it is definitely not shaping out to be that way. My interrogation of General Hoek gave me little insight into the world of Lord Doren Caldwell, but I did find that General Hoek cared very much for the victim. It was hard not to notice how many times the suspect's eyes became misty regarding his friend.

People who love their friends don't murder them. Unless they're sociopaths, then I have another story, but usually, erratic or psychotic behavior can be determined within a matter of minutes, and even though I goaded General Hoek, he did his best not to show any form of weakness or emotion—besides the fact that he was truly distraught over his friend's death.

I did; however, take into account that General Hoek never once said he *didn't* kill Lord Caldwell, which I find to be supremely interesting. If he didn't kill him, then why not say that? I know General Hoek didn't kill him, but that is beside the point. Everything he said is on record, and lawyers will easily jump to the conclusion that he is the murderer. Does that mean he knows who the murderer is and he's trying to protect them? Or is there a deeper secret he's not willing to share yet? I lean back in my chair, my fingers fumbling with the rose brooch on my jacket's lapel.

I look at the name at the top of the list. Despite my initial assessment of the case, I failed to ask General Hoek about a certain Lady Leya Caldwell. Did they have any history? If so, could he be protecting her? I shake my head.

No, I've already determined that the suspect is not a woman, unless she manipulated someone else to murder her husband, but then what would she get out of it? Her husband's estate? I don't think that's the case either because I've heard her father is one of the richest men in Higher Seperium.

People do stupid things because of greed, the thought echoes in my mind, and I can't argue with the truth I find there. I won't rule out any of the suspects until I have spoken with them all—not even General Hoek.

I take a deep breath, looking over the names once more. Tomorrow, Chief Lecten will be taking me to Claren Hill to interrogate the wife and her family. That ought to be interesting since the Barretts decided not to make an immediate statement or testimony about that night. Could they be hiding something? Or do they just not care because they are insanely rich?

I take a wine glass in hand, swirling the dark red liquid before inhaling the scent of the liquor. It's floral with spicy undertones like cardamom, or a late-night dalliance with a mysterious young woman. I glance at the list again—Rosea Dierich. What in Inferium was that infuriating woman doing at the Caldwells' house that night? Wait, why do I even care? She's the one who left me.

No, I left. I will never admit that I let her drag me through the mud because she didn't. She is a chapter of my life I've forgotten, or tried to forget . . . I won't admit that I haven't. I won't admit that I still wear a rose pin on the inside of my jacket, or that I avoid Crémant wine at all costs, or that I still have the signature of a promise burning a hole against my heart from where it hangs around my neck. I won't admit that seeing her name brought about emotions that I have clearly *forgotten* about.

No matter, the case will still be solved, and if she is involved with Lord Caldwell's death, I won't hesitate to incarcerate her like I failed to do three years ago. I grin while taking a sip from my glass. The wine is exquisite, almost as interesting as this case, but not quite. I try not to think about the weight of the name on that piece of paper. I close my eyes and revel in the thrill of the case—and the wine.

CHAPTER 26
Before the war: 1854-S: Michele Barrett

I stare at the grand clock in the sitting room. A warm fire crackles be-side me, lighting up the dark room and leaving shadows, like little monsters behind the furniture. Monsters don't scare me though, but the *tick-tock* of the clock does, an ever-present reminder that my hus-band isn't home yet. It throws my heart into a frenzy of panic. Where is Wellan? He missed dinner, and he's never done that before. He's al-ways home on time.

Something terrible must have happened to make him so late, but does it involve the company or his health? He hasn't exactly been taking the best care of himself lately. There has been too much unrest in the factories down below, and he has been worried about me and the baby.

I sigh, the needlework in my hands doing little to calm my overac-tive mind.

Tick, tock . . .

I need to stop the ticking. The clock has to go. I grab the bell ly-ing on the end table beside my chair but remember everyone has gone home already. There is no one to call except Leya and Gabriel, who I'm certain have fallen asleep in Leya's room by now, and they aren't strong enough to move a giant counting menace.

Tears clog my throat as the endless ticking settles into the room. I'm alone. I'm so alone. I have no one. Nothing to make this feeling go away. Why hasn't Wellan sent a message if something is wrong? What if—the door to the sitting room bursts open, startling me out of my seat.

Wellan and Lord Hoek stumble into the room.

"Wellan," I gasp, rushing toward him and falling into his arms. He smells putrid—nothing at all like the smell of ink and paper that usually settles around him. I pull away and notice the streaks of soot and ash across his face and clothing. That smell . . . it's destruction, disease, death. I try not to gag as the tears from earlier clog my throat. I clear them away. I can't show weakness. Not yet.

"What happened?" I gasp, pulling Wellan over to a chaise. He and Lord Hoek sit. Their faces are far away, their eyes lifeless—broken. Why won't he say anything? Why won't he speak? Doesn't he know how scared I am in their silence?

Tick, tock . . .

Wellan sighs deeply. "There was—" he starts. "There was an explosion at the factory this morning."

Fear forces a gasp from my mouth and my hand flies up to my lips. "Oh dear." That's why they look the way they do; they had been in Lower Inferium.

"We got the message, and there was no time to think, all we could do was act. So, we went down to assess the damages," Wellan continues and looks at Lord Hoek.

"There were forty-four wounded. Nine of those were killed in the blast," Lord Hoek says, his voice as grim as a reaper's.

I can hardly speak. It's so much worse than I ever could have imagined. In all honesty, I had been hoping that my dark thoughts would prove to be wrong, but instead, I am the one who is fooled.

"Which factory was it?" I stutter. Was it the weapon's factory? Or the steel?

"Mine," Lord Hoek speaks. "We are still under investigation on how the explosion happened, but the inspector believes that it was one of the workman's errors when handling the gunpowder for the bullets. Everything went under with one wrong spark. We're still not certain how the spark occurred. My workers are usually very careful . . . They are all trained not to smoke or light a match anywhere near the facilities. Unfortunately, someone did, and nine people have lost their lives because of it."

"What will happen if they find out it was a workman's error?"

"My company will go under review by the High Council, and if they find that my company is liable for not administering proper protocols, I will be shut down and owe millions of SEM for the damages caused. If they find it was a workman's error, even though they have been trained properly, the training process will have to be reviewed and updated before they'll allow me to start rebuilding and get my workers back on the job." He runs a hand through disheveled hair before continuing,

"My company's hearing will be at the end of the week once they've gathered enough evidence. It wasn't my only facility, but all production has been halted until the Council hearing." He looks at Wellan. "As I was telling Wellan, I don't expect you and your company to uphold our contracts and help me out of this nightmare. No amount of foresight could have prepared us for this, and our contracts exclude case liability. I completely understand if you want me to take Gabriel and leave."

"Nonsense," I hear myself say, surprised that those words have even left my mouth. "You and Gabriel have been a part of our family for over five years. I don't think we can just forget all that and kick you out of our home. We will wait and see what the verdict is." I hold my composure against both Wellan and Lord Hoek's shocked faces.

Despite all my initial hesitation, I've grown quite fond of Gabriel and Lord Hoek. I don't want to abandon them at the first sign of trouble. Plus, I know Leya will be heartbroken if I send Gabriel away. She'll hate me forever, and I can't allow that.

"Thank you." Lord Hoek stares at me with grateful eyes. "Thank you for your extreme amount of kindness."

I nod. "You and Gabriel should stay here for the night. It's already very late. I'll get a bath drawn up for you." I look at Wellan as tears of relief flood my face. "I'm glad you are both safe."

He takes my hand and kisses my knuckles.

CHAPTER 27
Before the war: 1854-S: Leya Barrett

Gabe and I pull away from the grate we are kneeling in front of, our faces contorted in horror. His father's company could be in big trouble, especially because people *died*, but also, what will happen to Gabe and his father if the Council decides they did something wrong? But they didn't. I'm certain they didn't. I look back at Gabe, but he has disappeared. I stand, finding him by the hall window, looking up at the stars outside.

We were supposed to be in bed. We should have never heard any of that.

I walk over to him and wrap him in a big hug. "I won't let them take you away. No matter what."

"I'm scared, Leya." His voice is full of tears.

"You don't have to be. I'm right here."

He pulls away. "But what happens if they decide that my father has to go to jail? What will happen then? What if I have to go with him? You won't be there, and I'll be alone."

I take his hand into mine. "I'll never let that happen to you. I—I'll go to jail with you. You'll never be alone."

"You mean it? Even if I'm not rich anymore?"

"Especially then. Besides, why would you be thinking about money? You're not made of it. I'd rather have you than all the money in the world anyway."

"Promise?" He sticks his pinkie finger out.

I hook mine with his and then snap three times before slapping his hand against mine. Gabe does the same, sealing our promise before we knew what promises even meant—before we knew they could be broken and betrayed.

CHAPTER 28
During the war: 1861-S: Gabriel Hoek

"These are to protect you at all times," the general says, referring to the masks lying on the metal tables in front of us. I sign to Riel, who stands beside me, so he can understand what the general is talking about even though I know he can read lips pretty well. "Most of you have never stepped foot in Lower Inferium. It is disgusting. A cesspool of human filth and waste. Disease runs rampant and bodies line the streets.

"Don't get caught off guard when you step onto the feces-lined pavement, and if you see something that might be blood, don't stop and stare because it probably is. You won't want to breathe the air, hence, these"—he stops and holds one up—"If you lose or damage your mask, you will regret it immediately. You're dismissed. Don't forget to take one before we are shipped down there. I won't tell you again. If you forget, it's not my problem."

I study the masks lying on the metal tables in front of me. They are long, narrow beak-like things that look like they were designed from someone's horrific nightmare, not something used to protect you. Part of me wants to leave it here just so I don't have to put the terrifying thing anywhere near my face, but if what the general said is true, then I don't want to risk not having one at all. Other soldiers take their masks and move on to the mess hall where dinner is about to be served.

'They're ugly.' Riel signs, and I stifle a laugh. He's not wrong.

'I know.' I sign back.

'What are you two chatting about?' Doren signs.

I nearly jump out of my skin when I look up to meet his eyes. He already wears one of the terrible masks, and just like I assumed, they make you look terrifying. I wonder if the design has anything to do with the fact that we will be stifling the rebellious efforts of the Lower Inferium citizens. Were the masks supposed to scare the wits out of them first?

'Get that ridiculous thing off your head.' Riel rolls his eyes at Doren.

'But it's comfy.' Doren signs back.

Again, I try not to laugh, leave it to Doren to bring some light-hearted laughter into a dark situation. Sometimes I wished I had his positivity. He takes the mask off, shaking out a head of golden hair, and slapping a hand against Riel's back, who jumps and shakes Doren's hand off.

Doren signs. *'It's okay to laugh sometimes, my friend.'*

Riel sighs, glaring daggers at his mask. *'Not in this situation. It's bad enough that we have to head down there in a few hours to stop a rebellion, but these make it even worse. We're just cowards who will be hiding behind a mask made by a rich society of tyrants.'*

'Unfortunately, we belong to that society of tyrants.' Doren clasps a hand on Riel's shoulder, and this time Riel doesn't shake him away.

Doren's right. We all grew up in the rich society of Higher Seperium. Doren grew up as the heir to Caldwell Textiles. Our gray uniforms had been crafted using his father's very fabrics. Riel's family owned a prosthetic business in East Seperium City. His father hand-crafted beautiful prosthetic limbs that members of the rich society literally mutilated themselves to be able to wear.

And me. My father used to own the biggest weapon manufacturer in High Seperium. The gun strapped to my thigh burns with the weight of what it stands for—a gun I will most likely have to use against people who never had a chance to be anything different.

Riel's features harden as he throws the mask back on the table. *'If the people of Lower Inferium are rebelling against us, isn't there a reason for that?'*

'I guess we're about to find out.' Doren signs, before strapping his mask to the pack on his back.

I have to agree with Riel, especially if what the General said about Lower Inferium proves to be true; then I can definitely understand why they would want to make what they have better, or at least try to. I'm not certain a rebellion is the way to go, but maybe they had no other choice. Maybe we left them with no other choice . . .

CHAPTER 29
Before the war: 1854-I: Vienna Sinclair

I know something is horribly wrong as I hurry through the streets to Lower Inferium Hospital for my shift with Dr. Greenwood. The smell of smoke and bits of ash linger heavily in the air today and cause my eyes to water and itch. As I near the hospital, I notice there are way too many people standing around the front entrance. I walk to the back and hurry inside.

What I see stops me dead in my tracks, freezing me to the white-washed hardwood floors. Men and women, covered in soot and blood, line the halls of the building as if the rooms spit them out. My fellow nurses hurry past patients, stepping over them and trying to help the ones who are bleeding the most—like those who lost an appendage or two.

"Vienna!" Jodi, a plump dark-skinned nurse, rushes out of the staffroom, nearly bowling me over. Her arms are full of bandages and ointments. "Get out of the way, girl . . . and hurry up and get ready. Greenwood needs you in two," she calls over her shoulder as she hurries down the hall.

Her words pull me out of my stupor, and I rush to get ready. As I'm washing my hands in the nurses' station, I overhear two nurses talking about what happened.

"An explosion, I was told."

"Really? Where?"

"Hoek Weapons." My heart plummets at the words. My father works at Hoek Weapons. I still for a moment, remembering that Hoek

Weapons is made up of several factories.

"The big one?"

"From what I heard, yes. They lost nine people." I feel like someone stabbed me in the gut, like when I found my father five years ago. I can't breathe. What if my father was injured? Or . . . I stop the thought before I can continue. I bend over my knees, breathing in deeply. I have to get a grip. Dr. Greenwood needs me, and right now, I can help someone stay alive. If my father is injured, he'll be here.

The tangy scent of blood assaults my nose as I step out of the nurses' room and into the hall, heading toward operation room number two. Since joining the hospital ranks a few months ago, Dr. Greenwood has me assist in suture surgeries and other operations. He told me that a lot of the other staff found the job to be too gruesome, and a few actually fainted.

He said he needed someone level-headed, who could think clearly and didn't falter or shake at the sight of blood. I was apparently that someone, and so far, I hadn't fainted. There is only one time I faltered, but the details are too gross for me to elaborate and have to do with a lot of spewing blood.

Strapping a cloth mask over my face, I step into the room.

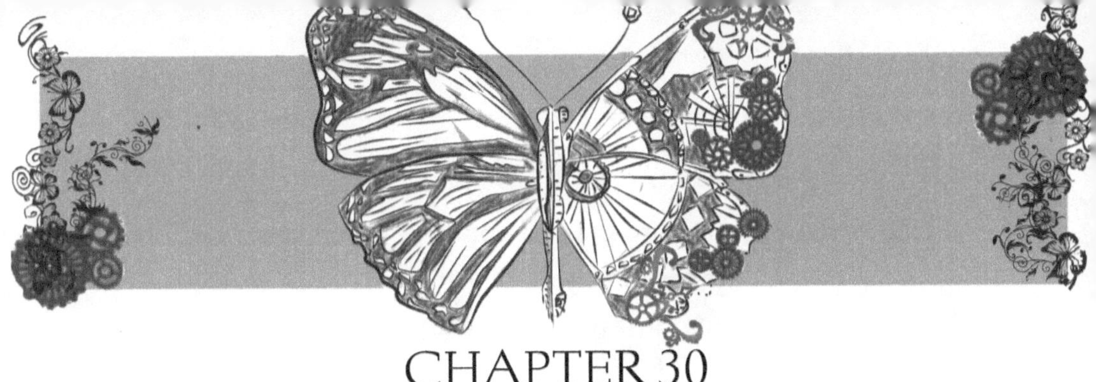

CHAPTER 30
Before the war: 1854-S: Riel Mjorn

My jaw drops in disbelief as I stare at the newspaper headline. I only bought a paper to read the word of the day and articles on Seperium's High Council—the only justice system we had. Even though I'm only fourteen, I've always enjoyed reading about the cases and their verdicts or punishments. I like reading in general, but that's beside the point. Today, the headline causes me to stop in the middle of the sidewalk while people push past me.

Factory Explosion! Mayhem in Lower Inferium!
Read all about how nine factory workers lost their lives!
No comment from the factory owner, Lord Samuel Hoek.

My heart sinks as my fingers move to fiddle with my mechanical necklace. Hadn't the people of Lower Inferium been through enough already? Nine people lost their lives in a truly tragic way, and the news reports of Higher Seperium are blasting about the *exact* details of their deaths. How is that okay? Those people and their families deserve better than this. They don't need their loved ones' deaths being talked about all over Higher Seperium—their names being spoken by the condescending mouths of the rich.

My stomach twists in revulsion. I can't imagine the gossip that is going to come from this. Everyone will say that it was some stupid factory worker's fault, but is that actually the case? Surely, some people are going to make quite a bit of money from this disaster, and I'm almost certain their names have got to be in the High Council.

I clench the paper in my fist and continue down the street. The things people would do for money, even if they already have loads and loads of it. Sunlight hangs low in the sky while I huff my way to Breve and Daniella Michalesen's house.

After meeting Breve, the conductor from the Seperium elevator last year, he arranged for my parents and me to have dinner with them so I could meet his wife, Daniella. We got along so well that ever since then, I spend one dinner a week at their house, but now, I don't even want to go. The turmoil in my gut is enough to steal my appetite. Besides, how am I supposed to make nice conversation with Daniella and Breve when my mind is spinning? I know, I can't carry the weight of the world, but that doesn't seem to stop me from feeling upset.

Flicking dark brown hair from my eyes, I stop in front of their house, which is smashed against other apartment buildings—a sweet two-story with a little yard that faces the street before leading to the front door. Five windows stand like silent sentries keeping watch over the house—two on the first story adorning each side of the door, and three on the second story. I consider turning around and pretending that I forgot, but I never forget dinner with the Michalesens. Our dinners are a pleasant idea of what my life could look like one day—a nice house and a loving wife.

I step to the door, knocking to announce myself before I open it. A set of stairs sits next to a hallway directly in front of the door. Two halls on either side of me lead to the kitchen and dining room on the left, and the parlor to the right. Delectable scents of chocolate and garlic waft through the cozy house. I take a left, heading toward the kitchen where Daniella stands over a large pot. She has dark hair that is pinned up into a high bun and tawny skin that only makes the smile she sends my way even brighter.

'Almost ready.' She signs, before pulling rolls out of the oven.

I sit down on a stool just on the outskirts of the kitchen, eyeing the plate of chocolate chip cookies sitting on the counter.

Daniella notices me looking. *'You can have one you know.'*

'I know.' I sign back. *'But I don't want to spoil dinner. It smells amazing.'*

Gentle aromas of chicken and sage with hints of yeast permeate the kitchen and make my mouth water.

She smiles. *'Thank you. Aren't you glad my cooking skills have improved since the first time you were here a year ago?'*

I laugh. *'I'm very glad I don't have to suffer through any more burnt meals, but if that were the case, I would still come to dinner.'*

'I know you would.'

'Where's Breve?'

'He's still at the elevator. Things have been tense since . . .' her hands stop short as a distressed look settles over her face.

'I know. I saw the paper. It's a terrible tragedy, and they're blasting it all over the place like it's everybody's business. Do you know they included the details of the deceased? What family wants to deal with that? Have your loved one's death broadcast to people who don't even know you.'

'That's terrible. I haven't read the paper yet. They don't even treat them like human beings, they're just . . . expendable bodies.'

'It's disgusting.' I sign. *'I wouldn't be surprised if the owner had something to do with the fire, but the papers will never cover that side of things. The coward didn't even have the gall to make a statement for the reports.'*

Daniella narrows her eyes at me. *'You shouldn't assume things, Riel. The owner is in a very detrimental time right now. Many lives were lost in his company, and even though the Council doesn't care if one person dies on the job, they care when something like an explosion happens because it's too big to hide. He will be under trial for several weeks and the Council will most likely halt production until the matter is settled, leav-*

ing hundreds without work or pay. I'm sure he never wanted something like this to happen, so let's not be so quick to judge.'

I look down at the tile floor in shame. *'I'm sorry. I'm trying to get better at not . . . judging, but there is so much hurt in this world that it's so easy to become angry and blame it all on the ones who have the money and power to change it—because they did nothing.'*

She continues, *'I know, but I think there is so much more that we don't understand. We should hear and know all sides of the story before we make a decision. We live in a world where we can't afford to do something rash. Someone will always be watching, and what we do can destroy or rebuild something beautiful. Don't forget that.'*

I nod.

'Have you heard anything from Seperium Landing yet?' she asks.

Oh, right. With all the terrible news, I completely forgot about the letter I received this morning.

'I got accepted.' I say, fiddling with my mechanical necklace.

'Riel! That's wonderful! You're going to do wonderful there!'

'Thank you. I'm excited, but a little nervous.' I sign before grabbing the necklace again and popping open the locket and then closing it again.

'It'll be an adventure for sure.'

'Did you ever go to boarding school?'

She shakes her head. *'No, my parents weren't brave enough to enroll me. They thought I would get taken away because I wouldn't know how to survive.'*

'You think I'll be able to survive?'

She laughs. *'I know you will. You can read lips. Plus, our abnormalities aren't as unacceptable as they used to be.'*

I smile before it drops in confusion at smelling something that isn't right.

Daniella's eyes widen in fear before she turns to the stove. She looks back at me.

'Oh well, I guess you have to eat a burnt meal after all.'

'Oh well, I guess you have to eat a burnt meal after all.'

CHAPTER 31
After the war: 1864-S: Inspector Leo Pim

Chief Lecten won't shut up. He's done nothing but jabber since I got in this motorcar with him. How much farther can Claren Hill be, because I will risk personal injury and jump out of this car to get his grating, droning voice out of surround sound. I don't even know what he's talking about anymore because I tried to drown him out by humming Concerto 117, but that lasted all of two seconds. Somehow Chief Lecten made my favorite concerto annoying.

Gloriously, the motorcar chugs to a stop, and I jump out as the driver puts it into park. Immediately, my eyes focus on the giant steel building in front of me. Claren Hill is nothing like Dwell Hall. It looks like a whimsical castle of old. Swooping and spiraling metal, like lily stems, snake up the front of the house to uphold the third-story balcony. Glass windows look out from underneath large metal sheets, like blinders that are split open in the middle. Gears anchor them to the ground, and I assume, it's what opens and closes them.

The stairs leading up to the door aren't even stairs at all, but an escalator. I sniff, *it's rather classy*. I like the Barrett family already, but of course, their money has had trails of blood smeared on it before. Who's to say they're not responsible for Lord Caldwell's blood? Chief Lecten steps onto the escalator, suddenly silent. I sigh happily for my ears— he's finally run out of words . . . or maybe this elegant, colossal house has scared him into silence.

A butler opens the door for us, and we step into a grand entrance. Windows behind us, shine natural light into the space, illuminating the cerulean blue rug and flags that adorn the room. The inside, unlike the outside, is garnished with beautiful ebony wood, complimenting the blue. Directly in front of us, a huge portrait of the Barrett family greets the foyer.

Their menacing faces look down with an air of confidence and pride. Lord Wellan Barrett is in the background with his hand gently holding his wife's—Lady Michele Barrett. Their daughter, who appears to be sixteen or seventeen, stands just in front of her father—Leya Barrett, now Caldwell. The youngest, now deceased, member stands in front of his mother—Casen Barrett.

What I find most interesting about this portrait is the young man standing next to Leya, a boy who looks very much like General Hoek. His long hair is slicked back in the photo, and he stands as if he is a part of their family with that same prideful look in his eyes.

"Sirs, if you would follow me, the Barretts are expecting you," the butler says, walking into a hall directly below the portrait. This hall is almost as large as the entryway with more pictures and portraits of the family and ancestors. The butler takes a right and introduces us to the people in the room. It's a parlor with a marvelous onyx fireplace and deep blue curtains like the rug in the foyer. The family sits on furniture made out of ebony wood and light blue and black upholstery.

A man with a large gray beard and mustache, glowing hazel eyes, and a face filled with grim lines stands to greet us, his hand extended. He has a slight limp like it hurts him to walk.

"Lord Wellan Barrett," he introduces himself. I stare at his hand. Thick hands, strong hands for a man who has never seen factory work like those he employed. Interesting.

"Inspector Leo Pim." I shake his hand, and he moves to greet Chief Lecten.

I look over the other family members. Lady Barrett looks up at me, her brown eyes rimmed in red and filled with knowledge she may or may not be willing to share. Her black dress compliments the dark details in the room. I move toward her. She lifts her black lace-covered hand, and I place a short peck on top.

"Nice to meet you, Inspector Pim," she says, her voice pinched like she's in pain.

"And you as well, Lady Barrett." I move on to the next person— Leya Caldwell. Brown eyes, much like her mother's, meet mine behind a layer of black lace. They are blurry and red, but there is something else in them that I can't quite place, and it leaves me full of intrigue. Worry? Perhaps, but her face doesn't look worried, it looks broken and exhausted. This tells me *nothing*. I have to find a way to separate every member of the family for singular interrogations. I need to break them. I need to study them in an environment that isn't so formal and perfect.

"Leya Caldwell, I presume?" I ask.

She lifts her hand. "Yes, Inspector."

I kiss her hand. "Might I ask you some questions?"

Her brown eyes glance toward her mother, who seems to be watching us with rapt silence. Lady Caldwell opens her mouth. "I—"

"Leya will be taking no questions at the moment, Inspector," Lord Barrett interjects. "She's still . . . recovering."

I glare at Lord Barrett. Something isn't right here. They know something. Something they don't want to tell me. "Excuse—"

"We've come to update you on the case," Chief Lecten says, taking a seat across from the family.

I frown, my eyes narrowing at Chief Lecten. I'm not sure if I'm upset that he cut off my words without an apology—how rude—or that he's lying. I'm here to interrogate them. What in the world did Chief Lecten drag me out here for then? Surely, I'm not supposed to tell them what I've found? That's supposed to be his job, not mine.

"Excuse me, Chief, but I am not here to update the family. I am he—"

"Well, why not? You are the inspector on the case, correct? My daughter's husband was murdered in their peaceful home," Lord Barrett starts. Frustration barrels down my throat, if someone cuts me off one more time . . .

"It must not have been a very peaceful home." I stare at Lord Barrett. The family's faces study me in shock. While they are recovering, I continue, "A murder happened in a home which all of you have access to, correct? And you were all there for a dinner party the Caldwells were hosting . . ." I leave the words hanging in the air, daring them to question my judgment.

"Are you sayin—"

"You are all suspects in this case, and I have to ask questions, even if you are not fully *recovered*," I say, successfully cutting Lord Barrett off. Ha, for small victories, because this interrogation seems to be going nowhere. I look at Lady Caldwell, whose brown eyes study me. Suddenly, I recognize what I couldn't place before. Vengeance. A fire that burns in a consuming rage. Lady Caldwell is a lit cannon, ready to explode. Now, does her fire burn for or against a certain general? I can't wait to find out.

CHAPTER 32
Before the war: 1855-S: Wellan Barrett

"This is not what we agreed on!" Samuel screams as he smacks a piece of paper onto my desk, disrupting the letter I had been writing.

"We agreed to nothing, Samuel." I glance at the paper he had slammed on my desk.

"You promised you would help me recover Hoek Weapons! Not buy it behind my back!"

I glare up at him. "I didn't buy it behind your back. The Council was going to sue you for negligence. I convinced them to let me buy Hoek weapons and keep you out of jail. Would you rather have had to pay an exorbitant amount of money and still lose your business? Where do you think you would be then?"

"That's beside the point. I want my company." He leans over the desk, his eyes blazing in madness.

"Either way, you weren't going to have it! I did you a favor! I kept you out of jail, your son off the streets, and put a pretty penny in your pocketbook to help you provide for Gabriel! Shouldn't you be happy that your company is in the hands of someone you know?"

"That was only when I respected the man standing before me. I have no more respect for you! You took everything from me! You could have consulted me first! You could have told me what you were planning before ripping everything out from underneath me!"

I stand. "There was no time! The Council called me before them to give my testimony. I told them you taught your employees well, and that you were always fair to them. They then told me that they would be prosecuting you and suing for negligence, and if I wanted to keep my nose clear I should break all ties with you immediately. I told them they were being ridiculous, and offered to buy the company instead, and pay for all damages so they owed nothing and had nothing to answer for!"

Tears glaze his eyes. "I never did anything wrong. I always did what I was supposed to. I took care of my people and now . . ."

I move around my desk, clamping a hand on his shoulder. "I'm sorry it came to this, but I did what I had to. I promise I will take good care of Hoek Weapons."

"What will happen to Gabe and me? I'll have to move him into the city."

"I'm willing to offer you a position in the company as overseer, but I have to wait until everything settles down—at least a year. Michele and I have plans to send Leya to boarding school, and if you want, we will do the same for Gabriel while you get settled."

"You would?"

"Yes."

He sighs. "I'm sorry for yelling. I just—I—"

"I understand, but everything will be okay."

His dark eyes look at me as if he believes those words, before nodding his head.

CHAPTER 33
Before the war: 1855-S: Leya Barrett

"Boarding school?" I stare in disbelief at my parents. "You're shipping me to boarding school?"

The dark green trees painted on Mother's sitting room walls seem to dance around me in a taunting merry-go-round. *You're going to boarding school. You're going to boarding school*—around and around.

"Leya, please stop with the tantrum," Mother starts, wincing as she shifts in the seat. Her stomach is huge, and I know the baby will be born soon. I'll be a big sister. "You're thirteen now, almost a lady. You're ready for the next phase of your education. Plus, I went to boarding school when I was your age."

"Just because you went doesn't mean that I want to." I cross my arms over my chest.

"Leya." Father's voice admonishes my dramatics. "Listen to your mother."

I gesture to my mother. "But what about the baby? I won't be able to get to know my little brother or sister if I'm not here."

"Leya, you're being dramatic. You will get a full month between semesters, and you'll be home in the summer. And with your father having to oversee everything with the new company, and me having to take care of the baby, it's just—it's not a good time right now. Your education needs to be improved, and that can only happen at this school. I won't have time to continue your and Gabriel's education."

Fear plunges to my gut at her words. "Wait, what will happen to Gabriel? You're not sending him away because his father is moving to Seperium City?"

"Quite the opposite, Leya," Father says. "We're paying for Gabriel to go to boarding school as well. It's an integrated school, and you will most likely see him in between classes and whatnot."

"We're going together?" I sit back down on the chair across from my parents, feeling more at ease with the situation. If Gabe is coming with me, I'll be fine. Besides the baby, Gabe is my next biggest concern. There is no way I'll be able to face boarding school without him.

"You and Gabriel will be leaving at the end of the month. Everything will be fine."

But it wasn't fine, and nothing could have prepared us for what was to happen next.

CHAPTER 34
Before the war: 1860-I: Rosea Dierich

I stop, admiring the mural painted on the side of Barrett Industries. Sunshine streams down from the hazy sky, illuminating the bright colors. Some workers are out on scaffolding, trying to erase the image. Six years ago, Barrett Industries became the biggest fat cat in the business when their partner Hoek Weapons went up in flames . . . literally. Since then, things down in Lower Inferium have gotten worse.

To compensate for the loss, the factories put a lot of people into overtime, working many to death. A disease broke out, leaving millions scarred, and ready for a change. I watched my best friend lose everything. She's okay, and honestly, the way that girl stands the sight of blood unnerves me—but we got through the loss together. We watched as others broke the same way we had, but they didn't have each other like Vienna and I did; their brokenness has become fodder for the fires of rebellion.

Even now as I stand here looking up at the work that was inspired by the cost of hundreds of lives, I feel the weight of the unrest forcing me to conform, but conforming was never my forte. I bite my nail, picking at the little flecks of paint still lodged there.

The mural is a picture of a long-haired blonde girl with tears in her eyes. Her mouth has been sewed shut with thick black string, her hair blowing in the wind. Behind her, a factory blazes in big blue and orange flames with black smoke billowing out of it. A rose is clutched in her hands as the words *Never Silent* in big red letters bleed down the front of her light pink dress.

It's gruesome, and yet, insanely gorgeous at the same time. So many are starting to believe in this vigilante they're calling Crémant Rose, and the seeds of rebellion she's planting. *"It only starts with one,"* Grams' voice rings in my head. She's right. One spark. One voice. One action to set the world aflame with light or burn it down.

What trick shall I pull to get you to hear my plea? The song plays in my head, and I look down at my other hand which still holds a bag full of mended dresses. Right. I'm supposed to be delivering these and then—

"Oh no," I say aloud as Grams' sweet face pops into my head. I got to go. I rush through the streets.

What trap will you find to fall in love with me? I make a left turn and then another. The grim buildings cast ominous shadows against my path.

Capture you in my jeweled gaze. The apartment I'm looking for starts with an A and ends in 235.

Turn your head with my talons. On the right. I knock on the door, and before I know it, I'm walking back down the alley with a small handful of SEM notes.

Whatever will do with me. To the right twice, and I'm back near the main square of Lower Inferium. I can find my way to the theater from here, usually. Grams taught me this system when I was really young. She'd sing a song from a popular play or performance piece, and then she would teach me the way by using the song as directions. It worked well for me since I seemed to get lost, turned around, and confused everywhere I went.

Now, I use the same system to keep my mind focused, so I don't ever lose my way again. I look around the busy afternoon square as I wait for the trolley. People rush past me with their coats pulled tight around them, their eyes cast to the floor where they walk. Dark soot lines every inch of the square, with large piles of trash scattered here and there. Feral dogs gnash and bite at passing ankles, fighting over anything they can possibly eat. Smoke pours out from chimneys and keeps a constant dark cloud bearing down over the citizens.

The trolley pulls up, showering sparks into the dim sky as people spill out into the street.

"Young man, I already told ya. I don't need ya 'elp. Just because I'm ol—"

That sounds like Grams, but I don't recognize the other voice.

"Woman, let me help you down, and then I'll have to remind myself never to help another unfortunate soul again."

"That's quite a rude thin' to say. Fine, ya may 'elp."

"I—"

Suddenly, my Grams, being led by a handsome man, steps off the trolley. I can't stop the sly smile that spreads across my face, it's my victim from last night. *He's here.*

Grams notices me. "Rosie! I thought ya'd be 'ere. I was gettin' off and this young man offered to 'elp me." She pinches the man's cheek, and he noticeably cringes.

I hold my hand out to him. "Rosea Dierich."

He stares at my hand, his lips curled into a snarl. Finally, he takes it. "Leo Pim."

I yank his arm, and he stumbles, nearly crashing into me. I bring my lips close to his ear. "The wine you left me last night was quite wonderful."

He jumps, smacking my head against his. Whiplash, and a few sparks later, I find him groaning and holding his head almost five meters away. Well, that's what he gets for trying to run away again.

Grams starts clapping. "Wonderful performance," she calls, referring to our debacle.

I bow to her, soaking in her praise, but Pim doesn't seem to notice.

"I think I'm bleeding," he mutters to himself. "Oh goody, I'll now get an infectious disease and probably die in this rotting hellhole." He notices me looking and straightens, clearing his throat. "You owe me."

"What? A new head? I don't think they make those."

"I—"

"Do you want me to kiss it? That will probably make it feel better."

"Don't you ever put your lips anywhere near me again!" He takes several steps back as if I'm one of those rabid dogs about to bite his ankle. He notices the dog and screams—literally screams. A grown man. *Screaming.* I burst out laughing, picking up some trash on the ground and throwing it at the mutt.

"There are worse things," I say, heading over to Grams.

"Excuse me?" His voice rings across the bustling square. "You still owe me."

"What? For the wine? I called dibs on it after you left. That's some expensive wine you bought last night, and you just left it. That means you must have money. You're from Higher Seperium, aren't you?"

He ignores my question, those bright blue eyes blazing. "No, for bringing your grandmother here."

Who says the word grandmother anymore?

"I never asked you to do that."

He stares at me, his mouth opening and closing like a fish.

"Come back when you've got something real to pin on me. Ha-ha, pin Pim. Pin Pim. Pin Pim," I start to hum.

He stares at me with a confused expression. "What in Seperium's sake are you talking about?"

I feel a hand on my shoulder and stop my muttering.

"Come on, Rosie. Thank the gentleman and let's go," Grams says, turning toward the direction of our apartment.

I bow to the gentleman, almost all the way to my knees. "Thank you." And with that, I take Grams' hand and leave the curious Mr. Pim flabbergasted on the side of the street.

CHAPTER 35
During the war: 1861-S: Gabriel Hoek

My heart palpitates with fear as I march beside Riel and Doren. The Seperium Elevator looms up ahead. A metal beast that would be taking us down into the heart of Inferium. Doren glances sideways at me, looking as pale as I feel. Are we ready for this?

My feet move instinctively. No, of course, we're not. We're just rich kids who have never lived without anything before, and now, we're scared. Scared that there might be a chance that the luxuries we have will be taken away.

As we near the station, our line of fellow soldiers shuffles to a halt. Riel turns to look at us. *'Looks like the line has stopped,'* he signs, before moving his fingers to fidget with his locket, averting his gaze.

Doren smacks his lips. "It's gonna be a long night," he says, signing for Riel, but Riel isn't paying attention. He's already lost in that place of la la land he likes to visit. A place where he's stuck in an endless loop of spiraling thoughts.

"Have you ever been to Lower Inferium?" Doren asks.

I shake my head. I never had a reason to go down there. I had a dream once that I created a pair of wings that could help me fly from Higher Seperium to Lower Inferium, but in the dream, Lower Inferium was beautiful—as beautiful as Higher Seperium, not like what I had heard from other people. Perhaps it was because I had never known anything different, but it made me wonder why Lower Inferium was so bad. How did it happen? And why didn't it look like Higher Seperium?

'I've been there . . .' Riel signs. So, he is paying attention.

'What was it like? Is it as bad as the General said?' Doren asks, his green eyes shining with curiosity.

'Worse.' Riel's face contorts into a mask of grief. Poor Riel, he always takes on the weight of the world but his twenty-year-old shoulders can't uphold it.

'Were there rats?' Doren asks.

Riel shoots him a withering look before answering, *'Yes, big ones… bigger than my head.'*

Doren smiles, elbowing me in the side and covering his mouth with his other hand. "Cool. We all know Riel's got a big head. So those rats must be ginormous."

I try not to laugh, but a smile creeps up onto my face in spite of myself.

Riel notices finally, glaring at us. *'What are you two giggling like schoolgirls for? Are you talking about me? Why do I always get left out of the joke? Why do—'*

His hands move so fast that I barely understand what he's saying, and it only makes me laugh harder.

'Sorry, Riel.' Doren starts. *'I made a joke about your head being big.'*

Riel's hands stop dead. He looks between the both of us. *'You two suck.'* He starts to walk away.

I reach for his arm. *'Sorry, Riel. We didn't mean to laugh at your expense. We should have included you. You were just so serious about the rats, and we thought it was funny.'*

'What's so funny about rats that are bigger than my head? People live around those rats.' He signs, still missing the point of Doren's and my joke.

'Nothing, there is nothing funny about it. Please just stick with us. I

don't want to get separated before we have to head down.' I sign.

Riel sighs. *'Fine, but no more jokes about rats, unless we're comparing them to your head.'* He shoots me a sly look, before walking back to Doren.

That little— I stop the thought; glad he finally got the joke.

CHAPTER 36
During the war: 1862-S: Doren Caldwell

I want to scream because I live in an impenetrable prison. I'm on the hospital floor again with my face smashed against the tile.

"One more time, Mr. Caldwell."

I glare up at the nurse. One more time? Can't she see I'm at my limit? Can't she see that I can't go any farther? That I don't want to? I don't want to try again. I don't want to get back up. It hurts, and I'm so tired of everything hurting. I want the pain to go away, disappear, but that means I have to die. I don't want to die, but I don't want to live in this hell either.

I'm stuck in a prison with no way out. No matter how hard I try. I can't move my legs. I can't lift myself up and out of a wheelchair. I'm too broken. I'm too damaged. I have nothing to keep fighting for. No one. No one to push me through this. I want Gabriel and Riel. I need them, but they are fighting. They are protecting their city because I'm a cripple who can't. I'm a cripple who can't even lift himself out of a chair.

"Get up." The voice that speaks strikes fear in my stomach.

I turn my head, meeting the menacing eyes of my dad. His dark green eyes glare at me from behind bushy gray eyebrows. "No son of mine lies on the floor like a beggar. Now get up. Have some self-respect, Doren. You're a Caldwell for Seperium's sake."

I glare at him. Now, I definitely don't want to get up because he told me to. If he told me to lie down and die because that's all I'm good for, I would have immediately tried to prove him wrong, but I've played this game long enough. It's time for me to grow up. It's time for me to get up.

I sit up, reaching for the chair. The nurse holds it steady while I shakily lift myself by my arms. Pain spikes up my spine as I use my abdominal muscles to help my hips into the seat. I clench my teeth, willing myself not to scream. I won't scream—not in front of my dad.

I'm gasping in shaky breaths as I look up at Dad from the wheelchair. I did it. I did what a Caldwell would do. I got back up.

Dad looks at me, and he still doesn't even look a little bit pleased. That's my dad for you. Never satisfied. He reaches into the inside pocket of his jacket, pulling out a letter.

"This arrived for you. It's from the army." He hands it to me. "I'll be back in three days to take you home. Make sure you don't end up on the floor again. People who are content to stay on the floor never move again."

And with that, he's gone, leaving me with the ominous letter in my fingers. I open it.

Doren, it's me, Riel. I'm writing this letter to let you know that Gabriel has been reported missing in action. He went on a separate assignment with some other men after you were shipped home—and they never came back. Some others were sent after them, but they didn't find Gabe's troop. We have no idea what happened to him. They're saying he's most likely dead. I just wanted to let you know. Please write back to me. Let me know that you're okay because they won't tell me anything. No one seems to know anything. Things are getting worse. A terrible virus has broken out among the ranks. We're all dropping like flies. I'm afraid something terrible is going to happen. Please just let me know that you're okay. I don't think I can keep fighting without you guys.

Your friend,

Riel

My fingers shake as I fold the letter back into the envelope. Gabriel is missing—possibly dead, and Riel is fighting for his life—a life he's afraid of living alone. Tears clog my vision, blurring objects around me. I have to write to Riel. I have to tell him that I'm okay. I have to tell him that I'm rooting for him—that I just want my friend to come home.

CHAPTER 37
After the war: 1864-S: Inspector Leo Pim

"That is ridiculous!" Lord Barrett screams as he stands. "*We* can't possibly be suspects in this case. The murderer has already been taken into custody. Why are you not prosecuting him?"

"Because, Lord Barrett, the murder weapon has not been identified, and just because General Hoek and your daughter were the only two, supposedly, in the house during the murder, doesn't make him liable. In fact, that makes them both prime suspects, and your daughter isn't in custody. Would you rather I file a warrant for her arrest? Or can I interrogate her here while Chief Lecten is present?"

"Why would my daughter kill her own husband?"

"Why would General Hoek have any reason to kill him?"

"Because—"

"Father!" Lady Caldwell stands. "Stop speaking about me as if I'm not here! He's right. I will speak with Inspector Pim, and if you try to stop me, he can go get a warrant for my arrest. I should have been taken into custody too. I thank you for not letting the police take me, but this has gone on long enough." Lady Caldwell glares at her father, who mumbles something under his breath before storming out of the room.

"Well, that was eventful," I mutter, looking at Lady Barrett who has stayed silent throughout the whole exchange.

She notices, her nose sticking up in the air. "I'm not going anywhere. If you wish to speak with my daughter, you will speak with me present—"

"Mother," Lady Caldwell cuts her off. "Leave."

"Leya! That is no way to speak to your mother!"

Lady Caldwell rolls her eyes. "Would you rather me be dragged to the police station? Don't you want me to have some dignity? He could have come with a warrant for my arrest, but he didn't. He's allowing this to save us the embarrassment, and we've already had enough of that. So, get out."

Lady Barrett huffs, glaring at her daughter as she stands and leaves the room.

Lady Caldwell breathes a sigh of relief as if her parents' presence had suffocated her. What she said is completely inaccurate. I don't care if their pride is intact or not. I didn't want to deal with the waste of time it would take to get a warrant, but at the rate it took to get Lady Caldwell's parents out of the room, it probably would have been worth it . . . On second thought, that's a stretch. I rather enjoyed watching Lady and Lord Barrett swallow their pride.

"I'm sorry about that. My mother is a spitfire," she says, pulling her black-laced veil from her face and sitting back down.

"You're a lot like her."

She grimaces. "Unfortunately."

"Lady Caldwell," Chief Lecten begins as we both sit. "Why don't you tell us everything that happened that night?"

I glare sideways at the Chief. Is this his investigation or mine? I can't break her with simple questions that will become arduous and long. Is she supposed to remember everything from that night? Because if so, we'll be here longer than a quick visit, and I have a hot bath with my name written all over it waiting for me at the hotel.

Lady Caldwell purses her lips before beginning. "Doren and I threw a dinner party for General Hoek. If you don't know, he'd been missing for two years. Enough to where everyone thought he was dead. Suddenly, he appeared. Doren and I were shocked because we had already grieved his death. He had nothing when he arrived, so Doren offered him to stay with us. We threw the dinner party just to welcome him home. We invited my parents, who were practically Gabriel's parents, Doren's war buddy, Riel, and his friends, Rosea and Vienna.

"The dinner went smoothly, and no one had any qualms with anyone else. In fact, we got along as if we had all been friends for years. After dinner, we had drinks and talked for a little while longer, and then our guests Riel, Rosea, and Vienna left because they had to get back to their hotel in the city. Doren and I saw them out. My parents lingered for a minute longer, hearing all the details of Gabriel's journey, while I retired to bed, and Doren went to his office to finish up some last-minute work.

"I read for a while before I thought it odd that Doren hadn't come to bed yet. And then—" her voice chokes for a minute. "And then I went to his study, and there was blood everywhere. I screamed and Gabe came running. He telegrammed the police. He told them what happened, and before I knew it, they were there and arresting Gabe, and everything happened so fast . . .

"I was supposed to go with the police too, but my father came and told them that I would make a statement later and that I should go home with him until I was stronger. They agreed as long as we had a deputy watch over us, and that's it. That's all I remember."

I study her in silence for a minute after she has finished. From what I could tell, she only lied about one thing. Her hands fidgeted, her voice cadence hitched, and her eyes shifted when she said she had retired to bed. Something pulls at my gut, begging me to poke and prod holes into her little story.

"You went straight to bed while your parents talked to General Hoek?" I question, watching her mannerisms carefully. She swallows. There. Got her.

"Yes, I got ready for bed, and then sat down to read."

I start to shake my head. "Please be blunt with me Lady Caldwell.

If you have any information, besides what you have shared, I suggest you say it now. Someone's life is on the line, and from the way you are trying not to breathe, you know it too. You saw something. Something you weren't supposed to."

"I—" Her breath speeds up, a cornered rabbit with nowhere to run. "I—I can't."

I turn to Chief Lecten. "Please leave us. What Lady Caldwell has to say will stay between us."

"But—"

"Chief, I mean no disrespect, but I kindly ask you to leave."

"Fine." Chief Lecten stands, leaving the space to Lady Caldwell and me.

Her face is pale when I look back. "If it has to do with General Hoek, you can tell me. I have a feeling you are closer to him than a woman married to another man should be."

Tears flood her eyelids. "We didn't—I—I couldn't take it any longer. I waited for him outside his room so I could talk to him the second he was finished. I had to tell him I still loved him. I had to tell him I never wanted to marry Doren. That I wanted him, but he wasn't there, and then, we—we kissed, and I wanted—but Gabe said he wouldn't do that to Doren. He was right, and I felt so guilty that I ran and hid until I could compose myself. I waited up for Doren so I could tell him what happened, but then he never came." Tears stream down her face before she continues.

"Please don't tell my family, they don't know how much I still love him. Unfortunately, my testimony doesn't exonerate him because there was still time from when I left Gabe to when I found Doren. That's why I didn't tell you because it wouldn't have mattered. There is still no evidence that he's not the killer. I—I don't think he is, but I . . . but that could just be wishful thinking. A man can become damaged, broken, and destroyed after being gone for two years. He didn't hurt Doren or me the first few days he was staying with us, but who's to say?" She grabs a handkerchief, rubbing her eyes.

"So, you think General Hoek is capable of murdering his friend?"

More tears cut paths down her cheeks. "Yes, he is a general after all. You have to kill people to get that far, but the Gabe I knew would have never hurt a fly. I know he got through the war because of me. I know he fought and came back because of me, and now I'm afraid that because of me, he did something he can never take back."

I nod before I stand. "Thank you. I won't tell your family what you've told me. Continue to tell them your version of the story."

She stands, grabbing my arm as I turn to the door. I stare at her hands in revulsion, and she gently releases me.

"Please tell me if . . . do you think Gabe did it?" Her brown eyes hold so much hope that I wish I don't have to squander it.

"I have no opinion. I can't have thoughts or feelings in the matter of a case because it'll cloud my judgment. Right now, the evidence is stacked against General Hoek."

She gasps in pain, doubling over as if my words have physically delivered a punch to her gut.

"I have more suspects to interrogate. Chief Lecten will keep you updated with the details," I say and leave the room.

CHAPTER 38
Before the war: 1856-I: Vienna Sinclair

My hands shake as I place a clean white cloth across another victim's face. The disease we are calling "Black Rot" is sweeping across Lower Inferium faster than it takes us to blink. It is characterized by black boils that infect the surface of the skin and soon eat away at the body until limbs start to fall off. Of course, many don't make it to that point because once it infects the lungs, people don't survive long.

Dr. Greenwood and I are on a mission to discover a way to figure out how it spreads and stop it before everyone in Lower Inferium dies. Already, I have covered the faces of twenty-one victims. I haven't left the hospital since the first case was discovered a week ago. The disease seems to spread outside since none of us nurses or doctors have fallen ill yet, but we're overwhelmed and spread thin. We have over one hundred patients that need to be attended to.

I'm exhausted, and so far, those who have been infected have not recovered. Not a single one. Frustration clogs my throat as I head through hopeless halls trapped with weary whispers. Once in the nurses' station, I lean my back against the bright, clean walls, closing my eyes for a rest. The tears come without warning. In fact, I don't even know I'm crying until my cheeks are covered in precipitation. I quickly wipe them away, chalking the display up to exhaustion.

People are dying. I can't afford to be idle. I have to do what I can, while I can.

"Vienna!" Dottie, the receptionist, rushes into the station, her face pale with worry.

I look up from the sink I'm washing my hands in. "What is it?"

"It's your family," she chokes. "They—they're here . . . with black rot, all three of them."

All the air leaves my lungs at Dottie's words and my vision blurs.

No.

No.

This is a dream. I'm dreaming. This isn't real. I must have fallen asleep, and the nightmare of the last few days has bled into my head. I can't escape it. It's just a dream.

Dottie's hands shake my shoulders. My blurry vision sharpens, focusing on her kind face. Her lips are moving, but I can't hear what she's saying.

"Vienna!" My name in her voice shatters me back to reality, my world fracturing into a million pieces.

"Tell me it's not true."

"I'm so sorry, Vienna. I wish I could lie to you. I wish I could tell you that it's not real." Drops of moisture fill her eyes, decorating her lashes.

A scream wells in my throat as the nightmare bleeds into the broken glass of everything I once knew to be true. I have to get out of here. Ro. I need Rosea. I change out of my nurse's outfit as quickly as I can and race through the broken streets of Lower Inferium.

Wails and cries from people mourning the loss of their loved ones rise up from the streets. A stench chokes the air even more than usual from all the rotting bodies littering the streets. Most of them had been left in the streets by families too poor to cremate or bury their loved ones.

I hurry to the theater where Ro works and lives with her Grams. I hope she's here and not gallivanting around with the troupe—like anyone could be gallivanting at a time like this. I think she was supposed to be back from Seperium now.

I open the door, rushing into the dimly lit old theater. I'm sure it was very beautiful once. Red velvet seats, gold-trimmed marble stands and booths, and a roof covered with ornate paintings of cherubs and people dancing in the clouds. The stage features dancers and actors rehearsing for the next big set of shows, their steps and calls echoing from the stage.

I don't see Rosea among them, so I head to the stairs just outside the lobby. A fading "no trespassing" sign hangs haphazardly from a rope. I pull it away and continue up the worn-away velvet stairs.

"Ro!" I call as I push open the door to their flat. "It's me."

Ro stands on their dining table with a pair of metal, wing-like boots strapped to her feet.

The sight of the contraptions stops me dead in my tracks. "What is that? What are you doing?"

Ro squeals. "Ah! Vienna, quick. Watch this masterpiece at work. These babies are gonna get me back to Higher Seperium."

"But you just got back from—"

"I know!" Her face glows in happiness. "I met the—" she stops, studying my face. Her features fall. "Vienna, what's wrong?" She jumps down from the table, the giant boots clunking on the hardwood floors.

Tears well in my eyes as she pulls me into a hug. I start to sob, thinking about my family lying on hospital beds—dying. "I—my family—they're all dying from black rot. There is no cure. I—" Weeping takes hold of me, and I can't finish the thought for Ro.

She holds me close. "I'm so sorry, Vienna."

I pull away, looking into the warmth of her blue eyes that have filled with tears. "Anything you need, I'll be there. Grams and I'll be there." Her voice cracks. "I promise."

I nod. She hugs me again.

"I s—should probably get back to the hospital. I—I should get back to them. They don't hav—" I start, but the tears consume me once more.

Ro pulls away. "Of course. We'll come by later and bring you anything you need, okay?"

I nod again, clearing my throat and asking, "Why do you need to go back to Seperium?"

She looks down, embarrassment flushing her features. "Right, I—I met this guy."

"Oh, what's his name?"

"Well, I actually didn't meet him. I just—stared at him from across the room—on stage, and then, I found him later and kissed him . . ." she trails off.

I raise my eyebrows. "You didn't even meet him? Wait? You kissed him? And you're willing to risk your life to go back to Seperium? On those?"

Rosea smiles widely. "Yes!" She giggles. "You don't understand, Vienna. He just—" Her dramatic acting from the shows she's been in reveals itself as she sighs. "He had the most beautiful blue eyes, and I just know he's the one. So, I have to go back to Seperium to find him. I even made his red-headed friend jealous." She wiggles her ample figure.

I have to smile at her antics, forgetting for a moment the nightmare of reality I still have to face. "Will those boots even make it to Seperium?"

"I don't know, but I'm gonna find out." She laughs.

"You're crazy."

"I know." She hugs me again. "I'll drop by later."

"Okay," I say, and leave Ro alone to daydream about beautiful blue-eyed boys.

CHAPTER 39
Before the war: 1860-I: Rosea Dierich

From my perch at the top of the theater, I glare down at the man hurrying along the streets of Lower Inferium.

Inspector . . .

The man who helped my Grams and seemed almost too expensive for my taste is a Higher Seperium inspector. I overheard the other barmaids talking about how the High Council in Seperium had sent an inspector down to find Crémant Rose. I almost laughed out loud once I connected the dots. Why did the Council send down the prissiest, most abhorrent man they could have? Is it all part of a joke to them?

"They must have said, 'Hey, let's see how long the prick can last.'" I mutter to myself with a smile. "Do they find you as annoying as I do? No . . . they can't. Because I don't find you annoying. I find you—" I stop thinking of the right word. "I think you're more like a child's new toy. Something fun and interesting to play with." I want to cackle to see if he'll hear it, but I'm certain from up here, he won't. He's too . . . in his own thoughts to notice, or precisely that's what he would notice—an eerie cackle in an already eerie world.

I resist the urge, wondering instead why I find him so annoying. It's not like he did anything to me. In fact, he even helped Grams against his better judgment. Perhaps, it's because he's from the privileged society of Higher Seperium, but that never really bothered me before. They are just people too, stuck in a prison of their own superiority with no clue of what's actually happening down here. They're told that everything is fine and dandy, and they just believe it, lapping it up like starving animals. No, it's not because he's from there.

"Maybe it's because he's trying to find me?" I question aloud. "Hmm, I don't think it's that either." *Perhaps, it's because he reminds you of . . .* I stop the thought before my mind can take it and run with it.

Fear pools in my gut, and my hands immediately become clammy. My mind doesn't want to remember, but my body does.

"You'll never be anything but an Inferium rat. No one will hear you scream . . ."

"No," I say out loud, forcing my hands over my ears as if that can stop the memories flooding me. I feel his hands on my arm . . . his breath in my ear. I feel—"It never happened. Not everyone from Seperium is like that vile creature who is not even worthy of being called a man."

"Breathe, Rosie." I hear Grams' voice in my head. I drop to my knees, taking deep breaths like Grams taught me to.

After a minute, I stand back up, looking for the Inspector, but he's moved on in the time it's taken me to freak out. I won't try to compare the Inspector to anything anymore.

"Just because he's rich doesn't make him a monster. You don't know anything about him, but you could find out. In fact, he could be the best thing that happened to you—and he's not that bad-looking. It's not a crime to look," I tell myself as a thrill fills my heart at the thought of all the ways I can thwart the handsome inspector. How long can I get Leo Pim to chase me? But will I have him chase Crémant Rose? Or Rosea Dierich? He seemed to show interest in the normal girl I usually am, but he is also on the hunt for the alternate ego I had created for myself.

A gasp settles in my mind as a new thought takes place. *What if he chases us both?* Me getting close to him as Rosea, and me leaving enough clues to have him tailing his own tail as Crémant—hehe, tailing his own tail. A wry chuckle escapes my lips at the thought. This is going to be fun. Who knew that choosing one random victim at the Drunken Pig would lead to the greatest game of the century? Even if the extraordinary game never leaves the confines of my mind, it will still be the greatest. Maybe he won't see it that way, but . . .

"Let the games begin."

CHAPTER 40
Before the war: 1860-I: Inspector Leo Pim

I *swear* it's supposed to be here. My calculations can't possibly be wrong. I've never been wrong, but I am, and I hate this feeling. It's a stupid feeling when you're wrong. Instead of finding what I had hoped to be Crémant Rose's lair, I've found a dark dead-end alley where I'm certain a homeless man is asleep. I can't tell for sure though.

I sniff, feeling the weight of the gun against my hip. It's late and pitch black in the middle of Lower Inferium. I don't know why I thought it was a good idea to come out here right now. I just had to prove my hunch correct . . . *or wrong.* Nope. I refuse to admit that I'm completely wrong.

"Vat do ve have here?" a voice calls in the dark, startling me almost out of my skin.

I look up in the hazy moonlight, and find someone in a red suit, hanging upside down like an acrobat from a ladder that's attached to the side of a building.

Crémant Rose.

First of all, ew; second, I'm not wrong after all. I knew I shouldn't have admitted defeat so easily.

"Crémant Rose, I'm Inspector Pim. I'm here by order of the Higher Seperium's Council. I've come to arrest you." I flash her my badge.

The voice giggles, the form shaking in the darkness. "Zat's funny. I seem to recall zat if you vant to arrest me, you have to catch me."

What the—no. I am in no way shape or form to run through the disgusting streets of Lower Inferium chasing after a criminal. "My dignity won't allow me to chase you."

"Zen you can't arrest me."

"Is this a joke to you? You're a criminal. You have to answer for your crimes."

"Vat crimes? I zink you have to tell me vat I actually did vrong."

"You—" I stop, trying to plan my next words carefully. If I don't say something right, she might run away, and then I'll have to find her all over again. I'm tired and haven't had a proper bath in ages, so I don't want to do that. I just want to arrest her so I can get out of this horrid place. "You are under arrest for upsetting the peace of Lower Inferium."

She laughs, a bubbly sound that reminds me of raindrops. A shiver breaks across my chest, but I try to ignore it. The sound is beautiful. I shake my head. What the hell am I thinking?

"Inspector, I zink you have a very misconstrued idea of peace, zat or you haven't spent much time in Lower Inferium. Nozing is ever peaceful here."

As if to prove her point, a gunshot rings through the dark alleys, followed by a crashing bottle and a scream.

"I noticed," I mutter. "And it's only getting worse because of riffraff like you."

"Perhaps it's getting better—have you ever zought of zat?"

"I don't waste my time with nugatory thoughts."

She giggles. "Only someone from Higher Seperium would use ze vord nugatory."

I roll my eyes, placing my hands on my hips. "Please let's stop with this idle banter. I have things to do, places to be."

The shadows seem to creep closer, the smog growing thicker. As ridiculous as it might be, I fear if I stay too long the night will trap me in its vicious claws.

"Vell, so do I, Inspector, and unfortunately, I can't conform to your vishes." She spins in a blur of crimson and climbs higher up the rusty ladder. "You'll have to catch me."

Then she's gone, disappearing over the soot-covered roofs. I groan in frustration, contemplating if I should chase after her, then think better of it. I'm in no shape to leap from building to building, but next time I encounter Crémant Rose, I will be.

I spin on my heels, heading for the apartment the police acquired for me to stay in. Beaten-up motorcars grumble wearily along the lonely roads. I hear a mew from somewhere beside me. At first, I freeze, thinking it's a drifter who wants to lure me in, but then I hear it again—a kitten mew. I shake my head, continuing down the path. I have no interest in animals, especially ones from Lower Inferium. *Mew* . . . the little scared sound tugs on my heartstrings, and I turn around, heading for the place I had first heard it.

There, lying on the ground is the ugliest cat I've ever laid eyes on, but it's dark so I can't really tell. I think it's been mauled and hurt. I groan. I can't leave it here. Tugging my jacket off, I wrap the creature up. The menace screams bloody murder as I bundle it and hold the ball far away from me. I start down the path again, but stop and jump into an alleyway, hiding from the abhorrent woman heading my way—Rosea Dierich. I glance back making sure I haven't just imagined it. A lantern illuminates the features of her round face. It's definitely her.

Blast it! Why is she out here in the middle of the night? *Cause she's an entertainer . . .* I grumble. Right. Of course, the only person I actually don't want to find always seems to find me. *Breathe, Pim. She probably didn't see you.* Her footsteps start to pass me by. A meow, the sound of a warning siren, escapes from the bundle I'm holding. I glare down, hoping she didn't hear it.

The footsteps stop.

"Ah, Inspector Pim!" Her cheery voice disrupts the quiet night, and

I hold back a groan. *Blasted cat*! I don't turn around. Maybe she'll go away. "Are you stalking me?" she teases.

I spin around. "I am most certainly not! I was on my way to my apartment." I sniff, accidentally squeezing the ball I'm holding. A trembling mew escapes from the animal.

"What do you have there?" Miss Dierich leans closer.

I back away, holding the ball from her. "Nothing, at least, it's none of your business."

"Sounds like a cat to me. Are you trying to murder a cat?"

"I—why do you immediately jump to that conclusion?" I reveal the cat to her. His face is bleeding and covered in pus, leaving stains on my jacket. Yuck, this jacket is getting burned the second I finish helping this animal.

Miss Dierich says nothing, looking at the poor creature. "Ah, poor baby."

I pull the bundle closer to me. "I found him first. I'm taking him home so I can help him."

"Well, if you're dead set on it, he'll need some food. Make sure to stop at Bernie's tomorrow morning. It's the only place with fresh goat milk. It's expensive, but I think you can handle it."

I look at her skeptically. "Why are you helping me?"

She cracks a smile that reflects the yellow light of her lantern. "I'm not helping you; I'm helping the cat."

"Fine. I will do as you say."

"Let me know how it's doing." She smiles, turning to continue down the sidewalk, muttering some song under her breath.

I stare after her, confusion molding my face. Part of me wants to say that I will never consult her for anything, but . . . the encounter was quite nice, and she did genuinely seem concerned for the cat's well-being.

CHAPTER 41
Before the war: 1856-S: Leya Barrett

Birds flutter and chirp in the trees surrounding the outer courtyard of Seperium Landing after lunch. With it being early spring, the outside air is still cool, but crisp—a perfect day. Or it would have been perfect. I glare sideways at the three girls approaching me. The middle one, who I can't remember the name of, is the apparent leader, while the two girls flanking her seem to be her perfect clones—they even look the same, with their pinned blond hair and blue eyes.

It's hard not to look the same in our gold-colored school uniforms, but still. I think even their names are similar, perhaps that's why I can't remember what they're called. Generic names for generic girls who all sound the same, act the same, and will forever be the same. They even bully the same—every day they pick on whomever they deem fit. I have been no stranger to their harsh words in the last six months since coming here.

"Is he your boyfriend, or your brother?" The girl in the middle prods in reference to Gabriel, who just left. "To be completely honest, I can't tell the difference. Wouldn't it be—oh, what's the word again?" She trails off.

"Incest." The girl on her right offers up.

"That's right, *incest*, if you were in love with your brother?"

I try to ignore them like Gabe advised me to do after I told him about their bullying, but ignorance is most certainly not bliss.

"Is that what happened in your family?" I spit, dropping my book and standing. "Your mom was in love with her brother, and that's how you came out to be such a horrible human being?"

The girls' jaw drops. All of them in *unison*. I barely stifle the laugh that crawls up my throat.

"You little t—"

"Sorry, I'm late." A strange boy, with long golden hair falling into his eyes, puts an arm around my shoulders. "I hope you weren't waiting long, *Darling*." He draws the word out, looking at me.

The girls standing in front of us glare, their lips curling with envy.

"Come on, girls," the middle one says, arching perfectly placed blond brows before spinning on her heels.

After they're gone, I glance up at the boy, meeting gorgeous green eyes. "And who might you be? *Darling?*" I challenge.

"It looked like you needed some help there." He smiles, taking his arm off my shoulders. He didn't answer my question.

My eyes narrow at the odd boy. "I think I had it covered."

"I heard." He laughs, a sound that spills over the bright day like a bird cawing. "I just always wanted to try something like that, and you standing there all by your lonesome seemed like the perfect opportunity." He puffs out his non-existent chest. "Did you see their faces?" He guffaws, slapping my back like we've been friends for years.

"I saw that they all looked the same."

He stops for a minute, cocking his head as if he hadn't considered the possibility. "That's true." Finally, he looks me dead in the eyes as his laughter dies away. He sticks a hand out. "Doren Caldwell." He smiles again, a boyish grin that causes my own smile to appear.

"Nice to meet you, Doren. Leya Barrett." I shake his hand.

"A girl who shakes hands?" He stares aghast at our clasped hands.

I rip mine away, my cheeks flushing in embarrassment. "Right. I—I forgot it's not *proper* for a woman and a man to shake hands." I roll my eyes.

"Sounds like you don't care for a peck on the hand either." He laughs again.

This boy really likes to laugh. I scrunch my face in disgust.

"Sorry, I didn't mean to make you feel embarrassed," he continues.

"It's nice for a change."

"I guess, I forgot you're not like Gabe."

"Is that your boyfriend?" He cocks an eyebrow, looking overeager.

I glare at him, the memories of the girls' words lingering in my head.

"I'm her best friend." Gabe appears beside me, sparing me an answer.

Doren looks at him with a huge smile. I'm starting to think he never stops smiling.

"Gabriel Hoek." Gabe introduces himself, holding a hand out to Doren.

Doren gently places his hand on top of Gabe's like a woman would. I can't help but giggle as Gabe bends down, placing a peck against the top of Doren's hand. They burst out laughing and slap each other on their backs.

"I didn't think you would actually do it!" Doren hoots as they both turn to address me.

"Leya," Gabe starts. "I'm sure you two met in my absence, but this is Doren. He's my roommate."

Oh, he's *that* Doren. How come I didn't connect the dots earlier? *Because you had been enthralled by Doren's laugh . . .* I wouldn't say I wasn't, but I will never admit that to him.

CHAPTER 42
Before the war: 1856-S: Doren Caldwell

Clayson Bradly pushes in between Gabe and me as we head to the main building. Sunlight shines low around us, giving away to dusk. The dinner bell rings in the distance.

"Get out of the way, you imbeciles," he sneers, heading toward a lone guy, who sits against the retaining wall outside the main hall of Seperium Landing. He's wrapped up in a book, undisturbed by the world around him.

"I hate that guy." Gabe glares at Clayson.

I nod, watching as Clayson approaches the kid on the wall.

"Hey! Deaf boy," he yells, flicking the boy's book out of his hands and dropping it in the dirt.

The boy looks up with the nastiest glare I have ever seen, putting fear into my own gut.

"We should help him." Gabe steps forward, and I nod, flanking him as we step toward the duo.

"Dirt bag," Gabe mutters, smacking shoulders with Clayson and picking up the boy's book. The boy looks at Gabe in astonishment, taking the book.

Clayson pushes Gabe's shoulder. "Get out of my way. This doesn't concern you."

Gabe stands up to him, chest to chest. "I think it does. Someone needs to put you in your place, and it might as well be us."

"Us?" Clayson turns around, finally noticing me. "You idiots are gonna defend this guy?" He points to the other boy, who is studying our exchange in earnest. "He's deaf and dumb. He has no idea what I'm saying to him."

I raise my eyebrows. "I think he does."

Clayson turns back to the boy with no time to react as the boy's fist connects with his face. Clayson immediately falls to the ground, blood spewing from his nose as he lifts a hand to his face.

"You little rat!" Clayson jumps up, throwing a punch at the boy. I step into it, his knuckles smashing against my face. My head reels back. That hurt.

Gabe jumps in front of me, kneeing Clayson in the gut and pushing him away from me.

Clayson coughs on the ground.

"I think you need to learn some manners," I grunt.

Clayson stands, gearing up for another swing.

Gabe holds his hands up, standing in between us. "That's enough for now. If you don't stop, I will tell Principal Adams that you fought us for no reason and hit someone who wasn't defending himself," Gabe says, deflecting Claysons's raised fists.

"I—" Clayson stops, realizing he hit me without me fighting him back. He wipes the blood from his face and spits on the ground. "Fine, then," he says, before hurrying into the main hall. He'll probably tell the principal, but I don't care.

I turn to the boy, sticking my hand out toward him. His dark eyes size me up and down wearily. "Doren Caldwell." I smile, even though my face is starting to swell and is already puffier than my left eye can see over.

The boy shakes my hand but doesn't say anything. His hands suddenly start flying like a raving madman. I step back, glancing at Gabe who stares with a question mark on his face. The boy's hands stop, and he turns to his bag, grabbing a notepad and stencil. He writes something and turns it toward us.

My name is Riel Mjorn. I am deaf, but I can read lips. I just tried to speak in sign language, but I forget that not everyone knows it.

Sign language? So that's what he was doing.

Gabe chuckles, holding his hand out to Riel. "Gabriel Hoek." They pump fists, and then Riel talks in sign language again.

"What does that mean?" I ask.

He writes in his notebook. *I said, "Nice to meet you."*

"Oh, that's cool! Can you show us again?" I grin, studying Riel's hands. He does, and I copy him.

I look over my shoulder at Gabe. "Look, I spoke in sign language." I do it again toward Gabe. "Nice to meet you." He rolls his eyes with a shake of his head.

Riel scribbles in his notebook. *Actually, you said, "Nice to sweat you."*

Gabriel bursts out laughing, and my bluster falls.

"I really thought I had it," I mutter, kicking a clump of grass.

Riel taps my shoulder. *You'll get it.* His notepad says as he cracks a huge grin.

CHAPTER 43
After the war: 1864-S: Inspector Leo Pim

"Well, that was an utter waste of time," I groan as Chief Lecten closes the motorcar door behind us.

Chief Lecten grunts a response, looking as tired as I feel.

I run a hand over my face, catching stubble. I grimace. I need to shave. I need a bath. I need wine. Yikes, this day was a disaster.

The Barretts' testimonies led me to solve absolutely *nothing*. Lord and Lady Barrett were masters of misdirection. After they threw a tantrum for an hour over having to be questioned, I finally was able to get them to sit down and tell me their side of the story.

I look outside, watching the green rolling hills covered in wildflowers as the motorcar breezes by. They're pretty, but I wrinkle my stuffy nose, remembering that wildflowers create pollen, and pollen causes allergies.

Of course, there was a lot of ridiculous banter with the Barretts telling me over a hundred times that they shouldn't be questioned, but I finally got them to tell me the exact same story. They came to the dinner, caught up with Gabe, and left before the murder happened. End of story. Except—it's not the end of a story, it's the beginning.

Stupid allergies. I sniff, blowing my nose with a rose-embroidered handkerchief—and no, it has nothing to do with *her*. I deposit the handkerchief, watching the countryside blur by from the safety of the motorcar.

My thoughts go back to the Barretts. They're hiding something—that much is certain, but what can it be? Lady Caldwell spilled her guts in the first few seconds, clearly, she didn't have the same gift for misdirection that her parents did. Lady Caldwell is an open book while her parents are like stone sarcophaguses—impossible to seal, and equally impossible to open.

I tried to get the Barretts to crack like their daughter, but the task had almost driven me to insanity. No, that's wrong. It did drive me to insanity. That is why I am in a motorcar heading back to Seperium High Countryside prison without any clues or answers—just a stupid hunch, a sore neck, and a grimace I hadn't been able to smooth out of my face.

I'm so tired. I need a good meal, and—never mind. I already said this. Pristine shops, getting ready to close for the night, appear out of the countryside as the motorcar pulls into High Seperium Countryside—the name of this quaint village. Our car pulls into the prison courtyard.

I jump out, eager to get to the hotel just around the corner. The sun hangs low in the sky, illuminating the little specks of dust and pollen I am so allergic to. I wrinkle my nose. Even though we're in town, pollen still invades the streets.

Chief Lecten steps out of the car, looking at me. "You can get some rest, Inspector. I'll type the report for Lord and Lady Barrett. I'm assuming you'll be working on Lady Caldwell's—since you kicked me out of the room?"

I nod. "I'd like to type all the reports up to make sure I didn't miss anything." I put my top hat on. "But I will do that after a hot meal and a warm bath."

Chief Lecten nods. "Have a good night, Inspector." He tips his hat and steps into the prison.

I turn in the direction of the hotel I'm staying in. The little village of Seperium's High Countryside is set up like a grid, perfectly square, and easy to tell where everything is at—not even Rosea could get lost here . . . I shake my head. I've forgotten about her. Paved streets covered in a glistening sheen of iron are smooth and clean, pristine. Closed shops display beautiful merchandise and gifts in their large windows.

As dusk falls, little gas lights illuminate the street, flickering like mini suns in my path. I step toward the hotel, ready to order a scrumptious meal from the kitchen. Perhaps, I'll have it brought up to my room. The doorman paves the entrance for me. My feet stumble, and I nearly fall onto my face when my eyes light on the past I had tried so hard to run from.

The curvy blonde woman standing at the front desk shoots me a heart-stopping smile. "Inspector, fancy meeting you here." She turns, her right hand clasped with a chubby little girl's.

My whole world comes crashing down as I stop frozen in the middle of the foyer, looking at Rosea. The girl looks just like me—dark hair, bright blue eyes. I'm gonna throw up. I need to eat. I need rest. I need—

CHAPTER 44
After the war: 1864-S: Rosea Dierich

Hmm, I didn't think my smile would scare him that much. I stare at Pim's wilted body lying on the floor.

The doorman checks him. "He's out cold," he laughs, skirting around Pim. "I'll get the smelling salts."

"Mommy, what happened to tha man?"

"Nothing, my little acorn. He's fine," I sigh. "Or he will be." I pick up Priscilla, cradling her on my hip as we walk closer to Pim. I stare down at him. "Good to know you haven't changed one bit," I mutter as the doorman puts the smelling salts in front of Pim's nose.

Pim gasps awake, locking eyes with the doorman. I stand behind him since he hasn't noticed us again yet.

"What happened?" he asks the doorman.

"You fainted," the doorman answers, hurrying out with the smelling salts.

Pim holds his head in his hands, muttering to himself. "I—It was just a dream. Just a bad dream. It's forgotten—forgotten." He takes a deep breath. "I can get up and go take my bath."

I roll my eyes. Pim, and his baths. I bend myself over him, his face appearing upside down in my vision. "Hiya!"

He screams, trying to stand up, but instead smacks my head against his. I see stars in my vision and stumble backward.

"Rose!" Pim scrambles up, rushing over to me as I blink away the spots. His long slender fingers brush my arm and leave gooseflesh behind.

"I—" He looks so worried.

I hold a hand up. "I'm fine, not to worry." I set Prissy down and take her hand in mine again.

Pim looks from me to her to her to me and back again, his face as pale as snow. He opens his mouth, then closes it again, like a fish out of water. He holds a hand up, points it at Prissy, and then drops it.

"I'm glad that after all these years, I still leave you speechless," I titter, not even acknowledging the elephant in the room—namely, our three-year-old daughter.

"H—how?" His voice finally comes out in a squeak.

"We slept together, and nine months and six days later she popped out. Not a hard concept Pim." I can see the gears turning in his mind. *We. We. We.* "Yes, I said 'we'," I reiterate at the look on his face.

"So you didn't—but I mean—" he stops, swallowing the words that won't quite form. "I need a drink."

"Now, that I can oblige." I smile. "I'll leave Prissy with Grams."

"Grams is still alive?"

"You say it as if you've thought she was dead this entire time, but she's still kicking, nothing can kill that woman." I laugh, picking Prissy up. "Wait here. I'll be right back."

"Like I can go anywhere else," he mutters. "I don't think I can take a step without keeling over."

Dramatic, Pim. I head to the room Grams and I are renting.

After leaving Priscilla with Grams, I head back to the lobby where Pim still stands in the exact place.

I grab his arm. "Come on, Pimster. I'll explain once I've gotten a glass of wine into those gorgeous hands of yours." I take a right out of the lobby and head to the bar and restaurant.

"Are you seriously flirting with me right now?" he asks as we sit up at the bar, his long legs wrapping around the tall bar stool. I have to admit, he looks good. Better than I remember even. "That's how we got into this mess in the first place."

"Excuse me? Mess? Did you just call our daughter a mess?" I say loud enough for everyone to hear. Some rich Seperium citizens look at us with raised eyebrows. I smile to myself. *Nice, Rosea, nice.*

He shushes me, glancing around. "Be quiet. I don't need the entire police force knowing this by tomorrow morning, and I didn't call *her* a mess. I called *us* a mess." He orders a glass—bottle—of wine from the bartender. He looks at me. "Whiskey neat, right?"

I stare at him, flabbergasted that he even remembered that. I thought he was trying to forget. I nod.

"And close your mouth. You seem astonished or something," I whisper to myself as he orders my drink. I close my mouth, thinking that I told him we should talk, but now I just want to kiss him. What is wrong with me? I thought I could do this, but I can't. The second I laid eyes on him, all my feelings for him came back tenfold, but maybe that's good, right?

The light glints off the array of exquisite bottles in front of us, their colors bounce off the bar lights and onto my light-blue dress. I had chosen the dress specifically with Pim in mind—to match those eyes. Since I knew I would be seeing him tonight.

The drinks arrive, and he looks at me, those blue eyes scouring every inch of my face. It makes me feel vulnerable, open. Like Pim is the writer, and he is describing me while I am being formed by new words, but what words is he using to describe me? The kind, beautiful, perfect Rosea Dierich, or the woman who had viciously ripped his heart out and fed it to the wolves? Kind of dark imagery there, but I wouldn't put it past him. In his mind, that is exactly what I had done.

"We are a mess." I take a sip of my whiskey.

Pim downs his entire glass of wine and then pours another all the way to the brim. Finally, he looks at me. "What are you doing here, Rosea?"

"I was called to testify at the station tomorrow."

Pim shoots me a withered look. "That's not what I meant, and you know it." He takes a sip from his glass.

You knew this was going to happen. Don't be a chicken. The smell of orange-glazed chicken on a passing plate fills the air as a waiter hurries by. The irony. I wonder if it would taste good enough for Pim's prissy taste.

"Well, this is the only hotel in Higher Seperium Countryside."

Pim rolls his eyes, turning to leave. "Why do I bother? If you don't want to tell me, fine."

I grab the sleeve of his maroon suit. Golden light, like the warmth of sun rays, reflects in his blue eyes as he looks back at me. I feel like I could just drown in them but now is not the time or place. "I'm sorry. I want to tell you. I just—don't know where to start."

"An apology would be nice but I'm not going to put words into your mouth." He sits back down. Hushed murmurs of guests, the clinks of crystal, and the soft warmth of lamplight all begin to fade away at his gaze—even if that gaze is upset and hurt, it's solely on me.

"I did what I had to do, Leo. I had to . . . keep her safe."

He glares at his wine glass. "When did you find out?"

"A few weeks after I went back to Inferium. By then, the war had started, and there was no way I was ever going to be able to tell you . . . but I wanted to, so many times, and I thought, I—"

"You didn't even give me a choice, Rose. The war ended over a year ago, why didn't you just tell me the truth?"

"I—"

"Do you know ever since you left Seperium, I've been trying to forget you? Do you know that I threw myself into work—into meaningless things, just to make it all seem worth it? But it didn't work. It felt terrible. When you told me you didn't love me, I wanted to die . . . and it seems you still don't love me." He turns his face away, looking toward the red draperies hanging from the windows to our right.

"Leo, it goes both ways." All my anger from the past three years wells and culminates in the next few words. "You could have contacted me too. You could have come back down. You could hav—"

"I did!" He glares at me, his voice cracking with those two words—it makes my heart break because I did that. I hurt him.

He continues, "After the war, I went to every place in Inferium that I thought you might be. I scoured Lower Inferium, but you had disappeared. I later learned that you were in Higher Seperium becoming an Inferium Council member. I just couldn't understand how you could fight for the world, but not us. I didn't want to accept that you didn't love me, but it was a futile attempt, and my pride wouldn't let me keep trying. So, I worked, and I forgot about you."

"I never stopped loving you, Leo."

"Why don't I believe that?" he chokes, tears welling in those eyes.

I want to wipe them away, but I'm the one who put them there. So, I keep my hands to myself. "There was no one else—ever. After Priscilla was born, Inferium was in turmoil. Black rot was everywhere, so I laid low to keep her safe. After the dust settled, they asked me to become a part of Inferium's Council . . . isn't that funny? The criminal you were chasing becomes the first member in a new decision-making Council?"

"Hilarious."

I down the rest of my whiskey as I stand up. "I've said my piece. You can take it or leave it." I turn to leave.

"Rosea, wait."

I stop, hearing him say my name sends a flurry of emotions through my heart. For him, I would wait. Always. I turn around and find myself face to face with his chest. He towers over me like a wilted skyscraper—broken and beautiful and held together by bits of nails and glue. Nails that have been removed, and glue that has worn away. He is wearing away in his attempts to forget.

"I—" His blue eyes well with trapped words. A million he wants to say, but none make it past as he bends down and kisses me. My heart explodes in my chest, and my fingers instinctively cup his cheeks.

He pulls away, his blue eyes engorged in tears, his fingers caressing my cheek, running through my golden locks.

"Goodbye, Rose," he whispers and leaves me ravaged and gasping for air in the middle of a hotel bar.

CHAPTER 45
Before the war: 1856-I: Vienna Sinclair

Find a way, Vienna. I know you can do it. Save us . . . Papa's last words ring in my head, sounding like a failure—a broken promise, because I didn't do it. I hadn't been able to save them. I stare at the porcelain boxes holding my family's ashes, little beautiful boxes holding so many memories. People who had been so full of life, now confined into tiny containers.

Three of them. Mama, Papa, and Yosef—my little brother. I'm so numb I can't cry anymore. They went quickly. I didn't even have time to worry about making them comfortable. I want to believe my father, but I have nothing left to save. I couldn't save them, so what was the point? Why would I even bother? I don't want to keep going. I want to die. I want to be with them. What is the point of fighting without them?

I became a nurse because of Papa. He was the only reason. He got me the internship. He worked extra hours to put me through school. He cheered me on when I thought I couldn't do it, and now . . . he is gone—ripped from me by a horrible virus, in a horrible world. I want to scream. I want to cry. I want them to be alive. I want this nightmare to end. I want so much, but I have no strength to act. No way to reverse what has already been done.

My glass heart that had been formed to live and fight now lies on the ground, bleeding through the millions of shattered pieces—sharp, jagged, and cutting.

The door opens behind me, and Dr. Greenwood enters into the

grief-filled space. "Vienna." He holds his arms open, letting me know that he is here, that I'm not alone.

I fall into him, needing his assurance, needing his comfort. "It hurts so much. I don't want to keep going—not without them. I couldn't save them. I couldn't—" Tears finally break through the floodgates of my torn-up wounds.

Dr. Greenwood holds me close, patting my back gently. "I know. I know," he whispers, his raspy voice bringing comfort to my fractured heart. After a moment, he steps back, wiping my tears with his smooth fingers. He pulls out a letter from the inside of his jacket pocket, holding it out. "Your father left this to me after you came to work for me. He asked that I take care of you in the event that anything happens to him, and I want you to know I will do my best to fulfill his wishes."

I take the letter, vaguely remembering my father mentioning something about it when I first started.

Dr. Greenwood pats my shoulder. "Take as long as you need, but remember, people are still dying. They still need someone to save them . . . and I think we can find a way if we try."

"I'm not worthy to save anyone."

"I don't think any of us are worthy to save anyone, Vienna. I think we're just at the right place at the right time. 'Yet who knows whether you have come to the kingdom for such a time as this?' It's a quote I read from a book once. We're here because we're supposed to be because no one else can do it but us. Don't forget that," he finishes and walks out the door, leaving me to the quiet.

What he said only made me angry. Were my family's lives worth nothing? No. They were worth it to me. I'm the one who has to carry on their legacy. I'm the one who has to preserve their memory. I'm the one who has to keep going even if I don't want to.

"I'll keep fighting," I whisper to their boxes. "I won't let your lives be in vain. I will find a way to stop this virus. I will continue on—for you."

CHAPTER 46
Before the war: 1859-S: Gabriel Hoek

The music flowing from the piano at the prompt of Leya's fingers sends shivers throughout my heart. The refrain sounds like heartbreak. A melody of gut-wrenching loss and devastation. Tears well in my eyes, but I blink them away. You could hear a pin drop in Seperium Landing's Music Hall. We're all enthralled by the piano's haunting song.

The melody changes, and Leya's fingers start to move faster over the keys. The sound becomes thrilling, like an adventure—like fear before you step into the unknown. Leya wrote this song, and the passion that flows from her to the piano is apparent as we all listen with open-mouthed wonder. I smile to myself, knowing what this song is about. It's about us. Our friendship. Our years of mischief. The highs and lows. Throughout the years, we've had each other—ten in total. I can't believe it's been ten years already.

I still remember being that kid who was scared I had caused Leya to break her arm and thinking she would hate me because of it. Never would I have thought that she would become my best friend. My heart swells with pride.

The stage lights focus on her and the grand piano she plays. The audience around me is barely a whisper of sound to my ears as I stare, enraptured by her performance. Elongated shadows along the walls and railings are the only clue that it's not just Leya and me in the auditorium. Seperium Landing holds a student showcase every year, and the student with the most votes gets to perform a whole show for the entire school. Leya won this year. She's come so far. It makes me so happy I could cry, but I swipe the moisture away quickly.

Doren and Riel sit next to me, and I don't want to risk the teasing and snickering I'd receive if they saw me tearing up at Leya's concert. They'd laugh and taunt me, saying how much I "looooved Leya", but it's not like that—at least not yet.

Do I want it to be like that? I'm not sure. I love Leya, but I don't know if I love her like that—like how her parents love each other. Comparing Leya and me to her parents causes butterflies to flutter in my stomach.

I have to admit that she does look beautiful in her royal purple sequined dress. It's puffy at the shoulders with tightened sleeves that give way to ornate silver rings on her fingers, creating a web across her hands. Her dark hair is pinned atop her head with little curls escaping every now and then. Her brown eyes are captured with a thin layer of makeup, making them look big and gorgeous. Her pursed lips are scrunched in perfect concentration and—why am I staring at her lips? Is it warm in here? I think I'm sweating.

I shake my head, clearing my thoughts from the momentary lapse of sanity. She's my best friend. Best friends don't think about each other like that. They inadvertently break each other's arms and come up with hair-brained schemes. Just because we're older, doesn't mean any of that is going to change. It won't. I won't let it. I won't let intrusive thoughts destroy what Leya and I have. I won't lose her like that.

The song ends, the last note lingering like a lone wolf. It's sad, and it pulls at my heartstrings. What if Leya feels the same? The thought roots itself in my mind as I stand with everyone else, clapping loudly and whooping, joining the calls and whistles screaming Leya's name. But what if she doesn't? What do I even feel?

Leya stands, curtsying to us—her face is flushed with excitement.

Roses and flowers litter the stage from the girls tossing bouquets at the front. She blows the audience a kiss, whispering, "Thank you."

Her eyes find mine in the crowd, and her smile widens. My heart jumps at the bright display, and my mouth goes dry. Suddenly, there is no question about how I feel. Somewhere along the way, Leya became more than just a friend. She became my everything, and part of me wonders if she feels the same. Had I become her everything as well? Or was I still just a friend in her eyes?

The way our gazes lock over the hundreds of people in this room tells me it's the first option, but now what? How do you tell your best friend you're in love with them? *Yikes!* The thought scares me even more. I'm in love with Leya, but what does that even entail? How do I tell her the truth without ruining everything? Will it ruin everything? But if I try to just ignore this truth, our relationship might still be affected negatively.

No, I don't want to ruin our late-night conversations, or being excited over a new mechanical invention. I can't—

Doren claps me on the shoulder, bringing me back to the present. I realize I'm standing in his way to exit our row.

"Get moving man, I'm hungry, and I hear there is a nine-course meal waiting for me in the dining hall," he says, signing for Riel's benefit.

Riel rolls his eyes. *'They don't even serve nine courses.'* He signs, moving forward until he meets the exodus of people in the main row. He stops, waiting for an opening.

'They will for me.' Doren signs as we move into the line. *'I'm a growing man. I need my sustenance.'* He pats his stomach.

'Boy, Doren. It's an insult to men everywhere to compare yourself to a man.' I sign and laugh, using their banter to escape my feelings.

"That's insulting!" Doren exclaims, forgetting to sign.

'I'm sorry, but Gabe's right.' Riel signs.

Doren pushes past both of us, taking the lead. *'You guys suck, I will become a man one day! Believe it or not!'* He signs, sticking his nose in the air and hustling away from us.

We laugh together at his dramatics. We move out of the dim lighting of the music hall, and into the outer commons area. It's a beautiful room with silver and light blue carpets and curtains. Crystal chandeliers hang from the cavernous domed ceiling, illuminating the room with gas lighting. Like towering giants, marble pillars rise up to hold the roof together. Light blue ribbon and silver gears wrap around them as decoration.

A crowd of people have amassed in the middle, many of them talking and gushing about Leya's performance to one another. Leya stands in the middle of her adoring fans, and the feelings I felt in the music hall come rushing back. I don't know if I can face her right now. Plus, there are a lot of people around her. I'll wait.

'I'm gonna go find Doren.' I sign to Riel. *'She's really busy right now, I'll congratulate her later.'*

Riel nods, his brow furrowing in confusion. *'I'll go with you.'*

We sift through the crowd and find Doren in the dining hall, sitting at one of the white and light blue tables. Silver-crafted trees stand in the middle of the table, hosting little birds made of tiny gears that hop from branch to branch. Doren grabs one that has stopped, winding it up and setting it back onto the tree. The display reminds me of the first time I met Leya. I shake my head. I have to stop thinking about her like that.

I come up behind him, draping myself over him. "Sorry about that, Doren."

"Ew, get off me." Doren shakes his shoulders. Riel sits down on his lap, blowing him a kiss while I kiss his cheek. "You animals! Get off me!" Doren stands, but a smile has lifted his features. "You two have problems." He shakes out his hair.

"It got you to smile," I say.

'I just wanted your chair.' Riel signs, taking Doren's seat.

"I—*'gotta love you two.'* Doren sits down next to Riel, and I sit next to him.

'More than you love a nine-course meal?' Riel asks as a waiter places the first course in front of us and pours glasses of wine.

I look at the bottle. "Can you just leave the bottle?" I ask the waiter.

He nods, setting it on the table. We were allowed to drink as long as we stayed on school grounds and didn't get trashed on a weeknight—with tonight being Katurday it was okay.

Riel looks at me with raised brows.

Doren doesn't notice, his mouth already stuffed with salad.

Leya floats into the room and my heart spikes. Suddenly, I'm not so hungry. I have to get out of here before she sees us and walks over. I don't know how to act yet. All these emotions are too new, too raw. I grab the wine and hurry from the table.

"Gabe?" Doren questions after me, but I don't stop. I need to think. I need to get out of here.

CHAPTER 47
Before the war: 1859-S: Doren Caldwell

I shrug my shoulders after Gabe ignores me, stuffing more salad into my mouth. The concert was beautiful, and Leya, was a shining star, but all I could think about during the performance was how hungry I was.

Riel kicks me under the table.

"Ow," I exclaim. "What was that for?"

'Go after him.' He signs. *'Something is up, but I'm not sure what. He's completely ignoring Leya.'*

I scoff. *'Gabe would never ignore Leya.'*

'Well, he is. He bolted the second she came into the room, and he wouldn't congratulate her after we left the music hall.'

I look in the direction that Gabe went. *'You're right. I'll talk to him.'* I sign, my food suddenly forgotten as I head after Gabe.

"Doren." I feel a hand grab my sleeve. Leya stands beside me.

"Leya!" I exclaim, a little too eagerly. "That was a beautiful performance. You did amazing."

She smiles. "Oh, thank you. Um—have you seen Gabe?"

"I—I think he's using the restroom. He should be back soon."

"Well, if you see him, let him know that I was looking for him."

"I will." I nod, and she flits away. Whatever Gabe was avoiding her for must be something serious because Leya seemed worried, and I don't know why Gabe would do that to her. I walk out to the commons, searching empty lecture rooms until I find Gabe in the grand library.

It stands two stories tall with books crammed onto floor-to-ceiling shelves. A grand staircase in the middle of the room leads to the second-story balcony where more books are stuffed up to the domed glass ceiling. A giant clock hangs on the surface of the dome, so students never have to wonder what time it is. Desks with little lamps fill the inside of the room where bookshelves don't take up space, and that's where I find Gabe.

He sits at one of the desks, swigging from the wine bottle. I pull a chair up next to him, taking the wine from his hand and gulping down a mouthful.

"You weren't even gonna share?" I say, setting the bottle on the desk.

"Sorry, I—" He takes another drink.

"What's eating ya, man?"

He shrugs. "I don't know."

"Liar."

He sighs. "I just needed to gather my thoughts. I—I think—" He folds his hands together, twiddling his thumbs. "I think I'm in love with Leya."

I blink. Not what I was expecting to come out of his mouth. "You think or you know?"

"I . . ." he trails off, clamping his mouth shut.

"How about this, what if I asked Leya on a date?"

"Absolutely not."

"Why?"

"Because you—and she—and I don't want her to be with anyone else."

I smile. "Well, there you go. You're in love with her. Now what?"

"I—I don't know." He groans, rubbing his eyes and setting his elbows on the desk. "I don't know if I want to tell her how I'm feeling, and I don't know how to act around her now. I know she'll see right through me, and then what? What do I tell her? What do I say? I'm afraid she won't feel the same. I—I'm afraid that everything will just be awkward, and so, I'm hiding here until I can find a solution."

"I think you're overthinking this, man. I think you just tell her the truth because if you don't, things are just gonna get worse. If you avoid her, she might think you hate her or something, and then—then she'll wonder what she did wrong . . ." I trail off, thinking about my parents, about my mom. She lost everything when my dad started acting distant. She didn't confront him, and now she—emotion cages my throat thinking about that time.

I cough to cover the tears forming. "Just tell her the truth," I say. "Now, come on. I'm hungry." I stand to leave, but Gabe grabs my arm.

"You can't just leave without telling me what that was about."

Crap. I was hoping he wouldn't see my tears. I stare at him for a moment. I don't want to tell him, but I do, so I sit back down. Waterworks form in my eyes again as I think of the story.

"You know last summer, when I went back home, and you came to see me because my mom died?" He nods slowly. I continue, "My dad released to the press that she died of an illness, but . . . a few days before she died, I went to her room to talk to her, and she told me, 'Doren, don't let anyone ever think you hate them. If you have a chance to fix something, do it.' I asked her what she meant, and then she explained that things hadn't been good between her and Dad for a long time. She thought she had done something wrong. Something that made him hate her because he started to avoid her, and when I went to boarding school, she noticed it even more." I stop as rivulets make their way down my cheeks. I wipe them away, grimacing.

"She—she killed herself, Gabe," I whisper, slamming my hand against the desk, my lips quivering. "I found her. M—me. She drank poison. She was so pale. She—I thought, but then I checked, and she was—" I break down, setting my head into my hands. Gabe grips my shoulder, squeezing it. I feel like a weight has been lifted off of me. I had been keeping that secret for so long.

"My dad pretended it never happened. He said that she died from an illness, and that was that. He didn't want to be the cause of her death, you see. He didn't want to admit that it was his fault." My tears turn to anger. "I learned later that he was being unfaithful to my mom. He was going down to Lower Inferium and paying or *targeting* young women to sleep with him. My dad is a monster, and I'm afraid I'm gonna be just like him."

"No." Gabe gasps, his own tears coating his eyes. "You are nothing like your father. You could never be. You're too kind, too funny. You see life. You see the hard things, and you find the good in them. You could never be the one who destroys hearts or ruins lives. You got it?"

I nod. "I know, it's just—he is my father, and I can't help but think that I might be like him too." I wipe my face with my hand. "Thanks, Gabe. I—I needed that."

"Thank you for coming after me. I will tell Leya. She deserves to know. She doesn't deserve to think I hate her." He stands and offers me a hand. "Come on, let's eat."

CHAPTER 48
Before the war: 1859-S: Leya Barrett

I glare at the door Gabe and Doren had disappeared through a few minutes ago. After I had said goodbye to my parents and Casen, I came into the dining hall to find Gabe booking it for the door, and Doren not far behind him. They were ignoring me. I had seen Gabe evade me twice since the concert. Usually, he's the first to greet and congratulate me.

Why is this time different? Maybe it's because I saw Mary Ilser chatting him up before the concert, twirling her hair and looking at him all starry-eyed. Oh, brother. If he would date anyone, why would he date her? She's not even nice. She just likes him because he's cute and smart. No, he wouldn't date her. He can't because she's not—

Riel taps my hand. *'If you glare at it long enough, it might burst into flame.'* He signs before shoving a huge bite of roast beef in his mouth. *'Eat some food. They'll be back any second.'*

He's right, and the food does look and smell amazing. I take a bite of my roast, and it bursts in my mouth with an explosion of juices and savory pepper. I look back to the door, finding the two boys walking toward me. I dab my face with a napkin.

Doren plops down with a sigh. His eyes alight on his food. "Ooh! Roast. My favorite." He smiles, shoving food into his mouth.

Gabe moves around the table, gently tugging my shoulder. His dark eyes meet mine. "Can I talk to you?"

My eyes narrow. Why is he acting so strange? "Are you going to explain to me why you've been avoiding me?"

"Leya, don't be stubborn."

"Oh, I'm being stubborn? I watched you run away from me twice." I hold up two fingers.

He groans. "And I'll explain. Come on." He tugs my arm in exasperation.

I stand up, following after him as we head back to the commons room. He takes me down a darkened hallway that leads to the lecture rooms. He stops with a sigh, fidgeting with his hands. He only does that when he's nervous. Why is he nervous? It's just me. My heart plummets with a realization. What if he has bad news? Did he hear or receive a telegram before the concert and he doesn't know how to tell me? Does it involve his dad?

I reach out, taking his shaking hands into my own. He gasps, the sound echoing in the empty hall, his nerves steadying for a moment. I'm staring straight at his chest. When had he become so tall? We used to be the same height.

"Gabe, what's wrong? Whatever it is, just say it. I can handle it." I look up at his face.

His dark eyes search mine, and I see a plea in them—a desperate prayer that needs an answer, but what is the correct answer? What answer will extinguish that dream or ignite it? His hands have turned over in mine, caressing my skin. It feels oddly intimate.

My heart starts to pound, my thoughts racing. How many times had I dreamed of this moment? How many times had I wished it would happen, and then shake my head, saying it wouldn't? That I would be his friend forever, and that I would love him from afar. I know he doesn't have any bad news to give, but will he be brave enough to say it? Like I wasn't.

"I—I'm—I'm in love with you, Leya," he chokes out. "I think I always have been. I just didn't realize it until tonight when I saw you up there. I was thinking of how proud I was, and then I—and then, your eyes met mine and I just knew. An—and I avoided you because I didn't know how to act, and I didn't know how to tell you, and I just needed to gather my thoughts. So . . ."

My heart swells almost as if it might burst. He's in love with me.

Me. I get to have him. I get to keep him. Mary Ilser can eat her heart out.

"Please say something." His quivering voice is back.

I want to speak, but I have no words to say. I lean on the tips of my toes and gently kiss the corner of his lips. I lean back, studying his reaction. He stares at me in shock before his features soften.

"I—"

"Leya! There you are!" one of my classmates, Ila shouts, cutting me off. Gabe and I jump away from each other. She rushes over, grabbing my wrist. "Principal Avery is about to congratulate you! He's asking you to join him on stage!" She starts to pull me away.

"But I—" I start, glancing back at Gabe.

He looks after me with understanding. "I'll be fine."

I rush out with Ila before she pulls my arm out of its socket. I glare daggers into the back of her head. I couldn't even tell Gabe I felt the same way. Although, I'm sure he knows because of the kiss—more like a peck—*dang it!* I was hoping to tell him the same, and then really kiss him. Why did Principal Avery have to call for me now?

Ila rushes me back into the dining hall.

"There she is!" Principal Avery says into the microphone at the front of the room. Cheers erupt from everyone, sounding like a deafening cadence. I smile and hold my head high as I glide toward the stage. "Leya Barrett, everyone!"

He smiles widely as I join him on stage. Principal Avery is a wiry man with a thin, narrow face, and an even thinner mustache with blond hair that has been slicked back way too many times with pomade. He gestures at me, waiting for the cheers to die down.

"It is one of my greatest honors to host such a talented student at our music hall. Miss Barrett, congratulations on winning the showcase. You have an amazing gift, and I know your music will take you far." I nod in gratitude. "Wasn't she wonderful everyone?" he calls, instigating more cheers from the crowd. He holds the microphone out to me.

"Would you like to say a few words?"

I nod and carefully take the microphone, centering myself to look out at the crowd. "Well, this is wonderful. I—thank you for this opportunity. It was a dream come true to play for you all, and I hope you enjoyed it, and—" I stop, my eyes meeting Gabe's who had just appeared through the open doors. Suddenly, it's just me and him. No one else matters. "And I love you too," I whisper before I can overthink saying those words out loud.

Gabe smiles, his eyes sparkling with love and pride, a bright reflection of his heart.

I tear up before everyone's shocked faces suddenly come back into focus. I clear my throat. "Sorry, I'm much better at standing behind a piano instead of a microphone." I laugh, dissolving some of the awkwardness before I hand the microphone back to Principal Avery.

He laughs heartily. "Well, enjoy the meal, and don't forget to congratulate Leya in person." I hear him say as I step down from the stage.

Gabe still stands by the doors, and I ignore the stares of my peers as I march right up to him—twinkling chandeliers, dark suits, and frilly dresses blur by me. I don't care if the whole school knows I love him because I want to shout it to the whole world that he is mine—that I am his, and that no one else can have him. I wrap my arms around his shoulders, hanging off his neck like jewelry.

His hands wrap around my waist, pulling me close, and it feels right. Perfect. Like he's the missing puzzle piece to my heart. I lift my lips to his, this time giving him a real kiss, not an insufficient peck. He kisses me back, filling my heart and soul with so much joy.

CHAPTER 49
After the war: 1864-S: Inspector Leo Pim

I'm going to hate myself. I just know it. What am I saying, I do hate myself. I kissed her. *Kissed her.* What in Seperium was I thinking? I have to interrogate her today, and now—I rub a hand down my face, leaning back in the chair of my temporary office in Higher Seperium Countryside. I look out the window, watching motorcars pass by on their way to wherever.

Why did I kiss her? *Because you wanted to . . .* No! Absolutely not! I've forgotten about that woman, or I had before I saw her in that hotel lobby, and *sweet Seperium,* she looked good! Why am I admitting this? She's the one who left *me.* She broke my heart, and she didn't even address that issue during last night's drinks.

My fingers fumble with the rose brooch. I never forgot about her. Ever. I wanted to, but I couldn't. After the war, I tried to find her. I wanted to fight for her, but she was nowhere to be found, and then I heard she was in Seperium, and all my searching seemed futile. I didn't want to find her anymore. I just wanted to forget her. I just wanted my heart to stop hurting. I just wanted to never care about anyone ever again. But now—

Get it together, Pim! She'll be here any second. Any second. Fear traps my stomach, but I will it away. I'm not afraid of her. I've never been afraid of her, and I won't be now. I take a deep breath. Everything will be fine. Everything—an image of the chubby little girl that Rosea had been holding pops into my mind.

Priscilla . . .

I'm a father. A *father.* Never in a million years would I have thought this could happen to me. Men like me don't become fathers. We become critics or inspectors. We enjoy a glass of wine and play board games alone because no one else can match our brilliance. I never meant to fall in love, but that infuriating woman made me. I was intrigued by her mystery, by the way she saw the world. I fell right into a trap set for fools, and like a fool, I thought it would last. I thought I could keep her, but you can't hold onto a hurricane; the winds will blow you away, or the floods will drown you. I still feel like I'm drowning.

"I never stopped loving you, Leo." Her words from last night come back to me. She hadn't been lying when she said it. I had been watching for all her normal ticks—wringing her hands, running fingers through her hair, or humming. She didn't do any of those, but if that was the case, why did she break my heart? If she loved me so much, why didn't she try to find me?

"Pim, Rosea Dierich is here." Chief Lecten stands in the doorway to my office. My heart jumps at his words. Foolish heart . . . It doesn't know what's good for it.

I stand and follow the chief to the interrogation room. She sits there, tapping her nails on the metal desk. Her dark blue eyes meet mine—an ocean of unspoken words and regrets. I take a deep breath and step into the room.

She smiles. "Looking good, Inspector. I guess that wine didn't hit you too hard."

"Miss Dierich, I would refrain from referencing last night. I'm here to speak with you about Lord Caldwell's murder. The other guests placed you at the dinner party that night. Now, can you explain as to why you were there?"

Rosea tsks. "I don't like it when you're being serious." She sighs. "I was there because I was invited by my best friend, Vienna Sinclair. Her beau was a close friend to the lord of the house and General Hoek. I only came because she asked me to."

"Did you murder Lord Caldwell?"

Her eyes are dead set, unwavering. "No." No tells.

"Do you know who did?"

"No."

She's not lying, and I just have one more question for her. Something I remember from when we were together. Something she told me because she trusted me. Something only I would know to ask her.

"I hear you have a history with Lord Caldwell's late father—Hyam Caldwell."

Hurt slashes across her face, and I immediately feel guilty for asking it, but a motive is a motive. She may not have killed Lord Caldwell, but I wouldn't put it past her if she manipulated an accomplice who did.

"I can't deny that *Lord* Hyam Caldwell did find an interest in me and that he did take from me things I can never get back, but I would never kill his innocent son over it. That scumbag is dead—and I don't care that I called him that on record—his dues are paid. There's no one to get revenge on, and even if there was, no amount of revenge will give me back what was stolen." She glares at me.

With anyone else, I would overanalyze that answer, but with Rosea . . . I can't. I'm speechless because I know how much it hurt her to answer those words truthfully. I feel like the grimy streets of Lower Inferium, and that's saying a lot. *Low blow, Pim.*

"Thank you, Miss Dierich. You are free to go."

She stands with a huff and stops beside my chair. "I understand that you're angry. I would be too, but I never thought you would stoop that low," she whispers, her voice quivering.

I hear her footsteps head out the door. *Go after her . . .* I jump to my feet, rushing after her as she treads through the narrow hallway. "Rosea!" I gently nudge her elbow.

She whirls around. "Don't touch me! Don't you dare!" Tears stream down her round, dimpled cheeks.

"I—" I stop, not sure what I should say next. I was just doing my job.

"Say it, Leo."

Silence fills the space between us, before Rosea sniffs, wiping snot with her sleeve. I try not to openly grimace. "Never mind. I don't know why I got my hopes up. The case was always more important to you anyway." She turns around.

"I'm sorry," I whisper, loosening the tie around my neck. I feel like I'm choking, or maybe I'm still adrift in her ocean, gasping for air.

"How much did it hurt to say those words?" She doesn't turn around.

"Not as much as it hurts to watch you walk away again."

My eyes widen. I can't believe I just said that. Why does all my sense go out the window when it comes to her? Why do I always lay my heart at her feet? Why am I surprised when she steps on it? Maybe part of me is scared of what it will feel like if I'm not drowning anymore.

She looks back at me with red-rimmed eyes—it only accentuates her dark blue irises more. "Oh, Pim." Her eyes swell again, and I look away, because High Seperium, I'm not going to cry in front of her again.

"I—" she starts. "Priscilla is in the lobby. If you would like to . . ."

I nod. "Yes," I hear myself say and follow Rosea to the lobby. The three-year-old girl sits in a chair playing a roll-up chess board by herself. The sight makes my heart soar. I do that.

"Mama," she calls and runs up to her mother, dropping chess pieces on the floor. Rosea picks her up and turns to look at me. Priscilla has my dark hair and brilliant blue eyes while she sports hints of her mother's round face and dimpled cheeks. I see my reflection in those big eyes. I look terrified. "Mama, who's daat?" she asks.

Rosea jiggles her a little. "Prissy, this is Inspector Pim. He's helping Mama."

The little girl waves a chubby hand, before sticking a finger in her mouth. My heart melts. This is my daughter. Mine. And even though I hate kids and never wanted to be a father, I find myself thinking that I want to be this little girl's father. I find myself believing that I can do it, just for her. Only for her.

CHAPTER 50
Before the war: 1858-I: Vienna Sinclair

I wrap my coat tightly around me to ward off the frosty night air. Puffs of crystalized breath float in front of me like a welcoming friend. When it's this cold, Inferium is beautiful because you can't breathe in any putrid smells. The temperature halts the rot and decay. Of course, that means I have to walk over frozen waste and feces, but when am I not? I take a deep breath, my lungs enjoying the crisp atmosphere.

I am on my way to see Rosea perform tonight. She's singing at the Drunken Pig—at least that's what she told me a few nights ago. Inferium still bears the scars of the black rot pandemic that swept through two years ago. Dogs lick and chew on bones left over from the bodies that had been laid to rest on the streets. Bile rises in my throat. After six months of hell, Dr. Greenwood and I found a cure for the black rot, but by then over 100,000 people had already lost their lives.

Higher Seperium ordered the residents of Lower Inferium to throw the dead in a mass grave, but not all the bodies made it there. I shiver just thinking about it. We distributed the immunization as fast as we could by giving it to underground vendors and traveling performers, like Ro and her troupe.

Many were skeptical at first, but once word got out that it worked, everyone went crazy trying to find out who made it. We didn't tell people where the vaccine came from, because if we had, we would have been overrun with desperate people, and we didn't have the capacity for that.

I turn down a grimy street, the gas lamps barely illuminating the path through the smog as I reach for the back door of the Drunken Pig. A long rickety hallway greets me as I step over the threshold. To my left, a swing door leads to the kitchen where smells of over-greased and grizzled foods assault my nose. To my right, a door with a hand-carved sign saying "backstage" stands.

I reach for the door, wanting to hype Ro up before she gets on stage. I turn the knob but find that it's locked. Odd. This door isn't supposed to be locked. I look around for a key before heading out to the front.

"Hey, Mit," I greet the bartender. He's a big guy with a constant scowl set between his dark brows, causing him to squint unnaturally green eyes. "Do you have a key to the backstage room? The door is locked, and I wanted to make sure Rosea's ready."

Mit snarls, before reaching under the bar for the key. He hands it to me. "Don't take too long. Rosea is supposed to be on in a few minutes."

"Always a pleasure, Mit." I palm the key and head back to the door.

The door clicks and creaks as I open it. The main room stuffed with costumes of every size and color is void of any living human. She must be in one of the separate dressing rooms. I step past the racks of clothes and head for one of the three doors set in the wall on the other side.

I hear a crash, followed by a muffled gasp from the door on the far right. My heart spikes in panic as I rush toward it.

"Ro!" I call, reaching for the door. It catches, and I have to slam my shoulder into it to get it to budge.

What I see causes my heart to plummet. A man with blue eyes and light-blond hair stands over Ro, locked in a lover's embrace, his hands holding up Ro's skirts. Ro turns her head to look at me, tears streaking her face, her mouth agape in pain. I grab a metal prop sitting on a table to my left, raising it high.

"Get away from her you filthy monster!" I screech and race into the room. My presence dumbfounds the man enough for Ro to escape his grip. I throw the prop at the man's head. I miss, but it's enough to distract him as Ro comes back into the room with a revolver in her shaking hands.

"Get out or I'll shoot!" she screams.

The man's eyes narrow. "You can't shoot me," he says, his voice a mixture of arrogance and condescendence. He's from Seperium. I grab the gun from Rosea.

"She won't, but I will," I say. "I'm a nurse. I know exactly where to shoot so I can leave you in miserable pain and suffering before you die."

The man glares, but skirts around us, heading for the door. I put a hand in front of Ro as if that would possibly block her from the horrors she's already faced. I turn, aiming once more at the man. I won't shoot to kill him, but I will make it very miserable for him to live. I hold the barrel steady and pull the trigger.

The gun goes off, whiplashing in my hands. My ears are ringing from the sound, but when I look at the man, I find that my bullet has hit its mark—a space just between his hips. A bladder wound. It won't kill him, but for the next few years, he'll have blood in his urine and possibly pass out from the pain every time he has to use the bathroom.

Hopefully, it will be enough to keep him off any more undeserving young girls. He screams, dragging himself out into the hall and calling for anyone to help him, but he won't find help, not down here.

Once he's gone, Ro falls to the floor, shaking. Her dark blue eyes look at me, welling with tears. "Th—thank you," she whispers.

I drop down beside her, setting the gun down and pulling her into a hug.

She falls into me, sobbing. "I—I can't. I didn't. I—can't perform tonight."

I smooth her blonde bob. "Don't worry about it. I'll take care of it," I say, thinking about that creep. Why had he targeted my sweet friend? Ro didn't deserve this.

She pulls away, sniffling, and I notice a purple bruise forming above her left brow. "Thank you. I—he came in a few minutes before you did, and he—he forced himself on me. I didn't know what to do. I tried to fight back, but I wasn't strong enough. And I—couldn't scream and—"

"You don't have to explain it. I know it wasn't your fault. Did you know him?"

She nods, wiping at her tear marks. "He started coming in a couple weeks ago. He was nice at first, giving me small tips and being friendly. He said he really enjoyed my performances. Then he started coming almost every night I performed, cheering me on. He was always so excited, and then his tips started getting bigger. He tried to hand me wads of SEM, but I always refused them, and then tonight, he said he was gonna cash in his favors, so he . . ." Her eyes well with tears once more as she trails off.

"Oh, Rosea, I'm so sorry. I should have been here sooner. I should have—"

"It's not your fault. I should have been more careful. I—I should have known. If you hadn't come in when you did, maybe he would have killed me or something."

"But he . . . did he—"

A sob escapes her lips as she nods. "Yes."

I glare toward the door. "I should have killed him."

"No, Vienna, you're not like that. He will suffer for what he's done, and whether that's now or later . . . at least you shot him."

"Yeah, it was a good shot too."

She cracks a smile. "I'm assuming it won't kill him then?"

"No, but he will be in severe pain for a while."

"Good." She wipes at the snot falling from her nose with the back of her hand.

"Come on, let's get you outta here." I help her up. She leans into me as if she's not strong enough to stand.

Mit comes stomping into the room. "What in Inferium is going on here?" He looks at us. "Rosea, you were supposed to be—" he stops, looking between the both of us.

"Please tell me you threw him out into the freezing cold alleyway—

maybe strip him of his clothes too. He won't remember, especially if he wakes up outside a bar," I say.

Mit nods. "I will. Get her home safely." He heads back into the main bar area.

I look back at Ro, whose face has gone incredibly pale. Part of me hopes that man does die in the alleyway tonight, but I know that letting him die will be a mercy he doesn't deserve. Instead, I hope he lives out the rest of his days in terrible suffering.

CHAPTER 51
Before the war: 1860-I: Rosea Dierich

"Your beau is here," Teresa, one of my performer friends, says as I step into the backstage room of the theater. She wiggles black eyebrows with a laugh. I walk to the wings and peer out into the audience. Inspector Leo Pim stands in the middle of the empty torn-up chairs with a cage in his hands. A cage? What an odd thing to bring to a theater. Perhaps, he has a bird he wants to perform here or a secret kink that I might have to expose.

Or—and then I remember. The cat. That's right the cat he found the other night when I taunted him as Crémant—not that I haven't taunted him since—I just forgot about that occurrence. I couldn't believe a pompous High Seperium citizen would care about a hurt cat. Perhaps, there is a soul under that sullen exterior.

I smile to myself, thinking how it would feel to crack open that shell, and expose the beautiful person underneath, or maybe just get to know him, and see if there is enough to him for me to get to know. I step out onto the stage.

"Welcome to the Traveling Troupe of Lower Inferium!" I shout. "Prepare to have your senses dazzled, and your mind trapped in a state of astonishment. All scoundrels, pimps, and pims are not allowed to see our show, so if you identify by those names, you must leave. If not, enjoy the show! Woo!" I shout, throwing little pieces of confetti out toward the audience, becoming my amazing one-woman show for my singular audience.

Pim studies me, looking completely disinterested with my antics. Hmm? What's it gonna take to get this guy to smile? He doesn't seem like a guy particularly interested in the charms of a woman, in fact, he seems only interested in Crémant, wine, Seperium, and cats. An odd combination if you ask me. An idea pops into my head so I drop down on all fours, meowing like a cat and pretending to lick my paw—hand.

"My name is Rosie the kitty," I start in a high voice. "If you feed me wine, I'll let you—"

"Will you please stop?" Pim cuts me off as he heads to the front, holding the cage as far away from him as he possibly can. "Can you just act like a normal human?" He sets the cage on the edge of the stage . . . Hehe, that rhymes. Also, what he said is a total insult to cats everywhere.

"But I'm not a human, I'm a cat."

He pinches the bridge of his nose. "Fine, I just wanted you to see the cat you helped me save, but I can see that coming here was clearly a mistake." He grabs the cage again, sticking his nose in the air and walking toward the entrance.

I hustle to stand. "Wait!" I call, jumping off the stage and racing up past him, blocking his way. "It was a joke." I smile. "I didn't mean to— I'd love to see the cat."

He wrinkles his brow in skepticism but places the cage down and opens the door, pulling out the ugliest cat I have ever laid eyes on. It has no hair and is completely wrinkled and mangy. It's missing its left eye, part of its tail, and a right back leg which Pim has wrapped in gauze.

The one-eyed creature looks at me with an expression of boredom, surprisingly a lot like Pim's expression a few minutes earlier. Has this cat already learned from its rescuer? Please, as if, it's a cat.

"That's the ugliest cat I've ever seen."

Pim covers the cat's ears with one hand. "Shh, he'll hear you."

"I thought you hated ugly things."

"I never said I hated ugly things. I just hate gross things, and yes, this animal was disgusting when I found him, but he's doing much better. He even enjoyed his bath today."

I stare open-mouthed. "You taught a cat how to like baths?"

"Roosevelt was made for baths."

"Roosevelt, seriously? You should have named him Fluffy."

Pim shoots me a withered look.

"What?" I continue, scratching the cat's head. "You should have."

He puts the cat back into the cage. "I just wanted to let you know that he's okay. Now that you've seen him, I'm leaving." He starts for the door again.

I can't let him leave yet. I have to pop the question. Okay, not the question, but a question. "Wait a minute!"

He groans, turning back to me. "What now?"

"I just—I was wondering if you would like to get dinner or drinks with me tonight. I don't have any performances till tomorrow, and I know a safe place to eat."

He narrows his eyes at me. "What's the catch?"

"Does there have to be a catch? I think you're hot, and a girl can ask a hot guy out, right?"

His cheeks flush. "I—"

"Just say yes or no, Pim. It's that simple."

He takes a deep breath. "Fine, what time can I pick you up?"

"Fine? It's not like I'm forcing you to have dinner with me. If you don't want to, you can just say no." I roll my eyes.

He takes a step toward me as if to prove his point. "I want to—yes."

I smile. "Great! Be here by 1900."

He nods and then turns toward the door, muttering something to himself about being completely crazy.

CHAPTER 52
Before the war: 1860-I: Inspector Leo Pim

What am I doing here? I think as I stand in front of the theater I had met Rosea at earlier today. I couldn't find anything nice to give her besides a rose. The irony. The one flower I don't want to parade around the city, I am.

Wait? Why did I even get her a flower? I only agreed to the date to find out more about this insufferable woman. She's crazy and mysterious, and probably full of secrets. Secrets that could be helpful for my investigation.

I reach for the door, but it is suddenly thrown open, revealing Rosea in a royal purple dress with a tight bodice and flouncy, black-lace skirt. It's not a bad outfit, considering this is Inferium. The dim city kerosene lamps shine down on her blonde hair, making it glisten like a halo—like an angel. Although, I would never—in my right mind—call her an angel.

"Well, aren't you going to tell me I look nice?" she banters.

I hold the rose out to her, and her face lights up in surprise. "You look fine, at least, not like the filth of Lower Inferium."

Her blue eyes look up over the flower she is smelling—the red contrast only accentuates the dark blue of those gems. I swallow, refusing to admit that she is quite beautiful.

"I take offense to that," she says, tucking the rose into her hair.

"Take offense all you want."

She closes the door behind her. "You know, you're really bad at this date thing."

"I take offense to that."

"I think we can agree that anything that comes out of our mouths will be offensive to both of us, so let's agree to only say offensive things." She starts down the sidewalk.

This woman is so weird. I stumble, nearly falling face-first on my dark blue suit as I catch up to her and walk beside her. "Where are we going?"

"Just around the corner." She smiles.

Well, just around the corner turned into four miles—four—with Rosea muttering some song under her breath the entire way. If I would have known it was going to be that long, I would have hailed a cab! Now my feet hurt, and my once-perfect loafers are covered in so much grime, I will never be able to remove it. These were a good pair of shoes too, *sweet Seperium!*

I shuffle behind Rosea, pouting.

She turns. "Come on, you big baby, it's this one right here."

She points to a building with a mechanical sign that reads Seperium's the Limit. The word Seperium is stacked atop the other two words, and every once and a while, a small metal air balloon pops up from behind the sign and floats to the word Seperium and then settles back down again. Warm yellow light spills from the windows of the restaurant, and I can hear people laughing and clamoring inside.

It sounds happy, unlike the racket of a bar. I finally get close enough to peer into the windows and my heart soars. This looks like my kind of place. People, with their hair done up or gelled and combed, sit at white table-clothed square tables eating delectable food and drinking expensive wine. I gape, my woes from earlier forgotten. I didn't even know a place like this existed in Lower Inferium.

"Are we gonna stand here gawking, or are we gonna go in?"

"What is this place?"

"It's the fanciest eats in Inferium. It's actually a place that a lot of the rich factory owners frequent. They spend a pretty penny here to be able to eat good food and drink exquisite alcohol."

"I didn't even know this was here, and I searched—" I stop. It probably isn't a good idea to tell a civilian about the wine I had been looking for. How come this place hadn't come up in my search?

"You gotta belong to an exclusive club to hear about this place. I know about it because I live in Inferium," she says and pulls the door open.

The most heavenly smell wafts to my nose and makes me think of home. Finally, something that doesn't smell like death or rotten trash.

"Welcome," a hostess greets us. "Table for two?" she asks, and I nod, taking in the crystal chandeliers and painted ceiling. Draperies of white and gold hang along the walls, accentuating the tables. We follow the hostess to where she seats us at a two-person table toward the back.

I pull a chair out for Rosea—not because I care, but because I'm a gentleman.

"Would you like a full selection of our available wines and liquor?" the hostess asks.

"Yes, that would be marvelous," I answer, taking my seat across Rosea. The hostess leaves us alone, and Rosea picks up a menu, flipping through it.

"This place is expensive. Do they take kidneys as payment? I think that's the only way I can eat here."

I sigh. "Would you like me to pay for your dinner?"

She lights up, looking over at me. "Would you?"

I nod with a roll of my eyes.

"Yay! See you're getting the hang of this date thing." She wiggles her eyebrows, and I try not to cringe.

Why do I do this to myself? I should be looking for Crémant, not sitting here with a woman whom I found to be as much of a mystery as the vigilante. I glance at the menu, immediately picking out what I want.

"Why do you sing to yourself when you walk on the streets?"

She looks up. "I get lost easily. I always have, ever since I was a little girl. So, Grams came up with this system to help me memorize routes the same way I would memorize steps to a dance number, and it stuck. Now, I make up my own routes, and when I need to go somewhere, I sing so I don't get lost."

Interesting.

"You must have a lot of maps," I say, as a waiter brings me a drink menu and takes Rosea's order of a whiskey neat.

"Yes." She laughs. "A lot. Some of them are incomplete, so sometimes, I have to look at multiple ones."

"Do you know anything about Crémant Rose?" I study her reaction.

Her head snaps up. "Of course, everyone knows about her."

"Have you heard if she started with her following—The Rosaries? Or did they just come to be?"

"From what I heard, she started painting murals around town. People loved them and the messages they brought. So, when the vigilante signed their name Crémant Rose, they came up with a name for her followers, but most of them do radical things, like starting riots and strikes. Things—as far as I know—she doesn't participate in, but I could be wrong. You know, you hear rumors . . . but who doesn't?" She takes a sip of her drink that arrived while she was talking. "I'm assuming, since you're asking, that's who you're on the hunt for."

"Yes, to put an end to her tyranny."

The waiter comes back, taking our orders and menus.

Rosea leans against the table, her elbows propping her up. I try not to be repulsed by her table manners, who puts their elbows on the table? "I wonder. Have you considered what she's fighting for, or trying to bring awareness to?"

I study her, looking deep into those blue eyes. They're like an ocean, big and mysterious—dark and full of secrets, but always reflecting the sun's light. The golden tapestry frames her, and the room's peaceful chatter hushes, almost as if I'm hearing it through a tunnel—as if the people stopped at her words. *That's stupid Pim, she can't possibly have commanded a whole room.*

"Of course, I have," I say, answering her question. "She's an instigator, starting riots and causing turmoil."

"I thought you would say that, but you didn't answer my question—what do you think she's fighting for?"

I huff. "I don't know—better wages? More jobs? Whatever it is that can give others incentive to cause trouble and raise hell."

"Have you ever thought this was already hell for them? Perhaps, raising hell is the only way to get out of hell. Ha! A play on words!" Rosea smiles, showing off bright teeth and causing her skin to dimple and crack her makeup. Little red splotches appear in the breakage. I hadn't noticed it before, but now I see she has terrible acne that she covers up with makeup.

I shake my head. "Who's interrogating who here?"

"So, you admit that you were interrogating me?" she asks, taking a sip of her whiskey, blue eyes narrowing.

The food arrives, and I cough to cover my embarrassment, running a finger underneath my collar. "I'm an Inspector. Interrogating people is my job. So even though we're . . . on a date. I can't seem to stop interrogating people." *Phew, nice save.*

"So, you only agreed to this date just to interrogate me?"

"I—you said yourself that I'm bad at this dating thing, and isn't dating an interrogation anyway, two people who spend hours together just asking each other questions?"

"I—well—" This time her face flushes, and she takes a bite of her salad.

I look down at my salad, taking a few bites. Mm, fresh greens topped with thyme balsamic and olive oil. It melts in my mouth, and I try to ignore the sweat dripping down my neck. That was too close. She almost found out that I couldn't care less about getting to know her romantically. I'm just curious as to who this crazy woman actually is.

"Wait . . ." she starts, her mouth full of masticated greens. I cringe, and don't try to hide it this time. "How many dates have you actually been on?"

"I refuse to answer that question."

She smiles, flecks of green stuck in between her teeth. Gosh, this woman is a disaster. "Aw, Pimmy, am I your first?" She tears up, clutching a hand to her chest. "That is so sweet."

"You are not my first date," I defend as the waiter takes our empty salad plates, replacing them with what looks like pumpkin soup.

"Really? What was her name?"

"Uh, Aleetha Färrin."

"You're lying. I know those names from a book I read once."

"Well, her parents were very fond of this book." I gulp a mouthful of wine. I swallow it wrong and start to cough like a madman, splattering wine on the clean, white tablecloth.

"Don't die. If you die, I can't enjoy flustering you anymore."

"You most certainly don't fluster me!" But even as the words leave my mouth, I can feel my face heating up.

"You're blushing!" She smiles, glee sparkling in her eyes.

I grumble, shoving soup in my mouth. Delectable flavors of cinnamon and cloves, mixed with a hint of pumpkin burst in my mouth. The food here is amazing, but I'm not sure how much longer I can sit here. I knew agreeing to this date would be a mistake. Rosea is so infuriating I can't even enjoy the meal.

"What? You have no comeback for that one? So, that means I'm right."

I slam my spoon on the table, leaving splatters of orange next to the red spots. The colors look good together, but I pity the person who will have to clean this tablecloth—they'll probably curse my name while doing it too. Even though I pride myself on being exceptionally clean, I notice Rosea hadn't even left one mark on her side yet.

I lean toward her. "We're here to eat as well, right? Can we please just enjoy the meal, and drop the subject? I've had enough idle banter." I sigh, taking another spoonful of soup.

She grumbles. "You're no fun." She takes a bite of her soup. "Mm, this is wonderful."

"You like it?" I ask, thinking that her palate couldn't possibly be refined enough to enjoy gourmet soup.

"You don't have to seem so surprised."

"Lord Caldwell! Fancy seeing you here!" a voice in the front room exclaims.

I groan. I don't want to deal with Lord Caldwell's patronizing, pompous temperament. I look at Rosea. Her face has gone pale, and the spoon she has suspended in midair comes crashing to the table as her fingertips release it. Her eyes are feral, searching the room for an exit, like a cornered animal.

"Rosea?" I reach out, and she flinches before my fingers touch her hand.

Her eyes come back into focus, tearing up, sweat clinging to her brow. "I—" she starts, her breaths coming out in rapid spikes. She places her hands on either side of her head, trying to breathe. Something's wrong. I have to get her out of here.

I stand and throw a wad of SEM onto the table before walking over to her side and gently taking her shoulders into my hands. She nearly elbows me as one of her arms leaves the table and jabs toward my side. I jump away, but don't let her go.

"Stop it," I whisper. "I'm trying to get you out of here. Let's go. We have to go."

Her tearstained eyes meet mine, and she stands, allowing me to guide her to the exit behind us. We stumble out into the disgusting night air of an alleyway, and my heart plummets. For a short second, I had forgotten we were still in the filth of Inferium. Rosea bends over her knees, trying to breathe.

Noticing I still hold her, I release her shoulders, waiting for the urge to wipe my hands on my suit-pants to come, but it doesn't. Odd? Usually, it does. She breathes in silence for a minute before I reach out again, patting her back like a dog who has done a good job.

"You don't have to console me, Leo," she whispers, her voice laden with tears.

"I just—"

"You should go. Unless it makes you happy to see other people in pain."

"It's called comfort, or is that a foreign concept to you? I just wanted to be sure you were okay."

"Like you care."

The words feel like a stab to my heart. She's right. Usually, I don't care about the situations of others, but today, just now, for some reason, I care. I care enough to help a scared woman out of a bad situation, or maybe I had over thought the whole ordeal. I thought she would appreciate the help, but maybe that's what upset her—the fact that someone, a stranger even, saw her at one of her most vulnerable moments.

"I can't stand to see others in pain, but maybe your pain isn't what I thought it was," I say, turning down the alleyway, leaving her behind.

"Wait." She grabs my sleeve. I turn, glaring down at her. "I'm sorry. I didn't mean to say that. I just—you're right. I was hurting. Thank you."

"You're welcome." I start down the alleyway again with her beside me.

"Do you know how to get back? I—memorized a song, but I forgot it after—" she trails off, biting a broken nail.

I sigh. "It's a date, isn't it? The gentleman has to bring the lady back home safe and sound for it to become a successful date."

She smiles. "I guess you're right."

CHAPTER 53
During the war: 1861-I: Riel Mjorn

It's worse. It's worse than I ever could have imagined. The general hadn't been lying when he said that you'd need a mask to survive in this squalor. The smog is ten times thicker than I remember from coming down a few months ago to see Vienna. Vienna.

My heart sinks as I look around. How is she doing? It seems so much darker than it once was. Not that it was any walk in the park to begin with. The atmosphere feels heavy—like the weight of death. Perhaps, that's why they were revolting, they can't stand the weight anymore.

White flags painted with blood-red roses dot the silent streets and hang from windows—the only amount of color besides the fires that rage from the factories to our right. That's where we are headed. To the factories, where riots and strikes have broken out in the intensity that they are getting people killed. Fear grips my heart. I don't want to do this. Why should we try to stop them? Clearly, from looking at this place, they have every reason to want to change what they have for the better.

We're not to use weapons on them, but I can feel the gun strapped to my hip. I dread the thought of using it. I don't think I can ever kill another human being—even ones desperate enough to kill others to get what they want. I'm just a scholar. A lover, not a fighter. I want to be home with my books, with my words, with pen and page. In a place where I can bring change to the world, and awareness through my thoughts. Not here, not with a gun burning a hole into my skin. Not against people who are trying to change what they have.

I look at Gabe, who stands beside me, but I can't see his face through the ugly mask. I notice that his hands are shaking at his sides and find a little comfort from his display of fear. I wonder if he's thinking about using his weapons too. Or if he's thinking about being back in Seperium with Leya and his father . . . if he's even thinking about anything.

The smoke grows thicker as we approach the factories. A haze that brings with it a never-ending stench. It smells like war—it smells like death.

CHAPTER 54
During the war: 1862-S: Doren Caldwell

I knew he would do this. I'm still bed-ridden, and yet, he's forcing me to attend this dinner with the rich and elite of Seperium City. I tie the bowtie around my neck, tightening the loops with shaky fingers. The butler helped me into my maroon suit—as if that wasn't embarrassing enough—but I refused to let him help me with the tie. The door opens behind me.

"Just a second," I call over my shoulder.

"It's just me." The soft voice fills the empty, gray room—sparking it with a little bit of color, and my heart jumps. It's a voice I recognize—a comforting voice. A voice that brings me back to the past, back when I was just a teenage boy, who had all the time in the world, and the best friends. I reach for my tires, spinning my wheelchair to look at her. Leya Barrett stands there with her hands folded against the fabric of her emerald-green dress, silver lace complementing the sleeves and embroidery.

Her dark hair is pinned on her head with little silver vines wrapping around it. Her brown eyes are rimmed in red, raw from the tears filling in those spaces. My heart hurts because I know those tears were for someone we both loved so dearly.

"Leya," I whisper, and she moves closer, hugging me tightly. I hug her back, glad to have found someone close, comforting. She has to lean down to hold me, but the gesture is like a thick shield, cloaking me away from the rest of the sorrowful world.

"Oh, Doren, it's so good to see you." She pulls away.

"You too. I feel like I haven't seen a friendly face in a while."

She nods, tears streaming down her cheeks. She reaches laced gloved hands up, dabbing at the tears. Her emerald engagement ring blinks underneath the fabric.

"I'm sorry, I—" she starts.

I take her hands into mine, tears forming in my own eyes. "It's okay. I miss him too."

"Is he—I can't believe he's gone. First Casen and now him, I . . . They should keep looking for him. They should look until he's found. Why—it would be better if they found his body, or something, then I would at least know that he's truly gone or not. But this . . . I hate this." She sobs.

I avert my gaze at the mention of her little brother, who got sick and died just before I got back. "I know. I've been in contact with Riel, but he said it's pointless. Inferium's in turmoil. I wish I could be down there looking, but I—"

"I agree. I would be down there in a heartbeat, but my parents keep saying that I should just accept that he's gone. Even if he survived the riot, he would need superior medical attention to save him . . . and that doesn't exist in Inferium." Her fingers caress her ring.

"I'm glad you're here, Leya. I don't think I can get through this dinner without you."

"Me too. I'm glad that you're still alive. I'm sure it hasn't been easy, but just don't give up. I'm here."

"Thank you." I sigh. "Ready to brave this dinner?"

CHAPTER 55
After the war: 1864-S: Inspector Leo Pim

I hate this. *Hate* this. They still haven't found the murder weapon, and now I have to traverse through the terrible green hills covered in dust and pollen again. Maybe I should wear a mask. Maybe it'll protect my mucous membranes from being assaulted. I glare out the window of my temporary office, procrastinating getting in a motorcar and heading to the crime scene.

Chief Lecten said that Dwell Hall was scoured from top to bottom, but the weapon still hasn't been found. I asked him if they knew what they were looking for, and he said a dagger. A dagger? Yes, the blade was thin, but daggers aren't the only weapons that sport a thin blade. They should be on the lookout for anything that could have been narrow enough to cause those cuts.

This is why I have to go out there and do it myself. My last two suspects are still on the way, having been taken into custody last night in Lower Inferium, but that also means that I won't be able to question them until tomorrow morning. How can I wave the murder weapon in front of the suspects if I don't have a weapon to wave? I groan in frustration.

Everyone seems to have the same story from that night, and they couldn't all have conversed together before questioning—they came, they ate, they talked, they left. So, either someone is lying, or General Hoek really did kill his friend. I run a hand down my face. This case is proving to be impossible. Especially, since the one man whom I don't believe killed the victim is looking very guilty right now, but I'm up to the challenge. No case is impossible.

"Not for the likes of Leo Pim!" I shout, putting my knuckles on my hips and puffing my chest out as I look over High Seperium Countryside.

"Inspector," Chief Lecten calls from the doorway, and I nearly scream in fright, looking back at him. Jeez, this man has a way of sneaking up on me or being so annoying I can't stand him—both are terrifying.

"Rosea Dierich is here to see you."

I huff. What can that insufferable woman want now? She still hasn't apologized to me for what happened all those years ago. Wait? Do I forgive her? Should I? I shake my head, none of its important right now.

I nod. "I'll take it from here. Thank you."

He shrugs, moving out of the doorway so I can go greet my guest. My long legs hurry along the narrow hallway. Is it just me, or do my steps seem lighter? I push away the thought. They can't possibly be. Muscle, bones, flesh—don't just become lighter.

Rosea stands in the lobby with her hand clinging onto Prissy's. Rosea's blond hair is pulled back into a messy bun. Her dark blue eyes are hooded under a cloud of exhaustion. Her face is void of makeup, showing off the red splotches of acne that decorate her face. What happened? She was here only yesterday, and she looked fine then. Why does it look like she fell from Seperium to Inferium and back up again?

"Rosea, I didn't know you were coming today."

"I—wasn't but—Grams is running a fever, and I was up with her most of the night. I don't want Prissy to get sick, and I can't watch them both. Is there . . . anyway I can leave her with you, just until Grams' fever breaks?"

I stare at her with a mix of horror and disbelief. She wants to leave me with a *child*. Is she crazy? Yes, the child is mine, but that doesn't mean I know how to keep her alive yet. I have to study these things. I have to make sure that I know everything—all the ins and out and ups and downs, anything that can possibly go wrong.

"I'm working. I have a small amount of time to look for the murder weapon. I can't take Prissy there. She might—"

"Please, Leo. It's not like I asked for many favors."

"You have to be around to ask for favors," I mutter.

"What?"

"Nothing, I said nothing." I backtrack before sighing. "Fine. I will take Prissy with me today, but if she accidentally catches sight of human blood and freaks out, it's not my fault."

"She's from Inferium, Pim. I'm certain she's seen worse."

I cringe. "How comforting. What a lovely childhood she could have had if she knew her father."

Rosea rolls her eyes. "Will you take her or not?"

I stare at the blue-eyed little girl, crouching down to her eye-level. "What do you say, Prissy? Would you like to spend the day with me?"

Prissy backs away, hiding behind her mother.

I huff, standing up. "See, she doesn't want to go with me."

"She's a child, Leo. You have to give her more than two seconds to get used to you. You're still a stranger to her."

"Gee, I wonder whose fault that was?" My own daughter is scared of me. What kind of a father does that make me? Granted, I haven't had the chance to actually be her father, but still, it feels like a sickening twist in my stomach that Prissy is terrified of me.

"Will you stop? I'm giving you a chance to get to know her." Rosea's tone becomes exasperated as if I'm a young child in need of scolding, but who's supposed to scold her? She's the one who kept my daughter a secret.

"Hand her over," I begrudge.

Rosea picks her up, cradling her on her hip. "Prissy, I'm gonna leave you with Mr. Pim. Now, you be good for him, okay?"

Priscilla nods. "But Mommy—" she starts, glancing at me with those blue eyes that are so much like my own. She sticks a thumb in her mouth.

"You'll be back with me before you know it." Rosea looks at me. "Hold your hands out." I hold them flat out toward her. She frowns. "Like you're gonna hold a chi—like you're gonna pick up Roosevelt."

"She's not a cat."

"It's close enough." Rosea holds Prissy out to me.

I groan, grabbing the little girl's waist and tucking her against my chest. She's heavier than she looks. I shift her weight to my hip, looking down at her. She sticks the wet, spit-covered thumb up my nose, and I yelp, backing away and nearly dropping her. She giggles loudly. Oh, she thinks it's funny? Disgusting.

Rosea tries to stifle a laugh. "You two are gonna be just fine. Bring her to the hotel when you're finished at the scene. Also, introduce your-self."

"As who?"

"As who you are to her. Otherwise, she'll never know." Then she's gone, walking out of the steel front doors.

I look at Prissy again. "Prissy, I'm your father. I know you don't know what that means yet, but I hope to teach you. I hope to become the man who will always be there for you. The man who loves you un-conditionally because that's what you deserve."

"Okay." She smiles. "Fader." . . . and my heart melts.

CHAPTER 56
Before the war: 1860-S: Samuel Hoek

I don't regret it. I did what I had to, to save my son, to keep him safe. That's all any father wants—to keep his children safe. I did wrong by him when I went into business with Barrett Steel. Wellan took everything from me, and I became scared that I would never be able to provide for him again, but I have been able to do just that.

"The assets have been saved in your account, Lord Hoek," the kind teller at the bank says as she sits back down at the desk across from me. A stack of papers in her worn hands. She looks over the top of her glasses, brown, wrinkled eyes shining warmly at me. "The trust fund can only be opened by your son, Gabriel—not you, nor anyone else. If you are one hundred percent certain you want to proceed, please sign and date these documents." She holds the stack out to me.

I reach for the quill and ink, smoothing my hand down the first page. Yes, I've done what is right by him. Gabriel is my only son, and now, he will be set for life, and Barrett Steel will suffer for what it has done to me. The sins of Wellan's past will catch up to him, and he will be found guilty of all his crimes. I smile to myself as I sign the paperwork, my cane tapping on the ground with a sickening rhythmic frenzy.

Wellan is the only other owner of this particular cane. I only ever made two when Hoek Weapons was still mine. No one knows they exist. No one knows the secrets they've been through. No one knows that I gave it to him as a gift when I thought he was still my friend.

What a fool I had been to give something so precious to someone who would never care, but I won't regret the past anymore. I will look to the future. I will make the past right by correcting the future.

Nothing lasts forever. Wellan Barrett taught me that, and I intend to teach him the very same thing. His fall is just going to hurt a whole lot more.

CHAPTER 57
Before the war: 1860-I: Rosea Dierich

Sunlight beats against my back, blue paint splatters across my face and the mask that covers my eyes as I run the loaded paintbrush across the murky bricks above my head. The scaffolding I stand on bends and sways as I wave the brush to and fro.

Last night someone came into the bar I was waitressing at and said Barrett Industries couldn't pay him for his weeks' worth of wages. He said they had been one of the few companies still providing higher than normal wages, but he heard that some internal investor pulled his stocks out and caused Barrett Industries to lose a lot of money, and in turn, not be able to pay their employees. To the left where Barrett Industries main factory stands, I can hear the calls of protests groaning and clawing like a raging beast.

The people of Lower Inferium are tired, breaking under the weight of the tyranny forced upon them. They just want to be treated fairly—better wages, better lifestyles, but the protests are starting to become more than just that. The people are realizing they want to be free of Seperium's rule altogether. They are realizing that Seperium depends on us—not the other way around.

For years, Inferium has provided all of Seperium's food and products, and the throne of Seperium can't stand without the commodities they need to uphold their lavish lifestyle. Sure, they provide us money for our livelihood but it's not enough to matter. Not when Inferium could be completely independent of Seperium.

That's what my new creation depicts. In a world of dark blue, factories rise up from the ground, billowing gray smoke and in the middle of it all, a man portrayed in blue with his back facing me, lies on his knees staring at the scene—a bright red rose peeking from the brim of his top hat. Gold bills of SEM are spread out around him, some of them burning in little balls of fire like the factories he's looking at, others clasped in the fingers of disembodied hands rising from the ground.

I reach down to dunk the brush into the paint once more, noticing the small crowd that has gathered below me in the street. They're whispering and pointing at me, looking like little bugs from the two-story scaffolding. Bugs that are so easily squashed, and yet resilient when confined to dark places, but we are a people fed up with being nothing more than insects.

I add the final touches to my mural as a motorcar pulls up behind the crowd. A few policemen file out, setting up a barricade and pushing people away from the building I'm painting on, as if I am a precious talisman they need to protect. How special it makes me feel. I turn around, waving at the people who stand below me. Some wave back, garnering a shove from a nearby policeman. I glare downward at the officers. Well, that's rude. They were only returning a friendly gesture.

Finally, Inspector Leo Pim steps out of the motorcar, sniffing in disgust. It's odd to see the tall man from way up here. Flashes of memory rush through my mind as I study him. He likes to put up this facade that he is a pompous pain in the rear who hates everything that doesn't initially benefit him, but I have seen a different side of him as Rosea. He is a kind soul—someone who cares about others. Someone who will help them in a moment of weakness and vulnerability.

Perhaps, that's why he is an inspector, fighting to bring justice to those who deserve it, but I fear his sense of justice has become skewed by the views of the Council who sent him. I didn't get to ask him as Rosea, but I wonder if he really believes what the Council told him about Inferium, or if spending a few weeks down here has allowed him to see a different perspective of the story? At least, if he hasn't yet, I can show him the way and plant seeds of doubt in his mind against the Council—

as Rosea of course. But as Crémant, I get to tease him for the pompous nature of his lifestyle.

He looks up at the scaffolding I'm standing on. I lean against the sun-warmed railing, the dark blue brush dangling from my fingertips.

"Well, would you look at that! By golly, if it ain't Inspector Pim. Howdy!" I call, donning another fun accent to further confuse the blue-eyed gentleman.

He glares up at me. "Halt! With your hands above your head, you're under arrest by the High Council of Seperium!" he shouts, taking a revolver out of the holster on his hip.

"Boy, this Inspector's got me shiverin' in my boots!" I knock my knees together in mock fright, garnering some snickers and smiles from the crowd.

Pim scowls, marching up to the ladder underneath the scaffolding. "Drop the contraband and put your hands above your head!" He aims the barrel of his gun at me.

"Did ya have to move closer to shoot me better, Inspector? And what contraband?" I wave the paintbrush. "This poor defenseless paintbrush? Well, darlin', it sucks to be you," I say to the brush before letting it slip from my fingers.

While gazes are diverted at the falling painting tool, I jump, grab onto a rung of the scaffolding hanging above me, and climb to the roof. I start toward the edge, ready to goad the Inspector some more, but just then, long, slender fingers clinging to a revolver appear at the border of the roof.

"By golly! He's catchin' up with me, but he's gotta be faster 'en that!" I call back, racing along the rooftop and jumping onto the next building.

"I'm not letting you get away this time!" Pim follows me over to the next building.

The warm sun rays caress my skin, filling me with wonder and excitement. The thrill of the chase fills my bones. I turn on my heels, running backward for a second.

"Try 'nd keep up ol' man!" I take a running jump onto the next rooftop, tucking and rolling when I land on the other side.

"I'm pretty sure I'm not that much older than you!" he yells, following me to the other side.

"You can't seem to catch up, so in my mind that equals an ol' man!" I grab onto a ladder at the edge of the rooftop we are currently on, saluting him before I slide down metal rods.

On the ground, I look back up to see him staring at me from over the edge, then the disgusting, rusty ladder, then back at me. Come on, Inspector. Chase me! Catch me.

He nearly gags as he sets his hands on the bars, long legs swinging over the edge. Ooh! I should keep running, but I am enjoying the view.

"Nice butt fer an ol' man." I bite my lip.

He glances over his shoulder. "Don't stare at my butt!"

"Too late!" I start running again before I get too distracted by him.

"Oh-oh there the fox goes . . ." I take a left turn but run into a dead end.

Oops, I must have gotten off on the wrong rooftop. I had forgotten to sing, and now that I am, I'm completely lost. I turn back around, running as fast and as hard as I can. He spots me as I rush out and is soon on my heels. Fear palpitates my heart. None of this is familiar. I'm so lost. I hate being lost. I hate—*Get it together Rosea. If you don't find a place to hide, he'll catch you, and then you'll never have to worry about being lost again.*

I keep running, taking any zig zagging patterns I can. I run into people walking home, in front of oncoming traffic, trip over feral dogs that bite at my heels. I just have to evade Pim. I take a tight right, squeezing through a small alleyway. When I come to the end, I find myself in a large clearing, staring at a factory that is blocked off because of a strike—the dark bricks look foreboding and dismal in the sun's light.

No one will be in there. I'll run through the factory and out the other side. I heard enough stories about factories to know where most of the exits and entrances are. I race across the clearing, heading for the back door. I hear the strikers shouting from the front of the building. Hopefully, they don't see me.

I wrench the backdoor open, squeezing inside. It's dark. Adrenaline fuels me as I run and crash into crates or barrels or something. I don't know. I stand, limping as I try to find any bit of light to help me see. The darkness starts to close in.

My heart sinks in my chest. I can't breathe. I suck in air, but it immediately disappears—my asthma causing my breaths to wheeze like a growling lion. I can't—I close my eyes. *"It's all in your head, Rosie. Just breathe."* Grams' voice fills my mind before I hear the door bang shut behind me, followed by a crash. He found the same pile of garbage I had moments earlier.

"Ew, what even is this?" I hear him say.

I quiet my breaths and crouch where I'm standing, my eyes slowly adjusting to the dim light. I see the hazy outline of machines and piles of material lying on pallets to my left. To my right, an elevator and stairs lead up to the attic where I'm almost certain the offices are located. I hear Pim shuffling closer, but I have the advantage for the moment—I can see.

I tiptoe to the stairs, gently stepping onto the first one. A small, almost imperceptible creak, escapes from the metal. I glare up at the spiral contraption. This is going to be loud. I have to move fast. My feet fly up the stairs, the metal groaning and squeaking with every footfall. When I reach the top, I find that I'm right. It is a landing filled with office rooms.

I glance around, looking for the next place to make an escape, but I'm trapped. Unless . . . I race into the office directly in front of me. It's large, and just like I expected there is a window that overlooks the factory floor down below. I hope I don't have to run much farther because if I do, my asthma will get worse, and then I really won't be able to breathe.

Reaching into the slit of my suit, I grab my knife from where I have it strapped to my thigh. Palming it, I smash the blade into the window. Shattered glass rains over me. I look over the edge, and my heart sinks. I can't jump down from this height. I'd break something, or worse, but maybe I can reach the beams just above me. As I'm gearing myself to jump, a pair of slender hands grab me by the waist, pulling me away from the ledge. We tumble to the ground and land with a collective grunt, swearing at each other.

Crap! I scramble away from him, adrenaline fueling me as my feet fly for the open office door. My breaths heave, stabbing pain into my chest. My vision blurs.

"Not so fast!" he grabs a small bit of fabric from my suit, ripping the garment a little and causing me to stumble—or perhaps it's the lack of air in my lungs. He pins my wrists down. "I got you now," he laughs, his voice robbed of breath. His face is covered in snot, his eyes red and blurry. What the heck happened to him?

"Allergies, I—Inspector?" I ask before spitting in his face.

He yelps, immediately releasing me to swipe his face. I stumble for the exit, but he grabs my ankle, dragging me down again. I land on my hip with a gargled scream. He pushes me down face first so I can't spit at him again. Stradling my legs, he forces my arms behind my back, strapping cuffs against my wrists.

The pain in my chest is back tenfold, and I close my eyes to avoid the red spots crawling into the edges of my vision. I start to wheeze again. My own lungs are trying to kill me. I can't hold air . . . I'm gonna die. I'm gonna—

"Crémant Rose, you are under arrest for inciting violence and treason against the High Seperium Council." He pulls my wrists forcing me to my feet. Lack of breath begs me to double over in pain. "Any last words?"

I want to retort something, but all that makes it past my lips is a wheezing breath. I fall against him, the pain forcing me to concede. To give in. To die.

"Crémant?" Pim's voice edges on concern, his blue eyes meeting mine with worry.

"I—" I gasp. The breath I take in is immediately void in my angry lungs.

He sets me on the ground. "I can't have you dying on me now," he grunts, two fingers checking my pulse. "I—I have to—" He swallows, clearing his throat. He pinches my nose, his lips waving over mine in uncertainty. *This fool!* Mouth to mouth is not going to help me in this situation. If I could slap him, I would, but I wouldn't dare waste my energy. His lips meet mine, and before he can breathe into my mouth, I bite his lip.

He jumps back. "What are you doing? I'm trying to save you!" He winces, touching his lip.

A commotion down in the factory below causes him to look up at the sound.

"Crémant Rose!"

"We know you're in here."

"I know I saw her—"

"I saw her too—"

"I saw her being chased by that fancy Seperium Inspector—"

"Do you think she got out already?"

"We would have seen it."

Voices down below carry up through the broken window.

Pim looks down at me, light blue eyes questioning.

I stare at him. "Y—you should go. If they find ya—" I wheeze out.

Despite knowing that Inspector Pim is a prissy, rich man from Seperium, I don't want him to die. I want him to change. I want him to see that he can change. His eyes meet mine with a hurricane of conflict. He completed his mission. He caught me, but he can't possibly fight his way out of here alone. He has to let me go, and I know it hurts his pride to do it, but I'm sure it will be fine because his pride needs a good knocking down—at least two pegs.

"Go," I gasp. "I—I can't s—stop ya."

He grumbles. "I will catch you and turn you in, Crémant Rose. This will not be the last you see of me."

I nod, trying to calm my tight nerves. The Rosaries find me not long after he's gone.

CHAPTER 58
Before the war: 1860-I: Inspector Pim

Music flutters throughout the room like it's being carried on the thrilled heartbeats of those in the audience, taking us to the moon and back. The song is a chase. I can feel it in my blood, begging to be met, and my mind wanders to thoughts of Crémant, and our crazy chase through Inferium.

I hadn't heard much from her in five days. No new murals, no new issues. As far as I knew, the asthma attack—as I later learned is called and can't be solved by mouth to mouth—didn't kill her. I shudder, thinking how my lips *touched* hers. I only tried to save her because you can't incarcerate a dead criminal, and I had no interest in making her a martyr. That's what her followers would have done—use her death as an excuse to cause more trouble.

I know she's alive because her loyal Rosaries blabbed about saving her. Those fools even tried to find me too, but by that time, I was long gone. I'm glad I escaped. I'm also glad she survived because that means she can be found again, and then, I can turn her in. Justice will be served. This case will be closed, and I can finally return to my home in Seperium and take a hundred baths until I'm certain that the grime of Inferium has been washed away.

I look beside me, studying Rosea's profile. Her white-blonde hair frames her face like the halos painted on the cherubs above our heads.

Her deep blue eyes are glued to the opera singer and the whole orchestra backing her. I can't help but stare for a short second. Rosea's wonderment fills my stomach with butterflies—wait? Butterflies? I'm not a twelve-year-old girl. I don't get butterflies, but I can appreciate someone who has an apparent love for the opera.

Shame. I brought her here because I thought she would hate it or get bored. I had to pay for extra tickets—one to Seperium and one to the opera. I even picked out the dark blue dress she wears. She doesn't know it, but I did. I thought her eyes would complement it nicely—and I was right. I had to ask her Grams for the correct sizes, but in the end, we pulled it off. I don't know why I wanted her to hate it; I just thought someone from Inferium wouldn't appreciate the elegance of the opera.

Although, now that we're here, Rosea doesn't seem all that out of place like I thought she would. She looks like she belongs here, and I wouldn't say that anyone from Inferium belongs here, but I can see her living in Seperium. I'm not sure why the thought causes my heart to pound inside my chest.

I smile, eyes fixing back on the stage that is trimmed in gold and marble. A sparkling chandelier hangs above the singer and orchestra, washing the stage and font rows with golden light. Gold and black tapestries hang behind the orchestra, complementing the gold-covered seating.

The song ends on swelling high; our hearts having fluttered up to the moon to be left there—or the sun, but I'm certain one hurts more than the other. I stand clapping with the audience. I glance sideways at Rosea. Tears dot her blue eyes, reflecting the golden light of the stage. She smiles at me, a tear falling on her face, and I have a sudden urge to wipe it away. *Get it together, Pim! What the hell are you thinking? She wouldn't let you touch her anyway.* Wait? Why do I want to touch her?

I gulp, finding my heart hammering inside my chest. Odd, it only beat to the music playing earlier, but now—no. *It's just a temporary high from all the excitement surrounding you.*

The applause dies away, and I help Rosea into the crowd of exiting people and out of the music hall. The commons room seems so bright now that we are out of the dim hall. Blinding chandeliers wink down, illuminating the marble and metal pillars surrounding us. Filigree gold and copper flowers decorate the pillars and walls, creating the illusion that the walls are on fire.

Rosea dances around me, humming to the tune stuck in her head and flouncing her dress.

"That was wonderful!" she exclaims, and I have to will my eyes not to follow her around. It's starting to hurt my head.

"Indeed, I'm rather surprised you enjoyed it."

She stops. "What, you think Inferium scum can't handle classy music?" She steps closer to me, invading my personal space.

I take a step back. "I never said that. I'm just—glad you enjoyed it."

She smiles, backing away. "Thank you. No one has ever done something like that for me before. It was wonderful to witness another beautiful performer. You could just tell she loves what she does."

"You're welcome." I nod at her kind words. "And yes, Clarissa has had a love for singing and music since we were in school."

"You were in school with her?" Her eyes grow wide.

"Yes."

"Do you know all of these people here?" She looks around at the perfect society of Seperium that seems to have squeezed themselves into one common room, forcing Rosea and I to stand against a wall.

"Most of them, none that I care to talk to right now, but the hounds will sniff us out soon enough. I'm sure many of them will be wondering about you."

"You mean they'll be dazzled by my quick wit and alluring beauty?" She flutters blonde eyelashes.

"I'm sure they'll be dazzled by something." I roll my eyes, thinking of how highly she saw herself.

She's not that pretty. Is that a horrible thing to think? Okay, she's not amazing or strikingly pretty. She's—well she's more like a delicate pretty. I won't call her alluring or mysterious, but I will call her delicate and welcoming. Easy on the eyes—a flower amidst a bush of thorns. Perhaps, that's why she is named Rosea, for her beauty only rivals that of a rose.

"Earth to Pim." Rosea snaps her fingers in front of my face. "Are we gonna go eat some fancy food now, or whatever it is you rich people partake in?"

"I—uh—yes," I stutter, leading her to the door of the theater and trying to take my mind off thoughts about her beauty.

I shake my head. Why do I find this infuriating woman even remotely attractive? She's from Inferium. How can I be attracted to someone who's not from Seperium? It just doesn't make sense. *I don't think attraction makes sense, Pim.* At least, that's what Rosea would say. I shake my head. I have to stop thinking about her. Nearly every thought begins or ends with her.

She stands on the sidewalk, looking back at me. Elegant lanterns light the path to her as if welcoming her into my world. "Where are we headed, Pimmy?"

"Please don't call me that," I grumble, waving for a cab.

"Would you prefer Primpy? Primmy? Pimster? Pimpster?" She bursts out laughing, and I turn to glare at her. "I'd call you that last one, but I don't think you're smooth enough around women."

"I—" I start ready to yell the perfect retort, but just then the cab arrives. "If I wasn't even a little smooth around women, you wouldn't be here." I open the door, taking Rosea's hand and helping her into the back.

"I seem to recall that it was me who asked you out first," she shoots back.

I follow after her. "And you wouldn't have asked me out if you didn't find me a little smooth and attractive, so ha!" I settle beside her.

She shakes her head. "I do—" she starts. "Never mind."

I chuckle, feeling quite pleased with myself. I've won this round. "Pim or Leo is fine," I mutter as I close the door, giving the driver the address of Où L'aube Rencontre le Crépuscule—where dawn meets dusk. It's a beautiful rooftop restaurant that overlooks the whole of Seperium and is decorated with beautiful gardens—fake ones, of course—and fountains.

Sometimes people like Clarissa, the opera singer, or Halen Jeol, the famous actor, appear there for fine dining—a place I think Rosea will love. Of course, I originally thought she'd hate it, but after her reaction to the opera, I'm not so sure now.

Rosea watches the buildings flash by, her eyes glued to the glass. I see now that she loves Seperium, and who wouldn't? It's a beautiful place. It makes me feel a little bad that Rosea didn't grow up here, but it only stays beautiful because no low-life scum is here to taint it. Although after spending a few weeks in Inferium, I'm not sure it's all their fault that they're lowlifes. It's not like they had rich aunts to take them in and raise them—Rosea certainly didn't.

I shake my head. I'm thinking about her again, but part of me is starting to wonder if she's thinking about me, or am I just a meal ticket into Seperium? What even are we? Are we dating? Am I seriously dating someone from Inferium? Somehow, this turned from me getting to know her because I was suspicious, to me actually dating her.

"Are we dating?"

She turns to look at me. "It depends. What entails dating? Are we going out on a few dates together? Are we dating to spend the rest of our lives together? Or are we dating to get under each other's sheets?"

I wrinkle my nose, thinking how particularly unsanitary it would be to share sheets with someone. I grimace as it dawns on me, she hadn't been talking about sleeping in a bed.

"I don't know," she continues. "It can be whatever you want it to be, I guess. I already made my feelings clear. I told you that I found you attractive and asked you out. Now, you, I'm not so sure where you stand, or what you think of me—if you even think of me."

"I think of you," I whisper. "I think of you when you're right beside me."

Her eyes widen in surprise. "And what do the thoughts say?"

"They say you were born to live in Seperium. They say you love it here. They say—say you are beautiful. Not perfectly beautiful, but delicate, like that of a rose," I say so softly it's a wonder she even hears it. Has she moved closer to me, or is it all a figment of my imagination? Is it warm in here? Why does everything seem so hyper-focused, and why is it only focused on Rosea?

The High Seperium Tower that I used to love observing passes by in a blur of steel and gold. All the wonders of Seperium seem lost to my eyes even though I haven't seen them for several weeks. Perhaps, in just a few hours, Rosea had stolen away its splendor and bottled it into her gaze.

She leans closer. Those dark blue eyes filled with questions I'm not sure I can answer, but maybe one day, if she gave me the chance, I could find the solutions. Maybe I could be the resolution she has been looking for, or perhaps, she'll become the resolution I've been looking for. I lean closer. Her lips meet mine with all the tenderness of rose petals, smooth, delicate, and insanely beautiful.

CHAPTER 59
During the war: 1861-I: Gabriel Hoek

A droplet of rain smears the ink on the page, and I groan, about ready to run a hand across the entire thing and call it a failure. There is no way Leya can read this jumbled mess of words, but that's what my heart feels like—a jumbled mess of everything.

I shot someone today. It's the first time I had to pull the trigger on another human being—someone who might have had a family, or worse, a loved one sitting at home worried sick that he hasn't come home tonight. Or the next night . . . or the next . . .

My stomach squeezes in pain, bile rising into my throat. I'm gonna be sick. I still see his face. I see the horror trapped in them. I didn't mean to kill him, but it had been a situation where it was either me or him, and I wasn't ready to let Leya or my father receive a telegram saying their beloved Gabriel died in battle.

Instead, I'm writing this letter to tell her what happened, to tell her that I had to kill someone to return to her. To tell her that this all seems so wrong. That everything we've tried to forcefully stop, only creates a million worse problems. I feel like a dog chasing his tail—like this is all pointless. Why are we even here to try to stop them? Why do we have to kill them? Why does it have to be us or them?

Doren sits down beside me, the kerosene lamp hiding under the eve with me whispers strange words of light over his features. I notice his eyes are blurry and red, and mud and soot streak his pale face. His green eyes meet mine as he looks over the paper in my hands before he takes a sip from a flask he holds. He hands the metal tin toward me.

"I hear it helps cover the stench. Is that for Leya?"

I take the flask, giving the letter to him. "Yeah, but I'm not sure she can read it. I—I wanted to tell her about today."

I take a sip of the liquor—it burns down my throat, warming my belly in the chilly, rainy afternoon.

Doren glances at the letter before handing it back. "Even if she can't read it, I'm sure she wants to hear from you. It's probably hard to be without the one you love."

"It's hard, especially because I'm terrified that I won't be able to make it home to her. I almost died today, and instead, I had to kill someone else to survive. How is that fair? Only because I have someone to go home to. Someone I don't want crying or drowning in sorrow because I can't make it back home to her. I'm scared, Doren."

His green eyes reflect the golden light of the lamp, dancing like fire. I close my eyes. I've seen too much fire in the last few days.

"I think that fear is what drives us. If we didn't have it, how would we know we're alive? We would just be husks of who we used to be, like chaff blowing in the wind. Separated from the wheat of our home and loved ones, hoping somehow to find a way back."

"But what if we never find a way back? What if we're stuck blowing in the wind and never ever land?"

As if on cue, the wind howls—a sorrowful moan that brings its own teardrops down onto dirty streets as if it can wash away all the blood stains. It leaves behind a cold that chills my bones and makes me crave home.

"Kinda depressing, but if we let go of the hope of finally landing then what are we actually fighting for?" He slaps a hand on my shoulder. "Stop worrying about getting home to Leya. You're gonna be fine because you have someone to return to . . ." his voice drifts off. "I'm only fighting to make sure you and Riel make it back safely, and possibly, maybe, find the one that I've been waiting for too." He smiles sideways at me.

I grin. "Thanks, Doren. Somehow, you always seem to put things into perspective."

He laughs. "Anytime." He stands, pointing at me. "And don't you go feeling sorry for me. I know that girl waits out there somewhere, so be sure not to lose the girl you have. Cherish her and send that letter, smudges and all because she loves you in spite of blurry words."

"That seems deeper than I think I can give you credit for. Who are you and what have you done with Doren?" I stand as well, stuffing the letter into an envelope.

"I'm not that much of an idiot, am I?"

I shrug. "It depends on the day."

He smirks. "I understand. Now go get the letter mailed. I'm sure she's checking the mailbox every time the mailman passes by."

CHAPTER 60
Before the war: 1860-I: Vienna Sinclair

The astringent tingles my nose as I douse the cloth in my hand and wipe the blood off the operation table. We had another amputee. Someone who got caught in the riots. A messy sight I have to say, but the patient survived and got a new prosthetic arm because of it.

It was the last prosthetic we actually had in stock at the hospital. Dr. Greenwood said earlier that our delivery for more should be here this afternoon—assuming the Council is still kind enough to provide them with all the strikes.

I'm not so sure. The Seperium Council doesn't seem like a group of people you want to mess with, and I'm sure they're upset over all the protests and halted shipments. I throw the cloth away, wanting nothing more than to get out of my blood-splattered apron and mask. I step out of the operating room and head toward the nurses' quarters.

Through the bright, white halls, I try to ignore the cries of hurting patients, and instead, focus on a man with flowers tucked under his suit jacket as he slips by, or the girl skipping through the exit on her way to be discharged.

As I reach the nurses' quarters, someone yanks open the backdoor of the hospital and grabs my wrist.

Rosea pulls me into the back alleyway, her blue eyes sparkling like a drunken idiot. "I'm sorry to bother you at work, but I had Grams distract Dr. Greenwood so I could sneak back here to wait for you."

I roll my eyes. For the last four years, Grams and Dr. Greenwood have had this flirting thing going on. I think they like each other, but they never seem to do anything about it besides talk. They met through Rosea, when her and Grams came to visit at my family's house that Dr. Greenwood and I moved into.

"I guess I'll take my break now," I say.

"Great! Let's take a walk." She giggles, grabbing my wrist into her hand again.

"Rosea." I pull her back. "I can't go out looking like this." I gesture to my apron.

She shrugs. "It's Inferium. Who cares? And you're a nurse. I have something I need to tell you, now!"

I sigh. "Fine."

We walk out toward the main road, avoiding piles of trash and homeless people propped up against the disgusting brick walls.

"I'm dating someone!" Rosea spins me around, and I yelp at the sudden motion. She giggles. "He's perfect and so kind, even though he'd never admit that."

I smile for my friend, her happiness reminds me of a jazz chorus dance, bright and full of energy. It crashes through the alley, almost as if enticing the sun to shine a little brighter on the grimy storefronts.

"What's his name?"

"Pim—I mean Leo. He's beautiful and tall, and he has long legs and blue eyes and dark hair and perfect hands and—"

"Wait? Pim? Leo Pim? The Inspector? The prissy, stuck-up, pompous jerk from Seperium? That Leo Pim?"

"Well—yes.

"He asked you out, and you said yes?"

"Actually . . ." she trails off, avoiding eye contact.

"You asked him out? Why would you do such a thing? He's trying to throw you in jail, you didn't forget that, right?"

"Of course not! But he's cute, and I really wanted to get to know him as more than just the inspector chasing me on the streets."

"But why would you do that? If he catches you—"

"He won't. I'll tell him the truth before he catches me."

"That's an even stupider idea. Once he knows you're Crémant he's gonna throw you in jail faster than you can say, 'I didn't do it.'"

A motorcar zooms beside us, kicking up dust and exhaust into our faces. I cough the stench away.

"Maybe it's stupid. Maybe I am just a simple fool who is starting to fall for the wrong guy, but—Vienna, there is just something about him. Something that draws me to him. Something that tells me to hold onto him, to never let him go, and I wish I could be smart about this. I wish I could deny what I'm feeling and hide it all away for the sake of my heart not being broken, but I can't."

I sigh, stopping our walk and hugging her. Over her shoulder, I see a scraggly rose bush fighting to survive among the dark stone bricks of Inferium. One lonely pink flower blazes brightly at the sun from between its leaves and thorns. Despite what is good for it, despite that it would be easier for it to just shrivel and die, it has chosen to live and bloom in a world of death and destruction.

Rosea is like that flower. When the world tells her to be complacent and die, she defies those words, believing in the good of someone she doesn't even know—believing that there is more to him than meets the eye, and finding the courage to fight for it. To see that change happen.

My heart swells with admiration for her, because my sensible mind would say, *"Run! Danger! If you go down this road it is only going to hurt."* But Rosea sees it a different way. She sees someone she wants to love, and she chases after him, despite the consequences. Despite that it might bring her immense pain and hurt.

I pull away. "I understand what you're saying, but I'm afraid he's just gonna break your heart." Tears form in my eyes. "Worse, I'm afraid he'll take you away when he finds out who you are. I'm afraid of losing you, but I understand why you want to fight for him. You're not afraid because you know what you want, but I'm terrified, and I will blame myself forever if I don't at least tell you how I feel. You can make your own decisions, and I know you won't give him up. You're in too deep now, but I can't, in good conscience, not at least warn you."

"I know the consequences, but I believe he can change. I believe he really likes me, and I believe my words and actions will speak to him. I believe he'll see my side, and I believe it will force him to think, to ponder, to fight for what we want—a world where we can live and love without the oppression of lower or higher class." Her blue eyes dance like a flickering flame, smoldering, growing, and blazing like a tango—passionate and filled with longing.

I hug her again. "I love you, Rosea. I will support whatever you choose, even if it hurts me to see it. I will endure it for you, and if he breaks your heart, I will destroy him. I will be here to catch you when you fall, sew up your heart, and implore you to one day love again with someone who isn't gonna throw you in jail."

She chuckles, pulling away. "I'll hold you to that."

"I know you will."

"Would you—I know—but would you want to meet him? Maybe you can see what I see."

"I would love to, but only to support you. If I don't like him, I won't hesitate to make my feelings clear."

We turn around, starting back the way we came. Sunlight tiptoes through the smog, creating whimsical patterns like a line dance. I smile at the beauty of it.

She nods. "I count on it."

"Do you need me to take you back to the hospital, or can you find your way back to the theater from here?"

"I—" she looks around. "You should probably take me back."

I chuckle. Even after all these years, she still doesn't have a good sense for direction.

As we near the hospital, two men carrying giant briefcases in each hand meet us from the other side of the alleyway, stopping in front of the hospital's backdoors—an older and a younger gentleman. The older one has thin gray hair peeking out from under his top-hat. Round wire glasses sit on the bridge of his hooked nose, and a large salt and pepper gray mustache takes up the rest of his face.

The younger man looks very similar to his companion—so they must be related in some way. He has long dark hair that falls almost to his shoulders and deep-set brown eyes that look like the mirth of the dance of life has died—like he's seen too much. They're beautiful eyes; sad, and yet, full as if he can tell you all about the mysteries of the world. He studies me, and I know he takes in my bloody apron because those brown gems widen in surprise. The poor thing looks like he might faint. All the color has leached from his face.

The older gentleman tips his head to us. "Lovely day, ladies. We're delivering prosthetics for the hospital." He smiles.

Rosea turns to me. "I'll be on my way," and then whispers, not so quietly, as she points to the young man. "You should talk to that one, he's cute."

I shake my head, rolling my eyes. "Get outta here. I'll talk to you later."

"Bye." She blows me a kiss, heading out of the alley and muttering a song to match her steps.

I turn to face the men. "Follow me, gentlemen."

I lead them into the hospital. Nurses and patients shuffle past us, clothed in white gowns and coats, stepping to the rhythm of the itineraries marked on their hearts.

Once I've shown the men to our prosthetic storeroom, the older gentleman reaches a hand out.

"I'm Ike Mjorn, and this is my son, Riel." He gestures to the young man.

I shake his hand and then his son's.

Riel starts to move his hands in odd gestures and symbols. I stare at him, concerned until I realize that Riel is deaf. We've had a number of deaf patients here the last few years. Some knew sign language, while others didn't. I picked up a little, but not enough to understand what Riel is saying.

Ike smiles. "He asked, 'Why is there blood all over your apron?'"

I smirk at Riel. "I like to bathe in blood . . ." I let the words hang for a second. His eyes look at me in horror, and I realize he can read my lips. "I'm just kidding. I helped with an amputee who got the last arm prosthetic we had. I didn't have time to change because my friend came by."

Relief sweeps over his face, followed by a wave of compassion. I can't help but stare because it brings a spark of life into those dark eyes, and all I can think about is how beautiful it looks. I think I'm starting to understand what Rosea meant—that feeling of being drawn to someone when you don't even know them, like a new partner who somehow knows all the steps to your dance of life. That's how I feel right now—that drawing, that pulling. The aching, the longing.

"You're beautiful." I feel the words whisper out of my mouth before I can stop them. "I mean I—" Warmth flushes my cheeks, and I swallow. *Stupid Vienna! Why didn't you think before you spoke?*

Mr. Mjorn raises his eyebrows, while Riel smiles. My mouth goes dry. What the hell? He's even more beautiful than before. He signs, and I notice no wedding ring on his thin, wispy hand.

"He says, 'I'm flattered you think I'm beautiful because I was thinking that you're beautiful—even though you have blood on your apron,'" Mr. Mjorn translates.

My heart leaps into my throat as I smile. He thinks I'm beautiful. This gorgeous man from Seperium thinks I'm beautiful.

"This seems like a very intimate conversation to be translating for my son." Mr. Mjorn laughs, curling the tips of his giant mustache. "Some people might think I'm the one flirting with you."

"He'll have to teach me sign language then," I say to Riel.

That gorgeous smile lights up his face once more.

"He says, 'he would be honored.'" Mr. Mjorn looks around. "I should be going. I think you two would like a little time to get to know each other, and Riel can write on paper."

"I can't. I have another shift, but maybe soon," I say. "Maybe, to-morrow."

"He said, 'he would like that very much.' He also would like to know your name."

I blush, feeling stupid. "Right, Vienna. Vienna Sinclair."

Riel mouths my name, the syllables glancing over his tongue and lighting his features once more. He signs, and this time I know what he says.

'Nice to meet you.'

CHAPTER 61
After the war: 1864-S: Inspector Leo Pim

I spin in my office chair, watching the world blur by in a collage of colors. Despite my frustrations with not being able to find the murder weapon, I had a wonderful day with Prissy yesterday. I could tell she is most definitely my child, because she was so well-behaved and proper while I worked to find the weapon. Though, I doubt I'll find the weapon until I find the killer, which makes things even harder—like finding a needle in a haystack.

Immediately after my fruitless search, I took Prissy back to town. As we were walking back to the hotel, I saw a giant plush cat toy in the window of one of the children's shops. I took Prissy inside, and of course, because she is *my* child, once her eyes landed on the plushy cat, she immediately wanted it. I bought it for an expensive 300SEM, but for Prissy, I would buy her anything, regardless of the cost. Rosea wasn't as pleased when I dropped Prissy off at the hotel, but she didn't tell me to take it back, so I called it a win on my end.

"Would you stop spinning in that chair like a child?" Chief Lecten enters my office without even a knock.

I grab my desk, skirting my spinning to a halt, ice-blue eyes glaring at him. "Always have to ruin the fun, Chief."

"Riel Mjorn and Vienna Sinclair are here for questioning."

"Ah, yes." I stand, my head rushing in a free-falling feeling and making me lightheaded. Not that I haven't stopped feeling lightheaded since Prissy and Rosea appeared, but still.

I glance into the window of the interrogation room, and sure enough, Rosea's best friend, Vienna Sinclair, sits at the table next to a man I assume to be Riel Mjorn.

I sigh. Miss Sinclair hates me, or she did, and I'm sure her love for me hasn't changed in the last three years. Rosea probably told her a bunch of lies about our parting—like how I broke her heart, etc, etc. I should get this over with. They're both suspects in the mystery of a Seperium Citizen's death.

I open the door, stepping into the dim room and taking a seat on the other side of the metal table.

"Nice to see you again, Inspector." She spits the title out of her mouth like it's made of poison.

I sniff. "And you as well, Miss Sinclair." I look at the man. "You must be Riel Mjorn."

He nods, his dark brown eyes never leaving my face.

"He's deaf," Miss Sinclair says, gesturing to the stack of paper in front of him. "The department provided us with enough paper to tell the story ninety times over, so he'll write everything down."

"Good to know. Well, let's get this over with." I look back at Miss Sinclair. "Ladies first."

She narrows her eyes, but I could care less—she can't commit murder in a police station. Unless she's crazy . . . and knowing Miss Sinclair, she might be crazy enough to do so.

"Tell me everything you witnessed the night of Oktobor 14th."

She sighs. "Well, I can't tell you everything because that would be inappropriate."

Mr. Mjorn, reading her lips, shoots her a look.

"Fine. Riel was invited to Dwell Hall because his long-lost friend, Gabe, was found. He apparently had been living with the Caldwell's for the last two weeks. Riel invited me, and I invited Rosea, especially because the Caldwell's are prominent people. As you already know, Rosea and I are on the new Inferium Council, and getting as many names as possible and support from Seperium will help us entice change in Lower Inferium. So, we went. Dinner was good, and we talked and laughed like we had been friends forever, except for Leya's mother, she was scary as heck." You're telling me, I think, trying to suppress a shudder at the thought of that terrible woman.

"Anyway, Rosea and I had an early appointment the next morning, so we left sometime before 2100. We went back to the apartment we were staying in, and that's it," she finishes.

Riel nods beside her.

I look at him. "And you? You're close to General Hoek. Do you think he would murder someone he was close to?"

He starts to write on the pages in front of him. Miss Sinclair leans back, glaring at me while Mr. Mjorn works. I hold her gaze. I won't allow her to intimidate me.

After a few minutes of Miss Sinclair and I staring each other down, he hands the paper to me.

Gabe is one of the kindest souls I know. The war was hard on him, and he did his best to never kill anyone, even in self-defense, although he was forced too sometimes. And when those dark occurrences happened, he would be riddled with guilt for days. I worried about him. I was afraid he would do something drastic to lessen the guilt, but Doren, Leya, and I helped ground him.

We were always there to remind him why he was fighting, but I think we soon learned that it was pointless. Inferium just wanted to be free of the cage they were placed into. Not long after that, he disappeared, and when they couldn't find him, I thought he killed himself. For years, I believed he was dead. Everybody else did too.

Then, he came home, and we were shocked. I had to go to that dinner just to see him for myself. He was so grateful to have made his way back to us. So no, I don't think Gabriel would kill someone he was close to. He felt immense guilt for killing a stranger. I don't think feelings like that go away.

Exactly as I thought. General Hoek isn't the killer, but then who is? Who would have enough motive to kill Lord Caldwell? At first, I thought it was General Hoek too, since he seemed to have the most motive. He came home to find the girl he loved married to someone else, and one of his close friends at that. Of course, all the signs point to him, all signs except one—General Hoek loved Lord Caldwell, and he never would have killed him.

"I heard he was stabbed multiple times. Sounds messy. If I were the murder, I would have killed him in a much easier way," Miss Sinclair remarks.

"You're a nurse, correct? How would you have killed him?"

"Yes, I am. I carry medical tools everywhere I go in case anyone gets hurt, and I need to help them. What I would have done is taken a scalpel to the notch at the base of his neck or made an almost imperceptible slit at the back of his neck right below the hairline. That way, he would have been diagnosed as dying of a heart attack, unless the coroner has a very sharp eye."

Interesting.

I smile. "A fascinating way to murder someone, Miss Sinclair. Sounds like you might have had practice . . ." I leave the words hanging in the air.

"I can assure you, Inspector Pim. There is only one person I have ever wanted to test it on, and I'm—"

Mr. Mjorn waves a hand in her face, forcing her to be quiet. Was she going to say that she wanted to murder me? In a police station? I don't remember Miss Sinclair being this bold—or stupid.

"Well, I sincerely hope you never have a chance to test it." I stand. "You two are dismissed." I turn to leave.

"You're a coward. I still hate you for what you did to Rosea," she says.

I spin around. "I think you need to get your facts straight, Miss Sinclair. Rosea left me. Not the other way around. She said she hated me. She said she didn't love me. She's the one who—you know what? Why am I even trying to explain this to you? You can think whatever you want. I don't care about your opinion. I care about Rosea. I always have, and I always will."

"Your actions would say less."

Her words feel like a punch to my gut. "I'm sure to you, they would."

CHAPTER 62
Before the war: 1860-S: Gabriel Hoek

Sunlight pours through the giant windows to my right as I stare at the portrait of a menacing Lord Barrett, avoiding eye contact of the real one sitting at his desk before me. Birds flutter outside the windows, casting shadows as they zoom through the sun's light.

My heart pounds like I've just run a marathon, and I can feel the blood rushing in my ears. I can't breathe. What the heck am I doing here? Why—I stop, letting my thoughts disperse.

I love Leya. That's why I'm here. I love her so much, I want to ask her father to let me spend the rest of my life with her, but why do I feel so scared? I think it's because I'm scared he'll say no. I'm scared he'll say I'm not good enough for his daughter.

I have no title, and I hardly have any money to my name. If I don't work hard, I won't even be able to give Leya a life in Seperium . . . but I love her, and I'll hate myself if I give her up.

My long black hair falls into my eyes as I lower my gaze down to Lord Barrett's. I push the ebony strands away, nervously tucking them behind my ear.

Taking a deep breath, I finally speak. "Lord Barrett, you and Lady Barrett have always been so kind to me, and I want to call on that kindness now. I've come to ask for your daughter's hand in marriage."

He sighs, his eyes growing sad, like a painter has taken the corners of his face and spread them downward. Fear strikes my heart. He's gonna say no. I just know it. Sweat beads in my palms, and I try not to swallow loudly.

"You want to marry my daughter?"

"Yes, I love her, and she loves me. We've loved each other for a very long time, and I want to promise her we will be each other's forever, and that I will love her until the day I die."

Lord Barrett nods. "I understand," he starts, causing my heart to soar. "But you're both only eighteen."

My heart sinks. He's going to say no. He's definitely going to say no.

"You've just graduated from Seperium Landing. She'll be headed to study music, and you will be going off to engineering school. You can promise to marry her, but I want you to wait until you've both finished college. I don't think that is a good basis to start a permanent relationship on.

"Marriage isn't an easy thing to manage, and if you two are trying to commit to this new step in your relationship while also trying to focus on your studies, it won't work. You'll become resentful of each other, and I don't want that. You can ask her to marry you, but you'll have a long engagement until both of you are finished with your studies, so both of you can give your all to each other."

I can't believe what I'm hearing. He's gonna let me marry Leya. Me. I can marry Leya. The breath that I had been holding since I came into the room releases from my lungs. My heart explodes in my chest as a smile breaks across my face. I feel as happy as the tittering birds outside the window—free and soaring through the sunny sky as if I had wings of my own. I smile at the memory of almost jumping off a barn roof with a pair of mechanical wings strapped to my back. It was Leya who had saved me then, and now, she's the reason I want to fly again.

"Thank you, Mr. Barrett. I promise I will take good care of her, for as long as I live," I rush through the words, still in disbelief.

Lord Barrett smiles as he stands and walks around his desk, pulling me into a hug. I yelp in surprise. He's never given me a hug before.

"I know you will, Gabriel. You've always been like a son to me, and I'm glad to be welcoming you into our family permanently as a son-in-law." He steps back. "Finish your studies well, and Lady Barrett and I will be honored to plan and pay for your entire wedding as a show of happiness and celebration of our beloved children getting married. I'm so grateful you both fell in love. I can't picture Leya with anyone else."

With anyone else . . . The words ring through my head. Had he and Lady Barrett always believed that Leya and I would become more than friends? Even if I had nothing to offer her? My head spins. He's allowing me to marry Leya, even though he knows I'm not good enough for her. He's allowing me because I'm a son to him already.

"Thank you. You and Lady Barrett's kindness has meant the world to me, and I can never express my gratitude."

He claps me on the shoulder. "We're very proud of you, Gabriel. Now, do you have a ring?"

"I—I wanted to ask you first," I stutter, my heart soaring high up into the sky. Rings. He wants me to get rings. Rings make it real—they make it official.

"Good, talk to Michele. She'll give you the perfect ring because she has been saving one for Leya for years." He smiles, his big bushy gray beard rising with the movement, his eyes shining with happiness.

"I will. Thank you." I bow my head slightly, skipping toward the door.

"Stop saying thank you and go get that ring, take your bride, and let her know she's all yours—that she will take your name and love you until the end of time."

I nod, opening the door and racing down the hall to Lady Barrett's sitting room. My feet slow to a halt thinking about Lord Barrett's words. Until the end of time, I will love Leya. I will love her with all my heart. Tears of joy well in my eyes as I gasp for breath. I'm so happy I could—I've already used this imagery, but how do I explain the happiness, the excitement of what I'm feeling right now? Leya's father approves, even though he could give her to someone ten times better than me—he chose me. He's proud of me—of us.

I reach the door to Lady Barrett's sitting room. How many times had Leya, and I crouched upstairs listening through the grate just to catch a word of Lord and Lady Barrett's conversations? How many times had we caused trouble through that grate like blowing flour through the entire thing and turning the sitting room into a world of white? I smile at the memory. Leya's mom grounded us for two weeks and banned all access to the kitchen after that one. The punishment was totally worth it to see Leya laugh so hard.

We even danced around in the falling flour, pretending it was snow. Leya loves snow. Maybe we'll have a winter wedding. We have to finish college first, but I'm sure she would love that.

My palms feel sweaty as I open the door to Lady Barrett's sitting room. Even though I see Lady Barrett as if she were my own mother, she still scares the crap out of me sometimes. But I'm not that little kid anymore, I'm a grown man who is in love with her daughter. I just don't know what she'll say when I tell her about Leya. I hope she'll be as pleased as Lord Barrett was because I value her opinion.

She sits in her rocking chair, working on some intricate embroidery with a pair of glasses perched on the end of her nose. The grand clock to my left tick tocks in steady rhythm, almost in sync with my heart. She looks up as I step into the room. It had been decorated like an enchanted forest, with dark green trees painted on the walls surrounding little bubbling brooks.

"Gabriel." She smiles, her dark eyes that are so much like Leya's fill with a shine as she greets me, lessening a little of my anxiety.

"Lady Barrett." I bow my head. "I—I just finished speaking with Lord Barrett, and—well—he—"

"Goodness, spit it out, boy." she pushes her spectacles up onto her face.

"I've asked him to marry Leya, and he said yes, only if we have a long engagement until our studies are over, but he told me to get the ring from you before I ask Leya," I gasp out, my heart pounding like a racehorse.

Perhaps, it is my anxiety, but it feels like the trees painted on the walls are reaching for me. The needle in her hand flashes like a wicked grin, even if it's childish to think she'd stab me. Although, Leya did tell me that her mother stabbed a pesky butler once, but I'm pretty sure she made that up.

"Oh," is all she says as she stands, moving closer to me. For a crazy second, I think she is gonna stab me, but instead, she pats my cheek, her eyes filling with tears. "Wait here," she says and is out the door before I can say, "okay." She comes back a moment later with a beautiful hand-carved wooden box that has been inlaid with light pink porcelain and amber.

She takes my hands into her empty one and places the box in my care. I open the lid, and a pair of copper and porcelain rings wink at me. The female ring has a gorgeous emerald centered in the middle of it, while the male ring has three small emeralds embedded into the base.

"That ring." She points to the female one. "Belonged to my mother. She passed away right after Wellan and I got married. So, I decided to hold onto it until Leya found the man she would spend the rest of her life with and commissioned a second one to be created. I think they belong to you and Leya now." Tears mist in her eyes once again.

"Thank you," I whisper, closing the box and giving her a hug. She startles for a moment before hugging me back, but she quickly moves away, like a stray cat.

"I'm so proud of how far you've come, Gabriel. To be honest, I didn't like you very much when I first met you, but as I watched you two—getting into trouble, throwing flour into my sitting room, smearing blood down the halls so that you could claim that a murderer had been in the house . . ." she trails off sighing. "I was about done with you, but then I watched how you loved Leya and took care of her. You always danced with her at the parties we attended. When she got sick with pneumonia, you stayed by her side every second until she was better. I watched you support her dreams, and you were always the first to clap at her concerts, even if those concerts were just our little family. And I—I couldn't ask for a better husband for Leya. I know you will always be there and will always take good care of her."

Tears well in my eyes. "I'm proud to be able to become her husband. I thank you and Lord Barrett immensely. Thank you for allowing me to marry her."

She nods, her brown hair bouncing as she clears her throat. "Now, go ask Leya, though, I don't think she'll say anything besides yes." She pushes me toward the door so I can't see the tears fall onto her cheeks.

CHAPTER 63
Before the war: 1860-S: Leya Barrett

"Gabe, where the heck are we going?" I ask, my hand gripping his tightly since my eyes are covered by a blindfold. Leaves crunch under our boots, and cool spring air wraps its wispy tendrils around us.

"We're almost there. I have something amazing to show you."

"Does it have to be so far away? And why am I wearing a blindfold? You couldn't have blinded me once we got closer?"

"You can see it through the trees. I couldn't risk letting you see part of it before we actually got there."

I grumble, nearly falling because of a tree root or a rock. "It doesn't matter. I'm gonna break something before we even arrive." I smell smoke and hear a fire crackling in the distance.

He laughs, gripping my hand and holding me still. "We're here," he whispers, his fingers untying the blindfold.

Firelight shines over my face, lighting up the little area surrounded by birch trees. Their green leaves flutter under the weight of a light breeze. Kerosene lamps in different shades of colored glass hang from the trees, creating an aura of rainbows against a background of darkness. Covered candles flicker from their perches atop tree stumps and rocks, surrounding a little picnic area that sits on the ground right by the fire.

"Gabe," I gasp. "It's beautiful." I look up into his dark eyes. Tiptoeing, I kiss his cheek. "Thank you."

He smiles, gesturing toward the picnic. "Let's go sit down."

He leads me over to the blanket. The meal consists of marinated chicken, fresh bread, pickled cabbage, and some kind of pie. I hope it's cherry pie. I love cherry pie. We sit down, and he pours me a glass of white wine.

"Wine?" I ask. "I think Seperium Landing ruined us when it comes to wine. It's all their fault I like it now."

"I know. I hated it when your parents used to give us a small glass at Merrytime." He laughs, his deep chuckle residing in his throat. He has a laugh like no other. It's quiet, but always gains my attention. It seems to grip his throat and slide off his tongue in a smooth manner, and I wouldn't describe most laughs as smooth.

"Have I ever told you I love your laugh?"

His brown eyes reflect the light of the flickering fires surrounding us. "As a matter of fact, you haven't. I take that as a high compliment." He puffs his chest out. "What does it sound like?"

"A hyena."

He slumps. "Really? I don't think it sounds like that, if anything, yours sounds like a hyena's laugh."

"Hey!" I swat his arm, nearly spilling wine all over myself.

"Abuse!" he shouts, his eyes swimming in mirth. "But I think your laugh is cute!"

"Even though it sounds like a hyena?"

"Yes, even then . . . wait a minute. See, you admit it sounds like a hyena." He laughs.

"I—" I close my mouth, swallowing my words. He's not wrong. "You tricked me." I take a sip of my wine.

He leans over, kissing my temple. "I love you."

I look up at him, setting my wine down and scooting closer to him. I wrap my arms around him, lying my head on the crook of his neck and shoulder.

"I love you too."

"Leya." His voice sounds unsure, worried. I sit up, releasing him. His brown eyes study me. I haven't seen him this nervous since he told me he loved me. Oh my gosh . . . is he—my heart starts to pound as I shake the thought away. I can't get too excited over something that hasn't happened yet because I'll just be disappointed if it doesn't.

"What's wrong?" I whisper, afraid that my words will break the moment between us.

The world around us seems to still. The sound of clacking leaves above us disappears. The crickets in the distance fall silent. He becomes everything, and all of my senses seem to focus solely on him—like there is nothing else in this world besides us, besides this moment right now.

"I—" He reaches behind him, his fingers fumbling with something. "Leya—I—wow this is harder than I thought it would be." He looks down, embarrassment choking his face.

Silence overtakes us for a moment. "Leya." He holds a little brown box that is inlaid in pink porcelain and amber. Immediately, I recognize it—Mother's rings. "I sing a song of gladness, for my heart will never feel this way a—again. I'll love you forever, but I know forever doesn't last. I—Leya, will you be my forever? Will you marry me?" He flips the box open, revealing the beautiful rings.

My mouth goes dry as I smile, tears filling my eyes. "Yes! I will. I will be yours forever." I throw myself into his arms. He laughs, almost dropping the rings as he catches me.

Tonight, the world is aglow just for us. Welcoming us, embracing us and the love we have for one another. Everything comes back into focus—the flickering candles, the smell of wood smoke in my nostrils, the creaking of the birch trees as they sway, as if they're an audience witnessing our love and congratulating us with a dance.

I kiss Gabe, my heart dancing with the trees. Tears stream down my face and fall onto his cheeks as I smile at him. My tears only make him seem more beautiful, more delicate, more mine.

"I'm so glad it's you," I whisper, kissing the teardrops on his face as he holds me close.

"I'm so glad you said yes," he whispers into my neck.

"It took you long enough."

"It's gonna take longer. Your father won't let us get officially married until we're both done with our studies, but I couldn't go another second without asking you." His dark brown eyes meet mine, reflecting the rainbow lights surrounding us. It makes my heart notice a song in his gaze—a song composed only for us. So much so, I can see the notes being written right before us. I'll have to play them one day.

"Then I will wait for you. I will wait until I carry your name as my own, for you already have my heart, and that is enough for me."

"And I will guard your heart well, as long as you do the same for mine. A breeze stirs beside us, tousling his long hair, and gently caressing our skin.

"Yes, our exchange of hearts will never allow us to be separated."

CHAPTER 64
Before the war: 1860-I: Inspector Leo Pim

"I knew it! I knew it!" Rosea's grandmother catches us pulling away in the dirty aisle behind the stage. Why I had ever let Rosea convince me to meet back here for a secret rendezvous is beyond me. I guess I like kissing her more than I will ever admit, but haven't I already admitted that by coming back here and hiding away like two teenagers who know better? I slap my forehead. Perhaps.

Rosea blushes, her cheeks flushed in red as she pulls a strand of blonde hair behind her ear. Her lips are swollen from our lip-locking, and her blue eyes gaze up at mine in the golden lights, almost like they're dressed in honey. It only makes me want to kiss her more. *Get a grip, Pim!*

Grams shuffles up to us, her blue eyes gleaming with glee. It makes me cringe. Why is this old lady so excited for us anyway? She didn't make her thoughts known before catching us, so she can't call this a win on her deductive skills.

"I knew ya two were goin' to get together!" she exclaims, pulling both Rosea and I into a huge hug. I squeal as she pulls my tall frame into her chubby arms, nearly knocking Rosea's and my head together. Rosea giggles, hugging her Grams back. I awkwardly pat the old lady, before pushing myself from her grasp and straightening my wrinkled suit.

Crew members and performers hurry past us in the dim hall as they head to the backstage door. The low murmur of their voices reminds me of the parties I used to attend with Aunt Madelyn, bringing me a small glimpse of home.

I sniff as my eyes wander around the rest of the space, taking in the dim, dirty hall. A thick layer of grime and dirt cakes the once magnificent red and gold rug underneath our feet. The intricate steel above our heads has rusted and bled orange colors down the gneiss walls. The musky smell lingers in my nose and leaves me grunting for fresh air— or perhaps, it was the kissing. I shake the thought. Rosea isn't the only thing that can take my breath away.

But you admit she is one of the things. I glare at the words in my head. No, I don't.

Rosea fights her way out of Grams' grasp, and instead, wraps her arms around my waist, clinging onto me like a chimpanzee. I can't tell whether I like it or hate it. My arm instinctively wraps around her, pulling her even closer to me.

My goodness, she is gorgeous. I will admit that her delicate beauty looks good next to mine, like we were made to complement each other for the rest of our lives. I don't usually admit things like that, ever, but somehow, Rosea is changing my thoughts, destroying them one by one like a beautiful disaster.

"I knew it too," Rosea whispers, those big blue eyes sparking up at me.

Blast it! She looks so kissable and beautiful, and—*stop!* I need to stop admitting how much I really like her because I don't quite understand all this yet. It's been a long time since I cared for someone more than I care for myself. I've been on my own for a while now. She's turning my world upside down, and I'm not sure how to feel about it.

I want her, and my ever-increasing desire feels like it might consume me. I have to stop or slow down before I'm in too deep. I feel like I'm teetering off the edge of a cliff about to jump, and Rosea waits at the bottom ready to catch me, but I'm not sure I'm ready to go. I'm not sure I want this, because what if I'm too selfish to care for her more than I care for myself?

What if I let her down because I never expected that I would fall in love with her? Wait? Have I fallen in love with her? Is that what this is? I hear Rosea murmuring beside me as she speaks with her grandmother, further proving the dilemma I am in. My eyes focus only on her, as if I have tunnel vision.

Do I love Rosea? What does that even mean? I thought love meant that you care for someone more than you care for yourself, and if that's true, do I care for Rosea in that way? Do I want her to be a part of everything I've ever hoped or dreamed? Do I want to share my favorite wine with her? Am I comfortable with letting her into every piece of my heart? Why would I be? I've only known her for a few weeks, but Rose has made a few weeks feel like forever, and every close moment we've shared seems to stretch out like a long lengthy road that has no beginning or end.

"Ya 'ave to go on in ten minutes, Rosie," Grams says, pulling me from my thoughts. Grams looks at me. "Ya've been mighty quiet over there."

I clear my throat. "I just have nothing to say."

"Aw, do I steal your breath away?" Rosea asks.

I run a finger under my collar. "N—no," I answer, and she giggles, laying her head against my chest.

"You always run a finger under your collar when you're nervous or you lie," she whispers.

I lean my cheek against the top of her head. "I'm kind of proud you noticed that."

"Kind of? You really know how to bring down a girl's self-esteem."

I lift her chin, my long fingers caressing her dimpled skin. "Will this make it better?" I lean in to meet those soft, red lips.

Grams clears her throat, pulling us apart before we've even had a chance to meet again. "Well, I'll be goin'. Don't forget yer cue, Rosie."

And with that, she's gone.

Rosea giggles, holding a finger up to my lips. "Hold that thought. You're all mine once I get done with my performance."

The echo of the crowd just behind the stage door resounds around us.

"All yours?" How can anyone truly be all of someone else's, like we're dogs or something?

"If you'll let me."

"Of course," I whisper, practically ripping my chest open and handing her my heart—still warm, bloody, and beating. I grimace. What a dark thought, and it's not even romantic. Disgusting. What have I become? What is this woman turning me into?

"I'll be back in a second." She giggles again, skipping to the backstage door.

I smile after her, but quickly wipe it away. I can't keep showing how much this woman is infecting me. I'm supposed to be here to find Crémant, but I haven't been doing a very good job of that. I've had no good leads to follow. A new mural popped up out of the blue yesterday. So, she must be feeling well enough to continue splattering her propaganda everywhere.

I don't want to miss Rosea's performance, so I start back toward the theater, but something catches my foot, causing me to stumble. I grumble. What in Seperium's sake—I turn around to find a little leather-bound journal lying in the middle of the hall. Hmm? Someone must have dropped it. I reach to pick it up, feeling the leather that has been worn smooth under someone's care. I smell the book, and it smells vaguely like . . . a rose. Not a common smell in the scum of Inferium.

I narrow my eyes. Roses seem to be a recurring theme in my life lately—Rosea, Crémant Rose, and now this journal. What if this has something to do with Crémant? What if she's here at the theater?

I untie the leather binding. I know it's rude to look into someone's private thoughts, but if my hunch is correct, I could find my missing vigilante, or at least, learn of their true identity.

A crazy thought strikes me as I glance over the first page. If this journal does lead me back to Crémant, then what will happen to Rosea and me? Will we be forced to say goodbye? Do I ask for a transfer to Inferium, or do I ask Rosea to come with me to Seperium? Or—I'm overthinking this too much. If Rosea and I are meant to be together, we'll make it work. I'll do anything to make it work, but right now, finding Crémant is my most important mission.

I focus on the journal again. Some of it is just thoughts, and little doodles, detailing what seems to be a girl or young woman's life—nothing super interesting, if I'm being completely honest, and it's not signed or addressed to anyone.

I keep flipping, breezing through the pages, stopping only to look at any drawings that might be incriminating. But what exactly am I looking for? I don't even know yet, suddenly I stop, my fingers halting along the pages. There it is. Something I wasn't expecting to find, but yet somehow did. This has got to be a coincidence.

A model drawing of Crémant Rose's costume stares back up at me from the page. I flip to the next page, there is another one, and another, showing off the different stages of evolution her costume went under until it got to the final entry.

My heart stops even through the excitement from the crowd on the other side of the wall, where their applause thunders underneath the building. Is this really Crémant's journal? But it can't be. Does that mean she is a part of the traveling theater? That would make sense. I do remember her hanging upside down off a scaffolding.

I slap a hand against my forehead. How come I hadn't thought of that earlier . . . *Because all of your thoughts have been clouded by a beautiful woman.* I growl. Or this book has been planted—a little thing to steer me off track. What if that's the case? Then who is trying to steer me off track? And are they trying to frame someone in the troupe?

I frown, going through the rest of the journal. I find other doodles of the murals or early versions, it looks like. There are entries in between the doodles, but the scrawl is too hard for me to read. I look around the dim hall, perhaps it would be easier if I had some better light.

I start for the door that leads into the foyer. A figure cloaked all in red steps out from the shadows, a mask captivating her eyes—Crémant Rose.

A vicious smile lights her lips. "Hello, Inzpector." She glances at the journal in my fingers. "It zeemz you've zomethingz of mine."

I hold the journal closer to my chest. "If you want it, you'll have to come and get it," I say, preparing myself to run.

She sucks her teeth. "Now, izn't zat extremely childish of you?" She leans against a wall, poking a hip out and showing off her curves. Why am I staring at her curves? I shake my head. *Get your head in the game, Pim.* "I'm not going to chaze you, Inzpector."

I march up to her, backing her into a corner. "Then I will chase you, I will chase you until you're in prison, where you belong."

She looks up at me with hooded blue eyes, and in the dim light they strike me as familiar, but I'm not sure why. I step closer to her ready to seize her wrist.

"If you come any clozer, I'll have to kizz you. Don't you zink ziz zetting iz a little romantic?"

I grimace. "No, this place is disgusting."

"Zats not what it looked like to me when you were locking lipz wiz your girlfriend."

Heat rises to my cheeks. She was watching us the entire time? "Who are you?" I step closer.

She stares into my eyes, tiptoeing before kissing me smack on my lips. I freeze. What the hell? Why is she kissing me? I mean she said she would but—wait? Why am I kissing her back? She pulls away, waving the journal in front of my face. I want to grab it, but I can't move. I'm too shocked.

"Don't look zo zurprized, Inzpector. I told you I waz going to do it.

Zank you for giving me back my journal."

I only half hear what she says as she slips out from underneath me, patting my shoulder as she goes.

"It'z been fun, Inzpector." And then she's gone, disappearing through the theater halls.

I finally come to life. *Why didn't you go after her, Pim?* Why did I let her kiss me? Why did—did I—no, I like Rosea, perhaps, even *love* Rosea. Crémant isn't going to destroy what I've just found.

So why didn't you arrest her? The thought wiggles itself into my mind. Because, because . . . I don't know. There is something about her. Something that's familiar, and I felt it even more when she kissed me, but why can't I place it? I always remember a face, a mannerism, something that makes a person familiar. I want to scream in frustration. How come Crémant is so elusive to me? How come I lose all sense when I'm around her? Twice I've let her escape. Twice. I've never let someone escape that many times.

I run a hand through my hair. I can't afford to let her keep disappearing from my reach. I have to arrest her next time I meet her, and then I can find out why she's so familiar. At least I have an idea where she might be now. At least I can re—

A scream from the backstage door pulls me out of my thoughts.

CHAPTER 65
Before the war: 1860-I: Rosea Dierich

I'm falling. The ground reaches for me like an angry beast's open mouth. The scream that escapes my throat is strangled as if I'm already locked in between its jaws. Darkness surrounds me as I hit the ground, but then it starts to move like water and I feel like I should start swimming, but all the air has left my lungs . . . I can't breathe. I can't—

I gasp awake. I can feel my chest tightening. *Breath, Rosea, breathe.* I try to suck in deep breaths, taking time to calm my racing heart.

"Rosea," Vienna says, sitting down beside me, a cup of warm tea in between her wispy fingers. I reach up until pain spikes up my left shoulder, and that's when I realize that my arm lies in a sling. Right. My nightmare had been real.

"How long have I been out?"

"Couple hours. I sent your boyfriend home. He wouldn't leave your side, and it was driving me nuts—always hovering over you." She sighs, checking my forehead. "You're not running a fever so that's good."

"Pim was here?" I ask as she helps me sit up. "You met him? What did you think?"

"Hold your horses, girl. One question at a time, please." She shakes her head. "Yes, he was one of the first few at the scene of your fall. He almost strangled the stagehand who didn't check your harness correctly. Grams had to pull him off."

"Aw," I sigh.

Vienna glares. "Not 'aw'. When he finds out who you are, you won't be saying that."

Dark curtains are drawn over the windows of the dim room of our flat as if they can hide the truth of the secrets I've buried for so long. The scratchy blanket weighing me down feels like a cage, trapping me against my will. I want to run. I want to hide. I don't want to deal with the weight of the choices I have made these last few days.

"He almost found out today."

"What?"

"I left my journal in the hall for him to read."

"Rosea!" Vienna gapes. I notice she's still wearing her once-white nurse's apron featuring a cross with blood dripping down and brown stains. Frayed dark curls poke out from her bonnet and frame her drooping eyelids and warm face. I suddenly feel a little guilty that she's here waiting on me. "Are you crazy?"

"He didn't get anything out of it, I came and taunted him as Crémant instead, but then he looked so good, and he was getting in my personal space, and I just had to kiss him."

"Seriously? You are crazy, and he still didn't realize?"

"No, he was dumbfounded. I paralyzed him with my beauty."

"You mean with your tongue."

"You don't have to be so vulgar, Vienna . . . but yes."

She gags, but I ignore it.

"So, what did you think of him? Did you like him?"

"Like him? He's a pompous jerk who was always getting in my way. I'd try to do something to make you comfortable, and he would be there. He did carry you upstairs, once I got your arm set, and he never left your side out of concern for you. So, he's not all that bad, and I could tell he likes you a lot." She pauses for a second, handing me the tea. "Is that why you fell? Because you were sauntering around as Crémant?"

"Probably, I should have double-checked all the lines again, but I was in a rush and I—I shouldn't have taunted him as my alter ego. I just have to tell him the truth. I can't keep living this double life, unless I want to end up with more than just a broken arm."

"Or it's time to just give up Crémant. I don't think it's wise for you to tell him the truth." Vienna swallows.

"But—"

"You can't have them both, Rosea. You have to choose, either him or Crémant."

My heart sinks with the weight of her words. She's right, but I want to keep sauntering around as Crémant. If I'm being honest, I love playing the role of the vigilante. It's like she's fused into my bones somehow. The me I never get to be. The me I can only be in a red suit with a dramatic flair to match. I don't want to give that part of me up, it would be like ripping my flesh in two, but then . . . I'd have to give up Pim.

Tears smart my eyes, I knew playing with hearts was going to be a dangerous thing, but yet, I still did it. I just wanted to change his mind, to get him off my trail, but if I'm being honest, that's not why I did it. I did it because of him. Because when I first saw him, I knew he would be mine no matter what. It didn't matter that he was trying to arrest me. It didn't matter that he wanted nothing to do with me initially, but somehow, he said yes when I asked him out. Somehow, the curiosity we had for one another drove us into this state of foolishness, and foolish it was.

Because now, his bright blue eyes are etched into my heart, the touch of his fingers is burned onto my skin, as if he took a hot ember and wrote his name so it can never be erased. The ember has ignited into a flame—no—a raging inferno as revelation rises up above the smoke. I love him. I love Leo Pim, and I don't want to douse the fire burning in our hearts, melding us together.

There is no way I can give him up now.

CHAPTER 66
Before the War: 1860-S: Riel Mjorn

I pace in the waiting room of the Inferium Hospital, not quite sure what I'm doing here. I came to find Vienna. At least, yesterday she said I could come back today, or did she? Maybe she was just saying that to be nice. Why would a busy nurse want anything to do with me? *She did call you beautiful.* That's true, she did like me.

Is that what this is? I've never had someone like me before. I don't even know what to do, or how to act, but despite my initial anxieties, I ventured back down here to see if maybe, possibly, she still wants to get to know me more—as my father had put it.

"—help you, sir?" I read the receptionist's lips, my face blanching. I should just go. Vienna's clearly not here. *Don't be a chicken. You didn't even ask her if Vienna's here or not.* I pull my journal out, hastily scribble across the page, and hand it to her.

I'm deaf. I'm from RN Prosthetics. I met Vienna Sinclair yesterday, and I came to see her. Is she here?

The receptionist looks up. "You must be Riel." I nod as she stands. "Vienna said you would be stopping by. She's already off for the day, but she told me to tell you that she would be at the Inferium Theater taking care of a friend." She draws a map on my journal, handing it back. "Follow that path, and you'll get there in no time flat."

"Thank you." I mouth and hurry out of the white-washed hospital.

Following the map, I take two rights and a left until I'm standing in front of a colossal building. Once upon a time, I'm sure this building was beautiful. Marble columns rise up to the roof decorated with gold and bronze statues that have worn away with weathering. I start toward the front doors, which are massive. The carved wood has been vandalized with nicks and cuts, destroying the once-beautiful engravings.

Pushing them open, I step into the dim-lit foyer. Mucky red velvet floors greet my feet, spreading out to what looks like a box office on my left and more open wooden doors that must lead to the theater itself. A broken crystal chandelier hangs above my head, and I shiver, thinking it could fall at any moment. I start toward the wooden doors, hoping to at least find another living soul in the dark place.

Past grim red velvet seats and rows, lights shine on a stage below me where actors and dancers step across the space, twirling and falling. I stop and stare for a moment, reading their lips as they call for "Over here!" "One, two, three, and twirl." "Keep with that pace, Elsie!" I smile at the wonderment of it all. Immediately, I can tell that these people love what they're doing, and it looks like they're doing it well.

A hand on my shoulder pulls me out of my reverie. I turn my head to find Vienna looking at me. Dark circles outline her tired eyes, which brighten as they study at me. It warms my heart more than she can ever know.

"You came." She smiles despite her apparent weariness, and she looks so beautiful, like I noticed yesterday.

I smile along with her, writing in my journal.

Is that okay? I wasn't sure if I was supposed to come. Or—

"It's fine. I'm glad you're here. If you had been a moment too late, you wouldn't have been able to find me at all."

I swallow. What is that supposed to mean? Is she saying she would have been kidnapped if I was late? Or possibly dead? But does that mean I'll have to protect her? Is she in danger? My eyes scour the room surrounding us, and suddenly the shadows look a little more menacing as if hiding sinister ideas that could destroy us. I wonder how many spiders live in those shadows. *You're going on a tangent, Riel.*

"It's a joke, Riel." Vienna looks so concerned, her dark brown eyes following mine through the room as if we can stop the shadows before they descend.

Oh, sorry. I don't pick up on . . . sarcasm very well.

She reads my note. "I noticed. Look—" she stops, pointing at her heart. "I'll do this when I'm joking. That way you understand. I don't want you to be concerned for my safety every time I say something stupid."

I sigh in relief, my heart swelling in happiness. No one has ever done something like that for me. I always have to decipher if Gabe and Doren are being sarcastic or serious.

I would like that very much. I write.

"Great!" She takes my hand, and I gape at her. It feels nice. Her hand sinks into the depression of my palm and the curl of my fingers, fitting like a glove. I hope she doesn't let go anytime soon.

"So, where are we going?" she asks.

I feel the blood drain from my face. I don't know. I didn't know I had to have a plan. *Of course, you have to have a plan! This is a date after all.* This is a date? Fear trickles into my veins. I don't know what to do on a date. What if I screw it up? What if—

"It's fine, Riel. This is my domain, not yours. I didn't expect you to have a perfect day set up for us. I'll show you around Inferium, even though there isn't much to see."

I think there is plenty to see, especially if I have you to look at all day—I shouldn't write that. I start to strike it out, but she's already seen it.

My heart pounds. She's gonna think I'm an idiot, or crazy, or—tears mist over those big brown eyes, dropping onto her brown freckled cheek. Instinctively, I reach up, wiping the lone tear. It's a tear for me, and I wish I had something I could collect them in, as a testament to every time I say something sappy to her. Is that weird? I don't think so. I just like to study things.

"I'm flattered you think so." I read the words on her lips, thinking how perfect they are. How can lips be perfect? I think it's the size or the curve or—*stop staring at her lips, Riel.*

She squeezes my hand. "Are you ready to paint this town?"

Paint the town? Where are we going to get enough paint? I mean, sure, Inferium could use a new coat or two, but still. That beautiful smile lights her face again, as if she's brought the sun into the dim theater. If I were the sun, I'd follow her anywhere.

"It's an expression, Riel. Let's get going. Time's a wasting, and we have lots to see!" She pulls us out of the theater.

CHAPTER 67
After the war: 1864-S: Inspector Leo Pim

I don't want to be here. So, why am I here? Something creaks above me, and I gasp in fright. I'm certain I will *die* here. Yes! That's it. The end of Leo Pim. Let all the newspapers say he died in a fiery explosion aboard an airship—not fright. How uncomely would it be to die of fright? I sniff, straightening my emerald green suit. No, I will *never* go out that way.

Even if it's to spite my old best friend, Sebastian. He'd die laughing if he could see me right now. His father's company probably built this airship. Ha! Let that be a testament to their bad engineering skills. Though they can't be that bad if the ship is still flying . . . if you can call this safe flying.

"Cap'n's right through here, Inspector," a burly crewmate says. He looks big enough to crush me with one fist. He takes me through one of the narrow hallways of the metal airship. I have to duck to keep my head from scraping the ceiling. I hold my luxurious velvet green top hat in between my fingers like a fidgeting schoolboy about to ask a girl out. The metal walls creak and moan like a lonely ghost wandering the halls of an abandoned mansion.

Seriously, how do these men work in these conditions—cramped quarters, metal rigging, darkness. I shudder, thinking about all the rats and mice that must live down here. Dim strips of bulbs light the pathway we walk. Something creaks to my left, grumbling like a beast that could destroy the ship whole. I hold back my scream and hurry after the crewmate, who holds a door open on the far side of the passage, spilling golden light into the tunnel.

I bend down to step into the room. To my right a huge map, depicting both Seperium and Inferium, spreads across the wall. Pins of all shapes and colors litter the map, and trade routes seem to be outlined in a pinkish color. To my left, a glass window takes up the entire wall, with bars crisscrossing each other. Directly in front of me, a man with an eye patch and a left mechanical arm sits at a desk, writing over yellowed papers. He looks at me, one bright blue eye glinting almost as white as the patchy hair on his head.

He stands, shuffling over to me. "You must be Inspector Pim." His voice sounds as grating and creaky as the ship surrounding us. He holds his left hand, the metal one, out.

I shake it. "Yes, and you must be Captain Larson Greik."

"Tis I!" he exclaims, clapping me on the back. I jump at the force of the blow and feel my lungs tighten. I cough, forcing air into my body. Captain Greik chuckles. "Ha! Stealing your breath away, am I, son? You need to put some meat on those scrawny shoulders of yours."

"Only one person can steal my breath away, Captain. Perhaps, it was the altitude." I take a seat across from his desk.

"Yes, yes, let's get this over with. I have shipments to make, and you have a case to solve." He settles back on the other side of the desk.

I pull a notepad out of my breast-pocket. "Can you tell me a little about General Gabriel Hoek?"

"Right, Gabe." His eyes seem to look far away as he recounts. "I found Gabe in Inferium. He was shuffling around the docks, tryin' to find somethin' to eat, even if it was fish guts." I gag at the image, not even writing that part down. "He looked like a strong, strappin' lad so I took pity on him and asked if he would like to join my crew. All he had to do was move boxes around. He was grateful, and soon told me what he could remember.

"Turns out the poor guy lost all of his memories. He woke up in someone's house in Inferium a couple weeks after bein' found in the aftermath of the Southside bombin'. Not a clue who he was, or where he was from—couldn't even remember his name. I could tell he was from Seperium. After the person who save him disappeared, he started scroungin', tryin' to find anyone who would help him out, but no one from Inferium would help Seperium scum."

Hmm, I take offense to that.

"And that's when I found him. He worked on my crew for a little over a year and a half. I was right. He was a strong worker—always did what he was supposed to, and kind to the other crewmates. They all loved him. He seemed to spread this light everywhere he went. Always tellin' us to be positive, always givin' us hope even though he had nothin' to hold onto. Perhaps, that's how he kept moving forward.

"A couple months after he joins me, I find him in the furnace room, tinkerin' away at somethin'. At first, I thought he was tryin' to sabotage the ship, but then he told me that the air vents weren't being properly maintained, and that's how our core kept overheatin'—we were havin' so many problems with that beforehand. I later started puttin' him on any engineerin' problems to see if he could figure it out, and what do you know, the boy was an engineer through and through."

"He didn't remember who he was after that?" Normally, something familiar from someone's memories helps them come out of the memory loss.

The captain shakes his head. "No, but we assumed he must have been a fancy Seperium engineer or goin' to school before the war. He found out who he was only a few weeks ago. A lot of my crew got sick, and so I needed his help haulin' boxes. We were commissioned to clear out an old Inferium warehouse, and in that warehouse were crates with the words Hoek Weapons stamped on 'em. At first, I thought these boxes were a rarity, and that we should keep hold of some of them, but the second he looked at them. His head snapped up and he screamed 'Gabe!' We were so startled, we thought he lost it at first," the captain laughs.

"But then he got all excited and started tellin' us that he remembered. That he remembered who he was—Gabriel Hoek, and my heart sank. I knew I was goin' to lose him as one of my best engineers, but the boy had gone on long enough. He wanted to see his dad and his fiancé. You should have seen how his eyes lit up when he said he remembered he had a fiancé, someone who was waitin' for him. So, I dropped him off in Seperium, and that was the last I saw of him."

"Do you remember what he said his fiancé's name was?"

He thinks for a moment, the white eye trailing around the room. "Lucy or somethin' like that."

"Leya?"

He snaps his fingers. "That's it! Leya."

They were engaged? Why didn't she tell me this? Probably because it is irrelevant to the case since she didn't end up marrying him.

"Interesting," I muse, setting my eyes on the beautiful clouds passing beside the windows and leaving water droplets behind on the panes. Sunlight filters through, casting little rainbows onto the floor. I can't help but think that Prissy would like it. Does she even like rainbows?

"You said something about the crates being a rarity, what did you mean?"

"Well, Hoek Weapons got bought out by Barrett Industries about ten years ago because of a fire."

Right. I remember this. I was in my second year of high school when I heard about it.

He continues, "That fire stole everythin' from Samuel. He was such a good boss, and always took care of us. He wasn't like any of the other owners. He came down to the floor to see how production was goin'. He took time to learn our names and got to know us," the captain's bright blue eye winks off in the distance, recounting the memory. Oh boy, he's gonna tell me his entire life story now.

"The Council blamed him for startin' the fire, but we all knew he was devastated, not because he lost money or production, but because thirty-five people lost limbs or could never work again, and nine others died. He cared about us. Even when he was under trial and hardly had any money, he sent the forty-four families the money they needed to survive while their loved ones recovered. That's how I got this arm." He shuffles his left prosthetic, and it buzzes and hums under the movement.

"I was there when the blast happened. You take a lit match to a vat full of gunpowder and boom! It's over. Samuel had a policy for no negligence. He treated us well and fair, even gave all the families gifts at Merrytime. We treated him with the same kind of respect and took good care of his facilities. I know he didn't start that fire, and I know none of us workers did."

Lit match, us workers did, he cared . . .

"You think it was sabotage from another factory?"

"Think? No, I know it was sabotage, but who would take the word of an Inferium worker with no money?" His white eyebrow bunches up at the question.

"Sabotage by who?"

"Barrett Steel, of course. They were in business together for a few years, and then everything went to hell for Samuel? I don't think that's a coincidence."

Barrett Steel? My heart sinks. Everything I once knew to be true comes crashing down around me. What if the rut between the Barretts and the Hoeks runs deeper than I initially thought? What if General Hoek killed Lord Caldwell because of a vendetta between the Barretts and his father? That doesn't make any sense because Mr. Mjorn said they were all good friends, and General Hoek clearly loves Lady Caldwell. No, there has to be something I'm missing. I've already concluded that General Hoek is not the killer, and with this glistening recommendation from the captain, that fact is further solidified in my mind.

"What happened to Lord Hoek after he lost his business?"

"Once the dust settled, he became an overseer at Barrett Industries. Just before the war though, he quit, and I never heard anything about him again, and then about the time I found Gabriel, I heard he had passed away. Maybe his son going missing had something to do with it . . . but who knows." His one eye trails off, winking in the sunlight like a fluttering butterfly. He gasps as if remembering that I'm still in his presence. "That's all I got for ya, Inspector. I got shipments to make before the days up."

I stand, buttoning my suit jacket. "Thank you, Captain Greik."

Thoughts swirl in my head as I leave the metal flying death contraption. If General Hoek isn't my killer, then who is? I have six possible suspects remaining, and only three of those are strong enough to have plunged the weapon into Lord Caldwell's chest eight times—Riel Mjorn, Vienna Sinclair, and Lord Barrett, and there is always the possibility that the remaining three suspects could have manipulated one of the men into murdering Lord Caldwell. But who? Who has merit? Who would want him dead?

Lord Caldwell was Lord and Lady Barrett's son-in-law, but that doesn't mean anything. I didn't ask them how they felt about General Hoek or Lord Caldwell, but perhaps, I should have. Did they want their daughter to marry Lord Caldwell because they had a falling out with General Hoek's father, or did Leya Caldwell truly want to marry Lord Caldwell?

Did she love him? No, she confessed that she told General Hoek she was still in love with him, and that she never wanted to marry Lord Caldwell. So, did she just marry him out of loneliness, or was there another reason?

My head spins as I stand in Seperium Port waiting for a taxicab to take me back to the train station. I have to get back to Higher Seperium Countryside. I also need a good glass of wine. I'm not sure which is more important right now. Perhaps, I should stop by my apartment to say hi to Roosevelt. No, Marisa, my secretary, is taking care of him. He'll be fine until I can come home for good and give him a nice rose petal bath.

"You taught a cat how to like baths?" The words ring in my head followed by the sound of giggles. "Only Leo Pim could make a cat like baths." I smile at the memory. Rosea always made fun of me for giving Roosevelt baths. I shake my head. I have to stop thinking about her.

I have to focus on the case. Who else is left? Mr. Mjorn seems to have no reason to murder Lord Caldwell. They are good friends who seemed to have kept in contact with each other after the war. Even to the point that Mr. Mjorn could bring his girlfriend to a dinner party, which in turn brought my w—I mean Miss Dierich to the party as well, which leads me to Miss Sinclair.

She is a nurse, and a good one at that. So good, she scares the crap out of me. She wouldn't be anxious over a little blood, and she is strong enough to have plunged the knife into Lord Caldwell's chest, but she made it perfectly clear how she would have murdered the victim. The way he was murdered was too messy. Unfortunately, that is one thing we can agree on, and she had no reason to murder Lord Caldwell.

Unless—unless Lord Caldwell was in love with Mr. Mjorn. I can't rule out that possibility, but she wouldn't have murdered Lord Caldwell that way. Maybe, it was just a ploy to get me off her tail, or she could have even got Mr. Mjorn to do it, but again, they were good friends, and perhaps, potential lovers. I don't think that would have happened. Now, Miss Sinclair seems to be a suspect, but that's only if I can confirm my motive and get her to break.

The cab arrives, blowing exhaust in my face. I cough to cover my disgust. It'll make my velvet suit smell. I hurry into the back.

"Seperium Station, please," I tell the cab driver as I settle back into my thoughts, watching the splendor of Seperium City blur by me.

The remaining suspect is Miss Dierich. Miss Dierich with those alluring blue eyes and beautiful pink lips . . . I shake my head, awakening from the daydream. She's a suspect and nothing more right now. The only motive she might have would be revenge, but Lord Doren Caldwell did nothing to her. The man she could be seeking revenge on is already dead. Plus, she has no prior connection to this group of people aside from Miss Sinclair. So, I don't think she's the murder.

I smack my head against the backseat of the cab. I hate myself for dredging up Rosea's past. I still see the hurt on her face when I asked. I know how hard it was for her to move past it, and I was the only man she felt safe enough around to give her all to me. She trusted me with those secrets, and yet, I used them against her. What kind of a coward does that make me?

I sigh, the weight of my sins settling in the pit of my stomach like a tank full of lead. When I get back to Higher Seperium Countryside, I have to apologize to her again. I don't want to keep pushing her away. I just want her to tell me the truth, and then, if all can be made right, I want to love her again.

CHAPTER 68
Before the war: 1860-S: Vienna Sinclair

I'm walking—no dancing on clouds. Okay. Not literally, but that's what it feels like. If this is what love feels like, then I realize why so many fools fall for it. I must be just like them, a fool. A fool for loving someone so much; just thinking about him makes my heart soar like I'm on the wings of eagles. Every time I close my eyes, I see his deep pools of sadness and longing—pools I want to wade in for the rest of my life.

When he looks at me, I know he sees me. I'm swimming in those beautiful eyes, and I never want to get out. I just want to stay there and unlock all the mysteries that make up Riel Mjorn—like he's looking at me right now.

He's frustrated because I can't make the right shapes with my hands to complete some words in sign language, and he's tired of showing me the shapes a million times. So now, he's standing behind me holding my hands, making the shapes with his fingers.

The golden lights of Seperium spill into the storefront of RN Prosthetics where Riel has taken me to learn. The dim kerosene lamps fill the space with an ambiance that makes me think of a starlight waltz; something to make stories out of, and yet, be intimate enough to fall in love—if we ignore the multiple prosthetic limbs littering the space.

I lean against him, wanting to just be a tad closer. We stumble backwards as he releases my fingers. I whirl, catching myself against his chest and stopping myself, looking up into those eyes.

"I'm sorry." I take a step back, my face reddening at being so close to him. I need to get a grip. I'm more sensible than this, blushing over a cute guy, but I think Riel is more than just a cute guy. At least, he's becoming more to me.

It's okay. He signs, and I understand. He says more, but I don't catch it, so he writes it down. *You startled me. I thought you fainted or something.*

I smile. "No, I just wanted to be close to you."

He gapes. *Close to me? You were close to me. Why would you fall against me?*

"You're so cute, because a girl wants you to hold her, and I didn't know how to say it without ruining the moment."

I was teaching you sign language.

"Holding me is too intimate for sign language? What about dancing? That's a form of communication too."

I don't know how to dance. How can I teach it?

I laugh, a bubbly giggle that makes me feel like a child in a candy store. "I can teach you if you want to learn."

But doesn't dancing require music? I can't hear music.

"Dancing only requires the music of our souls. We already know the steps. We just have to be willing to follow them." I take his hands into my own.

He freezes, and I can see the words written in his eyes. *But what if I follow the wrong steps?*

"You won't." I place one of his hands on my waist, and the other on my shoulder. "Now, pull me closer." He does. I smile because he's so tentative about it, as if he's afraid he might break me.

"Good." I step back, and he follows, looking down at our feet. I take my hand off his shoulder and lift his chin. "Eyes focused on me. Don't focus on our feet. Don't focus on anything around us, just me."

I feel the music flowing around us. The steps form before we even take them, and then he's moving with me without stepping wrong. I let go of the formality of our dance, breaking down walls as I wrap my arms around his shoulders, leaning my head against the crook of his neck.

I see his breath flutter in his throat like butterfly wings dancing in his skin. He would like that imagery since he loves bugs. He swallows as his arms naturally fall around my waist, pulling me even closer as we sway to the music embedded in our hearts. I glance up to find him looking down at me, studying me. Kiss me. But I don't know if he will get the hint. Perhaps, I'd have to kiss him first—

The sound of sirens startles us out of our reverie, destroying the moment before we've had a chance to explore it.

'What is it?' Riel signs.

"Sirens," I say, my nursing instinct kicking in as I hurry to the door. Who is in trouble? How far away is the danger? Can I do anything to help?

People run in the streets of Seperium, heading toward the Lower Inferium Elevator like phantoms in the night. I throw open the door.

"What's going on?" I ask the nearest person.

He stops. "There's been a raid in Inferium! The citizens are enraged! They've started a revolt! Some of them are overtaking the elevator. They're trying to come here!"

My heart stops. I have to get back down there. I turn to look at Riel whose face has gone pale.

"I have to—" He grabs my hands, cutting off my words. Tears glisten in his eyes.

If I go back down, I might not ever get to come back up, or he might never get to go back down. We might never find each other again. My throat clenches in pain, longing, and desire. Why did this have to happen now? I kiss his knuckles because we're out of time, and I don't care if he shies away. He doesn't.

"Find me. When this is over. Find me. Don't stop, and when I can—I will come back. I just can't leave them down there. Rosea and Dr. Greenwood—they're all I have left. You have to understand. We—we've only just met, but it feels like I've known you my whole life, and

I want to be close to you. I want more than what the world can offer us right now. So, find me." There are so many more words I want to say, but I don't know how to say them yet.

He nods. *"I will."* He mouths, and I turn to leave, but his hands grip mine, pulling me back toward him.

He steps closer to me, his hands caressing my cheek. His tears fall onto my face as he leans over me. His lips meet mine, and it's sweeter than I ever could have imagined, but I taste the bittersweet too. The taste that says we won't have this moment again for a very long time, if ever.

We linger longer than we should, and when I finally pull away, his hand slowly slips from mine until we're forced to let go.

CHAPTER 69
Before the war: 1860-I: Rosea Dierich

The sound of muffled shouts and screams rise up to the flat Grams I share. Over our dinner, she glances at me with raised eyebrows.

"Might just be a quarrel," she mutters, but the sound of objects crashing, and something being broken reaches our ears.

A huge snap reverberates our flat and the whole building seems to groan and quake with the force of the blast. Grams and I immediately stand up. Something is wrong. She races to the window, looking down into the street below. Red lights glint off the features of her weathered face.

She looks back at me. "The police are 'ere." My heart sinks.

"What?" I join her by the window, my sling pulling tight against my neck.

Pim is with the police. Does he know this is going on? Does he—I stop the thought, racing toward the door and wrenching it open.

"Rosie!" Grams screams after me.

The putrid smell of smoke and gas stings my nose and causes my eyes to water. The shouts are louder now.

"Check everything!"

"Don't leave anything unturned!

"Arrest any who resist! If they resist, they are conspirators!"

Smoke pours into our flat, and I hurry to shut the door, but just then a haunting figure steps out of the smoke, his hand stopping it.

I freeze. I know those hands. Those hands have caressed me so many times in the last three weeks. I feel like I've been punched in the gut. Betrayal is a ravaging and ugly beast, coming to devour when you least expect it. It takes you apart and destroys all that you once knew to be real. I feel like an idiot. An idiot who believed lies were real.

Inspector Leo Pim steps over the threshold, black suit making him look like an angel of death about to end my life. Tears smart his eyes, but I don't know if it's because of his betrayal or the tear gas.

"I'm sorry, Rosea. They called for the raid before I could stop them. They need evidence. They want it to end. I told them I found Crémant here and that was enough motive for them to move. Please just let me look around. Once I've searched, we'll leave. We can put this behind us." Those blue eyes will me to trust him, but the sting of betrayal already sours the air between us—even though I'm the one who has caused the most deception.

"No," I gasp, tears filling my eyes as I back away from him. "You liar." But I have no right to call him that—not when I'm the one who's lied to him from the beginning, and now Grams and the troupe are in danger because of me.

"Rosea—" he starts, but he doesn't know I'm about to betray him. He doesn't know what I've done is worse than raiding my home. He doesn't know this is the end for us. When I tell him the truth, he won't want me anymore. He'll turn me in, and that will be the end of us.

"No, Leo, we can't put this behind us. It's too late. I shouldn't have called you a liar because I'm actually a bigger liar." I laugh at the irony, feeling like I'm crazy as I utter the words I know will destroy us. It's an odd feeling, knowing you're about to sabotage something beautiful. It hurts, like someone has stabbed you in the gut. "I'm Crémant. I've always been her. I've lied to you from the start to fuel my addiction to the chase. I just wanted you to find out it was me." I sob. "And now my family is hurting because of it, but no more, I give in."

Disbelief crosses his features before his eyes narrow. "Rosea, this isn't the time for games."

I laugh, a bitter sound that chokes my throat. "I'm not playing anymore."

That seems to wake him up. His eyes grow glassy, and his face pales as he takes a step back. "No. I would have figured it out—I would have—"

Something smashes through the window, and I don't hear what he says as Grams throws herself against me, screaming my name. A blast shakes the room, and my ears ring from the impact. My vision blurs, and it looks like there is two of everything as I search for Pim in the dust-covered room. Plaster and bits of the walls fall from the roof. I feel my chest start to tighten. Oh no, not now . . . I find him lying on the ground, blood leaking from his temple.

"Leo," I gasp as someone pulls me up. I hadn't even seen anyone else enter the room. I turn my head, stumbling into the arms of a man who has a blood-red rose painted on his shirt. The Rosaries.

"I got you, Miss Rose. You're gonna be okay. We'll get you somewhere safe," he says, but his voice echoes around me, and I feel a spike of pain run through my head. I can't breathe. I can't. I turn my head again and see another man helping Grams up from the rubble. Our rescuers push us toward the window. I look back, trying to find Pim, gasping for the breath robbed by my asthma.

I'm sorry. I want to tell him as The Rosaries strap me to a harness, propelling me out the window. *I'm sorry I lied to you. I'm sorry I fell in love with you. I'm sorry I made you love me, but most of all . . . I'm sorry we ended this way.*

CHAPTER 70
Before the war: 1860-I: Inspector Leo Pim

"What the hell were you thinking!?" Chief Zorman roars, soot painting his box-like features.

The fire of what remains of the Inferium Theater blazes across the street, sending ash and smoke into the air. Citizens run back and forth with buckets, trying to contain the blaze before it spreads. Even from here, I can feel the heat, but I'm not sure I care anymore. I feel numb to everything, except for how dirty I am—I can never be numb to that. A makeshift bandage covers the hole in my head that was caused by the explosion.

"You had her in your grasp, and you allowed her to get away!" he continues, pointing a stained finger at my face. "We could have had this wrapped up and been home free! Now, we're back to square one!" A vein pulses on his forehead, his face as red as the fire burning behind us.

His screams fall on deaf ears, though, because I'm still there. I'm still in Rosea's flat. I still see the tears in her eyes. I still hear her bitter laugh. I see the red mask across her dark blue eyes. I hear her giggle matching the vigilante's. I see her in place of Crémant. The asthma . . .

"You're done with this case, Pim. I'm done with your incompetence." His words hurt, but I don't care enough to fight. I found her, didn't I? I just couldn't believe it until it was too late.

How come I never put it together? I can't tell if I'm angry at myself or Rosea, but I'm not even sure I'm angry at all. To be angry, you have to feel something, and I don't feel anything. There I was thinking that she would be hurt because I was the one leading the raid against her home when the joke was on me. She was the deceiver the *whole* time. Deceiving me into caring for her. Deceiving me into holding her. Deceiving me into loving everything about her, except who is she anymore? I feel like I don't know her at all now . . . and it hurts more than I care to admit.

"Chief!" A loud voice pulls me from thoughts about her. A young cadet comes running around the corner. "We have a situation," he heaves. "The Rosaries—they're attacking the elevator!"

Chief Zorman glares at me. "All units to the elevator! Let's get this situation under control, or the Council will have our heads!"

I perk up, finally something I can do to take my mind off her. I start after the group.

"Not you, Pim! I'm done with you for now. Once we get the situation under control, it's back to Seperium for you. You're on probation until then!" He starts running past me. "Let's get over there, you turtlenecks!"

I halt in the soot-covered street. My life feels like the fire smoldering a few feet away from me. Weary citizens covered in ash stumble past me with their buckets, mindlessly continuing to put the fire out. Once upon a time, I looked down on them, thinking that I had it all, that I didn't need anything. Now, I see them in a different light—broken people who have been forced to live in squalor.

I start to laugh like a crazy man. I get it now. Why she's fighting for them, because *this* is their reality. They were born into something terrible that they just wanted to change, and Crémant gave them a way out, something to fight for. All this time I had been trying to kill their hope and leave them with nothing.

All because I thought I was the better one. I thought they deserved what they got, but I would have been just like them if I lost everything too, and it feels like I have lost everything. I've lost her.

These people are like me. They have held hands and exchanged glances. They are real people. People who have loved and faced heartbreak just like me. People who have loved even against the darkest nights, even through scum and decay, because that's all they had left.

If only I had seen it sooner, perhaps she wouldn't have run. Perhaps she would have trusted me with her secret.

Tears start to stream down my cheeks. Now that it's too late, I understand. I wish I could tell her what I've found. I wish I could turn back time—stopped the raid, understood the signs, and told her that it didn't matter she was Crémant. That I would love her regardless. That I would stop hunting her, but it wouldn't have worked that way.

She still lied to me. She hid her identity because she knew I would stop her, and without this new revelation, I would have. I hate myself for it. Because returning to my pompous, lonely existence in Seperium would have been all I cared for, but that's not true anymore. I care for Rosea. I love Rosea, even though she lied to me. I get why she did, but it doesn't make it hurt any less.

"I get it," I say to the dark sky as drops of ash swirl down on my face, catching on my tears. "And now I've lost you."

But have you? Have you really lost her? The words ring in my head, filling me with a new sense of purpose. I can find her. I have to find her. I have to tell her that I understand. That it doesn't matter to me anymore because I love her. I need her, because I'm nothing if I don't have her to fight for. She was wrong. She's still playing the game. The chase is on, and this time when I find her, I won't ever let her go.

CHAPTER 71
During the war: 1860-S: Wellan Barrett

"Why did you do it? We were on the verge of greatness!" I scream.

Samuel Hoek stands to his feet, eyes blazing. "No! You were on the verge. I just took it away like you took it from me. I did nothing that you haven't already done to me."

What is he talking about? All I've ever done is help him. Unless—unless . . .

"You're being ridiculous!" I shout. "I've done nothing but take care of you and Gabe!"

"Don't give me that poison! I know what you did. I know you started the blast! I know you wanted Hoek Weapons from the very start, and you stole it from me just like you stole Soern Steel!" He glares, shaking from the weight of his anger. I cock my head. All documents linking me to Soern Steel should have been destroyed. How does he know about it?

He continues, "It doesn't take a genius to do a little digging. Almost a year after you married Michele Soern, her father's company suddenly gets inhumane and improper practice allegations? I don't think so. So,

266

I looked into the families that testified against him in court. They were paid off with enough money to move to Seperium. Isn't that interesting? You spread rumors, planted evidence, made up false witnesses, and bought her father's company to 'save' him the embarrassment. Just like you did for me. It wasn't enough that you got a beautiful wife with a large dowry to go with her, you had to take what her father built."

I start to laugh. Someone has finally figured it out, and now, Samuel is playing me at my own game. Having invested the money I gave him, and the money he got from selling his estate, he bought as many stocks of Barrett Industries that he could as a "ghost" buyer—someone who invests money with no intention of receiving the full amount back right away.

As Barrett Industries grew, so did his money. As he gained, he invested, and when the time was right, he pulled the plug, drawing all his funds out of Barrett Industries as fast as he could. My stocks dropped overnight, and my company lost more than half of its capital so that I couldn't pay my workers. Now they are revolting, like everyone else in Inferium, for not being paid their full amount of wages.

"What did you do with the money, Samuel? If you took it all, where is it?"

He scoffs. "You think I would tell you that? It's in a safe place. A place where Lord Wellan Barrett will never be able to find it."

I take a step closer to him. "Your son is in love with my daughter. He's asked to marry her. I can take that away in an instant."

"Good. I don't want my son to have anything to do with you or your family. You'll find a good match for her—someone with more money. I'm surprised you actually said yes to a penniless boy with his heart in his hands." He shoves an envelope into my hands. "This is what I owe you for his education. Now get out, I never want to see you again."

"Gladly," I spit, ripping the check in my fingers.

CHAPTER 72
During the war: 1861-S: Leya Barrett

"Gabriel," I whisper his name, feeling each syllable on my tongue.

We're standing at the gate outside of Dwell Hall. The motorcab will be here any minute to take him to Seperium City. I play with the engagement ring on my finger, twirling it around and around, like how I feel right now—around and around and around I go. The world hasn't stopped spinning since he told me he was summoned to fight in the Inferium War.

All men, ages eighteen through thirty, must report to Seperium City barracks by Kanuary the 12th. I didn't even know Seperium has a barracks. What is the point of a military when you don't have something to fight? Well, I guess we do now. We must fight for our livelihood. Fight people who have revolted against us, but will it change anything? What's the point of fighting if the damage is already done? Just give them what they want, and let's move on. Why do I have to send my fiancé off to war?

"Leya," he whispers my name like a lone note, haunting and not ready for goodbye. He takes my hands, kissing my cold knuckles. "I don't know what to say."

My next words choke my throat as I study those dark beautiful eyes that I know better than my own. "I think it starts with the word goodbye."

I swallow, finally taking note of the gray uniform he wears. It fills out his broad shoulders, and the cap that sits slanted over one brow shades his dark brown eyes. He looks so handsome, and it just makes me want to kiss him and hold him tight and beg him not to go, but go he must.

Sunlight bears down, and the chilly winter air rushes around us, crushing in its unforgiving embrace. I pull my shawl tighter around me. I can feel my cheeks stinging from the wind's force.

He enfolds me in a hug, and I have to stand on my tiptoes to wrap my arms around his shoulders. The shape of his body fits perfectly against mine as if we had been molded together before being separated, and to think that we almost had each other before being ripped away again.

"Goodbye, Leya." His voice quakes, and I can't stop the tears that cloud my vision. I don't want to say goodbye either, even though I told him that this is how it goes. I don't want him to go. I need him.

How can I go on if he isn't here? How can I live in this pompous world if he isn't here to convince me to do something crazy? How can I make it through without the sound of his voice, or the glint in his eyes that says he loves me? I've never been without him. Ever.

He starts to pull away, but I hug him again. "You can't go yet." I can't stop my voice from shaking.

He sighs. We both know he can't stay.

"I'm not ready to go either, but we'll be okay." He nods his head against my shoulder as if trying to convince himself. "We'll make it through this, like we always have. I'll try to write as much as I am able. Don't leave anything out when you write back. Tell me everything, as if I'm right there beside you, because I am. Don't forget that. I'll always be right here." He pulls away slightly. His hand resting on my heart. It's so cheesy I want to roll my eyes, but my stupid romantic heart loves it, and tears flood my eyelids instead.

"I will. I promise you'll get all the crazy details." I whimper, trying to swallow my tears before he sees them, but it's too late. His fingers gently caress my cheeks, wiping at the trails.

He leans his forehead against mine. "It's never enough for us, is it? The world is constantly at our door, forcing us to open it and face it." His warm breath leaves frosty puffs of clouds on my cheeks.

"No, it seems there is always something trying to pull us apart, and I don't want to face the world without you. We're supposed to face it together." I hold my hand up with the winking emerald ring. "That's what we promised. That's—" I gasp as his lips touch mine. A flurry of emotions floods my heart, ravishing me and leaving me gasping and broken. I love him. I love him so much it hurts.

He breaks our kiss, tears streaming down his cheeks. "I promise. When I get back, I will marry you. You'll be mine, and to hell if the world tries to pull us apart again." A fire rages in his dark brown eyes—a fire burning only for me—for us. For the promises we've made.

"Gabe—" He kisses me again, desperation filling every sense. It feels like the end of a concerto. The final note after a riveting climax. Is this all our climax will be? A string of promises forever unfulfilled? A taste that can never be satisfied. A thirst that can never be quenched. A song that will never be finished.

Our lips linger even after the contact has been severed.

"Goodbye, my love," he whispers, brushing my skin.

"I'll see you soon, my love."

CHAPTER 73
After the war: 1864-S: Inspector Leo Pim

I stare at the door to suite 220. The mahogany wood trimmed with golden cogs is an exquisite piece of craftsmanship. So exquisite it can keep me from actually knocking on the door.

I nod. Exactly! I came. I saw the door. I can leave now. *That's not why you're here.* I grumble at my self-intellect. Why can't it ever leave me in my state of procrastination?

I take a deep breath. I'm not here for myself. I'm here for Rosea. I'm here for Prissy. So why do I feel so scared? Perhaps it's because I'm afraid she'll leave me again. Perhaps I'm afraid she'll say no. Perhaps, perhaps, perhaps . . . I'm sick of perhaps. It's literally turning me green.

I grumble, ignoring the pounding in my chest as I rap my knuckles against the door. The gears and cogs creak as the door opens a crack. Grams appears in the wash of golden light spilling from the hotel room, her lined face and spectacle enhanced eyes taking me in.

"Well, if it isn't Leo Pim!" She smiles, opening the door wider. "Come in, come in." She drops her voice. "I just remembered that Prissy is 'sleep. Rosie will be gone for a little while longer now." She ushers me inside, taking my top hat and shooing me toward some foyer furniture.

"I'm only here to see Rosea," I mumble, remaining standing even at her behest.

She sighs, nodding. "I figured as much, but she's in Seperium City at an Inferium Council meetin'. She won't be back for at least another two 'ours, if even that."

"Oh, well then, I must be going," I say, practically racing back toward the door.

She grabs my hand as I pass her. "Now wait a minute. Ya can stay for a little while. I 'aven't seen ya in so long. Lemme just take a look at ya."

I sigh, stepping back until I'm sitting in the olive-green chair, she had almost forced me into earlier. Somehow, I can't say no to Grams. She reminds me of my late Aunt Madelyn.

She looks me up and down. "Still the same Leo Pim, and yer suits seem to be fancier too. I guess that's the style nowadays."

Her gaze makes me feel vulnerable. Guilty. Like I've done something wrong, but I know that's not true. I've done everything I'm supposed to.

Her eyes glance down at my hand. "Ya don't wear it anymore." The words feel like a stab in my gut. How can I wear something that resembles a promise? A promise that has been broken more times than I can count.

"Why would I, Grams? She's the one who broke the promises we made, not me." I look away, refusing to tell her that I have it tied to a necklace that sits just under my silk shirt, pressed to my heart where it will never be forgotten or revoked. Just not where the entire world can see. So they don't see me as a man whose promises have been broken by someone else. That my love was sent back, null and void.

She sighs. "Ya always were a daft one when it came to love, Pim."

"No, you have no right to say that. Yes, I'm daft, but I never left Rosea. I looked and looked for her. I never wanted to break our promise, but she forced me to. She left me alone, stuck in between two worlds with nowhere to call home. How is that okay?" I stand. "I'm sorry. I can't stay here and listen to you defend her."

"I never defended 'er, Pim. I never wanted 'er to break 'er promise to ya. I told 'er not to. I told 'er that ya two would find a way to make it through together, but she was convinced that she would lose ya for good—"

"She did lose me for good," I spit.

I hate the tears starting to appear at her words. They're all lies—lies to make me feel better, lies to soften my heart, but you can't soften a heart of stone. It's already been cemented.

"Well, unless ya're a ghost, she didn't lose ya for good. Whatever happened between ya—Rosie did it to protect ya."

"Yes, but protect me from what?" I scream. "No one can seem to tell me what she 'protected' me from."

"Shh." Grams' stern face forces me to clamp my mouth shut. "Ya'll wake the girl. She wouldn't tell me the details either. Rosie is the only one who knows the truth."

I chuckle, forcing the tears away. "Why do you think I'm here?" I start toward the door. "I guess when she's ready to finally tell me, she'll know where to find me—in my grave because by the time she makes up her mind, I'll be dead!"

Grams shakes her head with a little laugh as she stands. "Ah Pim, ya always 'ad a flair for the dramatic. I shoulda put ya in the troupe when I 'ad the chance."

I take my top hat, settling it on my head. "Not funny." I open the door.

"Come back soon. Prissy 'as done nothin' but talk about ya since the day ya took 'er with ya."

I halt at the threshold, turning to look back at the little old lady. "Can you kiss her goodnight for me?"

Grams sighs, a movement that seems to move her whole body. "I think that's somethin' 'er daddy should do."

"But I—"

"She is in that room right there." Grams points to a door just off from the foyer to the right.

I close the front door and move toward Prissy's room as if some invisible force is pulling me toward her, drawing me closer. I open the door without a sound, spilling golden light into the little room. A kerosene rainbow night light flickers gently on and off from its spot on the little bedside table, casting all sorts of colors onto Prissy's sleeping features.

My heart melts as I study her. She looks like a little angel with her fist smashed up against her face, her lips slightly parted. I tiptoe into the room, tugging loose strands of hair behind her ear before I bend down, kissing her cheek. I pull the small blankets tighter around her.

"Goodnight, my little petal. I'll see you soon," I whisper, and shuffle out of the room.

I wipe away tears as I stand in the foyer again. Part of me can't believe that something so beautiful and precious came out of the ruins of Rosea's and my commitment. I said my heart was made of stone, but that's not true. Despite all that's happened between us, I can never hate Rosea. My foolish heart will always love and want her, especially now that I have Priscilla. How can I ever let them go again?

Grams smiles up at me with tears of her own as I walk back toward the foyer.

"Don't say anything," I tell her, sniffling. "I wasn't crying."

She pulls a handkerchief out of her pocket and hands it to me before giving me a hug, but I have to bend all the way down just to give her a proper one. I blow my nose as we break our embrace, trying to hide my blubbering.

She pats my cheek. "Ya poor thing. I 'ope all can be made right between ya and Rosea. Because ya two created something so beautiful, and she needs both of ya"

"I hope so too," I whisper, handing her handkerchief back. "I'll head out now. Thank you, Grams."

"Anytime."

CHAPTER 74
During the war: 1863-S: Doren Caldwell

I smell something burning, and I don't mean in a good way. Never mind. If something is burning it's usually not in a good way, so I don't know why I thought that. Forget it, I know why. It's because I know it has something to do with Leya.

She's been hanging around Dwell Hall since Gabe died, causing trouble, and giving my father plenty of earfuls. I think he only tolerates her because he and Lord Barrett are trying to merge their companies. I smile at the thought—I've been trying to put my father in his place for years, and Leya has managed it in a few months.

The putrid scent wrinkles my nose once more. Whatever she has up her sleeve today, I'm sure will cause plenty of turmoil for my father. I just wish she would hurry up. It feels like I've been waiting for my breakfast forever. Something I'm sure Leya has a hand in, and there are only so many times I can stare at the ugly yellow and blue drapes accenting the window across from me. I just hate those curtains; they're so ugly.

When Dwell Hall officially becomes mine, those will be the first to go. At least, it's a sunny day, so I can't let the window coverings irritate me for too long. I pick up the Seperium Sun Times, fanning myself with the newspaper before setting it back down on the oak-wood table. I've already read all the interesting things anyway.

"What is taking so loooong?" I groan, closing my eyes and leaning my head against the back of my wheelchair. I feel a pair of hands cover my eyes, and I smile.

"You're such an impatient big baby." Leya laughs. "It's a surprise!"

"Does it have something to do with whatever is on fire?"

She scoffs. "I didn't light anything on fire . . . at least, not on purpose."

"What's that supposed to mean? And why are you covering my eyes?"

"I said 'it's a surprise.'"

"Well, why can't I hold my own eyes? It's my legs that are broken, not my hands."

"Because this way, I definitely know you aren't peeking." She giggles, and I hear things being placed on the table in front of me. The smell has vanished as well, now I'm starting to get worried. What did she manage to do this time?

"I won't peek."

"I don't trust that. Plus, we're almost done."

"We? Excuse me? We?"

She releases my face. "Tada!" she exclaims, making jazz hands at the breakfast table now piled high with all my favorite foods—fresh creme puff pastries, macaroons, bacon, fruit salad—only specific to just kiwi and pomegranates—orange juice, buttered toast, and coffee cake.

I stare, my face filled with astonishment. "Leya, how did you get all this?"

Since the war started, commodities and delicacies such as these have been hard to come by. Unfortunately, I have been eating a lot of oatmeal and porridge, which is basically the same thing—thick, gross, and tasteless.

"I pulled a few strings." She smirks, sitting down. "Happy Birthday."

Right. I'm twenty-three today. It seems like such a vast number, considering one of my best friends is dead, and I haven't seen a new letter from Riel in a long time. How am I still alive when they're not? How can I celebrate another year gone by when they're not here? Tears smart my eyes, and Leya stands, worry crossing her features.

She takes my hands into her own. "It's not a crime to celebrate your birthday, Doren."

"It's not that—it's just—they're not here. I miss them so much." I wipe my tears. It's a party. I shouldn't be crying, but now her eyes are smarting up as well.

"I miss them too, but I don't think they would want us to mope around. If they were here, they'd be celebrating, but . . . that's not going to happen. It's painful because goodbyes aren't meant to be easy. We have to learn to keep celebrating, even when they're not here a—anymore." She sobs.

I squeeze her hands. "Thank you. Thank you for reminding me to keep celebrating even when it's painful." I look at the array of breakfast, my hunger returning tenfold. "So, let's not let all this good food go to waste, especially since you went to such great lengths to prepare it. I can't deny I smelled smoke."

She sits back down, blinking away her tears. "What smoke? I have no idea what you're talking about. I'm an amazing cook."

I smile despite myself.

"Leya! Are you here?" The sound of heavy footfalls and slamming doors echoes down the hall to our right.

Leya jumps to her feet, hastily chewing the cream puff she just took a bite of as her father appears in the breakfast area with—with Dad. Lord Barrett stands almost a head taller than Dad. I don't remember him being taller, but maybe Dad has just shrunk in my memory because of his years of abuse.

"Yes, Father." Leya nods at her father, who steps closer to her, crushing her in a hug.

"I have some exciting news, and since you and Doren have become so close, I think the news will be of great happiness to you," Lord Barrett exclaims.

Leya's face changes, amusement gracing her features. "Well, are you going to tell us what it is, or leave us all in suspense?"

"Ooh! Is it a guessing game? I love guessing games," I pipe in, garnering a glare from my dad, who grumbles a low, "Doren" as if my name is the only disappointment he can utter.

"Caldwell textiles and Barrett Steel will be merging, but to make that happen, you and Doren will be married."

"Excuse me. I tuned out there for a second. Did you say, 'married?'" I ask.

Leya's face has gone pale, her fingers immediately fidgeting with Gabe's engagement ring.

"Yes, married. It's a duty you two will now have to perform. It has already been decided," Dad speaks.

"You didn't even think to consult us first?" Leya's voice sounds high as she directs the question at her father.

"Leya, it's almost been two years. It—" He places a hand on her shoulder, but she smacks it away, and I flinch at the contact.

"No," she gasps. "I promised him. I promised—I can't marry another. I can—"

"Leya," Lord Barrett speaks softly as if trying to soothe a frightened animal. "He's dead. Your promises died with him. If he was still here, you would be married to him, but he's not. Unfortunately, Barrett Industries needs this if we are going to survive as a company and as a family."

She breaks down into sobs.

He continues, "I'm sorry, darling. I'm sorry your chance at love and happiness was ripped from you, but perhaps you can find that again with Doren." He pulls her into a hug. "Please think about it." He rubs her upper arms.

She nods, trembling as she sits back down.

"Hyam, let's leave the children to discuss," Lord Barrett says, ushering for my dad to follow him.

Once they're gone, I look at Leya, who sniffles beside me, waiting for her to say something.

"I'm sorry," she whispers. "I didn't mean to make it sound like I would never consider marrying you. It's just—"

I reach across the table, taking her hand. "I know. I'm quite a catch, so I would be offended if you never considered me for marriage . . . glad to have cleared that up," I ramble since I didn't even garner a smile. "You love Gabe, and it's not like those feelings are going to go away, and now, you have to betray the promises you made to him. I'm sorry."

"You're right. I still love him. I love him so much. I can't let him go. My father was right too. It's been two years. Long enough to say goodbye, but how do you ever say goodbye to someone you've known all your life? How do I say goodbye to those memories?"

"You don't have to say goodbye to the memories. In fact, hang onto them, because that's how you knew they lived. Our memories are proof someone loved them," I whisper, tears glistening in my eyes as I think of my mom.

"Like your mom . . . like Casen." Her voice cracks at the mention of her little brother.

I nod. "And like Gabe. We'll both know Gabe loved and lived because we witnessed it. So, don't ever say goodbye to those memories."

She nods, more tears flooding her cheeks like a raging torrent of rain, and I know what she's going to say before she opens her mouth. "Then, I guess you'll be my husband, and I . . . would be lying if I said I wasn't glad it was you my father chose. Because I do care for you, and you have helped me get through losing Gabe, and I hope I have done the same for you."

I wish I could trade places with Gabe. Why did I have to be the one to live? If he was still here, Leya wouldn't be coerced into this choice. She would have the one she loves, and we wouldn't be forced to marry.

I pull her hand closer to me, kissing her knuckles. "You have. I—I probably would have ended it all if you hadn't been here to pull me through. You are my light in the dark, Leya, and I hope that's enough to build a marriage on."

She smiles, a sad smile that breaks my heart even more. "I think, maybe."

CHAPTER 75
Before the war: 1860-I: Rosea Dierich

The dim, dark warehouse seems to close in on me—a nightmare that has been bleeding into my heart since the raid. Every time I close my eyes, I see Pim lying on the ground with blood flowing from his temple.

Sometimes the nightmares are worse, and there is more blood pooling underneath him than a man can survive. Other times, it's the shock in his face that stabs my heart. The realization when he finally believed my truth. I hate myself for hurting him, for lying to him.

It was just a game when it first started out, a pull, an attraction I wanted to explore, but too quickly it became real. It became love, and by that time, I was in too deep to fix what I had already done. It's only been four days, but I miss him so much. I miss those piercing blue eyes. I miss those desperate kisses he reserved only for me. I miss those gentle caresses, and the way he would always hear me, even when he pretended not to listen.

It can't be three weeks since I met him, because who falls in love in three weeks? Who wishes for every second to be spent with someone they've practically just met? I guess I do, but now it's all too late.

I'm sure he's in Seperium by now, enjoying his baths and fancy food, and forgetting all about the vigilante who played with his heart. He probably hates me by now. Who am I kidding, of course he hates me. I hate me. I played him like a piano, and then took a sledgehammer to what was left of him.

Some part of me hopes he doesn't hate me. Hopes he still loves me and wants me, despite all my lies. It's a beautiful daydream my mind can float away on for days, but eventually the daydream ends and the fall from the clouds hurts way more than before the ascent. Maybe it would be better to stay on the ground and not allow my heart to rise to new heights, but I can't help it. Sometimes it's easier to believe the dream, but you can't live on dreams forever.

"Rosie," Grams' voice pulls me out of my reverie. "There is someone here to see you."

I sigh as I stand up from the pile of blankets I had been sleeping in. Since I was rescued from the raid, several of The Rosaries, my supposed followers, had been coming to me and introducing themselves and telling me how much I inspired them to fight—to change their circumstances. It's a weird feeling, knowing I have inspired others to act. It was never my intention, but somehow, it happened.

At least they gave Grams and me a place to sleep and food to eat, even if it was just a small corner of pillows and blankets in an abandoned warehouse. All of our belongings and our entire flat was burned to the ground. We literally have nothing, but at least everyone in the troupe is alive, and we are all safe.

I look around for the person I'm supposed to be meeting, but there is no one.

"Grams?" I turn to look at her, and she grabs my wrist, pulling me through the warehouse filled with huddled troupe members. Flickering lights leave flashes across our path as we head out the front door. I pull my tan coat tightly around me as we step outside. The cold days of Dekember have finally taken over, leaving us in the unforgiving world without warmth.

We trudge through dark, grimy alleyways for a minute before turning down one with a dead end.

There.

At the end of the alley stands the most beautiful, wilted flower I have ever laid eyes on. Okay, he isn't an actual flower, but to me that's what he looks like—a flower in need of some water and sunlight. He even wears dark green veined suit pants and a red silk shirt covered with a maroon vest. He must be cold. He doesn't even have a coat. My heart stops as those bright blue eyes pierce my soul. This is one of those happy daydreams, isn't it?

I stumble closer to him. What is he doing here? How did he find me? Fear strikes my heart. Is he here to arrest me? Well, if that's the case, I will brave a hundred cells if it means I can be close to him. If he was willing to keep looking for me after what I revealed, then he's probably not here to reconcile. He's here for revenge.

I move up to him, until we're standing only a foot apart. He takes a step closer to me, his beautiful, wilted form curling over me. The rose lapel pinned to his vest winks in the sunlight, casting a red glare over my face.

"You're not going to run this time, Crémant?" The way he says that name, like it's poison, stabs my heart.

"I said I'm done playing. You win." I hold my wrists out toward him. "You can take me to jail. Don't pass go. Don't collect two hundred."

He takes my wrists into his hands, rubbing small circles onto the flesh where my wrist meets my palm. It sends tingles all the way up my arms and back down again. Out of the corner of my eye, I watch Grams slip away.

"I understand now," he whispers. "I understand why you did it—why you didn't tell me the truth. I was blind. I would have never considered your feelings, and all I would have wanted was to arrest you and get the hell out of Inferium, but that's not true now. What's true is I just—" he pauses, and in the absence of his voice it seems like the world has stopped. Silent in anticipation, like a breath being held. There are no sounds of passing motorcars, no guns going off, no murmurs of wandering people—in this moment it's just us. "I just want you."

My heart stops. Me? He wants me? After everything I did to him, he still wants me. Tears break through my eyelids. I want him too.

"Nothing else matters. It's like you brought everything into focus and made me realize my pompous existence means nothing without you."

I sniffle, breaking a smile. "Only you would call yourself a pompous existence."

He sighs, rolling his eyes. "Can you not dwell on it? I'm trying to be romantic here."

I nod as he squeezes my palms, entwining our fingers together with warmth. His hands are so perfect—maybe that has something to do with growing up in Seperium, but it doesn't matter because I want to be the one who holds his hands forever.

"What was I saying? Oh, right. I don't want my life to be meaningless, and it feels like it would be if I ignore what I'm feeling for you and go back to Seperium. Let me live for you. Let me say every day how much I love you because I finally understand . . . I need you."

"No," I whisper, before I can even understand what I'm saying myself. The light in his blue eyes dims, and the hold of his hands slips from my fingers. "I mean. I can't let you only live for me. We're different people, and if one of us only lives for the other, it will tear us apart. I would rather you live with me, not just for me. Live each day with me. Help me fight for what I fight for. Love me by showing me.

"You say you understand and that you don't want your life to be meaningless. But your life isn't meaningless, and I'm not the only reason your life should have meaning. I can't—I can't let you do that," I whisper, feeling as if the words might break us apart. That they might take him away again. I want him, but not like this. If he just wants to disregard everything he once knew for me, then what makes me think he won't do it again? Or if he puts all of his trust in me, and then I hurt him again? If that happens, it will destroy us—I will destroy us. I can't put that kind of stress on our relationship. I won't become a reason to lose him.

"But you have given me something to fight for, you've shown me the world. You've shown me there is so much more to see and explore and enjoy and . . . yes, I want to do it with you. I want to take on the world with you by my side. I want to keep chasing you, because I want to be the one to catch you every time. You're right. I'm not meaningless, but everything has so much more meaning when you're there, and I just want that. I just want to be close to you, and if I have to brave living in the filth of Inferium, I will. I just—"

I kiss him, silencing the words coming from his gorgeous lips—not just because I want him to shut up, but because I believe him. If he's giving us this chance, then I don't want to waste it, because I will take a thousand chances if it means I get to love him and live my life right beside him.

I wrap my arms around him, bringing him closer. I feel it in his kiss—his understanding, his longing, his fear. He wants us. He wants to give all of himself to me, and I want to give him all of me. I deepen our kiss, not wanting to let him go. I have to give him all of me.

Suddenly, fear strikes my heart, and I feel my chest tighten under the weight of the past. The dark alley walls feel too much like the old dressing room. The nearby piles of trash seem to grow larger, closing in on me, and reminding me of the racks of costumes decorating the room that day. A flash of motorcar lights, and my heart stops—he's standing in the doorway, golden light spilling in behind him.

I take a step forward, pushing Pim against the grimy wall of the alley. I know he won't hurt me. I know he won't take advantage of me. He loves me, and I love him, and—my chest tightens as if a box of lead is weighing it down. I pull away, sucking in air, but the cold stings my throat, like a noose pulling tight around my lungs, voiding them of all air.

I swallow to keep the chill away.

"Rose . . ." Pim trails off, breathless, his forehead leaning against mine.

"I'm fine," I gasp, kissing him again. But I need air . . . it will be fine. *You have Pim now, who needs air?*

My chest constricts, like a snake wrapping itself around and around. I push away from Pim, hand on my chest as I try to breathe. Why does my asthma have to appear now? I just want to kiss him because we've been apart for four days. Four!

He leans over me, gripping my shoulder. "Rose? Are you okay? Did I—did I hurt you? Did—"

I shove a hand in his face. "Just—I need—" *Relax, Rosea. Relax.*

I fumble against the buttons of my coat pocket. My medicine. Vienna made me some. I can fix this, and then we can get right back to making out. I open the pocket, but it's empty.

No! I need to breathe. I need to kis—I look at Pim, my vision blurring. He scoops me up in his arms, and I fall against his chest, exhausted. I look up at his jawline, thinking how smooth and sharp it is. I didn't even get to tell him I love him back, though, I'm sure he knows.

CHAPTER 76
Before the war: 1860-I: Inspector Leo Pim

"Yer takin' 'er to Seperium for New Separation?" Grams ask as we clean up the warehouse after the Merrytime celebration.

Little gifts and pieces of dried fruit ornaments line the space. Everyone contributed something small and handmade for the holiday, and then we all exchanged them. Some lucky chap got a brand-new coat—my contribution, and I will say it made me quite proud. I even thought of getting gifts for everyone, but when I voiced my opinions to Grams earlier today, she told me that would be a stupid idea.

Because everyone, even though they are poor, loved to get heartfelt gifts during the holiday because it means so much more to them. It isn't about the things. It's about their families, their livelihood, and they give gifts to symbolize they've made it through one more year.

I never thought about Merrytime like that. In Seperium, everyone always gives the most expensive gifts to show off how rich they are. There is no rhyme or reason for their gift-giving other than to see who is better.

Once again, the people of Inferium have changed the way I see everything. They do everything they can just to survive one more day; meanwhile, people in Seperium spend their entire lives trying to find meaning. Maybe we should all come to Inferium, just to spend a day surviving instead of whining. I smile to myself. Everyone would hate that, but it is a nice thought. Wait? Is it? I know I would hate it, I mean, before I got to know Rosea.

I look over my broom handle, watching Rosea garner the little kids with garland decorations through their hair. She looks so happy, and in her happiness, it makes her look all the more beautiful. I smile, my heart swelling with love for her. If I hadn't come back, I'd be home in my giant Seperium apartment drinking wine alone and playing chess by myself. I'm glad I didn't have to give into my self-loathing.

"Earth to Leo. Come in Leo," Grams waves a wrinkled and dotted hand in front of my face. I take her hand into my own, placing a kiss on one of the brown spots as I bow my head.

"Yes, my most illustrious Grams?" What the hell is wrong with me? A few short weeks ago, I wouldn't have come anywhere near someone, let alone kiss their hand.

"Leo, stop it. We both know ya're not one to play the fool." She pulls her hand out of mine.

"But I am a fool. A fool in love."

"I can see that. Since ya can't even answer a simple question." Her blue eyes narrow. "And put yer tongue back into yer mouth, ya're droolin'."

I smile. "I'm sorry, Grams. What was it?"

"Ya mentioned before the celebration that ya wanted to take Rosie up to Seperium for New Separation."

I nod. "Yes, I—I have something important I wanted to ask her, and—and you." I scratch the back of my head.

Understanding fills her eyes. "It's not important to ask me, whatever Rosie decides. I'll go wherever she is."

I gape. "You mean it?"

She chuckles. "Yes, as long as ya cherish and love 'er well. If ya do anythin' to 'urt 'er, this ole lady can still pack some punch."

I squish her into a hug. "Thank you, Grams. I will cherish her until the end of my days." I laugh, lifting her up a little.

"Oh, put me down! I don't like to be manhandled." But she is smiling when her feet touch the ground. She pats my cheek with a sigh. "I'm so proud of 'ow far ya've come, Leo. I'm so 'appy that ya will be there for Rosie. Seperium knows I won't be around forever."

"Even though I destroyed your house and practically took everything away?"

"Well, ya don't 'ave to be so dramatic about it, but yes, even through that. Now, New Separation is tonight. Ya both better get goin', if ya're gonna 'ead up before they close the elevators."

I nod, turning to walk toward Rosea. The riots caused a lot of issues, but for the last few days, everything has been quiet. Maybe because of Merrytime, everyone didn't want to spill blood on the streets in an attempt to keep fighting. They had just been outraged because of the raid. I cringe, thinking some of that had been my fault. If I hadn't headed up the raid, maybe the citizens of Inferium wouldn't have snapped.

Hopefully, it will be secure enough for me to sneak Rosea up to Seperium for the evening I had planned. It would be an amazing evening, if I do say so myself—assuming she'll say yes.

My heart hammers inside my chest. What if she doesn't say yes? Impossible. She can't say no to me. I mean, I wouldn't say no to me, if I were her. *But you're not. So don't be so sure of yourself, Leo Pim.* My bluster weakens at my own thoughts, putting anxiety in my chest like a ravenous monster here to devour my courage. Why do I do this to myself? I need to stop overthinking things. I got permission from Grams. All I have to do is ask Rosea. It can't be that hard, right?

CHAPTER 77
Before the war: 1860-I: Rosea Dierich

The lights of Seperium blur in a polychromatic sphere of gold and blue—the theme for tonight's New Separation festivities. We've just finished a nice meal at Où L'aube Rencontre le Crépuscule and watched the parade from our balcony seats, which glorified King Randice, who originally separated Seperium and Inferium hundreds of years ago.

Inferium citizens hate him, and now after that gruesome reminder, Pim has ruined everything. Is this really happening right now? It has to be. My ears can't be lying to me. Did he actually just say this is our last date? What the heck does that mean? And now he's fumbling with the inside pocket of his gold suit-jacket.

I stand, thinking I should just go. If he doesn't want me here, why the heck did he bring me up here? To humiliate me? But that doesn't seem right. He said he loved me. He said he wanted to spend every second by my side. So, why did he lie? Revenge?

"I can't believe you're going to do this now. If you actually didn't want me, why did you make my heart believe you did? Why did you take me up here to get a taste of this life just to put me back down again? Is this just a ploy to humiliate me before you arrest me? 'Oops, Rosea, I'm sorry, I don't actually love you. I made all that up just to put you in your pla—'"

"Rosea." He stands, grabbing my hand. I rip it away. "What are you talking about? I didn—"

"Yeah, you did!" I cut him off.

Other diners are starting to look at us, but I don't care. His words have wrenched open a wound I didn't even know existed. "You said this is our last date, so let's just get it over with and end it. Stop playing with my heart. Stop making me think you actually care about me."

The golden lights all blur to gray, the luster of their brightness drained away with my broken heart.

"Oh, Rose," he says my name so tenderly, like I'm a delicate piece of glass he's trying not to break.

I scoff, turning toward the entrance. Why hasn't he arrested me yet? Why haven't the other police officers come to detain me and keep me from running?

I look back, and my heart stops. No, those aren't the right words to describe how I'm feeling right now. It's an immense feeling of elation. Immense surprise. Immense—any other word that can describe how incredibly happy I am at this moment.

Leo Pim's beautiful light blue eyes look over a velvet box, his long legs perched underneath him as he balances on one knee. A rose-gold ring with a rose made of rubies perched on top of the metal winks up at me from its velvet home.

A blush creeps up my cheeks as I rush back toward Pim, running into his arms as he stands, the force of our embrace nearly sending us over the rooftop edge.

He gasps, holding us steady to keep from toppling over. "Jeez, woman, you've nearly killed me for the hundredth time."

"I've never led you to death's door. At least, it can't possibly be a hundred."

"Oh, really? The warehouse, the mad dash through Inferium, The Rosaries leaving me to die in a burning building, stealing my breath away, killing me when you look at me with those mesmerizing eyes."

"I—the mad dash wasn't my fault; it was you for having no stamina whatsoever."

"You're the one who ran."

"You're the one who chased."

"I'm still chasing."

Those blue eyes drown me like a raging torrent, and I remember the ring he still holds in his hand. I grab the box, stuffing the rose-gold ring onto my finger. It fits perfectly. How did he know? It doesn't matter. He loves me. He wants to marry me—that's all that matters.

"I'm sorry for all the things I said. Please just forget I ever said anything about you lying. I'm sorry. I—" I start to kiss those most wonderful lips.

He smiles between our lip-locking, pulling his head away slightly. "I guess that's a yes?" he asks, setting me down.

I giggle. "Yes! Yes! Yes! A thousand times yes!"

Perhaps it's the lights, perhaps it's the contagious energy of the celebrating people down in the streets of Seperium. Perhaps it's a million reasons, but I just want to marry Pim now. I want to be his bride on the eve of New Separation.

"Will you marry me tonight?" I ask.

"Yes." He smiles down at me, taking my hand. "Despite all my better judgment, despite everything. I don't need anything fancy because you make me feel fancy already. You make everything beautiful, and I will marry you tonight if it means I get to be the best-dressed man in Seperium."

Before I know it, we're in a motorcab on the way to Seperium's courthouse. I don't even know if there will be someone there to give us paperwork to sign, but here's to wishful thinking. It seems to have propelled Pim and me this far.

Like when I was hoping he would find me, and still want me. Like when I was hoping I would be able to water that wilted flower and watch it bloom and grow. Both of those things have happened, even if they were only thoughts that miraculously blossomed into fruition.

Everything blurs by in an instant, and all of my wishful thinking appears to have become true once again. For right in front of us, a table with a marriage license stares up at us. A man named Kladvii helped us get the paperwork, saying people did this all the time on New Separation.

The pen in my hand trembles as I sign and print my name on the line, right next to Pim's. That's it. It's finished. My name is officially Rosea Pim. My heart is screaming. I love my new name. I love my husband. My husband! What a crazy thing to think. I am Leo Pim's wife, and I forever will be.

CHAPTER 78
After the war: 1864-S: Leya Caldwell

I found it today. My father told me not to go back to Dwell Hall, but I couldn't resist. I had to go back there. I had to see it one more time—believe it. And then . . . and then I saw it. The weapon. The one that killed Doren. I can't breathe. My entire world has been shattered more times than I can count these last few weeks. I can't take it anymore. I can't. It just can't be him.

It can't. Because he was—we were—

My vision blurs as tears cover my eyes. This is all a dream. I've been dreaming for the last five days. All of this is a lie. It can't be real. What should I do? Should I tell the Inspector? No, I can't. I can never do that to Gabe. I have to protect him. I have to keep him safe. He didn't do it. He didn't—sobs choke my throat. I want to keep believing the lie because it is easier than the truth. The truth is a broken and twisted beast, ugly and ready to devour me whole.

It's chasing after me, trapping me like a caged rabbit, and I can't run anymore. I have to face it, and all the evidence points to Gabe. The weapon, the timing . . . but it doesn't make sense. Why would Gabe kill one of his best friends? Because of me? Because he was angry about Doren and me? If he was so angry, why didn't he take my life instead? Is it all my fault? If I hadn't married Doren, none of this would have happened. I promised Gabe I would wait, and I didn't, but what was I supposed to do?

I thought he was dead, and I had to marry Doren. Father made sure of that. I had no choice. I told him the truth so why didn't he understand? Why did he do it? Doren didn't deserve it. Doren was—was perfect, and now he's gone, ripped away by jealousy and greed.

More tears make their way onto my face as I turn to look out the window of the motorcar I'm sitting in. Dark gray skies gloom the day, sending droplets of rain onto the panes. It makes it look like the entire world is weeping—matching how my heart feels.

I want to talk to Gabe. I want him to tell me why he did it, or maybe I just want him to tell me that he didn't do it. That this is all a lie. That the last five days have been a dream. That he will be resolved, and we can forget all of this happened. I want the pain to go away. I want things to go back to the way they were before the war, but most of all, I just want this nightmare to end.

CHAPTER 79
After the war: 1864-S: Inspector Leo Pim

The world blurs by in a spinning world of crazy, kind of like my life recently—crazy and constantly spinning. Someone murdered Lord Caldwell, and I can't find the killer—spin. My wife is a suspect—spin. It turns out I'm a father—spin. I still can't find the murder weapon—spin. I don't think it's ever going to stop, and I'm not sure my head can take anymore dizziness.

"Will you stop spinning in that chair? For Seperium's sake, it's like you're a child." Chief Lecten opens the door to my office.

I let my chair start to lose momentum, glaring at him every time the chair looks in his direction. "Does anybody knock anymore? You know, it used to be a way of introduction, but now, it's just a forgotten formality so my boss can barge in when I'm deep in personal thoughts."

"Well, unless your thoughts are out loud, they're still personal, Inspector. Besides, I could care less about your thoughts. I just wanted to let you know that Leya Caldwell is here requesting to see General Hoek." I stop spinning, my interest piqued. "I have half a mind to send her away, but I wanted your opinion since it is your case," he continues.

Interesting. The wife of a murdered man wants to see the man who could possibly be her husband's murderer. Hmm, a lot of murder in that sentence.

"No. Don't send her away yet. I want to see how they interact. It could be very crucial to the case."

Chief Lecten shrugs. "Whatever you say. I'll tell the receptionist she has clearance to see him. Do you want them in the interrogation room?"

I nod, contemplating. Of course I'm going to eavesdrop on their conversation. I have to, especially if I'm going to find out the truth, but why does the thought make me feel so dirty? Like I've been rolling in the grime of Inferium. Perhaps it's because they were almost married, and they have an intricate past—almost as intricate as Rosea's and mine. Maybe if someone was eavesdropping on my love-life then they would feel dirty too.

I almost laugh. That person's ears would bleed if they got even remotely close to hearing anything about my love-life. Well, actually, my love-life has been dry as of late, but I'm hoping that will change soon.

I shake my head, dispersing the thoughts as I fumble with my rose pin. What will Lady Caldwell speak with him about? Why would a grieving widow find it so important to come talk to the main suspect in the case? She must have an ulterior motive that doesn't include angsty make-out sessions in the dim interrogation room—not that I would let it get that far, because ew . . . Who knows what that room has been through, but to each their own, I guess.

I stand, heading to the interrogation room. This time I would be on the other side of the glass. They won't be able to see me, but I'll be able to see them. I'll be able to watch for their ticks. Lady Caldwell is an open book, easy to read and decipher. While General Hoek conceals his thoughts a bit better, but he wears his heart on his sleeve. When those emotions bubble to the surface, that's when I get a good read on him.

General Hoek sits in the empty gray room, his wrists chained to the table. The door opens, ushering the forlorn Lady Caldwell into the space. The second he recognizes who is in front of him, he tries to stand, but his chains settle him back to his seat as he utters a gasping, "Leya."

She sits down. When their eyes meet across the table, I watch the weight of their past fall between them like a rushing river—the currents pulling them under and bashing them against the rocks until there is nothing left but raw and broken flesh. Laid bare, and with no hope that it can ever be mended.

"Gabe," she whispers his name as if it's a broken promise, severed throughout the years of neglect and loss.

"What are you doing here? Why—" General Hoek's emotions are already crawling to the surface. Shame. I thought he would last longer.

"I—I came to—" She breathes in, tears making their way to her face. "I came to ask why. Why did you do it?"

"Leya, I—"

"Just tell me truthfully, Gabe. I can't take anymore secrets. I can't take this anymore. If you did it, just tell me why. I need to understand."

"Do you really believe I murdered Doren? Do you think I'm capable of that? I loved him like a brother."

"I don't know what I believe anymore. Just tell me the truth. Did you kill him?"

"No. Never in a million years would I ever think of doing something like that to Doren—even if it meant I could have you because it wouldn't matter. If I have to destroy one life to live mine with the one I love, then it's not worth it—not at the cost of someone else I loved."

Tears stream down Lady Caldwell's face, falling down and echoing like a ticking clock, reminding them that their time is almost up. That every clue led closer and closer to someone being proven guilty.

"I'm just so tired, and I—I don't know what is true anymore. This whole thing—you coming back, Doren's . . . death has me questioning everything, and I don't know what to do anymore. You are the main suspect, and all the evidence lining up toward you just has me questioning if maybe it's true. I just had to see you to know for sure." She wipes her tears.

"And am I telling the truth? Do you believe me? Because if you believe me, I can brave this. I can brave the accusations. I can know at the end of the day that the one person I want to trust me does."

She nods her head. "I believe you because you're not lying. You've changed, but you haven't changed that much. I still know you, even if it's been three years."

He sighs, letting the river's current wash over him and take him downstream. Maybe it will destroy him in the end, but I don't think he cares anymore. He just wants to be close to her, and if the river will wash him on the shore at her feet, then he'd take it. I can see the longing in his body language.

I've felt the same all too much in my lifetime. When I was just wishing for anything to take me back to Rosea, but nothing ever did—until now. Ironic how it took a murder case that ripped others apart for Rosea and me to be brought back together.

"Good." His fingers reach for hers, and she takes them into her own.

I look away for a moment, thinking how strangely intimate the scene is.

"I should go. I hope the Inspector can find enough evidence to exonerate you. I don't think I could take it if you were found guilty. I will go to jail with you if that happens."

"Leya—"

"No, I'm done hiding like a coward. I married Doren because of my father. I did it despite my heart. Because even if you were dead, I would have waited until I was old and gray. But—"

"I know." He squeezes her hand. "I don't blame you. I would have never wanted you to be alone because I was gone. I would have wanted you to continue living your life, even if it meant living and loving someone else."

"I never deserved you, Gabe, and if it helps him find the truth, then I have to tell the truth."

"What do you mean?"

Lady Caldwell looks up at the glass, looking right at me. Shivers break out on my skin. She knows something. Something very important.

"I found the murder weapon, and you're not going to like what it is."

CHAPTER 80
After the war: 1864-S: Gabriel Hoek

The truth embedded in my mind comes crashing down around me in a fiery blaze of brimstone and smoke. The impact of the explosion reverberates through my heart. My chest tightens as anxiety creeps into the open cavity left in the wake of the collision. My breaths come all too quick, and the only thought that resides in my mind is . . . Did I really kill him?

My hands shake as I look down at them. I don't even have the strength to keep looking Leya in the eyes. How can I? I don't even know what's real, and what's not anymore, and I'm starting to believe I really did kill Doren.

"Gabe." Leya reaches for me, but I jerk my hands away, or at least as well as I can in my chains. Chains that cage me like a roaring lion, devouring me whole, reminding me I still don't know what is real or not. It feels like I've been living in a dream since I got arrested. No, before that, when I remembered who I was and came home. When I found everything I once remembered to be true was, in fact, not.

I remember Leya's words a few weeks prior when I found out my father died in my absence. *He left it for you. He wanted you to have it . . . along with this.* She had handed me a savings bond worth a fortune—a fortune my father didn't have before I left Seperium, and a beautiful hand-crafted talisman my father always carried with him—one so rare, only two existed in the whole world . . . and I owned the only known one.

All the evidence is stacked against me now. Even if Leya believes me, it doesn't matter because we will never be together. Everything points to me. That's why I'm the one in chains—not anyone else. I didn't kill Doren, but I'm starting to believe I did. I've already lost my memory once, who's to say I didn't forget something horrible I did just to relieve my conscience? Just so I could be with her.

I finally look at Leya. Her brown eyes are rimmed in red. The hurt weighing her down over the last few weeks causes her once straight shoulders to hunch. Dark circles decorate the lower parts of her eyes. She's lost so much, and I will never forgive myself if I am the reason for that hurt. Seeing her like this breaks my heart—and we've been broken for far too long already.

"Gabe," she whispers my name, filled with longing and love, as if that will make the pain of the past go away. As if that can unlock the chains wrapped around me. "You didn't do it. I can see that now. Don't believe the lies just because everything points to you. It—it doesn't, and we'll find a way to prove it—we will."

"Leya." Tears well in my eyes, blurring her face and the dark room. "I'm afraid it's already too late. They clearly believe I'm guilty. I'm the wildcard here. I should just accept it."

"No." Leya chokes. "No, you said you could bear it if I believed you, so let's bear it together. I'll be right here until you're proven innocent. I'm not leaving."

"I can't ask you to do that."

"You didn't ask. I'm doing it. I'm not giving in like I did the first time. I'm not—" The door behind Leya bursts open, smacking against the adjacent wall with a bang.

Inspector Pim's tall, lanky form steps over the threshold. His burnt orange suit fills the dim room with a burst of color. His ice blue eyes lock on Leya, malice rolling off his form, and I try to stand as if I can defend her, but of course, I'm chained.

She stands up, braving his presence with her head held high.

"You know what the murder weapon is?" he asks, towering over her like a formidable skyscraper.

"Yes, and I know where it's at too. I'll take you there, but . . ." Leya trails off.

"But?" Inspector Pim quirks his head.

"But you have to tell me truthfully if you think Gabe is the murderer."

The Inspector's gaze trails from Leya to me, and back again. "No, I don't think General Hoek is the murderer, but unfortunately, I don't have any other leads as to who is. I have to submit the evidence to the Council. They are the ones who will condemn him guilty, and unfortunately, all the evidence points to him. So, if you know what the murder weapon is, it might give me some leads—it might help me save him, and I know you, of all people, want that."

Leya nods at his words. "I will take you there. Just promise me you can prove he's innocent."

"I can't promise that. We're wasting time. Let's go," Inspector Pim huffs, stalking out of the door like a phantom.

Leya looks back at me.

"We'll find a way." She nods her head. "I won't stop until you are home safe in my arms. I—" She breathes a shaky breath that seems to rattle her entire being. I know what she's going to say, and I don't want her to say it, but then she smiles, and my heart starts to believe she will find a way. I will be exonerated, and the chains of our past will finally be broken.

"I love you."

CHAPTER 81
Before the war: 1861-S: Rosea Pim

I stare at the floor, finding the crisscross patterns of granite and marble fascinating. I'm happy I'm married, ecstatic really, but my heart hasn't stopped hammering since Pim brought me back to his apartment. I mean. It makes sense that we would come back here as husband and wife and share in a night of bliss. But would it really be a night of bliss, or would all the terrible monsters of my past come back to haunt me? *He's not here. Pim is here. Pim loves you. Pim is your husband.*

I had never seen an apartment quite like Pim's. It is bright, even at night. Everything is contorted in a color scheme of gray and white, fading into the darkness of my past and feeding my anxieties.

Pim walks back into the bedroom, a robe tossed over his thin frame, and two glasses of rosé in his wispy fingers. He looks so adorable in his dark blue silk robe. Part of me wants to forget about the night of bliss and just draw him in all his perfect glory.

I shift from my seat on the chaise, wringing my hands together and glancing at all the doors and windows. If I need an escape, I have to know where—I stop the thought. I won't need to escape. Pim is here. He won't hurt me, but no matter how many times I tell myself that, I can't get my heart to believe it. My rational brain knows he won't hurt me, so why can't I convince my body?

He hands me a glass of wine, sitting down beside me, and pulling me against him. "Are you all right?" he asks, sipping from his glass.

I gulp half my wine down, nodding. "Fine." I burp.

He sets his wine down, taking my hand into his. Our wedding rings blend together like a beautiful sunset.

"You don't seem fine." He twines our fingers together.

"I—" I look at him, my mouth going dry as I realize I never told him about my past, about what happened to me. Will he still want me after I tell him? That's ridiculous. Of course he will, but what if I can't love him the way he wants me to? What if I can't—I breathe in, trying to disperse the thoughts.

"Is it the wine? Is it the apartment? Is it too warm in here? Are you comfortable? If you're not comfortable I can—" He starts to stand, ready to adjust whatever he thinks is making me uncomfortable.

"Leo, it's not that."

He sits back down. "You only call me Leo when you're upset."

"I'm not upset. I—I'm scared." I look away from those gorgeous blue eyes.

"Why?" he asks, and I'm not sure I know how to answer him.

"Because I—because do you remember our first date? When I took you to Seperium's the Limit?"

He nods, his brow wrinkling in confusion. "Yes, you got scared. You—" Understanding crosses his features, and fear strikes my heart as I watch the gears work in his mind. I can practically see the steam coming out of his ears. "Someone came in that night, and you had to run. You couldn't stand to be there another second."

Tears flood my eyes as I nod. "I was—a couple years ago, I was raped, and I—I'm scared that when we—I'm scared all those memories will resurface, and then I will hurt you because of it."

"Oh, Rose." He takes my hand again, squeezing my fingers gently.

I fall into his arms, spilling my wine. I don't care anymore. I just want the memories to stop. I want the pain to go away. I want to be perfect for him. I wish I was perfect for him. I wish I could fit in the perfect world of Seperium that has tried so hard to keep the darkness of Inferium out of its streets, but I can feel the darkness creeping in, even through the perfect black silk curtains. "We don—"

I kiss him then, willing my anxiety to disappear. Willing the memories to stay forgotten. Willing my heart not to freeze, because I don't want to be frozen for him. I want to be alive and breathing because he is the one who melted my frozen heart. He said I am the one who cracked his heart of stone, but he's really the one who saved me, and I don't want to be scared in front of him anymore. I don't want to be defined by my pain. I don't want that to define our marriage.

"Rose," he gasps, pushing away from me. My heart sinks. No. He's gonna say I'm too broken. He's gonna say I'm not good enough for him. He's gonna— "Stop. I don't want you to use this night as an excuse to cover up how you feel. If you're scared, I don't think you should force yourself to sleep with me. I don't want you to drown your monsters in me."

"But I want you, Pim. I want to be your perfect wife, but—" I lean away from him, gesturing to my wine-stained robe. "I'm already stained, and you hate stained things," I utter, even though I'm not talking about the wine. As if on cue, Roosevelt limps beside the chase.

Pim scoffs, pointing to the three-legged cat. "Look at Roosevelt, never in a million years would I have thought I would love a cat that ugly . . . or even save one."

"You're comparing me to a cat?"

"Stop cutting me off. I'm trying to say something important, and you're making me lose my thought. I—my point is, if I can love Roosevelt for his imperfections and scars, then I can love you. I want to love you, and you are by far more beautiful than Roosevelt"—he stops, looking over his shoulder at the cat—"No offense, Roosevelt."

He looks back at me. "In my thoughts, I compare you to a rose—the irony, I know—but maybe your petals have been scarred and bruised, but they can grow back. They can be mended. I love you, and you made me promise to live life with you, not for you. So, I'm here to live with you—never in a million years would I have thought that I would say those words either, but here we are."

"Oh, Pim." I fall into his arms again. "I love you so much, and because I love you, I want to do this, and if I can't handle it then . . . can we stop?"

I want to believe I can fit in this perfect, unstained place—that my face will hang from pictures against white walls. That our memories will be stored along the rooms, but I don't care about that anymore, because houses fall apart. No, I would forever make a home in Pim's heart—where those memories would never be forgotten or destroyed.

"Of course," he whispers against the top of my head.

I lift my lips to his, letting my pain bleed into him. Relinquishing all my brokenness to him because I know he isn't scared of it. He wants it, and I want him to have it all, because I love him, and I don't want to hide behind the beasts of my past anymore.

CHAPTER 82
Before the war: 1861-S: Inspector Leo Pim

I've never wanted to murder anyone more than I do at this moment, and his initials start with an H and end with a C.

She's crying in the bathroom. She's trying not to let me hear it, but I do. It only makes me feel guilty. I knew she didn't want me to do it. So why did she say it was okay? Why did she go through with it? I hate myself right now. I hate that I didn't stop and ask one more time if she was okay. I hate that I never knew about her past, and most of all, I hate that I wasn't there to protect her. I should have seen the signs.

What good am I as an inspector if I couldn't even figure this out? It's like all my training and perception goes out the window when it comes to Rose. I should have been there alongside her, helping her mend those wounds. I know damage as deep as that doesn't just heal overnight. It takes time to heal, but I still wish I could have been there for her.

I want to destroy him. I mean, I always knew he was a self-righteous creep, but to have forced himself on a young woman? What kind of a psycho does that? Apparently, his name is Hyam Caldwell, and I hope he gets everything he deserves.

I shuffle out of the sheets, pulling my robe over my shoulders. I head to the bathroom, tapping on the door. A golden light spills from underneath it. A shaky "yes" greets my prompt.

"Can I come in?" I whisper. I hear sniffles.

"I—"

"Don't hide from me, Rose. If it was too much, why didn't you say—"

The door opens revealing Rosea in one of my oversized silk shirts. *Sweet Seperium.* She looks beautiful, standing there framed in the doorway like a pastel painting of a girl who didn't deserve to be in this wicked world. Even the little red bumps that creep across her skin only manage to bring out the flush of her cheeks. A blush creeps up my face. *Not the time, Pim.*

Her knuckles are white from where she grips the door, as if she thought reality would vanish from her clenched fists. Blurry red eyes meet mine before she leaps into my arms. I hold her close, whispering "I'm sorry" into her ear.

"Stop saying you're sorry. It wasn't as bad as I thought it would be. In fact, I actually liked it . . ."

I gulp, setting her down. "Good." *Good? Seriously Pim? That's all you can say?* "I mean, then, why were you crying?"

"Because I—because I'm messed up, Pim. It has nothing to do with you. I am just overwhelmed and trying to process the last few hours. I just—I have to cry it out."

My heart melts for her, and I lean my forehead against her's. "Cry all you need then. I'm going back to bed. Come and join me when you're finished."

She nods, and I leave her there. Somehow, I fall asleep dreaming of Rosea.

Sunlight streams through open windows. I slowly open my eyes, hating that the curtains are open. Why are the curtains open? I never open the curtains. A shadowy silhouette passes in front of the light, and in my groggy state, I almost scream. Someone is in my house.

I jump up, ricocheting blankets all over the bed and floor.

"Who are you, and what are you doing in my house?" I yell, suddenly aware of my bare chest. I reach for a sheet to cover it up.

"I'm the prissy Inspector Leo Pim." Rosea flounces around the room in one of my crimson suits. My jaw drops, and all the events of the previous night come rushing back. "I'm so bright I forgot that I just got married, and yell at my wife like she's a stranger." Rosea strikes a pose and wiggles a finger at me.

"I—what are you doing in my suit? And I am not prissy. You've got me completely wrong!" I fumble out of the sheets, standing.

Rosea looks me up and down, biting her lip. I have to admit that she does look absolutely amazing in my suit. I would let her wear it any-time, just so I could see it hanging around her curves. *Get a grip, Pim! You hate it when people touch your clean clothes.* I smile at her. I don't think I care anymore. She can touch anything in this room, and I won't be mad.

Morning light seeps through the window, settling over her blush-ing face as if to show me that no matter how dark the night is . . . Rose will be okay, she'll make it through.

"Now that's a view I don't think I'll ever get used to." She smirks.

I look down, aware that I am completely naked, and I don't feel ex-posed.

"Well, you better not." I lift my chin, puffing out my chest in pride.

She giggles, a beautiful sound that reminds me of raindrops falling on empty wine glasses. "Look at you trying to show off your non-exis-tent physique." She saunters over, poking me in the chest and leaving behind sticky residue. I cringe and forget about the jab to my manhood.

"What is that all over your hands?" I ask, smelling chocolate, sud-denly I notice it all over her face and teeth. The cake. She got into the cake. How long has she been eating cake? And with her fingers too? Disgusting.

"Cake." She smiles, licking her finger.

I want to gag. "Gee, I figured."

She scoops another handful of cake from the rainbow wooden box it came in where it sits on my pristine dark rosewood desk, and I blanche, bile rising in my throat. Okay, I take back what I said, she can't touch anything in my room, and she's wearing my suit! I want to cry. Is this what marriage is supposed to look like? Living with the other person's flaws and hoping you can actually learn to be okay with them?

"You want a bite?"

I grimace. "Nope."

She bounces closer. "Come on, Pimmy. Just one bite."

This time I do gag. "Only if you get me a piece on a plate with a knife and a fork—like a civilized person. Not . . . with your hands."

"You worry too much, or not enough." She smiles mischievously before shoving the cake at my face.

A million thoughts whir through my brain at that exact moment. I should have run. I should have just taken a freaking bite. I shouldn't have egged her on.

She's my wife, and I love her to pieces, but sometimes she scares me to the point of insanity—this is one of those moments as I watch my life flash before my eyes as the chocolate desert crashes into my face. Rosea doesn't know it yet, but she is going to pay for this moment . . . dearly.

CHAPTER 83
During the war: 1861-I: Vienna Sinclair

They came in droves. They came like locusts, here to destroy what we once knew to be our homes. Our livelihood. No one believed it at first, that Seperium would send soldiers to destroy what little we had left. Yes, to them we are a threat. Threatening their livelihoods by withholding their food and product quotas, but they did it to themselves. They never gave us a chance. They never even saw us as human. Everything we ever worked for went to Seperium.

We never got a taste of the decadent foods, or a chance to use any of the products we sent up. We couldn't afford them anyway. Sure, some people smuggled them, but that could only last so long, and they in turn would sell them for astronomical prices no one could afford, and the cycle continues.

My skin feels numb as I stand out in the cold alleyway behind the hospital—the place where I first met Riel. It's been three weeks since I last saw him, and his brown eyes haunt my memories like a beggar with no home. The feeling of his lips on mine in our final parting kiss lingers in my mind, and I can feel the broken pieces of my heart rattling around in my chest, like a caged animal desperate to escape.

I only knew him for a few short days, but in those days, he made my heart come alive like it never had before. It felt like hanging off the edge of a cliff, balancing each other in our newfound love, but our circumstances pushed us over the precipice. Destroying us before we even had a chance to step on solid ground.

Tears well in my eyes. I'm so tired of things ending. I'm tired of watching death. I had to get out there for a moment because of all the patients I had seen die in the last hour. Bullet wounds. Explosion wounds. Fear. Death. Destruction. The end of everything we once knew, and I had a front row seat to watch it unfold.

My Papa was wrong. I don't make a good nurse. I can't comfort people through this. I can't stomach the sight of death anymore—the permanent ending of all living things.

I just want it to stop. Sure, I helped accomplish good things, but what's the point of good things when the bad will always be there to counteract them? It's a vicious cycle, cogs spinning around and around and never breaking, resetting itself like a clock so the theory can play over and over again forever. I don't want to see anymore endings, only beginnings. But every beginning has an ending, and no matter how hard I try, I can't stop the endings.

I want Riel to be here. I miss him so much. Perhaps if he was here, he would tell me something about the endings not being important. That what was important is the middle, the tough road they walked, the memories they lived along the way. The steps they took and the dance they stepped to. He would have said something like that.

The cold breeze bites my cheeks, my tears freezing on my face. Snowflakes dance down into the dark alley, fluttering like a leaping ballerina.

To make matters worse, I haven't heard anything from Ro in weeks. *Weeks.* I last saw her briefly after the raid to make sure her sprain was fine, and during that time she told me she'd be lying low, but since then, I haven't heard anything from her. My heart clenches. I don't know where she is, or even if she's alive either. I need her, and she's not here.

I gasp, breathing in a breath of freezing air, burning my throat and lungs as if to remind me that I'm still alive, that my ending hasn't come yet—even though everything is falling apart around me.

I washed my hands so many times before I raced out here, but somehow, I can still feel the blood that spilled across them from my last patient—warm and the scent metallic. I breath in shakily. The patient had been young too. A teenager caught in the crossfire of a war on pride and riches. The Seperium soldiers are raiding any place of meeting—restaurants, bars, theaters, libraries. Anything to deter us, destroy us farther, but I'm afraid they're only adding fuel to an already enraged inferno.

It means I'll be watching more death, trying in vain to save those whose lives have met an untimely end. I want to run away. I want to find Ro. I want to get to Riel. I want so many things and yet, I can't have any of them.

The doors creak open behind me. Dr. Greenwood steps out into the cold, frosty clouds of breath lingering against his lips.

"Rosea is here to see you," he says, his eyes looking as haunted as I feel.

She's here? I nod in relief. She's okay—one less thing I have to weigh me down.

"Thank you." I rush to the door and open it for him.

"I'll stay out here a little longer. I need—I—" His golden eyes plead with the same horror I feel.

"I understand," I whisper, before leaving him in the frosty alleyway.

The whitewashed hall seems a little duller, and the usual dance of the hospital is broken today. My fellow nurses' steps are all out of rhythm, as if the song suddenly changed on us midway through the performance. We're all feeling the effects of Seperium's display of hate and power. I walk out into the waiting room, which I immediately realize as a mistake.

Several—no—hundreds of people with bloodied wounds and bandages sit all around the waiting room. Some on the floor, others in chairs, a few lying prone . . . my heart speeds up as if I've just danced a quickstep. Bile rises in my throat. I have to get out of here. I have to look away, but I can't. I'm frozen in a state of overwhelming disconcertment.

"Vienna." Ro's hand grabs my arm, pulling me back into the hallway past the waiting room. The feeling of her fingers against my arm burns, or perhaps it's just because my body is warming up from my outdoor excursion. She pulls me into a storeroom. Shelves that used to be full are now devoid of supplies like gauze and antiseptic. The emptiness only makes me wonder again why I'm doing this.

Ro shakes me. "Are you okay?"

Her dark blue eyes search my face, and I finally look at her. She's a mess. Her white-blonde hair hangs around her face in tattered waves. Her cheeks are clear of any makeup, and instead, are covered with more pimples than usual. Dark circles haunt her eyes as if she hasn't slept in days.

What happened to her? Did the police find her again? If the police found her, she probably wouldn't be here, but I'm sure they have their hands full with a war going on.

"I'm fine. What happened to you? Where were you? You said you would lay low for a while, but I didn't expect not to hear from you in weeks." I smash her into a hug. "I was so worried. Why didn't you contact me? Why didn't you—"

"Slow down." She pulls away. "I can only answer one question at a time ya know. I was—" she sighs. "It's a really long story."

After several minutes of tears, blubbering, and lots of hugs, Ro finally tells me the details of her disappearance. She lost. She loved. She lost again—a heartbreaking cycle . . . the cogs spinning round and round.

She idly touches her left finger now devoid of the ring I'm sure once decorated it—the place that used to seal her promise to her husband. *Her husband.* What an interesting concept. Her story breaks my heart and makes me think of Riel and me. It makes me jealous that we never got a happy ending, but I'm not sure I would want it after hearing Ro's story.

"I gave him up, Vienna. I broke his heart, and with the war, there is no way I can ever find him again, there is no way I can ever love him again. He'll never want me back, not after this. Not—" She breaks down into sobs again, her face red and splotchy from the well of emotions.

"I lost someone too." I wipe away my own tears.

"What?" Ro looks at me. "You met someone."

"I—" I start, realizing I never had a chance to tell her about Riel. "I did. That day you came here to tell me about Pim, before the raid and everything. It seems like so long ago now . . . anyway, the young guy you said was cute, well, we talked—I mean—signed and—I just—I fell in love with him. His name is Riel. He's deaf, and he's the sweetest, most innocent soul I have ever met, and now, I can never be with him—not when our cities are both so divided. So, I know how you feel when you can't be with the one you love."

Ro's lips quiver, and we pull each other close with sobs—our hearts breaking from the weight of losses. The dance in my heart feels like it has stopped, like I've broken my feet and I can't move anymore. I don't want to move anymore, but I can't stop either.

"There's something else too," Ro whispers into my ear. I pull away, looking in her eyes. "My period is late, and I've been throwing up in the mornings, and—"

"Cravings?"

"Even for things I haven't tried before. Don't tell me I—"

"I'm sorry, Ro, but I think you're pregnant."

"And he'll never know." She sobs, falling into my arms again. "What am I going to do? How am I going to protect the baby? How am I going to do any of this?"

"You'll be okay. I'll be right here alongside you. You won't be alone, and maybe one day after the war, you will get to tell him."

"I don't—"

"This isn't the end, Ro. It's the beginning."

CHAPTER 84
Before the war: 1861-S: Riel Mjorn

There are people *everywhere*. Most of them are guys around my age and a little older. They're all standing in groups, talking and laughing, as if this ordeal is anything to laugh at. I'm standing in the main hall of Seperium Barracks with my draft paperwork folded into the inside pocket of the uniform they sent with the summons. Somehow, they had the right dimensions for me—odd, and slightly creepy.

The building itself looks like a dance hall or something. My heart gives an odd little jump, and for a second I think I'm having a heart attack, until I realize I'm just remembering Vienna, and our dance. Our dance. She had been right. We didn't need music, because we already had the steps set in our souls, and then I kissed her. My first kiss. It wasn't how I imagined—rushed and desperate because the girl of my dreams was slipping away, but it felt right.

Part of me wishes I had kissed her before that, when she wrapped her arms around me while we were dancing, but I hesitated, like prey in the face of a predator—frozen and forever regretting the moment I let slip away. I tried to get back down when the elevator was momentarily open, but I couldn't make it. They wouldn't let us go down anymore because of what they were preparing us for—war.

I see Vienna's brown eyes, and my stomach rolls into knots. Knots? More like rocks. Heavy and weighing me down in all of their mass. I have to go down to Inferium soon and stop a war—a war that pompous tyrants caused.

Why can't we just help those in Inferium and move on? Why do we have to fight? Just to keep the lifestyle we want? How sickening is that? Vienna lives in Inferium, how can I, as someone who cares for her, go down there, and destroy what she loves? How does that make me any better than them?

A guy behind me ramrods into my shoulder, passing me with a glare. "Oh, now you acknowledge my presence? I said, 'You're holding up the line.'" I read his lips as he steps in front of me, his followers following after him like a bunch of baying sheep, pushing me in the process. I'm sure they make him feel good about himself. I roll my eyes. What a bunch of entitled idiots.

Everyone talking in their prospective groups does make me miss Gabe and Doren. It's been a long time since we all had a chance to hang around each other. At least for me, since I graduated first as the eldest, but if I hadn't been working with my father in the shop, I never would have met Vienna. I still remember how she looked—white pinafore stained with blood, amber skin, and dark curls that framed her face in a messy halo, like a reaper angel—formidable and yet gorgeous.

A hand grips my shoulder, and I nearly jump out of my skin, thinking the sheep are back, but when I turn my head, Doren smiles at me. His green eyes shine as he pulls me into a hug.

It's like my thoughts summoned him, but thoughts can't actually-ly summon someone. If that were the case, all the books I read about my favorite character would have come true or the books about bugs I devoured as a kid. My heart swells at the thought, it would have been wonderful to be surrounded by bugs. I'm sure my parents wouldn't have taken it lightly though.

'Riel, don't walk toward the light. Stay with me, buddy.' Doren signs before shaking my shoulders.

I push him off. *'Get off me. I'm paying attention now.'*

'You weren't a second ago.'

The line moves up, and he takes a step forward. I follow after him, remembering that I've been standing in line for longer than I should have.

'*Where's Gabe? Is he here?*'

'*I—*'

'*You guys can't talk about me when I'm not here.*' A pair of hands cut off Doren's words. I look up with a smile, seeing Gabe in front of us. His black hair is shorter than I remember it, and his dark eyes are dimmed with the sad weight of goodbyes and farewells.

'*But you're here now.*' I sign, before pulling him into a hug.

'*Do you always have to be a smarty pants?*'

Doren laughs before hugging Gabe as well.

'*Someone has to be.*' I sign, studying Gabe.

'*You haven't married Leya yet?*' Doren asks.

The mirth of the moment halts as Gabe nods with dismal eyes. '*We're engaged, but I don't know now. Her father wouldn't let us get married until I finished college, but if I make it back, we'll get married for sure.*'

'*How is she taking all this? I know my parents were upset to see me off.*' I sign in hopes of easing his fears.

'*Not well, our parting was . . . hard. I'm so scared I won't be able to make it back to her.*'

Vienna crosses my thoughts again. I'm so scared I won't make it back to her either, or maybe I'm scared I won't make it back in time to save her. What if she gets caught in the crossfire of this war? She is a nurse after all.

'*Me too.*' I sign before I can think better about it.

Doren smiles, wiggling his golden-brown eyebrows at me. '*You got a girl, or are you just referencing your mom?*'

I glare at him. 'Her name is Vienna, if you must know. She's a nurse, and she's from Inferium.'

'*A nurse. I hear they know a lot of tricks—if you know what I mean.*' Doren signs with a sly smile.

'What tricks could she know? She's smart. I get that, but what tricks exactly are you talking about?' I sign, feeling like I'm missing something important.

Doren laughs, white teeth flashing. *'I—'*

'Don't answer that.' Gabe cuts in with a less than amused expression set against his dark brows. *'Don't listen to him, Riel. He's being an idiot.'*

'A big one! I'm the king of idiots.' Doren places his hands on his hips, striking a ridiculous pose with his chest held high, and his nose in the air. I roll my eyes.

'Be careful, or you won't be able to walk straight due to that over inflated ego.' Gabe signs, and I snicker.

'Oh, that he gets.' Doren signs, a pleased smile on his face. *'I missed you guys.'*

'Missed you too, you idiot.' I sign.

'You may only address me as Your Highness.' Doren sticks his nose in the air.

'Shouldn't it be Your Majesty if you're a king?' I ask, and his bluster falls.

'He's got a point, Doren. Riel one, Doren zero.' Gabe laughs, chasing away some of the sadness in his features.

I realize now why the other groups of guys were laughing earlier, because it just gives us a little chance to forget. A chance for laughter to lighten a grim situation, because how else would we be able to face it? How else would we be able to go down there and destroy other people's lives?

CHAPTER 85
After the war: 1864-S: Inspector Leo Pim

I'm starting to believe the murderer and weapon are phantoms. Little ghosts of the past that don't actually exist, because it feels like every time I get a lead, it disappears without a trace like fog or a phantom.

Leya Caldwell walks in front of me, her steps echoing through the dim passages of Dwell Hall. I'm almost certain it's inhabited with ghosts—at least one ghost in particular. I wonder if he will haunt my dreams tonight because I can't find out who the murderer is. I shudder at the thought. I've never actually seen a ghost, but I'm sure meeting one wouldn't actually be pleasant.

Before we left, the police station received a telegraph saying Lord Caldwell's body needs to be buried as per Seperium law. *A body may not be held in limbo for longer than seven days. If th*—Blah, blah, blah. Yatta, yatta, yatta. Whatever else they want to yak to make their ridiculous laws seem even less ridiculous. I can't solve a murder if I don't have a body to study. They just like to make my job harder as if it isn't hard enough. *But it was your fault for calling this job easy, Pim . . .* I wave my thoughts away. Like I needed to be reminded of my own shortcomings, but who would have guessed that this case would take so many interesting turns?

I certainly didn't, and that's saying something because I can usually peg cases and their outcomes. This case has more plot twists than a game of chess against a genius opponent—not that I've ever had the privilege to play with one, but still.

The sound of a door creaking open shakes me out of my thoughts, perhaps there is a ghost following me around. Leya Caldwell stands in the doorway of one of the rooms, her body silhouetted against the frame. She ushers me into the space.

Sunlight pours in through windows with open crimson and gold drapes. Embroidered flags hang from the walls, depicting different historical scenes like King Randice raising Seperium and his loyal Order of Knights encircling him. Gorgeous mahogany wood accents the floors, tables, chairs, and four-post bed—what I would do to have them for my apartment . . . not that I'd want anything from this house. Sheer red curtains hang from the bed, calling out like an enticing whisper. How fitting that the crimson guest room could have potentially been inhabited by a murderer.

"Hmm, nice room," I mutter.

Lady Caldwell points to the wall and hanging from nails at both ends is a cane. A beautiful cane made out of polished blackwood and accented with hand-crafted silver on both ends. The handle is an owl carved out of quartz and silver with dark beads of onyx set as the all-knowing eyes. Its wings lie at its sides with its head turned slightly toward the left, a glare set into its gaze. It's a beautiful piece of craftsmanship, but I don't see how the piece is a weapon, unless . . .

I reach up to take it from the mantel. Built in between the bird's wings are the spokes of a cog. I stare at it for a moment before I place my thumb against the cog's edges and spin it.

Click.

Click.

Click . . .

The owl's wings spread out against my hand, and a thin blade propels out the other end with a little shining sound. I peer at the other end, running my finger against the flat part of the knife, but the tip of my finger touches the edge barely glancing it, and immediately, blood appears in the wake. *Yikes!* It's sharp, *very* sharp.

What an amazing specimen, and easily looked over. A gorgeous cane on the outside, and yet, a deadly weapon on the inside. I smile, clicking the blade back into its place. I study the other end, which immediately becomes covered by its silver cap again. No one would have ever known it was a weapon just by glancing at it.

I look at Lady Caldwell, questions brewing to the surface. "How did you know it was a weapon? And who does it belong to?"

"It was Gabe's father's—now Gabe's. I knew it was a weapon because he used to show us how the mechanism worked when we were kids. We would beg to see it."

"It's a beautiful weapon, and I bet if I compared it to Lord Caldwell's wounds, it would match."

Tears well in her eyes. "I know."

"Why would you show me this then? You know it will only give me more evidence against General Hoek."

"Because I'm about to give you evidence against someone else I love. Gabe's father made two of those. One he kept, and the other he gave to my father as a goodwill gift when they became business partners. My father sold his at auction sometime during the war, but who knows, if you do a little digging, you can find out if that's the truth."

"What happened between Lord Hoek and your father?"

"I'm not sure, really. Things were good until the war. My father even put Gabe through school, but sometime just before or during the start of the war, they had a falling out and never spoke again."

"Do you think it had something to do with Hoek Weapons?"

"It could have been. I know there was a lot swept under the rug during that investigation, which made Lord Hoek really upset. My father did his best to keep everything together by buying Hoek Weapons and then giving Lord Hoek a position in the company, but just before the fallout, he left his position and became a recluse. He only spoke to me on occasion because we tried to keep in contact while Gabe was in

Inferium.

"Suddenly, Lord Hoek was unresponsive to any of my telegrams or letters, and when I went to see him, I found out he was very sick. He gave me the cane and a few savings bonds worth millions of SEM to pass onto Gabe when he came home. He then told me how sorry he felt for leaving Gabe like this. Two days later, he died. I kept his things safe, even when I thought Gabe was dead."

The red drapes seem to strangle the room like a bloody nightmare closing in on the secrets being exposed in front of us. Who am I kidding? The secrets of this house did contain a nightmare marked by blood and animosity, but whose animosity, I can't seem to figure out.

I look at Lady Caldwell as another question comes to mind, "Why didn't you tell me you were engaged to General Hoek?"

She looks away, her dark eyes reflecting the red of the room. "I didn't think it was important. I was married to another, and you already knew Gabe and I were something more."

"Why did you and Lord Caldwell get married?"

A scornful smile glances her face. "We were forced to. My father and Doren's made a deal with their companies by pawning their children off. Doren and I had no choice. It wouldn't have mattered."

"What will happen to your husband's estate and his company?"

She breathes in a shaky breath, looking around the room. "After the funeral, I'm assuming it will all be left to me, but who knows what's in his will."

Interesting. With Lady Caldwell's revelation of the murder weapon, all the pieces are starting to come together, and some of them are starting to point at Lord Barrett. Unfortunately, I still have too many pointing at General Hoek. There is no clear reason why Lord Barrett would want to murder Lord Caldwell. If anything, he would have murdered General Hoek, but again, there is no real motive.

I'd need to catch him red-handed with the murder weapon, and to do that, I'd have to go back in time. Though I'm brilliant, even I can't accomplish such a feat. I have to find his supposedly sold cane, or I'm grasping at the wind—pointless and equally futile. Another thought nags at my mind as I study Lady Caldwell.

"Your father paid for all of General Hoek's tuition, correct?"

"As far as I know, yes."

"Hmm," I muse. How did Lord Hoek give his son a fortune when he didn't even have any money to pay for General Hoek's school? I look back at Lady Caldwell, who studies me with a confused expression.

"Thank you for showing me this. I have to submit the cane to evidence. You're certain your father got rid of his?"

"I'm not certain, but that's what he said happened to it. That's why I think you need to do a little more digging. I don't want the murderer to have been my father, but I don't want it to be Gabe either. I just want this nightmare to be over with."

"I'm afraid, Lady Caldwell, the nightmare is just beginning."

CHAPTER 86
Before the war: 1861-S: Rosea Pim

Bright lights shine down into my eyes, blinding me. Where am I? I close my eyes, but it does little to lessen the light flooding my senses. I panic as I try to remember the last thing I did. I was . . . I took Roosevelt for a walk. Is that really the last thing I remember? Is this a dream? Does Roosevelt even go for walks?

The light moves away from my face, and I blink in the darkness. I can feel my chest tightening with fear, creeping into my heart like the absence of the sun's warmth.

"Miss Dierich, thank you for joining me today," a voice speaks—a man's silhouette appears against the bright light. How does he know me? Where am I? What is going on? Where is Pim? Did something happen to him? Why can't I remember?

"That's Pim to you. Mrs. Pim. Where am I? Who are you?" I move my hand to point at him, but then realize my hands are cuffed together. What the—

"You don't remember, do you?"

I stare at him, trying to see any of his features in the obscure lighting, but besides a hook nose, a curly mustache, and a forehead that sticks out a bit too far, I have no idea who this man is.

"You didn't answer me. I said, 'Where am I?'" I ask again.

He smirks, bright teeth flashing in the dim light like a silvered moon howling to the night. He starts, "You're in Seperium City Prison. I came—"

Everything comes rushing back in a rush of fragmented images, cracking and shattering into a mosaic of hurt. Okay, it's not that bad, but this officer, chief, or whoever came up to me in Seperium Square when I was out wandering around, without Roosevelt. I was lost at the time but was trying my best to find my way back. I thought this officer would help me, but instead, he said I was under arrest for violating Seperium laws.

I freaked out and had an asthma attack due to the cold and my confusion. I knew nothing about Seperium laws, so I didn't realize what I did wrong until it was too late. I passed out, and that's why I'm here, chained in a police station. The man's voice drones on in the background of my mind, mumbling into words I'm not sure I'm ready to hear. It's probably important, but how would I know what is important and what isn't right now?

I just want to go home. Pim is still on probation, so he probably has no idea I'm here. I look around the drab interrogation room. It's clean, but also gray, boring, and with a singular light bright enough to give you a headache if you looked at it too long. Maybe that's what I'm starting to feel. I guess now he'll tell me why I'm here. I tune back into what he's talking about.

"—Chief Zorman." He sits down on a chair across from me.

"How do you know me?" I ask, finally seeing some noticeable features of his face—thin jaw, a dark mustache that curls at the edges, and salt and pepper hair slicked to his scalp.

"I've been following you for a while now."

Following me? My heart sinks as he continues. "Of course, I didn't know who you were at first—not until the raid." He was at the raid? "When The Rosaries went back for you, I knew. Pim didn't do what he was supposed to when he was ordered to incarcerate you, Crémant."

I try to keep my breathing still, my eyes focused on him. If I give him any hint of fear, he will ultimately use it against me, and I don't have time to come up with an adequate defense—but I can play a part if that's what he wants.

"Well, he got pretty close."

"Too close." The chief's eyes lock on my wedding ring, and I cover it with my thumb. He smirks. "Pim let his heart get in the way of his head, a pretty face was all it took for him to abandon his better judgment. After the raid, I watched him, and had some of my guys follow him. He led us right to The Rosaries, to your grandmother, and to you."

Everything around me freezes, and I swear I can see my breath forming in little ice crystals. He's looking at me like a hawk who has found a little field mouse to devour.

"I'm not here to be arrested, am I?" I whisper, cottonmouth drying out my lips.

"No." He leans against the table. "The Council is on me for not putting Crémant Rose behind bars before New Separation. They need a scapegoat. Someone to blame for what's going on in Inferium."

"And that's me, or rather, Crémant."

"Exactly."

"Then what is this conversation about? I'm in custody. You got her—Crémant."

"Not quite." The smug glint in his eyes takes over his whole being like a sunburn. "If I arrest you now, you'll become a martyr to The Rosaries. I have no interest in poking the hornet's nest and watching the peasants storm the castle. No, the Council has a better idea for you. You'll go out as Crémant and turn yourself in. It'll be a spectacle, and you will show all The Rosaries that you are done fighting. That the right thing to do, would be to turn yourself in—teach them right from wrong."

Is this guy serious? I can't believe the words he's saying. He wants me to turn myself in to calm The Rosaries, make them hate me, and get a show out of me—as a warning, as control. I don't do well with control.

"You think I'm going to teach them right from wrong? Are you serious? I think you'll find, Chief, that the hornet's nest has already been obliterated. I don't think turning Crémant in will do anything to calm the uprising. We're already there."

"Yes, but all it takes is a spark to ignite an inferno, or a downpour to dowse it to ashes. This is the dowsing part."

"I'm sorry, but I'm not going to go back on what I believe. The Council can take their opinions and shove them up—"

"Miss Dierich."

"Mrs. *Pim*. Pim." I roll my eyes. Can't this guy get it? I am Pim's wife, not his secretary.

"Fine. Mrs. Pim, I'm not asking you. I'm telling you. I can make things very difficult for you and Pim, mostly Pim in general. I can arrest you, and then ruin his life, his career, his livelihood, all it takes is one wrong move, and I can destroy it in an instant. While I'm at it, I can destroy everyone you love as well. I know where your grandmother is, the troupe, even your friend, Vienna Sinclair. Do you want all of those innocent lives to be ruined because of one person? I don't think that's a difficult choice."

He's threatening me? No, he's not threatening me. He's threatening my family. The ones I've loved my entire life, and my new love, my husband, and everything he holds dear. How can I do that to them? How can I destroy what they love?

"If I turn myself in, who's to say you won't harm them? I have no guarantee, and once you have me, you can do whatever you want."

"You're right, but if I hurt them after you're gone, I will only be obliterating that hornet's nest, as you say. So, you can call that insurance. I'll give you a day to think it over." He stands, turning to leave. "Oh, and about Pim."

"What about him?" My voice sounds harsh to my ears, broken and disheartened.

"If you want to protect him, you'll have to give him up." He looks back. "You know what I mean, because if someone finds out he is married to Crémant Rose, well, that could make things very difficult for him. I'll have one of my deputies show you out," he finishes. The door squeaks with the intensity of a siren as he steps out, spiking through my head and leaving a throbbing pain behind my eyes.

The anxiety from before grows, palpitating my heart and making my breathing speed up. I don't even realize I'm crying until a salty tear slides down my cheek. What am I going to do? He threatened everyone I love, and Pim . . . Emotion cages my throat, like a roaring beast cornering me against a sheer slab of stone. There is nowhere to run. There's no way to escape. This isn't a fantasy anymore. I'm not the red-clad vigilante who wasn't scared to fly from the rooftops and dance in the clouds—the one who played a game of hearts just for the thrill of it.

Because that's all Crémant had been, a fantasy. Something to put my bored mind to the test. Something to thrill me—until it wasn't. Until it became real. A symbol. A hope to a broken people. People who just want to live without oppression. How could I have known they would choose me to be their mascot? I was just trying to have some fun, and now, I have to pay for it—my loved ones have to pay for it.

Sobs of frustration and anger crawl out of my throat like angry vipers ready to strike. I don't care if anybody hears me. I just want the frustration to lessen. I scream, the sound reverberating along the gloomy gray walls. It's not my fault. I gave up the thrill. So why do I have to shoulder the responsibility of a revolution? I don't want the responsibility. I just want to keep my family safe. I just want to be with them . . . with Pim.

I stare at my ring, the rose ruby winking up at me. I hate it now. I hate that the rose is a symbol of hope. I never wanted this, but to be honest, I didn't really know what I wanted until I had it, and now I have to give it all up. I have to give it up for selfish rich people who think their way of life is threatened because of me. What a terrible way to live if your entire existence can be brought down by a rose.

I laugh derisively, like a madwoman whose reality has escaped her. Who am I kidding, it has. I don't hate this symbol. Without it, I wouldn't have met Pim. Ironic, the one thing that brought us together will be the thing that pulls us apart. I love this symbol for what it stands for—hope and love for others, but I hate that I have to be the one to shoulder it. I hate that because of it, I can't keep my hope and love. I hate that I'm forced to let go.

Pim's blue eyes swim in my vision, and it only sends more tears down my face. I love him, and my love is what will destroy him, or rather, his love for me. I have to let him go, because if I don't, everyone in Seperium will hate him. He'll be ostracized. He'll lose his job. Or—no, it's worse—they'll put him on trial for not catching Crémant and fraternizing with her by marrying her. He'll end up in jail, and if that happens—he'll die. Other inmates and criminals will kill him for what he's done to them.

I have to protect him, and if this is the only way to do it, then so be it. *I'm sorry, Leo. I'm sorry I can't live life with you like I promised. I'm sorry the cost of our love bought us a few moments. I'm sorry it didn't buy enough to last.*

CHAPTER 87
Before the war: 1861-S: Inspector Leo Pim

The scents of rosemary and black pepper waft around the kitchen as I simmer lamb chops over the stove. My chocolate cake baking in the oven collides into a decadent world of perfection. I hum, thinking Rosea is going to love this. She loves cake, and a cake made by her wonderful husband will be even better. I puff my chest in pride. I can't wait until she gets home. If she gets home. The thought nags at my mind. Where is she? I expected her back by now, at least because it's starting to get dark.

Oh no, what if she got lost in the streets of Seperium? They're unfamiliar to her. What if—*Pim! You idiot! You should have gotten her a map!* Now she'll be eternally lost, wandering and wandering until the end of time. Okay, that's not humanly possible, but it doesn't lessen my worry.

I start to unravel the dark gray apron tied around my waist. I better go out and look for her, perhaps she had half a mind to stay close, and she just got turned around somewhere.

The doorbell rings, an eerie sound that Roosevelt hisses at before he zooms out of the kitchen with a pained yowl. I walk to the door, opening it to find Rosea standing in the hall, a stack of paper in her arms.

Immediately, I know something is wrong, and my heart sinks against the initial elation of finding my wife at the door. At least, she's not aimlessly wandering the Seperium streets. Her dark blue eyes avoid mine as she steps into the house. Didn't I give her a key? I close the door. Why didn't she let herself in? She steps down the hall toward the kitchen, peering at the stove as I close the door.

"It smells good," she mutters, her hands trembling against the papers she held. Why does she have paperwork?

I step out of the foyer, heading toward her. "Rose?" I reach for her shoulder, but she flinches, slapping my fingers away with a free hand. My stomach drops. "What happened? Are you okay? Did something—did someone hurt you? Did—"

She starts to chuckle, tears suddenly streaming down her cheeks. "Yes, someone hurt me, and it was myself—no—it was you."

Her blue eyes clear, glaring at me. Everything blurs past me, until it's just Rosea and me. She's the only thing I see, and right now, it looks like the darkness of my nightmares surrounds her. It follows her like a shadow ready to destroy what I thought was something beautiful and light.

"This is stupid. I should have never done this. I shouldn't have come back here." She starts toward the door again, but I block her path.

"Rose, what are you talking about?" Fear creeps into my heart, but I can't let it tear me apart. I have to understand what is going on, and I can't let fear cloud my thoughts.

"You took everything from me, Pim."

What? What is she talking about?

"You destroyed my home—everything I loved, gone. I can't believe I just disregarded that because of passion, but passion won't carry us. It won't save us from the sins of our past."

"What sins? Rosea, where is this coming from? This isn't—"

"I was a fool to think I could do this. I'm still Crémant, and you're still the detective chasing after me, but now the thrill is gone. The chase is no more, and reality is here to destroy us . . . and reality bores me." Her blue eyes look into mine, now devoid of tears. A smirk lights her lips, the nightmare darkens her eyes—the blue disappearing in a black hole of regret.

I don't know what she's talking about. Everything was fine when I left this morning to run errands. Why is she acting like this? Did someone say something to her? Did someone do something to her? Because this isn't Rosea, this person in front of me is a broken monster.

"Rose—"

"Stop. Let me say this once, and let it be clear—I don't love you."

What? No. It's a lie. All a lie. Rosea would never say something like that. She loves me. She wouldn't have married me if she didn't love me, right?

"I never did." Her words are like venom, spreading throughout my body and leaving me paralyzed and dead. "I was in love with the chase, and now that you have me, you're not chasing me. The truth is so clear now. I shouldn't have married you." She slaps the paperwork onto the kitchen counter. Suddenly, I know what they are—divorce papers.

"No," I gasp. "No, who are you? Rosea would never do this. She would never—"

"Do you really know me though, Pim? We've only just met! It was all a game to me. I just wanted to see if I could make you fall in love with me, and I did! I got your heart and now—" she pauses, the darkness in her eyes taking over her entire being, manifesting into nightmares I never thought would become real. "I'm going to crush it while you watch."

She takes her wedding ring off and sets it on the papers. She is right. She is crushing my heart. I can feel it being smashed into little pieces that can never be made whole.

I close my eyes, pinching my arm to wake up. "This isn't real. It's a nightmare. I'm going to wake up, and you're going to be right there beside me. I'm just scared. That's all. I'm scared I won't be a good enough husband. I'm so scared, my subconscious is creating this nightmare to make me believe my insecurities. You're still he—"

"This isn't a nightmare, Pim." Rosea's voice forces me to open my eyes again, and she's right. I'm still in the kitchen. The papers are still on the counter. My skin is numb from pain where my nails dig into my arm.

"You liar. You promised we would live out our lives together. Why did you make me believe you? Why did you—" I choke, air gasping from my lungs.

She did it because of the thrill, stringing me along to fulfill her dark, twisted passion. She's crazy. I wipe my tears away. I won't let her see me cry anymore. The walls I broke down for her are starting to rebuild, covering my heart in a fortified stone castle—no, obsidian, black as this nightmare. Go figure, the one time I fall in love with someone she's a complete psycho—serves me right for falling in love with someone from Lower Inferium.

"Part of the game, Pim." She saunters toward the door, stopping only to whisper in my ear. "It was fun while it lasted. Goodbye, Leo."

Perhaps, I heard her voice crack on the last word. Perhaps, I should have realized the way she fidgeted with her hands the entire time. The way her eyes darted around the room when she thought I wasn't looking, as if the nightmare I saw was chasing her instead of me. The way she said my first name instead of my last. Perhaps, if I had been paying attention, I would have fought a little harder, questioned it a little more—made her tell me the truth, but I was a fool, and I was too late to change it.

CHAPTER 88
During the war: 1862-I: Vienna Sinclair

I was too late. Too late. I saw the blimps. I heard the whistle, but I had been too late to save them. I'm lying in the aftermath of what used to be Inferium Hospital. Ash and smoke billow up toward the dark sky, growing dimmer by the second. Smoke chokes my lungs making it hard for me to breathe. My eyes water, tearing down my cheeks. My ears ring from the impact of the explosion. I don't remember quite how it happened, but . . . they bombed the hospital. They actually bombed the hospital.

Disbelief strangles my thoughts even though I'm lying in a pile of rubble. The ringing subsides, and along with it comes pain. So much pain. My vision blurs as I watch the flames of a fire creep toward me. It looks pretty, dancing among the bricks. Perhaps, I could dance along with it. Allow its flames to carry me up to the sky . . . I blink.

What am I thinking? This isn't the time, or the place to dance. This is a place to cry. No, die. This is the place to die. I mean, why not? It's not like I haven't seen plenty of deaths here. It's not like I haven't watched the flames lick the remains of other's loved ones before—like my loved ones. How fitting. I'm going to die in the place they did. Lie to rest surrounded by the same bricks and walls, well not exactly, but rubble counts, I guess.

The pain is lessening, or maybe I'm just slipping. I watched so many patients go this way before. When they couldn't feel anymore, that's when I knew they would die. So, I'm ready. I should go now before the dogs eat my bones.

"Vienna." I hear my name whispered along the smoke. It rings in my head like a symphony. My vision focuses for a moment. Dr. Greenwood stands in front of me. "Not yet, kid. I'm gonna get you outta here. You're gonna be okay," he says, bending to lift me onto his shoulders.

I scream as pain spikes throughout my entire body. I don't even know where I'm hurt. I can feel everything and yet, nothing. My heart pounds in my chest as my head lulls. I'm screaming again, but this time it's not from the pain. Blood pours from my thighs where my legs used to be. Well, they're still there, smashed and matted from the rubble that crushed them.

Dr. Greenwood lied to me. I'm not going to be okay. He should just leave me here so I can die where my family died. At least then, I can go with them. My screams turn to gasps I can't stop. The smoke chokes me like someone gripping my throat. I'm going to die. Pain spikes along my skin again driving into my body like nails into wood, and this time when my eyes see nothing but blurred masses, I close them, drifting away into the place of darkness and pain.

When I open my eyes, he's there. Those brown eyes that pulled me in and held me close, dance like a waltz across my mind. He says I'm not done yet. He says I still have to find him, and then everything fades to

. . .

CHAPTER 89
During the war: 1862-I: Gabriel Hoek

"Congratulations, son, you've been promoted to general, well done," General Loens says as he hands me a sheet of paper. Everyone else around the dark brown dinner tent turns their heads to look at me. My heart sinks as I gently take the paper from his worn hands. I stand, saluting him as he salutes me back before moving on. I glance around the room before sitting back down. No cheers. No congratulations.

They all know why I'm a general now. It's because no one else is left to lead, and I'm one of the most competent. I've led enough raids to know how the citizens of Inferium work. I understand their mechanisms like the pieces of an engine. Every piece is where it belongs. Every piece can easily be taken away or replaced. Easy to navigate. Easy to control, but I always did my best to make sure that none of the citizens got hurt. Sure, there were casualties, but I couldn't live with myself if I killed them in cold blood.

I only killed those who pointed a gun and shot first. It didn't matter who killed who, but it mattered who pulled the trigger first. With the click of a gun, and the release of the trigger, that moment defines the rest of their lives, and unfortunately, it's never turned out well in their favor.

Doren reaches a hand toward my certificate. "Let me see." He takes it, pulling it toward him and reading in a pompous deep voice, clearing his throat before starting. "The High Seperium Council hereby grants this certificate to Gabriel Hoek—that's you—" He points to me, and I roll my eyes as if I didn't know. "The honor of being promoted to a first-class Seperium General. Keep this cer—and that's pretty much all the important stuff," he finishes, handing the paper back to me.

"Yay for me." I stuff the certificate into my inside pocket and turning to look at Riel. He's deep in thought again. His dark eyes pierce the roof of the tent as if he can burn a hole through it, his mouth set in a grim straight line.

Doren waves a hand in his face, shocking him back to reality.

'What?' He signs, glaring daggers into Doren instead.

Doren points at Riel's untouched dinner. *'You gonna eat that?'*

Riel huffs before sliding the tray over to Doren, who happily starts chomping away.

'Are you okay?' I ask.

'Peachy.' He moves to stand.

I grab his arm, forcing him back down. *'Please just tell me. I'd rather you tell me the truth than do something rash that you might regret later. I got to keep a close eye on everyone now, and if I think they're self-destructing . . . I've got to keep you safe, too.'*

His brown eyes grow even softer than I've ever seen them. Tears well and he looks away to hide them. *'I heard the hospital was bombed.'* His tears turn to anger, his features hardening like the cooling of steel. *'But you already knew that, didn't you?'*

'Riel. I just—'

'No.' He stands. *'Save your excuses for someone who cares. Vienna worked in that hospital, and now . . .'* Tears stream down his cheeks like silent footfalls of death. *'Why would they bomb a hospital? I knew Seperium was inhumane, but this?'* He sobs, placing a hand over his eyes.

Doren has stopped chewing, and we both stand, ushering Riel out of the tent. Dark gray clouds hang over the city of Inferium like a prediction of death as we stumble against muddy pathways.

He shoves us off once we've gotten away from everyone else. *Just leave me alone. I'm going to the hospital. I have to—maybe there are survivors. Maybe I'll find out if she's okay.'*

He starts to walk away, and we follow after him. *'No, don't follow me. I need to be alone. I—I know it wasn't your fault, and I'll come back. I just—I need time, please.'*

Doren stops, putting a hand in front of my chest to hold me back. *'We'll be here when you need us.'*

Riel nods, disappearing around brown tents and flashing gray uniforms.

"Why did you let him go? What if he—"

"If we push him, he might never come back. He doesn't want us there. He's hurting, just let him have a chance to breathe."

"I'm just worried about him. I can't imagine losing someone I've fallen in love with. I can't imagine—" I swallow, thinking of how I would react if I ever lost Leya.

Doren looks back at me, dark green eyes reflecting the gloomy hazy above us. "Speaking of love, have you talked to Leya recently?"

I sigh. "I need to write to her and tell her about my promotion. I doubt she'll be pleased. It only makes me a bigger target."

I look away from him, my fears welling in my heart like a dying machine with more and more broken parts. I'm so scared of losing Leya, or maybe it's the other way around, I'm scared of Leya losing me. I just want to be home in her arms. I want this war to be over. I don't want to be a leader. I don't want the responsibility.

Doren claps me on the shoulder. "It's gonna be okay. Riel will be fine. Leya will be fine, and we'll all be home soon."

I nod in agreement, because I do believe we'll be home soon.

If only I had known that at the time all hell was about to break loose. Maybe if I had foresight, I would have told Doren to run. Maybe I would have run. Maybe I would have saved the ones I cared about, but by the time I knew that it was too late.'

CHAPTER 90
After the war: 1864-S: Rosea Dierich

Today's the day. Today's the day I finally figure out why Pim is avoiding me. Well, besides the obvious that his wife left him—but why is he avoiding me now? I've sent letters and telegrams, but all of them have been returned, null and void. Now that the war is over, I can tell him the truth. I can tell him why I was forced to leave him. But what makes you think he wants to see you? He hasn't returned one of your messages. I stop at the thought. It doesn't matter anymore. Whether he wants to see me or not, I have to at least try to tell him the truth.

Sunshine bears down on the steel sidewalk of Seperium as I walk toward the police station. Motorcars rumble beside me in the streets, shines of bright metal blinding me as the cars reflect the sunlight. The air smells like any other day—fresh bread mixed with hints of oil. I breathe it in, but a horrible stench rots the normal scents, and I cringe, my insides closing in because the stench reminds me of Inferium.

I shake my head. Get a grip, Rosea. You're not down there anymore, and Seperium never lets their streets smell like anything besides—well, nothing like death. I lift my face to the sun, calming my nerves and wiping sweaty palms onto my dress. Everything will be fine. The chief can't hurt me or Pim anymore, because I'm no longer Crémant and after the last three years, no one remembers her anyway. She's no longer a threat because the war has already happened.

"Keep walking, Rosea. You don't want to go on without him anymore," I say out loud, before continuing on my way.

I . . . I can't see past these little lies. I sing to remember the path. Left turn.

I . . . I can't break through these promises. Two rights, and I'll see it.

Sure enough, the gold-gilded obsidian building appears. A little courtyard decorates the front of it with rose bushes and fountains because we all know police officers have time to take walks and smell flowers. I almost giggle at the thought. I know Pim never had any time for walks, especially when he was chasing me—when he had me in his arms. My heart clenches with longing. I just want to make this right. If I can make this right, then I won't be thinking about having Pim in my arms again, I *will* have him in my arms.

I start marching toward the entrance, but a tug on my heart causes me to look to the right. I gasp. It's like my heart knows, cause there he is—my Pim. Dark bags crowd the space beneath his bright blue eyes, but other than that, he looks amazing. His long legs stride toward the police station from the opposite side I'm walking from, almost like he's heading right for me. But I know he hasn't seen me yet because he hasn't stopped and gasped in disbelief.

A motorcar on the street beside him screeches to a halt, and two masked men stumble out of it, heading straight for Pim. My heart stops and I freeze while I watch the scene unfold. The men go after Pim, who barely has time to react as he reaches for the revolver he has strapped to his side. One with a wood block and the other with a knife clenched in his beefy fist. No . . . The one with the block smacks Pim over the head before he can gain a clear shot, while the other man stabs him in the back of his right shoulder.

"Pim!" I scream, starting to run toward him. This can't be happening. This isn't real. He must have gotten into some trouble. I have to help him. I have to call for help. I have to—

The man with the knife turns his head, staring dead at me. I halt at the dangerous look in his eyes. It dares me to come closer—dares me to save Pim. Officers pour out of the police station, and the two men on the street rush back to their car before they can finish him off. Tears stream down my face. This is what Chief Zorman meant, but how did they know I was coming to meet him? Do they have someone following me?

The officers reach Pim, and once they've confirmed he is still alive, they start to comb the square. I have to get out of here. I can't let them think I had a hand in Pim's assault. I turn tail and start away from the square. My heart shatters with every step I take away from him, but I tell myself it's for the best. I tell myself it's the only way to keep him safe. I can't risk ever seeing him again. I can't risk getting close. Because I would rather him be alive and safe, then dying in my arms.

CHAPTER 91
During the war: 1863-S: Leya Barrett

Everything is just as it should be. Perfect. Pressed. Clean. My family and his family wait patiently in the next room. They're waiting for me, waiting for the blushing bride to appear and marry her groom. Today, I'm getting married to one of the most wonderful men on the planet, and Doren is wonderful. I couldn't have asked my father to choose a better man for me to merge a deal with.

Tears swamp my eyes as I think about Gabe. This would have been our wedding day if he was still alive, but that is the harsh reality of it. He's gone, and I still have to move forward. I still have to carry on my family's legacy. So, I have to marry a man I don't love because the one I do will never come back.

The door opens, and my mother steps into the room. Her dark eyes sweep across my off-white lace wedding dress and corset that laces all the way up my back to my neck like a vice ready to suffocate me. She throws me a terse nod.

Even though my marriage is paying for her lifestyle, she's still not happy with me. I'm still a disappointment to her. Not a proper lady. Not someone worthy to marry a man from a wealthy, prestigious family. No, apparently, I was only good enough to marry Gabe—an engineer who couldn't have possibly helped carry my mother's greatest happiness—herself. Maybe that's it. Maybe she just wanted me to be rid of me once and for all. She didn't want me to be the one she would forever be indebted to.

"I hope it's good enough for you, mother," I bite, not caring if I make my feelings clear. Not anymore. I stopped caring when the love of my life was ripped from me. I shouldn't be wearing a white dress. White dresses are for clean things, and I don't feel clean.

"Leya—"

"No, I'm getting married, and I don't want to hear it. You're disappointed in me. I know that, but at least, the sacrifice of my heart and promises will be worth it for you. You'll get to keep what you've always wanted. I'm finally doing something worthy of your love and affection, and yet, I'm still just a disappointment to you."

I feel tears welling up my throat, but I swallow them down. She doesn't deserve my tears. Our relationship has always been a chaotic mess of a song that sounds like it's being played in two different keys—one going one way and the other heading in the opposite direction, like clothes tearing in two. Always dissonant. Always out of tune.

"Is that what you think of me?"

"You've never given me any reason to believe otherwise."

Tears well in her eyes. "I'm sorry. I'm so proud of you, Leya, but words don't make any difference because saying that means nothing to you if you've only ever believed I'm disappointed in you. I'm sad it has come to this. I'm sad you're marrying someone you don't love. I'm sorry Gabe is gone. When he asked me to marry you, I was overjoyed because the two children I loved and watched grow together were going to be each other's equals in love, and then . . . Your heart was breaking, and I didn't know what to do. I'd never lost someone like that."

Those words send my mind reeling. My mom had lost someone like that because what about Casen? Has she completely forgotten about him?

Her voice continues, and I tune in to pay attention to her. "And I'm sorry I made you believe I'm disappointed in you. That you aren't my perfect daughter, but those thoughts are all lies because you are perfect, and I'm so incredibly proud of your strength. The strength I see as I look at you right now, that you are standing in a wedding dress ready to marry someone for the sake of others. I never would have done that. I would have killed myself first, but you"—she smiles—"are so much better than me. I don't know where that came from, because I'm a coward who made her own daughter believe she hated her. You are so much more, and I hope I can do better to prove it to you."

She takes my hands into her own. My tears are back. She's right. I don't believe her because she has never done anything to support her claims. She's always been cold and upset at me, as cold and as dark as the navy-blue themed room we are standing in.

She continues, "So, allow me to do this one thing for you. Allow me to prove I'm not just your selfish, disappointed mother." She stops, taking a breath. "I taught you to be submissive, to be the perfect wife, but to hell with all that if you can't marry the one you love. You can leave right now if you want to. It will cost us the merger. It will cost us a fortune, but I won't blame you if you want to run away. I'm telling you to go because nothing will hurt more than watching you suffer for what you lost—not just in love, but choice. My trivial lifestyle means nothing if I have to sacrifice you to keep it."

Her brown eyes blaze with an unquenchable fire I have never seen before. They blaze like the build of a dramatic score. The dissonant notes that used to make up the song of our relationship starts to mellow as the chords and harmony start to coincide, erasing the dissonance and perfecting the pitch.

I hug her. "It's too late. Gabe is already gone. What else do I have besides taking care of my parents? And Doren will be good to me. I couldn't ask for anyone better to enter a loveless marriage with. I will be fine, and so will you. Thank you for offering me a chance, but I doubt Father will be pleased, and this is all I can do for you, so do it I must."

The blackwood door beside us opens, ushering Father in. He looks at me with sullen hazel eyes. We decided to host Doren's and my wedding at Claren Hill—finally, the large ballroom with crystal chandeliers and large copper-trimmed windows that Gabe and I used to run through as kids pretending there were ghosts lurking around every corner, will be put to good use. Tears flood my eyelids.

We would make up the most ridiculous things, and I wish we were still those two little kids who spent all day dreaming about fantastical worlds and how to make them reality. But today, there will be no shadows to hide behind in the massive ballroom. It will just be me and Doren in a room full of family and other privileged people we've never met. Oh, and carnations—we can't forget about the cream carnations with steel shreds interwoven inside that Mother had placed all over the room and overhanging balcony.

Father takes my hands into his own, squeezing them in anticipation before drawing my veil over my face. The off-white lace is covered in little flecks of gold, so when the light hits my dress, it shimmers like a halo. That's why there will be a big diesel-powered lantern shining behind me as I walk toward my fiancé. All the lights will go out, and the shadows will be eaten by me and my angelic dress.

The music starts, and my heartbeat rises with it. It's time. My brown eyes search for my father's, wishing for some comfort, anything to put my racing heart at ease, but he doesn't acknowledge my gaze as he places a kiss against my cheek. Mother places the wedding rings' box into my hands.

"We'll go before you," he whispers as if I don't know how a wedding works. He takes Mother's arm, and they stand in front of the door. It opens at their presence, as if sensing their movements.

I can feel my pulse pounding in my throat. The little porcelain and copper box in my hands shakes as I move in front of the door. It opens in what feels like a burst of fanfare, exploding around me like my heart. Everyone is standing. Everyone is looking at me. I feel the blood drain from my face as the music starts to play, haunting and demanding.

The lights flicker out, replaced by the giant light behind me. I can't move though. I can't—I look up ahead and see Doren's green eyes reflected back at me. They're brighter than I've ever seen them before, probably because of the light, but they're focused on me and only me. They seem to say, "It's okay. You'll be okay."

He stands at the front, his prosthetic apparatus holding him up underneath his velvet gold and off-white suit. His golden curls have been tamed into a ribbon at the nape of his neck, and his face is clean-shaven, showing off his chiseled jawline. He actually looks quite handsome.

He nods, a small, sad smile taking over his face. I lift my head, letting the gold veil shine across the room as I take a step forward.

This is the moment. The moment when one solitary note changes the course of the entire song. The moment in which my life seems to be moving at a snail's pace. The dark walkway dusted with white flower petals never seems to end as I walk toward Doren.

He lifts his head as I approach, nervousness taking over his features. I don't even think my feet are carrying me closer to him anymore. I'm not aware of my movements. I want to run. I want to hide, but I know I can't do that. Not this time.

CHAPTER 92
After the war: 1864-S: Inspector Leo Pim

She's waiting outside the hotel when I arrive from the police station, white-blonde hair pinned underneath a lace blue and black bonnet. Her dark blue dress reminds me of midnight excursions and moonlight dances, matching her eyes in an alluring pull of blue.

I entered the cane as evidence, telling Chief Lecten about the duplicate that could potentially be our weapon. He's pressing me for time though, saying the Council wants the case wrapped up as soon as possible, and if that means incarcerating an innocent man, then so be it. His words, not mine.

Seriously, what is the point of my job if I can't actually do it? Why hire inspectors at all? Just to put on a show? A wild goose chase, before they say, "Oops, it was all a hoax, folks. Put away your pitchforks and torches the case has been solved." Then proceed to put the wrong man in jail, so the real murderer can continue to roam free. I know Gabe isn't the murder, and if I can get enough evidence to prove it, I can absolve him—if only it were that easy.

I'm getting ahead of myself. Right now, I have to focus on her, and the promises she broke. The lies she whispered, and the heart she crushed. Will she explain it, or will she leave me in the dust? Golden light from Seperium's lamps and blimps flying overhead, cast a warm glow over Rosea's features, illuminating the bumps on her skin in little shadows. She's wearing makeup today, and the bright red lipstick across her lips reminds me of the rose red suit she used to wear—it's striking in comparison to her blue dress.

I meet her eyes, and my stride slows to a stop a few meters from reaching her. I see it in her eyes. She's finally ready to tell me. It's like watching a heart beating on a sleeve, but will she let me have it, or will she hide it in the depths of the ocean we were both still drowning in?

I move toward her. I don't want to drown anymore. I want to swim. No, I want to find myself on the shore next to her. Maybe we're stranded on an island we can never escape from—the last two people in the world. Perhaps that's more fitting.

Her dark blue eyes look me up and down, and I know she's taking notice of my gray suit with a lace ruffled vest and sleeves.

"Let's take a walk," she says, turning down the street.

I follow her, placing her arm in the crook of mine. "At least, let's make it look like I'm escorting you."

"You think I need a man to escort me, Leo Pim?"

I pull my arm out of hers, huffing. "Fine. You can't even lean on me a little, but I already knew that." I walk ahead of her like it's a race.

"Leo." The crack in her voice stops me, and I turn to find her standing a little way behind me.

The roar of a passing motorcar drowns out the sob I watch escape her lips. I move toward her. White lights from a blimp shine down against her, a broken and blue mermaid out of water—no, a siren. I reach to touch her, but I stop myself. I'm not here to comfort her. I'm here so she can tell me the truth, and maybe then, we'll find ourselves on the shore, and then, and only then, will I comfort her—will she comfort me.

"Just tell me the truth, Rose. I have to know, and if someone is after you, we'll . . ." I stop myself. I want to say we'll face it together, but I'm not sure that's true anymore.

She composes herself, breathing in before beginning. "Leo, before

I start, I have to tell you that I love you very much. I always have, but you know that, you knew it the day I left my heart back in your apartment. It was because of my love that I lost you—gave you away. That day, I was picked up by the Seperium City Police Department. It turns out, they knew I was Crémant, and they wanted me to take the fall for what was happening in Inferium.

"I refused, of course, because Crémant had done nothing wrong except paint a few murals, but they were convinced I could quell the masses by making a spectacle and turn myself in." She looks away for a moment, her eyes looking at a pink glass sign in a shop window, displaying the word love. Hmm, how ironic.

She walks ahead of me a few steps, before continuing, "Of course, I never got to do it. So, I lost a few things I loved, anyway. I—the chief then said that if I didn't do it, he would ruin your life, Grams', Vienna's, and anybody else associated with Crémant. He also said that an inspector being married to a vigilante was a bad idea. Because if word got out, you would immediately be stripped of everything you had, tried, and thrown in jail, and I refused to be the one who did that to you."

"So, break my heart instead? You didn't even ask me what I wanted—"

"What would have been the point, Leo? Both of us would have ended up in jail, and Grams? Vienna? How could I have sacrificed them? It wasn't just about us, Leo!" She runs a hand against her face, smearing the tears across a rainbow wash of lights cast from store signs above our head. *Sweet Seperium.* Even after all this time, she's still stunning.

"I know," I whisper, forcing myself to look away. "But I would have—I—"

"Don't tell me what you would have done, Leo. I didn't have a choice."

"Fine. You didn't have a choice, but what about after that? Why didn't you try to find me? Why did you just give up?" My ice-blue eyes pierce through her as if they could disperse all her secrets.

"After the war started, there was no way to get to you. Inferium was a bloodbath. They were bombing anything that could be of importance to us. They burned and destroyed homes and families. The Rosaries fought back at every turn, but all it did was cause more destruction. I found out I was pregnant, and Vienna told me to lay low with Grams. Anywhere that would take us. Anyplace that would hide us."

I look away, guilt curdling my stomach even though I know it's not my fault. I hate that she didn't have any safe place to survive. I hate that she had to live in squalor just to keep me safe.

"After Prissy was born, I started organizing The Rosaries, taking up the name Blood Red. Never in a million years would I have thought I would do something like that. We got a few good attacks together and depleted some Seperium supplies and resources. Then black rot hit again, and I had to hide to keep Prissy and Grams safe. We did our best until the antidote was created. When everything settled and Seperium surrendered, Vienna asked me to be on the new Inferium Council they were creating to delegate for Inferium. I agreed and moved Prissy and Grams to Seperium."

Tears stream down her cheeks as she swallows, taking a breath. It makes my own tears appear again because she loved me so much, she gave me up. She made me hate her just to give me a chance. Through all that, she was strong for Grams and Prissy, doing her best to keep them safe too, but Seperium—why didn't she find me then?

"I reached out several times once we moved to Seperium. I sent letters and telegrams to your work and the apartment. Somehow, the apartment ones were always sent back, and the work ones always sat without a reply. How do you think I felt? I knew I hurt you, but I couldn't believe you wouldn't let me explain."

She sent me letters. She tried to reach me? How come I never knew this? Were her messages being intercepted? Were mine? Maybe that's why I never received anything back for the efforts I put in to find her. Maybe my messages never made it to Inferium.

"Then," she continues, "and then I went to the police station to see you . . . I was there the day you were stabbed on the streets. I saw it happen, and—I thought the threats were real. I thought they went after you because of me. I watched while you received help. I watched until you were safe, but I couldn't possibly come anywhere near you. I couldn't help, and then, I didn't try to contact you after that. I just wanted to keep you safe."

The tears welling in my eyes start down my cheeks at her words. She saw me. She saw me and didn't help because she thought she was the reason I had been hurt. Suddenly, the spot where I was stabbed in the crux of my right shoulder starts to burn as if the wound has reopened at her words.

The anger and bitterness I felt toward her since finding out she was in Seperium disappears, filling with overwhelming regret and longing. Regret because our past had torn us apart. Longing for the future we never had, but now . . . but now I see it's possible. Now, I see we can be together, our past no longer hinders us, and our future is waiting to be grasped and held onto.

Her voice splits the silence our tears had created. "Finally, I was invited to go to the dinner party with Vienna, and then—miraculously, we were brought back together again. I hate myself for what I did to you, but if I had to do it again, I would. I would make you hate me. I would keep you safe."

Her words are rushed as if she's terrified she might not be able to get them out. As if she might spend three years holding onto them just to keep me safe. As if this moment might be torn from us in a second's notice, but I won't let it happen—not again.

Those dark blue eyes scrutinize me through wells of water. I breathe in shakily, because I think we've finally made it to the shore, together, but I have to hurry before the tide pulls us back into the depths. I stride over to her, my heart demanding that I don't let her slip through my fingers. I will pull her to solid ground, to a place where she can never be washed away from me. My fingers reach for her, caressing her cheek.

She leans into my touch, craving the feeling as much as I do. It feels good, right, to feel her skin under mine.

"Just promise me if something like that happens again, you will tell me the truth first. Don't make me wait three years to get it out of you," I whisper, looking into her shimmering eyes that shine like starlight—beautiful, and yet, achingly far away.

"I promise." She grabs me by my jacket, bringing her lips against mine in a torrent of passion and longing. I gather her into my arms, pulling her as close as I can without hurting her.

"I love you," I say against her lips.

CHAPTER 93
During the war: 1862-I: Rosea Dierich

She's so beautiful. I can't stop thinking that as I stare down at my baby girl lying in her crib. My little acorn—four months old today. She's got a crop of dark hair, just like her daddy. My throat clenches with emotions. Will Priscilla ever get the chance to meet him? I think she'd love him as much as I do.

"Pim as a dad?" I whisper to myself. "I wonder what it would be like." Tears spill down my cheeks, and I wipe them away, looking at the grim, black-bricked warehouse building Grams and I had made our home over the last few months. Drifters often come through, but it is safe in the upper offices, especially since we have a key. At least, it has kept us safe enough until I could give birth to Prissy. I curl a finger around her perfect, soft cheek.

I think Pim would love her too. I chuckle, thinking he would have passed out if he had been here through her labor and birth. He probably would call babies disgusting, drooling creatures until he held her for the first time, then—like me—he would be in love. He would never want to let her go. I turn away from Prissy as I sob into my hand. He never wanted to let me go, but I forced him to.

A spike of pain races through my chest at the memory of what I said to him. How could I have been so heartless? He'll never come back for me. He'll never want me again. So, how will I ever be able to introduce Prissy to him? How will she ever have her father?

The door opens behind me, and Grams comes in with a man from The Rosaries. I straighten myself, wiping my face. They both look stricken, like they've seen a ghost. Like they've seen death, but who hasn't in Inferium, especially now.

"Grams?" I move toward her.

"They bombed the hospital. Those snakes bombed the hospital," the man speaks.

What? I stare at Grams to tell me the truth. She nods with tears in her eyes.

Vienna.

No!

My heart sinks as I throw on my shoes and a coat, racing toward the door.

"Rosie, don't. Please don't!" Grams shouts, grounding me to the threshold of the front door. "There's nothin' to be done. They've already pulled the survivors. I'm sorry, Rosie. I don't know who 'as been accounted for, and who 'asn't."

"No!" I break down into sobs, falling to my knees, staring at the metal floor. It has little etched stars in it—stars like Vienna. She always reminded me of a star, shining bright against a dark world. That's who she is—was. Grams wraps her arms around me, holding me close.

"She can't be—she—"

"I know." Grams runs a hand down my hair. I don't know how long she holds me, but I don't think it's long enough as I look up, catching sight of the man from The Rosaries.

"Why is he here, Grams?"

She helps me up, leading me over to the middle-aged man. He has tattoos running up his neck, and his head is shaved to his scalp, reflecting the dreary yellow lights of our office warehouse.

He holds a hand out. "Lykan Vent, and I believe you are Crémant Rose."

I shake my head. "I've left that life behind. My name is—"

"Don't tell me. I have something to ask you, but it requires you to keep your true identity a secret."

"I'm listening."

"We want you to become the leader of The Rosaries. We need some-one to boost morale, plan attacks, and help us get back at Seperium for what they've done and what they just did."

"Me? Why would you want me? I'm no leader. I have a family to protect. Go find someone else," I mutter, turning away from him.

"They won't listen to anyone else. They want you. You can't keep running. All you've done is run. We can win this war. We can make life better for all of Inferium. We have to at least try. We owe it to those who have already been lost—in the past and in the present," he says, the weight of what his eyes have seen falling between our gazes.

I think about Vienna, Pim, Vienna's family, and my parents. They didn't deserve what they got. They didn't deserve to be killed and tak-en away in war based on greed and pride, and yes, this war has been go-ing on for a lot longer than a year—for me, it's been an entire lifetime.

"I don't think I'm the right person for this. I have a newborn to take care of, a daughter I would like to—" *protect*. I leave the word off as a new thought enters my mind. What if it's not about protecting her? What if it's about creating a better world? One where she can be safe. One where she won't have to be afraid of every solitary shadow.

"Fine," Larkyn starts. "I knew it was a long—"

"How do you expect I'll be able to help you, or even pull it off? I've never led anyone, let alone an angry group of wronged people. How can we control that?"

"We have to. If we don't, we'll lose Inferium for good. Seperium will slaughter us and start again. The people of Lower Inferium will have to understand that if they want to survive, they'll have to believe in you. They'll listen to you." His dark eyes are full of hope. Hope, I'm afraid I can't give.

"They believe in Crémant."

"Why are you talking about her as if she isn't you? Why don't you believe in her anymore?" The passion in his voice sends chills down my spine. *Because she stole everything from me,* I want to say, but I know without her, I would have never gotten here. I would have never met Pim. I would have never had Prissy.

He's right. Crémant is a part of me. A part I've tried to forget and reject. A part that didn't understand who she would become, until it was too late. A part I've tried to run from but running clearly isn't getting me anywhere.

"I do believe in her. I just didn't know she believed in me." I look back at Prissy's crib, then at Grams, who nods with tears in her eyes.

"Inferium needs you now. Just let them see you, let them know you're here so we can get everyone on the same page and organize precise attacks."

Everything in my mind seems to focus solely on this one moment. This moment I know will change my life, Grams' life, and Prissy's. Perhaps for the better, and if not, that means I failed in a way that can never be reversed or changed, but I can't sit back and do nothing.

"I'll do it. Let's show Seperium we're not to be messed with."

CHAPTER 94
During the war: 1862-I: Doren Caldwell

The scream lodged in my throat has become a hoarse reminder of the fear trapped in my chest. I can't move. The rubble crushing me is enough to suffocate me, but not enough to take away the scream. It haunts my thoughts, like an echo across empty skies, going on and on forever. The metallic smell of blood poisons the air around me, filling my memories with the blue eyes of the little girl I had tried to save.

Her endless scream sends shivers down my spine, or maybe that's just the pain coursing through my veins. Her blood coats my uniform and the rubble surrounding me. I had been too late to save her. Too late to save myself as well. I saw the bomb. I felt the ominous whistle in my bones, as if the missile had already claimed me as its victim. Moments before the bomb hit, I was standing beside a building we were certain had Rosary forces inside. I was sent to check it out, but the building was full of women and children. Innocents. We heard the blimps and knew what was coming. Most of them evacuated, but one little girl.

One girl without any family got trapped and left behind in the commotion. I went in to save her. I went in . . . tears stream down my face. The absence of oxygen starts to make my head foggy, or maybe it's just the falling dust, strangling my lungs and giving me no choice but to die. The sound of settling rubble above my head makes me think of a viper coiling around to strangle me.

"Doren!" The voice is muffled through the stone, but it cuts through the shrill scream piercing my head—just enough to put a spark of hope in my heart.

"Here! I'm here! I can't move! I—" I hold my breath in. I can't afford to waste what little oxygen I have left.

"Doren! I'm coming buddy! You're gonna be okay. It's gonna be okay!" It's Gabe's voice.

I hear the rubble moving above me, shifting and threatening to crush me at the wrong movement. Light appears above my head, blinding me against the world I had seen as dark just a moment ago. I was afraid I would get sucked into that void, but the light is here to chase away the darkness. I don't have to be trapped anymore.

Or so I thought . . . from that day forward, I lost all feeling from the waist down. I became a prisoner to my own body, a slave that could never escape the chains around me.

CHAPTER 95
During the war: 1862-I: Riel Mjorn

"Torch the houses. We take their resolve from them. House to house. Burn it all. Destroy it. Let's show these barbarians how disgusting they really are . . ." The words General Loens had shouted only a few hours before, punch a sick feeling into the pit of my stomach. The way the metal torch in his hand reflected orange fire over his face is etched into my mind—a constant reminder of the evil in this world. The evil I am no better than.

The ugly, elongated bird-beak mask settles against my face as I scramble through the dirty black streets of Inferium, heading toward sector three.

Are you evil if you don't try to stop tyranny as you see it unfolding in front of your eyes? I think so, because here I am marching through the dark streets of Inferium with a torch lighting my path. I'm supposed to destroy their houses—burn them to the ground.

How can someone be so heartless? Why did I take the torch without a second thought? Why didn't I try to stop them? Maybe it's because so much has happened in the last few weeks. So much so that I have no volition to be here. I just want to go home, and if I can save someone else before I go or . . . possibly end it all with them, maybe I can finally be free.

Doren is gone—home with no chance of ever walking again, and Gabe . . . unfortunately Gabe hadn't been so lucky. In fact, we can't even find his body to send back home so he can have a proper burial.

Tears clog my throat, the weight of his death is still too raw, crushing my soul because I hadn't been there. I hadn't been there to protect him. I want to go home, but how can I ever face his father or Leya? Even if I did get to go home, I would have to hide like the coward I am.

Hide from the fact that I couldn't save Gabe or Doren or Vienna. Hide from the fact that I'm still just a coward in a mask, ready to destroy what someone once called home. Everything I once cared for here has been stripped from me—my best friends and Vienna. Her name is like sweet nectar against my lips. I form the syllables with my tongue whenever I think of her, as if it would make her golden eyes miraculously appear back in my life.

Now, my fellow soldiers are getting sick with a disease the citizens of Inferium call Black Rot. A disgusting disease that eats you from the inside out. They said once there was a cure—an antidote to combat the illness, but it hasn't been around since the first bout, and no one can seem to tell me who made it. Even if the citizens of Inferium had the antidote, why would they tell us? I wouldn't if I was in their position.

The darkness of the nightfall seems to close in around me, but I'm not afraid. Ever since I was little, the shadows have never scared me. In fact, I welcome the shadows. The darkness helps me hide my disabilities from the world. That's how I used to think: that it would be better to hide in the darkness like a bug than be a human in the light, especially in a world that couldn't accept my handicap. Now, they live in a world full of people with handicaps, broken and damaged from a war they couldn't swallow their pride enough to stop.

I turn the corner, finding myself in the grimy third sector to the south. My sector. Destroy all the houses, leave nothing for them to call home. How ironic that I just want to go home, and the only way I can accomplish that is by destroying someone else's.

I hate this. I hate myself. I should have stopped it when I had the chance. I should have ended it all, but I'm just a coward. A wolf in sheep's clothing. So, I know I won't do what I have thought or even said. I'll just go home and hide like a recluse until the end of my days.

CHAPTER 96
During the war: 1862-I: Vienna Sinclair

The scent of smoke has choked the air for several weeks now. In fact, I honestly can't remember a time when I used to breathe fresh air devoid of the stinge—I'm sure there was a time, I just can't recall it. Maybe I should have compared it to dance, maybe then I would have remembered what it was like, but how do you compare breath to dance? The stillness of the house calms my nerves, telling my brain to settle down and rest, but I haven't been able to properly rest since the bombing. Not since we lost the hospital, not since I lost my legs.

Dr. Greenwood took me home and amputated what was left of my legs. He kept me alive, but sometimes I wish he hadn't. I can't move, and I can't actually live . . . I can't even dance anymore. The thought always sends tears to my eyes.

I'm just a broken stump. I don't even know if anyone besides Dr. Greenwood knows I'm alive. I haven't heard a word from Rosea in months. I'm sure she had her baby by now, assuming they are both still alive.

I shake my head. I have to stop thinking, but what else am I supposed to do when I'm confined to a bed for the rest of my life? Doc gave me plenty of books he managed to salvage, but you can only read for so long before the thoughts start to overtake your heart and soul, leaving you desolate and destroyed. He's working in a tent in the middle of Inferium, a place where a makeshift hospital and refugee camp has been set up. He goes there every day to help as many sick and injured as he can, then he comes here to continue developing the antidote.

If I had a way to stand over at the chemistry table, I would. I would just sit there and create the antidote until the whole world had enough. Okay, maybe not the whole world, but enough to start building immunity, but Doc and I haven't found a good way for me to get around the house without crawling. And no, no matter how bored I am, I will not suffer myself to crawl on the floor like a centipede.

I smile because that word makes me think of Riel. Who am I kidding? I'm always thinking about Riel, especially when the nightmares haunt me. It's his brown eyes that seem to bring me peace. I close my eyes, believing that if I think about his gaze enough, the dark will lull me to dreams instead of nightmares, but somehow, I'm always proven wrong.

The sound of a door creaking open downstairs causes my eyes to fly open. My heart starts to palpitate. Doc said he wouldn't be coming home tonight since Seperium issued a new order, and he wanted to be close to the camps when the order struck . . . maybe an intruder in my house is a part of that new order.

I roll off the side of the bed, carefully catching myself with my arms as I try to lower myself to the ground. I have to be careful since the stitching holding the skin of my hip together still hasn't set and can be ripped open at a moment's notice.

Once I'm on the floor, I crawl underneath the bed, doing my best to keep myself hidden from the intruder. The door handle rattles, sending my pulse almost to the roof as someone steps into the room.

I pull my hand in front of my face to stifle my gasp when I catch sight of him in the darkness. He holds an unlit torch in his hand, and the bird-like mask on his face looks like a nose that has grown two sizes too big. The man sighs before taking off his mask.

I scream, my heart bursting with joy, but I know he won't hear me. He flicks the torch on, and for a moment I think the Riel I knew is gone, and that he's gonna set fire to this place, but then he stares at it for a moment. On and off, like the flames might solve his problem. He reminds me of a moth, drawn to the flame of our disasters, those brown eyes glowing in the orange light.

I drag myself out from under the bed, and he catches sight of me, dropping his items and stumbling into the back wall with a shocked look on his face. His eyes are wide with disbelief and as round as saucers. I would laugh if I had the ability to, but I think that would just scare the crap out of him even more. I help myself up to a resting position, using the bed frame to prop my body up.

'It's me.' I sign, hoping he won't think I'm a ghost and run away, but that's what his expression says, that none of this is real, and that he won't believe me.

"Vienna." His lips form my name, tears streaming down his face. *'You're alive?'* He signs. *'Or this is just a hallucination I dreamed up because I miss you, because I want to die.'*

'Don't die. Please, I couldn't take it if you died because of me. Please, I told you to find me, and you have! Please, don't go now. Don't leave me alone. Not when I know you're here. Not when I know you're okay.' I sign. I'd been learning more of the language with another deaf lady who I knew from the hospital, so I would be ready when I saw him again.

He moves toward me, kneeling as his fingers reach for me. He touches my cheek, and I lean against his fingers. They are more calloused than I remember, probably from being forced to hold guns and destroy what was left down here.

"Vienna," he says again. Tears stream down his cheek as he pulls me into a hug.

I fall into the warmth and comfort of his shoulders. "Yes," I say even though I know he can't hear me.

He pulls away, looking me up and down—or what was left of me anyway. *'What happened to you? Can I help you up? Can—'*

I nod, wrapping my arms around his neck as he gently helps me back onto the bed's mattress. He sits down beside me, and I take his hand, kissing the back of it.

He starts to sob. *'I never thought I would see you again. I thought you were dead. It was chaos. No one knew if—'*

'I know.' I sign. *'But we're here now. You found me, and that's all that matters. In fact, it's a miracle you found me, and not someone else because they would have left me to die, but not you. You'*—I smile—*'are beautiful.'*

That gorgeous grin lights up his face. *'I'm flattered because I was thinking you were beautiful.'*

He pulls me into his arms, and I lean against his chest, drawing strength from the beating of his heart. We might never get the chance to finish the steps to our dance, but at least we can still sway to the music.

CHAPTER 97
During the war: 1862-S: Michele Barrett

I take Casen's cold hand, rubbing it between my fingers to warm them. Weak breaths escape his lips in little wheezes. The doctor said there is nothing wrong with him aside from a case of weak lungs. Well, the doctor is a complete fool. My son is dying. I can feel it in my bones, but I refuse to believe it. I will cling to him until my dying breath. He can't be taken from me. He was my little miracle, and I didn't go through his difficult pregnancy just to lose him.

The moon slivers blue light through the windows across from his bed. Maybe I should have the dark gray curtains drawn. Gray? I hate gray decor. Why is it in Casen's room? I ignore the question, watching a kerosene lamp flicker beside me on the bedside table. A bowl of warm water sits beside it. I pull the damp cloth on Casen's forehead off, touching his cool skin. His dark hair is matted to his small face. Seven years old and he isn't even strong enough to be outside most days. Leya takes him out for a walk as much as she can, but his weak bones can't sustain being in the open air for long. I've noticed the pain on Leya's face every time she brings him back to the house. He can't frolic with her outside when she's home from university. I know it grieves her.

She believes he'll die too, maybe he'll have no other choice . . . I shake the thoughts away, refusing to believe them. If I desire it to be so, my son will live. He will continue to survive, because nothing, not even death, will be able to take him from me.

The door behind me opens with a groan of ghosts long departed. "The bath is ready, Mrs. Barrett," Gertie, our family servant, says.

I nod, standing and pulling Casen from the warmth of his bed.

Gertie moves forward. "I can help—"

"No. I've got him," I tell her, and she backs away. No one can touch my son. I can't afford to let their negative thoughts take him from me. Wellan has already told me not to worry. *"A case of weak lungs is easily fixed with age and exercise."* I can hear his cheerful reassurance, but this situation is anything but cheerful.

Once upon a time, Wellan's voice was a comfort to me, but now it makes me incredibly angry. How can he not see that Casen's condition isn't just a case of weak lungs? He doesn't care though. He will never care, no matter how many times I tell him. All he cares about is his precious company he inherited from *my* father. It should be my company, but I'm a woman, and women aren't allowed to have their father's company.

Resentment has become my only companion these last few years, especially since the war started. Wellan has disappeared more and more trying to keep things running, and because of it, he won't even listen to me about Casen. That's where he is tonight, watching over the company. Always the company, never me. Never Casen.

Casen's skin feels like ice as I place my cheek against his. His breaths still come.

"Stay with me, my son. I will make you well. You will live. You will survive." I head down the hall. Tall portraits of ancestors long passed, stare down at me with morbid eyes and features, haunting me with thoughts of death.

"Casen will soon join us."

"Don't worry, we'll take care of him."

"Say goodbye while you can."

"Why would you want to fight for him to live anyway?"

"Won't he inherit instead of Leya? Won't that destroy all you've

fought for?"

I block the voices out, refusing to hear anymore. No. My son will live. I walk into the bathroom, the steamy interior hitting me with warmth even though Casen still feels cold in my arms. I set him into the hot water without removing his night clothes, ringing for Gertie to bring him a fresh set.

His dark brown eyes open, landing on me as he leans a pale cheek against the porcelain tub. "Mama? I'm so cold," he rasps.

I run my fingers through his damp hair. "I know." My voice cracks. I refuse to cry because he's not dying. He will be okay. He will survive. "Doesn't the bath make you feel better?"

"A little." He reaches a hand out, taking it into my own, but it's still cold as ice despite the warmth of the bath.

"Mama, wake up."

I gasp awake, the dark room closing in on me as I hear his haunting, small voice echo around me. I scream, pushing the covers off me and waking Wellan. Slivers of moonlight pool underneath our blackout curtains, but I can see shadows dancing in them. My heart leaps. What if Casen's just on the other side?

"Michele?" I feel his warm hand on my shoulder, but I jump, reacting by swinging my hand into his face.

He groans, and I finally realize I'm not in a dream anymore. I'm not living in the fantasy. Instead, I'm left with the sickening reality—Casen is gone. He died a few nights ago, and his face, his voice, haunt my every thought.

"I'm sorry." Though I'm not sure I am. It's because of him Casen is gone. If only he'd believed me. If only someone had taken me seriously, but I've never been taken seriously in my sad life . . . and I never will, because I'm not a man.

"It's all right. It was just a nightmare."

A nightmare? A nightmare, he says. As if my life isn't one manifested nightmare. You can't call your dreams nightmares when you live in one.

He tries to pull me into his arms, but I push him away, slipping off our bed. "Don't touch me. I—I just need a chance to breathe. I—" I look back at him, his dark eyes reflecting the slivers of moonlight.

He nods. "I understand. Do what you must."

I leave the room, closing the door and leaning against its solid exterior. What I must. I've already done that, and more. He just doesn't know it. He doesn't realize that I've always done what I must, and what do I have to show for it? A daughter who resents me and a dead son. I slide down the door frame, falling to the ground as tears appear in my eyes. What was it all for? Did it mean anything? Of course not, because I've never had anything in my life, and maybe that's a fate I'll just have to accept . . .

CHAPTER 98
After the war: 1864-S: Leya Caldwell

Gabe gave me a song—a beautiful song to play. Words and notes that formed into a melody. A harmony that flowed through the heart of our relationship, but the melody lost a note, and the dissonant chords rang out until it was grating on my ears. The harmony fell apart, breaking the song until the notes became destroyed and fragmented like an out of tune instrument. That's what our song is now—out of tune. I would say I don't know how it happened, but that's not true.

I realized it when Gabe disappeared, when his life ended. I mourned our incomplete song, but from the ending of our dissonant chords, a new song arose—a key change leading to a different signature. Healing created out of brokenness—brokenness that led to love. This new song played throughout my heart, leading to someone I never would have guessed, but found comfort and hope anew.

The knock on my bedroom door startles me out of my thoughts. The olive-green room with its creme wallpaper and depictions of leaves and flowers echoes the sound, and I can't help but think that it sounds hopeful, like the dawn of a new day. I set my journal down on my bed, shuffling to the doorway in my cream lace nightgown.

Doren stands on the other side of the door, his features distracted, his green eyes looking down at me. His prosthetic apparatus holds him up, keeping his feet on solid ground—although I know it's hard for him to stand in it for long. It must be so painful, but he never complains, not once. We've been married for about three months now, since Dekember.

"I—I came to say goodnight. I—um—I was just passing by your room. So . . . goodnight." He starts to walk away.

"Doren," I call after him. "You never say goodnight. Is something wrong?" I step into the darkened hallway, golden light spilling over us like a warm hug.

He looks back at me. "I—" He sighs, running a finger through blond curls. "This is harder than I thought." He swallows. "I never thought of you as someone I would love because I love Gabe, and he always loved you. We've known each other for years, but now my affection for you has grown. I've never had the privilege of falling in love with someone, so I don't know if that's what I'm feeling, but if I had to describe it, I would call it love. I love you, Leya." He stutters, his throat bobbing as he hurries to finish.

"And it's okay if you don't love me back. I just had to tell you the truth. I promised to take care of you when really, you're the one who has taken care of me. I don't want to hide my feelings because of sentiment. I want you to know the truth because you're my wife, and I don't want to lie to you." He exhales like he has been holding his breath the entire time.

Those green eyes are full of hope, and yet, despair because he knows I don't feel the same, but do I feel the same? I have immense affection and hope for what we could be—the new song rising from the unfinished one. I remember the words I wrote in my journal before he came to tell me this, my brokenness leading to love. Somehow, he felt that too.

"Thank you for being honest with me. I will be honest to you. Before you came, I was writing in my journal about finding hope and love renewed, and I think you are the renewal. Not that I want you to replace what I once had because that was a different song in my life, but I think you've grown into a place in my heart. I don't know if it's love in the way you are describing, but maybe it can be. I would want that because I don't want to be alone, and I don't want you to be alone, and if you love me, I'm willing to find you in that place and love you back."

At my words, it looks like the sun lights up his features. He marches up to me, tears wallowing in his eyes as he holds his hands out in a gesture that I know means, "Is this okay?"

"You mean it?" he asks.

I take his hands, entwining our fingers together. His hands feel safe, secure, and strong—not perfect, but beautiful, nonetheless.

"Yes."

He kisses me, gentle and yet full of reckless passion. I wait for the guilt to strangle my insides and leave me hating myself, but it doesn't. In fact, I feel at peace because I finally have someone to call my home.

CHAPTER 99
After the war: 1864-S: Inspector Leo Pim

I've already concluded that this isn't going to be fun, not that I ever think anything is going to be immense fun, but this in particular is definitely not going to be a theme park of joy and excitement.

Turns out, Lord Wellan Barrett never sold a two-of-a-kind cane. I checked with every auction and charity house I could find in Seperium, but none of them had any record of Lord Barrett giving them a cane to pawn off. They even let me read all their ledgers from the beginning of the war to the end, but there were no entries of a special death reaper cane. Unless he sold it privately? But then why did he tell Leya it had been sold at auction?

So, either he's a liar, or Leya is, and it didn't seem like she didn't want me to find her father's cane. If that was the case, she would have never told me about it in the first place. So, where does that leave me? In a dusty motorcab on my way back to Claren Hill to ask Lord Barrett some questions about the cane he once, perhaps still, owns.

The mansion, in all its castle-like glory, grows closer to the motorcab windows. It's still quite a beautiful structure, despite the fact that I would kill myself before living in the countryside. *Ya're such a drama kin', Pim.* I can practically hear Grams's voice in my head. I smile to myself, thinking about last night. After Rosea and I reconciled, we went back to her room and spent time with Grams and Prissy, and then had a chance to catch up on other things too.

I mess with the ring on my finger, spinning it around. It feels good to have it back where it belongs and not tied above my heart. I gave Rosea back hers—the smaller rose ring I left with my own. She was shocked when she found out we were still married.

Ha! I never signed the divorce papers. I couldn't let her have the last word, of course, and I'm glad I didn't, because now, she is back in my arms—we're back in each other's arms. While she was gone, I couldn't help feeling like a piece of me was missing. A broken piece that would never get the chance to find another perfect piece to fill it, but the pieces are all where they should be now.

The motorcab screeches to a halt, and before I know it, I'm at the massive, geared doors of Claren Hill, waiting for the mechanism to draw me in and ensnare me like a trap, but the secrets in this place won't trap me—not this time. The weight of the search warrant in my pocket burns with the heat of disuse. After I've hit the doorbell, the gears of the door grind and squeak as they open.

The butler from before stares at me underneath droopy eyelids.

I pull the search warrant out of my pocket, holding it in front of his face. "Inspector Leo Pim, you might remember me? I was here a few days ago . . . any who, I've got a search warrant to inspect the premises. So please step aside," I mumble, flicking the paperwork with my finger before skirting around him into the house.

He hurries away as I start to search for the cane. I have no idea if it looks like the other one with the owl, or if it has another animal as its muse. Either way, I will find it.

I've searched a total of three rooms by the time Lady Barrett finds me in a sort of oval room surrounded by plants. A glass roof shines warm sunlight over the two of us. She looks menacing in her ebony lace dress and lace cape that falls from her shoulders to the floor.

"May I understand what you're looking for, Inspector Pim?"

I turn my head, smiling at her. "Well, that would ruin the surprise."

"It's supposed to be a surprise?"

"If I find what I'm looking for, then yes." I turn, continuing to look behind the obnoxious foliage.

This search is like trying to thread a needle, not that I've had much experience with that, but still—tedious and ridiculous. Perhaps, I should have asked for the other officers to come sooner to help me. I shake my head, no, I didn't want to deal with their incompetence right away.

"I don't think you saw this surprise coming." The consonance of her voice changes, and I know I've screwed up by the time I look back at her.

A flash of metal and a reverberating crack across my head whiplashes my neck and sends stars to my vision as I stumble backwards. *Stupid Pim! Why did you turn your back on her?* Because I thought—I look up at her, seeing her duplicated in front of me three times. I would laugh if I actually thought any of this was funny, but it's not. This is a nightmare.

She smiles at my confused face, a cold gesture that sends my blood chilling to my toes. She points the barrel of the gun in my face, the hammer clicking back. I feel my breath catch in my throat, if I reach for the pistol strapped to my hip, I will die. She'll pull the trigger faster than I can flick a finger at my leather holster.

"You thought it was Wellan didn't you? Wellan was too weak to go through with murdering someone to get what he wanted—deserved."

My stomach shrinks at her words, a gripping vice of fear. Hopefully, my backup gets here soon, I just have to stall her long enough for them to rescue me. I came here to find the cane, yes, but in all honesty, I hoped my effort as a single inspector would draw the murderer out of his—her hole. Funny, I never quite saw it playing out this way, but when I had imagined someone holding me at gunpoint over this case, I expected them to be hairier and taller, and a man.

"Why," I gasp. *Play the fool.* "Why would you murder Lord Caldwell? What was in it for you?"

"You don't understand what it's like to be a woman in a man's world . . . how could you? I never got the chance to own or do anything of my own volition. Just sit there and look like a human doll and do my needlework, have children, raise children." She laughs, a sound that grates on my ears and sends shivers down my spine. "Wellan got more than he bargained for when he married me. I wasn't going to sit around and be a perfect wife. No, I told Wellan what he wanted, and then I went out and gave it to him—well, gave it to myself, but we won't stipulate on the details."

A maniac, she's a maniac. I never would have guessed the mastermind behind all this was Lady Barrett, but what about the other things that happened—the things I thought Wellan did? Like manipulating her father's company or destroying Hoek Weapons? Suddenly, it dawns on me. None of those things had been Lord Barrett. The entire time it was his wife, manipulating behind the scenes and taking what joy she could from it. All the while, if anything went wrong, it would be on her husband's shoulders, not hers.

"Wellan made a deal with Doren's father to merge our companies through our children's marriage. I thought it was a wonderful idea, until Hyam Caldwell died and left his entire fortune to his insolent son. We offered to buy Caldwell Textiles from the young lord, but he wouldn't let us buy it. Something about sentiment or memories worth more than the millions of SEM he would have made.

"When Gabe suddenly appeared, I decided to try to get Gabe to murder Doren, but Gabe wouldn't be swayed against his friend, even at the cost of getting the girl he loved back. So, that idea went out the window, and then I saw Gabe walking around with that cane." She stops the narrative, smiling like a kid in a candy store. "I used Gabriel to get what I wanted. Now, my daughter is the sole owner of a fortune."

The crazy glint in her eyes shines like venom against her face, and I see nothing but streaks of blood and red in my vision—the blood on her hands. The sins she had committed, all in the name of what she thought she deserved.

"So, will you murder your daughter next? Do you think she'll let you have the fortune she's inherited? Do you think she'll let you get away with this?"

"She'll do what I ask. With her husband gone, she won't want to deal with Caldwell textiles. We will buy the business and continue to grow our empire, setting up our children for the rest of their lives."

"Hmm, I was convinced it was a man behind it all, but now I realize men aren't crazy enough to scheme up a plan like this, or bored," I jab even though she's pointing a gun at my head. At least, it isn't the first time I've stared death in the eyes. "So how did you get the blood on the windows?"

She smirks as if pleased she has bested a man. "It doesn't take much to make sure some blood gets splattered; all it takes is a few drops. It's been fun, Inspector, but I can't have you destroying what Wellan and I have created. We won't let our fortune slip through our fingers just because of a petty murder, and I'm not about to let you take it from me."

I watch her finger, press the trigger . . .

CHAPTER 100
During the war: 1863-I: Riel Mjorn

The case in my hands wobbles as I hurry through the streets of Inferium. Over the last few weeks, I had been trying to find places to hide Vienna and Dr. Greenwood. After our emotional reunion, I had to get them out of there, because I knew if I didn't burn the house, someone else would. I hid them in a munitions warehouse I knew was mostly empty because no one was working to restock it. I stare at the ground, doing my best not to drop the case full of precious materials.

My heart soared when I decided to raid factories to find the parts I needed for Vienna. I had this brilliant idea to make her her own pair of custom-made prosthetics. She, above all, deserved only the best.

Of course, it took me a long time to find what I needed, but I snuck away every chance I could to be able to keep working on this pair of legs. They are perfect, or at least, I hope she will think they are.

Will she like them? Suddenly, I don't want to give her the prosthetics. They're not my prettiest work, but at the same time, I didn't exactly have the perfect parts to work with, and I had to guess how I would be able to even strap them to her.

What if they don't work? What kind of boyfriend am I if I can't even put my talent to good use? I'm her boyfriend. The thought brings a smile to my face. Never in a million years would I have thought we would ever see each other again, let alone date.

I look up, realizing I have stopped in the middle of the hazy street. Right, gotta keep moving. I have to focus and stop overthinking. She can't walk at all. I'm sure at this point, anything will be better than nothing. I reach the warehouse, setting the case down before I gently tap and slide my hand across the door in a series of codes that Vienna and I made up to let her know it's me coming through the door.

The door cracks open, revealing Dr. Greenwood. Dark circles haunt the shadows of his face. He always reminds me of someone who has seen one too many ghosts. Not that I'm certain ghosts exist, but you know, non-literal ghosts.

"Riel."

He opens the door wider, and I hurry inside. Vienna sits on a chair in front of a work-man's table trying to help Doc with the antidote for Black Rot. They make as much as they can in a day, but the demand and lack of supplies is making the task harder than it should be. Plus, there is talk that the previous antidote doesn't heal the disease completely, just lessens the symptoms, and it grieves Vienna and Doc to no end because they don't have the resources to figure out what could be wrong.

I run a hand along her back, kissing her temple. She leans into my chest, lifting her chin for a kiss. I oblige, my heart intoxicated on the feeling of being so close to her.

'I have something for you.' I sign, brushing my lips against her nose before I step away to unlock the case I left on the floor.

She smiles down. *'Is it a dead body?'*

I catch sight of the words on her fingers, and I stare up at her, aghast. How can she possibly think I would be carrying a dead body? I haven't even—I see her pointing a finger at her heart, and my face falls as I shoot her a withered look.

She smiles. *'Hurry up, I want to see what you brought me.'*

'I'm not sure I want to show you now.' I sign, giving into pettiness.

"Fine," she says aloud and turns to look back at her work.

I sigh, before unlatching the clasps and opening the case.

She immediately focuses her warm honey-eyes on the pair of porcelain legs lying in the case. Tears start to stream down her face as she smiles. Oh no, did I do something wrong? Why is she crying? She should be happy.

"Oh, Riel." I catch sight of my name on her lips before she covers a hand over her mouth. She wipes her tears, signing. *'They're beautiful. Thank you. I'm so happy. I—'* She breaks down into sobs.

I move over to her, pulling her into a hug. Her soft arms wrap around me, clinging to my shoulders. Relief swells my heart, at least she isn't upset at me. She's just so happy she's crying. I've never seen someone cry because they were happy before.

She lifts her tear-stained face. "I love you." I read her lips.

I mimic the words, breathing in her scent as I let the syllables glide over my tongue. *"I love you, too."*

CHAPTER 101
During the war: 1863-I: Vienna Sinclair

He's sick. *Sick.* The thought revolves around my mind like a dance centered around a maypole, twisted and wrong if you miss a step. It feels like a broken and jagged reality leading me down the dark path of death.

I see their faces. I see my family. The way their skin turned black—the way they started to slowly disappear because of a virus I couldn't find a cure for, but not this time. No, I know the old antidote now. I won't lose him. I can't lose him.

"Vienna." Dr. Greenwood shakes my shoulders, his golden-brown eyes fill me with strength as I focus on the ridges set in his irises—little canyons of hope. "We'll figure it out. You won't lose him like you lost them. There's still hope, and we will do our best to put hope into the hearts of those who need it. Once we have the antidote, we'll get it to them all. It will be okay. So put on your brave face—we have work to do."

He pats my cheek, and I nod. He's right. The shadows of the warehouse seem to grow around me, ominous monsters of doubt and fear, telling me that I won't accomplish it. Telling me he will die. Telling me I will fail again.

Save them, Vienna. My father's words ring through my head. My father believed in me, and I did it, not close enough to save them, but perhaps, close enough to save the man I love. I won't let the virus take any more people from me. I won't let it win. I won't let the monsters be right. I won't fail.

Dr. Greenwood hands me a mask and a syringe of the first vaccine we had created. "Go see him. Tell him you love him. Give him some of the other vaccine, and then get back in here. We won't rest until it's found. We won't rest until he's safe."

"Thank you," I whisper.

The dim lights of the warehouse we had been squatting in for a while cast shadows over his face as he nods.

"I'm going to scrounge for any supplies—anything we can use to start working harder. I'll be back tonight," he calls over his shoulder as I face the door to the little office where Dr. Greenwood stashed Riel.

My new legs wobble because of my unresolved heart, as if I believe the beautiful craftsmanship can't hold me up—as if I'll fall and stumble because of what I can't fix or stop. The failure feels too real, even though I haven't even failed yet.

My hand trembles as I reach for the metal knob. I knew it the second he came to visit today. I think he knew it too. I should have done more to protect him. I should have told him to desert the army since most of the Seperium soldiers were the ones getting sick, but it's all too late now. He's sick, and there is nothing I can do about it, unless I find the cure. The antidote in my other hand trembles, quivering under the force of my grip.

I push the door open, and it announces my presence with a groan. Riel looks up from his cot on the floor, those big brown eyes full of longing and hope. Large beads of sweat decorate his skin and soak the collar of his shirt. I know he can't see my face because of my mask, but his eyes stare at me, a beautiful reminder of the life he still carries. The life he still has left to live.

'I'm going to be fine.' He signs as if he knows I need to understand those words. *'You're going to find a way.'*

Tears cloud my vision. *'But what if I don't.'* I move closer to him.

'You will. I'm not scared because you're here with me.'

I kneel beside him. *'And I won't leave. I won't stop until the cure is found.'*

He nods. *'I know.'*

'You'll stay here. Dr. Greenwood already sent a message to your superiors to let them know you are sick in quarantine. That way your family doesn't believe you're dead.'

'Thank you.' His eyes shine. *'I wish I could touch you.'*

'Soon, Sweet. Soon.' I put a pair of gloves on and roll up his sleeve to administer the syringe's contents into his bloodstream. He sighs in pain, relaxing against the cot.

'Rest.' I sign. *'I love you.'*

He closes his eyes.

I didn't rest. From that day forward, I never stopped. I pushed and I pushed until I almost dropped from exhaustion, but I found it. In my last bit of resolve, I saved him.

CHAPTER 102
During the war: 1863-S: Doren Caldwell

He's dead. I would say I'm surprised or even sad. Or even . . . if I had any emotion to care, I would say something, but I don't care, but I do.

After all, he was my father. I mourn the relationship I never had with him—that's the only thing I'm sad about. That I never got a father who cared for me, but I guess he did teach me some things. Like how to be a terrible person who ruins marriages and sweeps his wife's ashes under the rug. Like how to be a great businessman who drowns in his own vices of sex and booze—just what I needed in a role model. I guess without him, I wouldn't even be here, so that's one little thing he gave me.

Before he died, I told him I forgave him. I don't think he believed me because I know he never thought he did anything wrong. Maybe he was thinking about it when he drew his last breath, but I'll never know now.

A hand slips into mine, the silk of her gloves smooth against my palm. I guess he gave me Leya, too. If he hadn't struck a deal with the Barrett's, I wouldn't have her beside me to ground me, to keep me from becoming like my father.

The incinerator's fire licks at the coals of his casket, glowing orange and yellow in the dim light of the morgue. Fitting that no one besides his son and his son's wife are here to attend his funeral, or even remember him. I guess that's what happens when you're a horrible person who upsets and offends people left and right, or maybe it's because he died of a terrible virus no one wants to get.

A virus that came from Lower Inferium—Black Rot. I was there when the soldiers first started to get it, and luckily, I evaded it when they shipped me home. Now, the virus has started to spread like the plague it is. There is talk of an antidote, but no one seemed to know where or who makes it, or even how to replicate it. At the rate we are going, all of Seperium and Inferium will be infected soon, and many of us will not survive.

Last I heard, Riel had it too. He's probably gone by now, and the thought brings more tears to my eyes than my father's death. I hope he's alright. I hope he is one of the strong ones who can pull through it.

Leya squeezes my hand, drawing my eyes away from the smoldering fire. "Let's go." She hooks my arm with hers.

We shuffle out into the broad daylight of Seperium, blinking to chase away the glare. Even the sun is shining to spite him. He never appreciated the sun, or his son. Huh, never compared the two. It doesn't matter now anyway.

"What will happen now?" Leya asks.

"Tomorrow, I will go to the office here in Seperium, and start to gather my father's affairs, and introduce myself as the new owner."

She looks at me, those brown eyes full of understanding. "Are you ready?"

I smile down at her. "Yeah, I just have to hopefully keep the company together through the rest of this war and pandemic, but who knows what will be left in the aftermath."

"I know. We'll just have to do our best, and I'm here if you ever need me—for anything."

"I appreciate that. The only thing you could possibly help me with is reading ledgers." I grin.

She shoots me a withered look. "I'm not that bored." She rolls her eyes.

"You said 'anything.'" I rub in.

"Smartass," she mutters, pulling her arm out of mine and walking ahead of me.

I race after her. "Well, you did."

CHAPTER 103
During the war: 1863-S: Rosea Dierich

"Rosie!" Grams hurries into the room with a two-year-old Prissy on her hip.

After I agreed to lead The Rosaries, we set up camp in the abandoned warehouse Grams and I had claimed while also moving periodically to keep the soldiers off our tracks. I even helped set up an underground system to be able to get messages across the ranks without the soldiers being able to tail and corner our every move. We were finally starting to gain some ground.

"There's someone here to see ya! Ya won't guess!" Grams exclaims, her bun of white hair bobbing as she practically leaps for joy.

I smile, taking her outstretched hand and allowing her to drag me down from the office area and into the commons.

"Grams, who is it? Why are you so—" I stop, not just because Grams has stopped, but because my heart has literally fallen dead and needs a restart to keep blood flowing.

I rub my eyes, blinking hard, because standing right in front of me is Vienna. My best friend who I thought was dead. I haven't seen her in two years. They never found her body.

"Hey, Ro." She smiles, tears flooding her eyes as she rushes forward enveloping me in a hug. She's real. Flesh and blood and warm and alive.

We start to sob as we hold each other.

"I thought you were dead. I thought—where have you been?" I mumble into her ear, not willing to let her go yet. I can't, not when she might disappear again.

"I was there when they bombed the hospital. I lost my legs because of it. I thought I was going to die, but Dr. Greenwood saved me and helped me stay hidden and safe for the next few years, and then . . ." she starts to pull away, but I cling to her like a koala cub. She chuckles through her sobs. "It's okay, Ro. I'm not going anywhere right now. I'm going to be right here. You can let go of me."

"No. If I let you go then you might disappear in front of my eyes like a phantom. If I let you go, I might never see you again, and I can't take that. I won't."

"So dramatic."

"You promise this is real? You promise you won't go away?"

"I promise," she says, and I finally let her go, taking a step to look at her. She wears a light pink skirt that is open in the front and drapes down the back like a waterfall, revealing the beautiful porcelain prosthetics holding her up. Tears well in my eyes anew.

"I can't believe you survived. I can't—you're so brave. I'm so happy you're alive. I missed you so much," I say, my voice shaky as I wipe away fallen tears.

"I missed you too." She blinks away tears with me before exclaiming, "Right! You haven't met Riel yet, I mean, not officially. You never had the chance before the war."

She turns her head, looking at the handsome young man who is perusing the warehouse. My heart melts with happiness for her—he's the same man we met behind the hospital all those years ago. He's here.

That means he found her again, even when she was probably bed-ridden without legs. Maybe that's how she got those fancy prosthetics. I do recall him delivering prosthetics that day. The thought makes me think about Pim. If Riel's here, maybe Pim could find me too. Maybe we could find each other and defy the cost together. Maybe—I stop the thought, not wanting to interject on the rest of this reunion.

He notices her looking, his eyes lighting up in adoration as she waves him over.

"Riel, I want you to meet my best friend," she says to him while also making signs with her hands. That's right, Vienna told me long ago that he's deaf.

Riel smiles at me, extending a hand.

"Rosea, meet my sweet Riel."

The love they had for one another seems to radiate through the room, making the dark warehouse a little brighter in their wake.

I take his hand. "Nice to meet you. Did you make those prosthetics?" I nod to Vienna's new legs. He nods. "They're beautiful."

He puts a hand to his forehead. "Thank you," he mouths.

"No, thank you. Thank you for finding my friend and taking good care of her. She's gone through a lot, and I'm glad she had someone there for her."

He signs something, and Vienna translates. "He says, 'he was almost too late.'"

"Almost and was, are two completely different things. You were there." I glance at Vienna. "Do you mind if I steal her away for a little bit? I miss her."

He nods, talking with his hands.

"He says, 'Take as much time as you need.'"

"Thank you." I grab Vienna's hands, pulling her off to the side of the warehouse, grabbing Prissy from Grams as we walk away.

Vienna smiles at her. "Is this—"

I nod with a smile. "Vienna, I want you to meet my baby girl, Priscilla."

Vienna waves slightly at Prissy, who giggles burying her face into my neck. "She's beautiful, Ro. And Pim?"

My smile falls as I shake my head. "I haven't heard anything from him since before the war. I'm sure he's moved on by now."

"Ro—"

"No reason to dwell on the past. I can't change what has happened, even though I want to." I look at the little girl in my arms.

She is a constant reminder that he will never truly leave my life. He will be here through her—a nagging thought ever plaguing me on what I lost.

"So, you've been running the show, huh?" Her eyebrows raise.

"If that's what you call it. I never thought I'd become a leader of hundreds of lost and broken people, but I guess they believed in me before I did . . ." I trail off for a minute, studying the features of her narrow face, dark curls circling around it like a crown. "Where have you been?"

She stops, pulling me further into the shadows of the warehouse as she grabs something from inside her bag—a small cigar leather pouch. She hands it to me.

"I was developing this. It's the cure for the mutated version of Black Rot."

I stare agape at the satchel.

She continues, "Riel got sick. So, Dr. Greenwood and I worked night and day to figure out the cure for the virus, and when we thought we had it, we tested it on Riel, and he survived. He lived." Tears shine in her eyes. "I almost lost him, Ro, but this time, I beat the virus before it claimed another thing I love."

I hug her. "I'm sorry but thank you. Thank you for bringing this here. I—" I stop thinking about all the opportunities this vaccine creates. "I will need more—a lot more because we're gonna use this to end the war."

"What do you mean?" she asks as I shift Prissy to my other hip.

"I mean, Seperium is reporting heavy casualties because of the virus. If we can get a message to them and tell them we have the cure, we can negotiate for the war to be over—for Inferium to win."

Excitement takes over my emotions. This war can finally be over. It's within our grasp.

"But they can easily duplicate it."

"Exactly, once they get a taste of the cure, they won't need us. So, we can only give the cure to Inferium citizens until Seperium agrees to see how it works and then accept our terms."

"You think they'll go for that?"

"If we show them it works, then yes. We can end this once and for all."

"But what if they don't?" Her eyes are full of doubts, glistening with just a smidge of hope. Hope that maybe we could live in a world without oppression and disease. Hope that it could finally be better, but doubt that we will never accomplish it.

Leave it to Vienna to rain on my parade. "At least we tried."

CHAPTER 104
After the war: 1864-S: Gabriel Hoek

My heart pounds in my chest, and I can feel sweat trickling down my back even though it's mid-fall. This is the place. Dwell Hall. Because I'm not ready to face Claren Hill, I can't bear to see her—not yet. I will soon, I just can't handle it right now.

Ever since I gained my memories back and arrived in Seperium, everything has been a whirlwind of crazy. I went back to my father's apartment, only to find that it had been sold to some kind older couple, and they were there to tell me that the previous tenant had passed away due to an illness of his blood. I knew things had changed in my absence. I just didn't realize how much.

Like now, I'm standing in front of Dwell Hall with no place to call home. Here, I'm hoping Doren is the lord of the house, and that he will let me stay here for a few days, just until I can access my father's accounts and will. I don't know where his personal belongings are, or if they're even still around.

After I've marched up the endless steps, I stare at the front of the house, trying to draw courage from the depths of my heart, but it feels like the depths are just a deep, bottomless pit that can bury me with darkness. I don't even know why I'm scared. I think it's just because I haven't seen him in so long. What will he be like? Will he be the same old Doren? Or a bitter cynic who hates everyone and everything because of what he's lost?

Finally, my courage fills the bottomless pit, and I ring the doorbell. An ominous echo resounds from the house, like a siren growing louder in an air-raid or bombs whistling through the sky. I shake my head. After my memories came back, it was hard to navigate through what was reality and what wasn't. What memories were vivid and front and center, and what were the others I had intentionally tried to forget, but there are some things you never forget. It's embedded in your bones like a fracture.

The door opens to a butler's kind face. He smiles at me slightly. "Can I help you, Sir?"

"I—yes, I'm here to see my old friend, Doren Caldwell." I step through the door, pulling off my top hat and coat and handing it to him. "Please let him know that Gabriel Hoek is here to see him."

"Of course."

He scurries away, giving me a chance to take in the house. It hasn't changed much since I last saw it, though there are different decorations and drapes. I smile, Doren always hated the previous drapes. I think they reminded him of his mother's death, or maybe they were just too ugly for him to handle.

"—the meaning of this? The man at the door can't possibly be Gabe. Gabe died two years ago in the war, Thom." I hear Doren's voice, and my heart starts to pound even louder at the sound. Part of me wants to hide, but that would be stupid because I'm already here.

He rounds the corner to my left in a wheelchair. His eyes land on me, and I see it the second he recognizes who I am—his eyes grow wide and his mouth parts slightly.

"What?" He shakes his head, blinking his eyes as if that would make me disappear or change into someone else. "Gabe." Tears well in his eyes. "This isn't—you're alive. You—I—"

I stumble over to him, kneeling beside his chair so I can pull him into a hug.

He leans against me. "This is the realest dream I've ever been in. I—but how? I—" He pulls back, looking me up and down. "It's you all right, but I never . . . how are you alive? We all thought that—"

"I know," I start. "I was crush—"

The footfalls of another person coming down the hall stops my thought because the voice is saying something about darling, about a concert, about—I freeze because the voice causes my heart to nearly jump out of its cage of ribs and run right into her arms where it belongs—where it's belonged for all these years, but what is she doing here? What—

"I'm sorry, buddy," Doren whispers as Leya appears in the hall saying,

"Oh, I'm sorry, I guess I didn't re—" She starts to turn around before stopping in her tracks as realization clicks with memories. She spins back around, holding in a shuddering sob as she moves closer to us like she's in a trance. Her brown eyes look me down, then up, and down again. She blinks tears away, her face a mixture of sadness and confusion.

"What? But—Gabe," she finally says my name, reaching a hand out to me.

A diamond ring winks on her finger, and it's not the one I gave her. My heart sinks, that's why Doren said he was sorry. He married my fiancé. I was naive to think she would still be waiting for me—especially when she thought I was dead. Her hand reaches for my face, but then stops before she touches me, probably remembering she is another man's wife. She pulls me into a hug instead.

"This isn't real. I can't believe you're alive. I spent all that time believing you were dead and I—how is this possible?" She pulls away, sobbing and sniffling.

I want to wipe away the tears fighting down her cheeks, but I have to force my hand to stay put. She isn't mine anymore.

"It's a long story. Maybe we should sit down, and then maybe you can tell me—catch me up on everything I missed," I stutter, refusing to be the one who addresses the elephant in the room.

CHAPTER 105
After the war: 1864-S: Inspector Leo Pim

The shrill scream is high enough to leave my ears bleeding for the next few weeks, that and paired with the sound of a gun going off, will definitely leave me wishing I hadn't prodded Lady Barrett. Or maybe it's making me wish I had prodded her more if this distraction was going to be presented.

Pain rips up my side from where the bullet pierced my skin, and I pounce as Lady Barrett turns her head toward the owner of the scream. My revolver is in my hand before she can even blink back at me.

Leya Caldwell stands in the doorway, her face pale as she takes in her mother holding a smoking gun, me pointing my weapon at the madwoman, and the warm blood gushing down my side. It trickles against my skin, filling the air with its coppery scent. It's fine. A scratch. If I think about it that way, then I won't panic and cause more blood loss. She did ruin a good shirt though. One hundred percent silk. I can't believe this. I knew I shouldn't have worn this shirt today.

I pull the hammer back, meeting Lady Barrett's eyes as she slowly gazes back at me. Fury sweeps her face, elongating her features until she looks like a sharp, jagged, and angry monster.

"Look what you've done." Madness screams in her gaze. "You had Leya waiting the whole time, didn't you? Turning my own daughter against me." Her hand shakes from anger, the metal of her gun quivering.

"Mother." Leya's voice carries across the room full of disbelief and fear. "What's the meaning of this? What are you doing?"

"I'm protecting our legacy." She cocks the hammer of the pistol back, steadying her aim at me.

"Mother, this is madness. What legacy do you have to protect? I'm your legacy. What you're doing isn't protection, it's madness."

"So, you heard the whole thing. I should have known he would turn you against me," she growls, keeping her gaze focused on me.

"No, Michele. Leya had nothing to do with this." Lord Barrett appears in the doorway, his shoulder slumped in what looks like betrayal. His form wilted and broken like a great tree that has been chopped from its roots, or perhaps trimmed of its canopy.

Lady Barrett turns her head slightly, her deranged eyes meeting his—the gun still pointed at my chest. Pain spikes up my side, and my vision blurs as I take a labored breath to keep my weapon from shaking.

"What?" he asks her. "Did you think you could keep me locked in the attic forever? Did you think I wouldn't piece it together? Leya looked for me, and she found me. I just can't understand, why? Why did you go to such great lengths? If you were trying to protect a legacy, why didn't you do it with me? I thought—"

"You thought wrong. We are not equals. I am just your wife, and in this society, that means nothing. You would have never let me have control. You never believed me when I said Casen was sick. I lost my son because you couldn't believe me. So, I stopped waiting for people to believe me. I went out and took what I wanted, and I'll keep on taking it." Her voice rises higher to a pitch of desperation as she swings the gun's barrel at her husband.

No.

I surge forward on stumbling feet, feeling the seconds move past me like a snail—one deliberate drawn out second at a time. This is going to hurt, but I'm not about to let someone die on my watch.

I tackle Lady Barrett. A tumble to the brick-paved floor, and the sound of another gunshot later, I have her gun secured in my other hand. I groan as she jabs a fist toward my wound, gasping as the pain steals my breath away. She smiles, a devilish crack of teeth as she prepares to hit me again. I fall backwards, missing her blow and trying to keep the guns out of her grasp.

Lord Barrett is suddenly there, pulling Lady Barrett off the floor and holding her hands behind her back.

"Let go of me!" she screams, her teeth lashing out like a wild dog.

I stand on wobbly feet. What is she going to do? Bite her husband? I mean, I wouldn't put it past her—feral animal that she's acting like. I stumble toward them, pulling handcuffs out of my pocket. "Lady Michele Barrett, you are under arrest for the murder of Lord Doren Caldwell."

She screams in frustration as I cuff her wrists. "I did nothing wrong. You would have done the same in my position. You can't be all high and mighty when you know what you would have done would have been no better than me!"

"Actually, Lady Barrett, I never would have murdered someone to get what I wanted. For one, it would be too much work to soil my perfect name over, and two . . ." I hand her cuffed wrists back to Lord Barrett, who nods. Where's Lady Caldwell?

"You're just a man. You couldn't understand what I've been through. You've never had to fight—"

I tune her out. Geez, I wish I could gag her, but that might look wrong on the reports. She didn't even let me finish my second thought. My gaze sweeps the room, finding Lady Caldwell propped against the frame of the door. Blood makes the fabric of her dress stick to her thigh. She's pressing a hand to the open wound. At least she's not dead, one less thing to put on my reports.

She smiles a small, weak smile. "Thank you." She looks over at her parents, where Lady Barrett is fighting tooth and nail—literally—to escape Lord Barrett's grasp. I'm sure they've had a fun marriage.

I lean against the wall next to her, pressing a hand against my side to pressurize my wound. "Don't thank me. I was convinced it was your father."

"Me too, until I found him locked up in the attic."

"People do that?"

"Nope, just my mother. I can't believe I'm surprised though. Maybe I just didn't want it to be anybody directly related to me, but I'm glad it's not Gabe."

I grunt, breathing through the pain that spikes up my side. "Me too. He should be released no later than tomorrow. I—"

The sound of footfalls rushing through Claren Hill stops my thought. Finally, it took them long enough. I honestly thought I was going to bleed out here. I look down at the paved brick flooring, studying the red and orange flecks. My vision blurs. Speaking of . . . I sway. The ground suddenly looks so inviting and—

CHAPTER 106
After the war: 1864-S: Leya Caldwell

The song had just started to settle, becoming a beautiful and flowing melody, nothing thrilling, nothing full of damaging heartbreak, nothing full of guilt—until now. Maybe it's just a nightmare—maybe it's a haunting sinister tune bent on destroying me, but this isn't a nightmare. I know because I haven't even slept. It's real. He's here. He's alive. I thought he was dead. At least, that's what they told me. Missing in action. Pronounced dead two years ago after a fruitless search for his remains.

Tears well in my throat as a pit forms in my stomach. My husband snores beside me, blissfully unaware that his wife is thinking about another man. Another man she loved and lost. Another man she never stopped loving. Guilt buries my insides and weighs heavy on my chest. I'm a married woman now. I'm not that little girl who fell in love with her best friend. I'm a wife—a wife to one of the most wonderful men in Seperium. A man I love too. I hate myself. I hate that I didn't even think twice before falling in love with Doren.

How could I have been so heartless? How could I have done that to Gabe? *But you thought he was dead.* Tears well in my eyes. That doesn't excuse it. That doesn't make any of this better.

His face. The look on his face when he realized I married Doren in his absence. The utter betrayal that sent a punch to my gut, leaving a grenade in the cavity, and exploding it into a million pieces. I may as well be dead for cheating on Gabe like I did, and now it feels like I'm cheating on Doren.

The second I laid eyes on Gabe, my heart burst open in my chest. The memories, the sentiment, the life we had dreamed for each other suddenly reappeared, wanting to become a reality once again, but I can't indulge in the fantasy, not when I have Doren. Not when he loves me, too. It wouldn't be fair, not after all we've been through to get here.

I shouldn't feel guilty because I didn't know. I mourned Gabe's death, and I found comfort in someone else who had lost him too. How does that make me a horrible person? Should I have lived out the rest of my marriage never admitting my feelings for the man I was married to? Plus, it wasn't even our fault we got married. It was to save our family's companies. Surely, Gabe will understand, right? Surely, he won't hate me for what I had to do, but I know I can't ask that of him, because if I were him, I would hate me.

I promised him that I would love him forever, and instead, I broke those promises after two years. I destroyed what we had, and I didn't even try to fight it. I laid down, and I accepted it, not caring if I damaged my heart in the process. What should I—I stop the thought. I know what I should do now. I'm Doren's wife. Not Gabe's, and I will remain Doren's wife.

I hold my breath, refusing to give into the sobs. I won't pick and choose because I've already chosen. I promised Doren I would be his wife, and I've already confessed that I love him. I won't let him go for the sake of what I once had with Gabe. Guilt be reproved because it's all too late now.

CHAPTER 107
After the war: 1864-S: Doren Caldwell

I can hear her muffled sobs. She's trying to hide it from me, but I'm not deaf or blind. Everything that has happened between Leya and I in the last few months flashed before my eyes like it was waving goodbye when she laid eyes on Gabe. I saw it on her face—the love she still has for him.

I understand, I guess, just because someone dies doesn't mean you stop loving them, but the green monster of jealousy has already poisoned my heart with its dart, spreading little minions into my blood to start poking and prodding at the friendship I once had with Gabe.

Even though I love Gabe like a brother, and he loves Leya, and they loved each other first—I don't want to give her away. She's my wife, and I won't give her to the man she never had the chance to marry. Maybe that's selfish of me, but I can't give away what I've found with her. I refuse. I wish I could be a better man, and for the sake of our friendship, tell Gabe that if he still wants Leya, he can have her, but I can't. I love Leya, and she loves me, or so I hope.

Her sobs say otherwise, or maybe it's just because she's conflicted. Hurt by the way she still loves Gabe and torn because of the new love she has for me. She can't erase those memories, and it's killing her— just like it's killing me to listen to her pain, but maybe, hopefully, I can show her I'm still here, and that I still love her, even though Gabe is here. Maybe I can convince her to keep loving me, and forget about— who am I kidding? She's not going to forget about Gabe. Not when she lost him once already.

I turn my head, placing a hand on her waist and drawing her closer as I trace the shape of her silhouette—the fabric of her nightgown bunching in my fingers. She turns to face me, placing her hands on my chest. I wipe her tears with my other hand.

"I'm sorry," she whispers. "I—this is all so hard to believe. I never—I don't want to do this to you, but I'll be honest. My heart—"

"Don't." I put a finger against her lips. "Don't tell me you still love him. Just tell me you love me. Tell me that you're not giving up on us because of the memories you once had with him. I know you don't ever forget how much you love someone, but please just tell me you still love me, and it will be okay. Then we'll be able to make it through."

She nods, breathing in shakily. "You're my husband, and I love you. I will stay your wife because your love has grounded me, and I've already promised to love you until the end of our days through a bond of marriage, and that won't change now."

Her words fill me with confidence. Confidence that she is mine, that we are each other's. I kiss her then, drawing her closer to me, just to make sure her kisses still taste the same—that there is no hesitation.

There isn't, and my heart settles with peace in my chest. I haven't lost her, and I won't.

CHAPTER 108
After the war: 1864-S: Vienna Sinclair

The giant High Seperium Council room grows around me like an exotic cage. The floor tiles create a mosaic of old King Randice and his Order of Knights— the first High Council. Glass and gold chandeliers above our heads shine down like a medical examiner's scrutinizing light.

The members of the High Seperium Council watch us from the platforms above us. There are twenty-four of them sitting on a platform in the shape of a crescent moon, looking down at us like a hawk sizing up its prey.

Gold robes garner their shoulders as if to assert their status more. I feel like an animal about to become a nice meal. Though I wouldn't want to splatter my blood on the pristine gold and quartz walls.

Rosea takes a step forward, her voice ringing loud and clear in the hollow room, performing like the actress she is—not afraid to do what she came here to do.

"Thank you for agreeing to meet with us. As you all can attest, the antidote we tested in front of you healed one of your own. If you want the rest of the vaccine, we kindly ask that you accept our terms and conditions."

Earlier today, Rosea had me administer one dose of the cure to a sick Seperium patient in front of the Council. An hour later the man was walking around without a trace of the disease.

The members nod at her words.

"It depends on what your conditions are," one answers.

Another stands. "Why should we listen to Inferium scum? Why

should we grovel and bend to their wishes? We can find the antidote ourselves."

"You clearly don't have any family members that are sick and dying, or dead already because of this virus," a woman with big, curly hair snaps.

"We are the most adva—"

"Enough!" a man in the center, highest platform yells. "We're wasting time by arguing. Despite all our efforts, we haven't found the antidote yet, and it could be years before we do. They have the antidote. We've seen it with our own eyes, and I will not sacrifice anymore lives because of petty pride. This has gone on long enough. Inferium deserves a chance—we deserve a chance, and if we don't give them what they want, we won't have that chance." He glares at his fellow members before finally setting his gaze on us. "Please proceed, Miss Dierich."

"To start, we want all Seperium soldiers immediately withdrawn from Lower Inferium. We will need help rebuilding Inferium. I had some architects draw up plans on how to properly format Inferium for the benefit of the citizens, and for the benefit of Seperium, adding proper drainage systems and sewage to keep Inferium clean and free of disease. You can have your architects look it over if you are still skeptical.

"We would like to create an Inferium Council to help run the city, and relay messages and laws between Inferium and Seperium—a delegation of sorts before things get implemented. With that, we'd like to start implementing proper wages and overtime for workers once they get the chance to go back to work after the rebuild. Those are our demands. If you accept, we are ready to ship thousands of vials of the vaccine to Seperium. If you refuse, we will go back to Inferium, and watch Higher Seperium suffer and fall." Rosea sets her gaze, resolve and determination echoing in her gaze.

The man in the middle meets her gaze like two lions dueling for the pride. He looks away, the battle over before it has even begun.

"We will convene and discuss," he says as a metal curtain falls from the roof in front of them, cocooning them in their little crescent moon.

I look at Rosea, who stares agape at the odd structure.

"Interesting." She smiles, racing over to touch the curtain. It doesn't budge under her fingers.

"Rosea," I scold, pulling her back. "Whatever happened to, 'if it's not yours, don't touch it?'"

Rosea grumbles. "Party pooper, I was just curious."

I sigh, looking up at the metal wall in front of us. "Do you think they'll accept it?"

She nods. "They have no other choice. We're leaving them with no choice, just like they did to us at the start of this war."

The curtain suddenly starts to rise, silencing our theories. When they appear, all of them are standing, looking down at us like a forest full of buzzards ready to start circling.

The middle man speaks, "We've decided to accept your terms on the condition that your Inferium Council members get approved by us, those families move to Seperium, and that the Inferium Council convenes here once a week with the Seperium Council. The members will have full access to move between Seperium and Inferium, and the other conditions . . . we'll agree once we've had several architects work with yours to instill the best plan for New Inferium. The higher wages will have to be negotiated with the owners of the factories, but I don't see how that would be a problem. Do we have a deal?"

Rosea looks at me, her dark blue eyes shining with hope and happiness.

Inferium is saved. Seperium is saved. We are saved.

I nod. "We have a deal."

CHAPTER 109
After the war: 1864-S: Rosea Pim

I hurry through the pristine halls of Seperium Hospital. My red heels pound to the beat of the music playing in my head as I hope I don't get lost within the maze of white walls, coats, and light. I have to find him.

The receptionist said he's here. My heart almost exploded out of my chest when I got the telegram that Pim was in the hospital, nearly dead, they said. Urgent, they said. Gunshot, they said.

That loveable idiot. How could he have done this to me? Nearly dying when we've just got back together, putting my heart into a frenzy. Why was he alone there anyway? Ugh, idiot!

I grumble down the hall, glancing into a room where I see a pair of long legs sticking out past the bed railing. I halt, backtracking, and peering inside. Sure enough, they're my husband's legs.

My heart explodes with joy, and surprisingly, anger, as I march into the room. He's dozing, his narrow, sharp facial features relaxed and at peace. The silk shirt he had been wearing earlier is missing, replaced with bandages wrapped all the way around the middle of his torso—blood leaves little spots against the white, tarnishing the cleanliness of it all. Pim would hate that.

Tears spring to my eyes, and I stifle a sob with my hand. I could have lost him again. Lost his snarky quips, lost the chance to make up for the years I couldn't hold him in my arms. The room is empty aside from him . . . empty like how everything would feel again if he was gone. One sad little window in the white room spreads light over his angled face. The thoughts sober my anger at him for putting himself in danger. I'm just glad it hadn't been worse. Glad that he is alive.

His black eyelashes flutter open, revealing those bright blue eyes. I hastily wipe my tears, rushing closer to him. I lean over, gently pulling him into a hug. He wraps an arm around my waist, sighing as our embrace melds us together.

I pull away, slapping his shoulder. It's more like an aggressive pat, but whatever. "You idiot. How could you do that to me? Do you know how scared I was when I got the telegram? Do you—"

His hand gently caresses my neck, bringing me close as his lips reach up to meet mine. The kiss is sweet like honey as his fingers dance along my arm, sending shivers up and down my spine. He breaks our embrace, placing his forehead against mine.

"You know a kiss doesn't fix everything," I mumble, hating myself for falling for that because now I just want to kiss him, and I hope I never have to come up for oxygen.

"I know, but it got you to be quiet." He smirks.

I pull away. "You're insufferable, Leo Pim." I stick my nose in the air.

"But you love me anyway, and I know you really want to kiss me again."

He's so confident and cocky, thinking that he's got me, and *dark Inferium!* He does. I step close again.

"Note that this is only because you almost died, and this is a thank you for not dying, but I'm still angry you went in alone. Let's just make that clear." I sit down, and he pulls me closer.

"Crystal." His lips brush against mine, and I melt into his arms.

CHAPTER 110
After the war: 1864-S: Gabriel Hoek.

"Do you love him?" The words I had uttered to Leya that night before Doren's death echo in my mind while sobs wrack her body as we watch Doren's coffin become enveloped by flames. I pull her into my arms, feeling her shoulders shake with emotion.

"Yes," she answered even though she had just confessed to loving me still. At the time, I concluded that those feelings never truly go away, just like how my heart still loved her even when I forgot for two years. She doesn't know how much it hurt when she uttered that word. She doesn't know that she drove a blade into my heart that night. Doren was the one literally murdered that day, but I had to pull an emotional knife out of my chest because, at the time, I concluded that I would never get to be with Leya. I would never get to marry her like I promised. I would never get to hold her again.

So, I kissed her in the last few hours of Doren's life, stealing one last embrace from her before I had to let her go to be with her husband. I immediately felt guilty for trying to taste something of Doren's and ignored the passion burning in my chest as I pulled away and told her I wouldn't do this to Doren. That I would walk away and leave them to their marriage. That I would watch as they loved each other, and I loved her from afar.

But I don't have to worry about that now. The thought sobers my heart and brings tears to my eyes. He's gone, and he'll never know about Leya and my stolen kiss. I'll never get to apologize for taking that from him. I can't believe he's gone. We went through so much together, and now, we'll never get the chance to go through more. We'll never get the chance to laugh or joke about stupid things again or have serious conversations about love and loss.

I start to sob against Leya, drawing hurt from each other's pain as we try to say a final goodbye. I feel a hand on my shoulder. I lift my head, looking at Riel. His sad brown eyes seep into my soul as he wraps an arm around my shoulder, crying with Leya and me.

I don't know how long we hold each other, but the casket is nothing but glowing ash when we finally have the strength to leave the morgue.

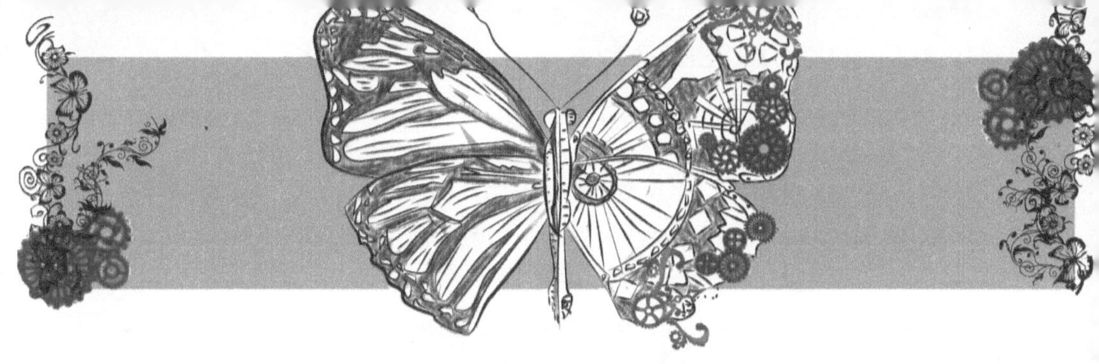

CHAPTER 111
After the war: 1864-S: Riel Mjorn

My hands shake and I clench them until they're sweaty. I wipe them on my pants, thinking I shouldn't be so nervous. I mean, it's only Vienna. Only Vienna. As if she's anything but only. To me, she's the sun rising to chase away the twilight, or she's the moon illuminating the night sky with her glow, or a candle blazing in the dreariest of places. Basically, she's my light in the dark—the person I want to spend the rest of my life with. So, maybe that's why I'm nervous.

She stares at me from atop the stairs leading into the High Seperium and New Inferium Council building. Her gold robe resting on her shoulders makes her look regal, like a queen, and I can't help thinking that she's the queen of my heart. That she will rule over it for the rest of my life—or as long as she wants to. Wait? Am I implying there will be a time when she doesn't? It's possible, but I hope for my sake, it's impossible.

She smiles as she descends the stairs, and her brown eyes glow golden in the setting sun's light. I wipe my palms once more as she moves toward me. I don't want my girlfriend to hold a sweaty hand.

'You're early. I thought we were meeting at the apartment?' She signs, before placing a kiss on my cheek.

I swallow, blushing at the public display of affection. *'I had another idea in mind.'*

'Oh! Are we gonna go toilet paper Lord Igrious' mansion?' Her eyes glow with glee.

I stare at her aghast. I have to get her to think of better pastimes. Honestly, who would want to waste that much toilet paper over a prank? I get that Vienna is rich now, but still, it seems a little excessive—

I watch her point at her heart, reminding me this is all a joke. *'Have I told you I love it when you tease me?'* I sign.

'No.'

'Good.' I smile before dropping my face. *'I don't'*

'Oh, Butterfly, don't be a stick in the mud. You seem a little worried or something. More so than usual.' She drops a kiss on my nose, and I try everything within me to keep my blush at bay, but it appears anyway.

"I love it when you blush." I watch her lips move.

'You just like torturing me.' I sign, ignoring her jab from earlier about being nervous. How can she always see right through me?

Her bright smile widens as if that were possible. *'Precisely. Now, where does my amazing Butterfly want to take me today?'*

Since we hit our one-year mark of dating, she's taken to calling me Butterfly or Bug or Beetle. Not that I hate those nicknames, it's just taken me some getting used to. The only problem is—she's leaving me no room to give her a cute nickname. What if I wanted to call her Butterfly or Bug or Beetle? No, I'm sure those nicknames wouldn't sum up my Vienna. I should call her Bright. Butterfly and Bright. I smile at the thought before I feel Vienna take my hand.

"Stop thinking so much. Take me where you want to go tonight—although, I'm not quite ready. I would have liked to freshen up." She fluffs her robe, shrugging her shoulders.

'You're gorgeous no matter what.' I sign, before sliding my hand around her waist and pulling her closer to me. It's her turn to blush.

We grab a taxi and pile in until we're outside of RN Prosthetics.

Vienna wrinkles her brow as we step out after paying the driver. *'Riel, I thought—'*

I grab her hand and pull her into the shop before she can finish, because once she sees what I have planned for her, she'll be speechless—or at least I hope she will be. Panic sets into my heart. Oh no, what if she hates it? What if she gets angry? Or what if she finds it insulting? I never intended it to be, so I hope she doesn't but—

Vienna gently pinches my hand—our little sign to tell me I'm overthinking again. I meet her gaze, and what I see tells me what I've done hasn't insulted her at all. Tears glisten in those beautiful brown eyes as she looks around the front of RN Prosthetics.

My father helped me set up hundreds of lights—dimmed to look like a starry night—all over the shop. At the very front of the shop, I hired part of the Seperium Orchestra to come and play for us tonight, even though I can't hear them. They're playing now. Their cue to start happened when we walked through the door.

"Riel." I watch her say my name.

I hold my hand out.

She stares at it a moment, before shaking her head. "I can't. I—I'm not ready. It won't be—"

'You're ready.' I sign. *'Remember dancing isn't about doing it right. It's about following the steps embedded in our hearts.'*

Tears stream down her face, and she takes my hand. We dance, swaying to the music, stepping to a melody that only we knew. She stares up at me with big, brown eyes, and I feel my nervousness dissipate.

I pull away. *'I have something to show you, but you have to close your eyes.'*

'Riel?'

'Please, just close them.'

She smiles before she closes her eyes. I take her wrists and place her palms over her face. Her body shakes with laughter, but she doesn't remove her hands. I can't afford to have her peeking and ruining the surprise. I look to where the musicians are, and they stop playing so they can grab the signs I made for them to hold. I smile when I find that it reads correctly.

I grab Vienna's wrists and lower her arms. I gently touch her eyelids and watch as her lashes flutter open. I know she can't see what the signs read because I'm blocking them.

"I love you," I mouth before moving away so she can read.

Vienna

Will

You

Dance

In

My

Arms

Forever?

She turns to find me holding the last sign with an open ring box in my other hand. A pink porcelain and opal ring lies on a bed of red velvet.

Will you marry me?

Her hands fly up to her face as tears start to stream down her cheeks once more.

"Yes! Yes! Yes!" She races toward me, and I barely have time to throw the sign away before she's in my arms and kisses me. She pulls away. "I will dance forever with you."

I take the ring out of the box and slip it onto her finger. It doesn't fit. Disappointment crushes me. No! I had the right dimensions! I double checked. I try to pull it back off, but Vienna, noticing my frustration, stops me.

'No! You can't take it. I love it. You're never going to get it off. Never.' She signs.

'But it doesn't fit, everything is ruined.'

'My sweet Riel, nothing is ruined. It's perfect, and we'll get the ring resized, but it's staying with me until then. You got it?'

My heart swells with love for her. How does this amazing, beautiful woman want to be married to me? *Because she loves you. Because you're her light in the dark too.*

I nod, and then she's kissing me again.

CHAPTER 112
After the war: 1864-S: Leya Caldwell

I never thought this song in my life would be completed. I never thought this would be happening again. I'm staring at myself in a full-length mirror. My white wedding gown flows to the floor in beautiful waves of gossamer, diamonds, and lace. It's even more beautiful than my first wedding dress, but some part of me believes I don't deserve this second chance at love.

Isn't that funny? In my first wedding, I thought I could never love again, and now I feel like I don't deserve to be loved again. So much has happened since that horrible day over three months ago.

Caldwell Textiles became mine. My mother was convicted to a life sentence in jail—my father gets to visit her once a week. It was later confirmed that she spread the rumors around her own father's company so Father could buy it, and she was also the one who lit a match to Hoek Weapons. Who would have thought she would do such a thing? I certainly didn't, and yet, I grew up around her. I saw the worst of her, but I never saw that? I couldn't have stopped her before she murdered my husband. Maybe that's why I don't feel worthy of a second chance at love.

Lastly, Doren left me a gift—a gift he doesn't even know he gave. I cup my stomach through the fabric of my dress. After the initial shock of the news, my father and Gabe were overjoyed when I told them about the pregnancy. At the time, I was terrified. Terrified I could never be a good mother. Terrified I would turn out just like my mother.

But Father and Gabe grounded me. They told me I could never turn into her because I knew I would never raise a child like she raised me. I would be a good mother who loves and encourages her child. They promised to be right alongside me through thick and thin, making sure I'm okay and helping me in any way they can. They even started getting a nursery ready for the baby at Claren Hill. I smile at the thought.

Gabriel gave me as much space as he could while we mourned Doren, and he got the last of his father's affairs in order. He waited until a month after Doren's death to ask me to marry him again. He even took me back to the spot where he first proposed to me. It was a reminiscent reminder of who we were before the war. I'd be lying if I said I didn't cry through the entire thing—he already knew I was pregnant.

"Are you ready?" Father asks as he comes into the room.

I smile over my shoulder. "Only if he's ready for me."

"He's been ready for several years." Father nods, his eyes growing sad. "I should have let you marry him right after he asked me. I shouldn't have made you two wait."

"Father—"

"No, I just keep thinking that you wouldn't have gone through so much heartache if—"

"It doesn't matter. I would have thought he was dead. I still probably would have married Doren, and"—I take Father's hands into mine—"I don't regret that you made us marry. I don't regret falling in love with him. I'm sad I lost him and I'm sad he'll never meet his child, but I wouldn't trade those few months with him for anything else in the world."

Father nods with tears in his eyes. "I know. I just—" he sighs. "Can I walk you down?"

"I would love that." I take his offered arm.

The light blares behind us, and I look up to meet Gabe's eyes. Tears glisten there, and my heart swells with happiness. Even after so much heartache, I finally get to marry my best friend.

CHAPTER 113
After the war: 1864-S: Inspector Leo Pim

I stare at the mirror, tying my pastel pink bowtie around my neck and creating perfect loops and swirls. There is no denying the fact that I look good. I smile at my reflection, humming happily to myself before releasing a pleased sigh. A perfect groom for a perfect bride. In a few minutes, I get to remarry the love of my life.

Well, technically, now after three years of being married, we finally get the chance at a real wedding. Nothing fancy, aside from hundreds of people waiting patiently in the ballroom at Dwell Hall.

Despite my initial grievances about living in the countryside, Rosea wore me down when Dwell Hall came available to buy. It was the rose door knockers that sold her . . . typical. I promised her I would buy it as long as she got rid of the ghosts for me. She agreed, though I doubt there are any more ghosts at Dwell Hall since I successfully solved Doren's murder. *Technically, she found you, not the other—*I silence the voice in my head, not today. I won't let my ego be brought down by my self-doubts.

Today, I get to renew my vows with Rosea, and we get to love each other like we never had the chance to. My heart swells, and I can feel tears crawling to my eyes. I blink them away. If my eyes turn red, it'll ruin the photos.

The door opens, ushering Grams in. Her white hair is bobbed

around her face in little curls, a giant emerald green hat atop her head. She clasps a hand to her chest as she sighs with happy tears in her eyes.

I smile, gesturing to my crimson suit. "Well, am I still good enough for her?"

"More than enough. Are ya ready? I'm walkin' ya down the aisle first and then Rosie."

"I know how a wedding works, Grams."

She clicks her tongue. "Don't get smart with me." She hooks her arm with mine, and I have to bend sideways so she can reach me.

The doors open before me, and I nearly faint as nervousness overtakes me.

Grams steadies me. "Don't create a scene, drama Pim."

I smile despite myself. Ohoho, she thinks this isn't my scene? Well, I'll have to prove her wro—I stop the thought, seeing Rosea peeking out from behind the door of her dressing room, grounding me even though she's not looking at me. I smile.

Right, it's not just about me. It's about us, proclaiming our love before the whole world. Rosea and I will be creating scenes together from now on. My drama queen and her king. What a beautiful love story.

422

EPILOGUE

Seperium Year 1866-S, AIA. STOP.
To Investigator Pim. STOP.
Murder on the ABC cruise ship, Crown of
Seperium. STOP.
Dr. George Caranaugh murdered around 1400 12th
of Kuly 1866-S. STOP.
One suspect in custody. STOP.
Requesting your immediate assistance. STOP.

TIMELINE OF CHARACTER AGES

1849:
Leya 7
Gabriel 7
Riel 9
Vienna 8
Doren 8
Rosea 10
Pim 12

1854:
Leya 12
Gabriel 12
Riel 14
Vienna 13
Doren 13
Rosea 15
Pim 17

1860:
Leya 18
Gabriel 18
Riel 20
Vienna 19
Doren 19
Rosea 21
Pim 23

1864:
Leya 22
Gabriel 22
Riel 24
Vienna 23
Doren 23
Rosea 25
Pim 27

INSPECTOR LEO PIM

VIENNA SINCLAIR

RIEL MJORN

GABRIEL HOEK

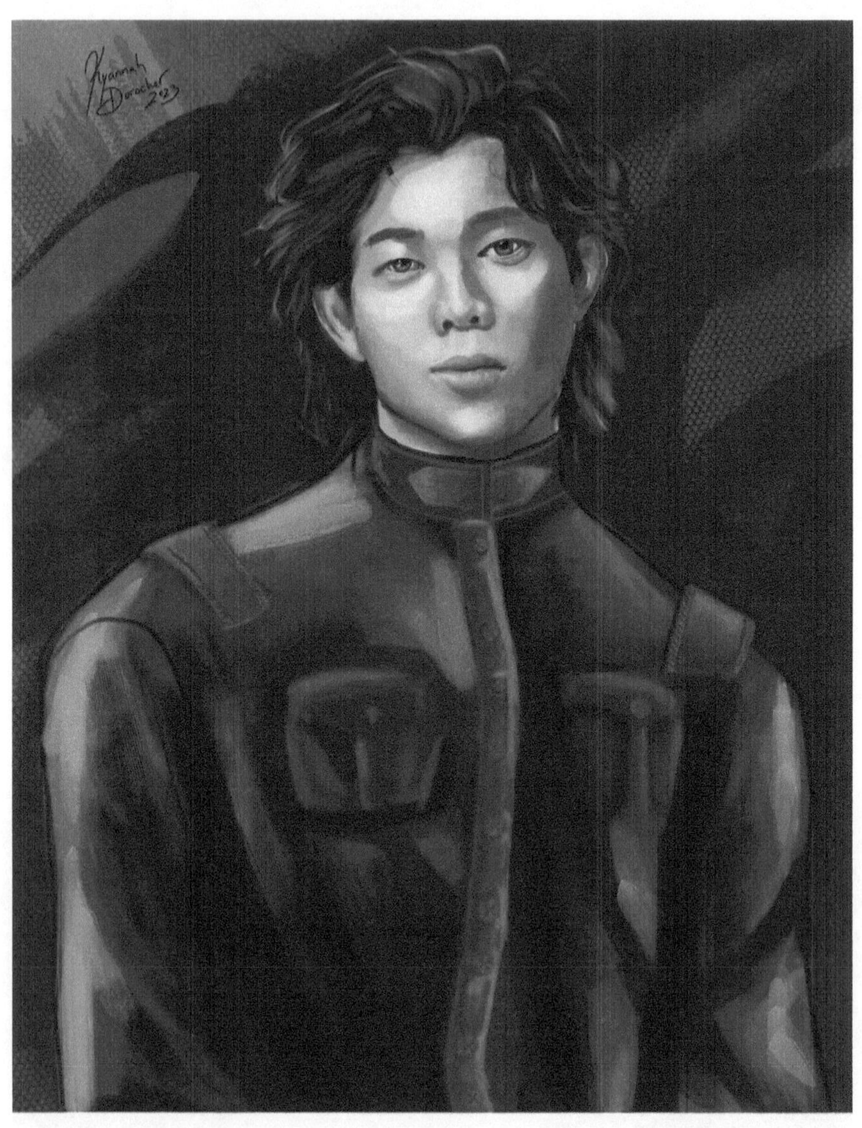

LEYA BARRETT

DOREN CALDWELL

ROSEA DIERICH

LORD AND LADY BARRETT

ACKNOWLEDGMENTS

Wow! There are so many people to thank for this book, but first and foremost, I have to thank my Lord and Savior, Jesus Christ, for without Him this book would have never been written. He gave me the ideas, strength, and perseverance to move forward with this book.

To my sister, Gaelle, thank you for all the ideas you graciously allowed me to use in this book. Without you, Vienna and Riel wouldn't exist and I know they are already fan favorites. You contributed to the idea of Seperium and Inferium and the malicious Black Rot that gave this story so much more depth. Thank you for letting me write while we watched movies and asking if I'd gotten my words in for the day. Also, for taking my author photo, which I adore. You're one in a hundred million.

To my sister in Jesus, Raphiel, thank you for all the 2:00 a.m. chats as we fangirled over Pimmy, reworked character depths, gave Pim a wife, and helped me plot and add characters for several sequels and spin-offs. Thank you for being the most fabulous Alpha reader and offering me so many wonderful suggestions. This book just wouldn't be the same without your guidance. Also, thank you for creating my chapter headers—I love them so much—and giving me a little song about a fox for Rosea.

To my amazing team of Beta readers, Autumn, Binny (Thank you so much for the Devil in Red song and allowing me to use it for Rosea!), Brie, Hannah (Both of you!), Jillian, Kat, Lia, and Loren. You all are amazing and this book wouldn't be the same without you. Thank you for the time and attention you devoted to this book.

To my critique ladies at Wolf Creek Christian Writer's Network, Cathy, Helene, Jessica, and Lynn, your work helping me polish this book for publishing was a gold mine of knowledge for me. Thank you for all the love and support, always!

To Quill and Flame Publishers, for without the incentive to submit a manuscript during open submissions, I never would have finished this book in time. A huge thank you to AJ Skelly and V. Romas Burton who so graciously offered endorsements even though I couldn't publish through their lovely publisher. I wish you both and the whole Q&F team the best.

To my Mom and Dad for believing and investing in this book and all my writing adventures. It means so much to me. Thank you for reading my books and cheering me on from the sidelines as I pursue this crazy dream of mine!

To Lorelei, for being my amazing editor! Your careful and quick attention to detail made this story ten times better. Thank you so much!

To Sera, for being my proofreader. I loved getting to work with you. Thank you for keeping me in the loop and helping me find those pesky typos!

To Kenzi, for creating my beautiful and ominous cover art. It was such a pleasure to work with you, and you exceeded my expectations!

To Kyannah, for all my beautiful character art! Seriously, you are so talented and I'm so grateful I got to support you. Keep doing what you're doing for the Kingdom!

To Susan, for creating my cover formatting. I thought I was a goner, but you swooped in. I couldn't have gotten this book ready without you. Thank you so much, my sweet friend!

ABOUT THE AUTHOR

Riley J. Perrie lives between the mountains of Colorado and the fields of Nebraska with her family and cat Sawyer. She's an avid reader and writer and you'll often find her soaking up sunshine with a good book or a pen and a page. She's been writing since she was seven and shows no signs of stopping anytime soon. You can connect with her over Instagram @authorrileyperrie or at authorrileyperrie.com.

Also by Riley J. Perrie
Partin: the Chosen

www.ingramcontent.com/pod-product-compliance
Lightning Source LLC
Chambersburg PA
CBHW031241310726
48971CB00004B/1127